WHATEVER YOU WANT

WHATEVER YOU WANT

WE WRITE, YOU DECIDE: A PICK-YOUR-OWN-ENDING ESCAPADE

RACHEL TIMMS AND LAURENCE HAYES

ReganBooks
Celebrating Ten Bestselling Years
An Imprint of HarperCollins*Publishers*

This book was originally published in Great Britain in 2003 by Pan Books, an imprint of Pan Macmillan, Ltd., U.K.

FIRST U.S. EDITION

Designed by SX Composing DTP, Rayleigh, Essex

Library of Congress Cataloging-in-Publication Data

Timms, Rachel.
Whatever you want : we write, you decide : a pick-your-own-ending escapade / Rachel Timms and Laurence Hayes.—1st U.S. ed.
p. cm.
ISBN 0-06-059163-3 (acid-free paper)
1. London (England)—Fiction. 2. Young adults—Fiction. I. Hayes, Laurence. II. Title.

PR6120.I55W47 2004
823'.92—dc22

2003069459

04 05 06 07 08 BVG/QWF 10 9 8 7 6 5 4 3 2 1

Warning!

Do not attempt to read this like a normal book.

You, the Reader, will enter the world of Whatever You Want *from within the body and mind of one of two characters. Start at the prologue, where you will decide whether you are best suited to navigate Barnaby or Barbarella through the social and sexual minefield.*

Rather than chapters, the book is broken down into scenes. Instead of starting at the beginning and reading straight through to the end, you will find yourself and the characters bouncing between scenes, depending on where your choices take them.

In all there are thirty-nine endings—but as in life, the Perfect Ending is hard to come by. Scraping through the surface of easy lays and drunken gratification, you will soon discover that these vulnerable heroes need all the help you can give them. Against deadly social enemies, Barnaby and Barbarella have only their quick wits, a few loyal friends, and your social expertise to guide and protect them.

So get ready. These are the golden days of Great Britain—a time when overtime is the norm, the tube is on strike, and pavements are slimy with lager sick—but the nights are long, your pay is soaring, and the only age to be is under thirty.

Remember, all *the events contained within this book are based upon the* actual *experiences of* real *people, but now it's your turn to take a grip on the tiller.* **BECAUSE LIFE WAS NEVER MEANT TO BE A SPECTATOR SPORT . . .**

Authors' Note

This book has been devised and developed by experts trained in the glossy magazine school of psychology to provide a unique psychiatric insight. Upon reaching any of the following endings, please notify your mental health practitioner immediately:

The (Premature) End
The (Sticky) End
The (Sexually Charged) End
The (Testosterone Free) End
The (Banged Up the Wrong Way) End
The (Disappointing) End
The (Bottled) End
The (Threesome) End
The (Blind Drunk) End
The (Forlorn) End
The (Silly Bugger) End
The (Disappointingly Dull) End
The (Humiliating) End
The (Sensible) End
The (Fucked Up) End
The (Uncomfortable) End
The (Elixir of Youth) End
The (Lads Together) End

The (Mud Glorious Mud) End
The (Crash 'n' Burn) End
The (Exposed) End
The (Evil Sinner) End
The (Bitter) End
The (Messy) End
The (Would You Adam and Eve It) End
The (Julie Andrews) End
The (Proper) Julie Andrews End
The (Boys' Own) End
The (Self-Love) End
The (Lonesome) End
The (Disturbed) End
The (Think of England) End
The (Soggy) End
The (Stunned) End
The End (of an Era)
The (Bloody) End
The (Dead) End

Remember, as in life, there is a (Perfect) end. It just takes some insight into human nature, and a little sharp thinking, to find it . . .

Prologue

Your alcohol-shrunken brain aches from lack of moisture. In the dark hours of Saturday morning, a sleep-groan slips from dry lips, and in the bowels of your subconscious you fight dream battles.

You're at a party in a gigantic country house. It's the recurring dream: you think you're lost, but you know you're chasing after an ex-lover, trying to explain that you made a mistake, that you can change, that it's true love.

"I'M SORRY . . ."

Your shout echoes through the empty hallway. Then, you catch sight of a slender white leg at the top of the stairs. A startling blonde smiles down—it's Maruskha, the Latvian, who serves you in Costa Coffee, and your beloved ex is leading her by the hand. You run up the stairs and after them, but they are too fast. The Latvian minx giggles as she disappears into a bedroom and kicks the door shut behind her.

Your sleeping body jerks violently as you dream-run across the landing and grab at the doorknob. A groan wails from within, smothering your feeble cries as you wrestle with the door—but as you struggle the handle slips in your grip and refuses to turn . . .

It's not just a dream; it's the story of your confounded life. Maybe when you wake you'll be able to rewrite the ending. But for the moment you're still slumbering. Even in a nightmare there are decisions to be made. What to do?

Never give up on love. And anyway, the stupid Latvian bitch needs to learn a lesson. Storm in, pour your drink over her head, give her a G-string wedgie, and steal your loved one back. **Go to Scene 202**

It's only a dream, for Christ's sake! You may as well make the most of it. Creep in, find a comfy chair, and enjoy the show. **Go to Scene 204**

This is all too yucky, beat a retreat. No, better still, jump out of the window. Your battered corpse will show the world the depth of your love. **Go to Scene 206**

Scene 1

It's the weekend. In that blissful state between sleep and wakefulness a tongue nuzzles your exposed ear. For long moments you take stock.

Who is she?

It can't be Raffles, your springer spaniel. She has never generated such pleasuring sensations. The teasing little tongue has all the dexterity of a nut-nibbling squirrel. And besides, Raffles doesn't knead your buttock at the same time. You feign sleep.

Who is she?

The bar after work, beers sinking, taxi to Camden, strange people—friends of Kamran. All unemployed aesthetes, mostly gay.

Is it a she?

Switch to vodka. On to a party. Small monstrous house, memory starting to wane. Vague images continue to flit. The intense actress with the eyes? Flirting lesbians? Surely not. Not both? Your brain flicks awake.

There was also the cute art student with the freckles and the upturned button nose, the pierced eyebrow, and the slightly lazy eye that made her look like she was thinking about sex. . . .

You can't help but turn, and with expectancy you open your eyes for the first time, smiling all the while.

Who is she?

No idea.

Scene 1

"Good morning" seems a little inappropriate, but you switch into the fake Irish accent you use to counter embarrassing moments. You kiss because it would be rude not to, but as you do a single thought grates across your brain: "Minger."

"I've got to go to the bathroom."

UgUgUgUgUgUgUgUgUgUGLY. Why do the ugly ones never have beds and houses of their own? A deft excuse and you could be home safe by lunch. But now? She had that grateful look in her eye. It could take hours before she decides to leave your nest, and you have neither the stamina nor a sufficiently darkened room to survive that long.

Think, Barnie. . . .

First moral decision of the day. This should test your mettle. She's a monster, no doubt about that. Her facial features look as though they've been thrown on by a capricious Creator.

But is there anything more reprehensible, more morally corrupt than the cut and run?

Are you a rascally rogue? Use all your villainous cunning to escape. **Go to Scene 219**

Or a chivalrous knight (with low standards). Go once more unto the breach, dear friend, once more. **Go to Scene 248**

Scene 2

It is not Sarah Cox who wakes you this morning. It is not one of your regular houseguests. In fact, it is not anyone you recognize at all. Not that you can really see his face, it's shielded by a heavenly spun mat of blond hair. His skin is acceptably bronzed and his hand is delicately caressing the small of your back. You maneuver yourself from under his arm, hoping that the familiar surroundings of your room might give you a clue.

Oh God, this isn't your room. But that's impossible. You never entertain away. Home advantage means makeup remover, a bedside pint of detox drink, and no humiliating reverse striptease. But think this through—where the hell are you?—and who the hell is lying beside you? The decor looks suspiciously eighties. But worse, you peek a proper look at your DiCaprio–boned Romeo only to realize he's no man at all—he's a baby. Barbie, what have you done? You have sexually inaugurated one of the new graduate trainees; this kind of training wasn't in his contract.

It's time to bury your face in the pillow and stop breathing. Alternatively, pretend to be asleep while your questions are answered. Who is he? Dave something. He joined the firm last week and was sitting next to you at the awards dinner last night. He impressed you with his knowledge of *film noir* and with the fatal line, "I don't think you're a real woman until you can masturbate in front of your boyfriend."

What did he do? He bought you doubles all night, held your

award, and then tempted you home with the promise of absinthe. What was the general consensus among colleagues? You're paranoid about your age and need to corrupt young flesh. Did you corrupt him? You certainly did, dominatrix. In fact, if you try and move right now, every muscle in your body will protest. Oh, and look out for the bite marks on his left buttock. But you can feel the back of your neck being kissed; he's gently coaxing you to turn round.

"Look, Dave, I really shouldn't be here. I'm out of my tube zone, and frankly, I feel uneasy." That was supposed to be a joke, but Dave laughs at you not with you.

"Barbarella, relax, the bus is totally reliable." He runs a hand up your thigh and ducks his head under the duvet.

"Do you have taxis round here? I need one now, I need, need . . ."

Enough's enough, Barbie; it's time to extract yourself from this god-awful mess. Be firm with Dave and make him call you a cab immediately, even if it does break his heart. **Go to Scene 235**

Dave's twenty-one—he doesn't know the meaning of the word "enough." Let him have his head. **Go to Scene 114**

Scene 3

You gulp the contents of the glass in one. If you must drink of the poisoned chalice then do it swiftly, and live not in doubt. In half an hour you will venture forth, either with a beautiful and aroused young woman on your arm, or a permanent erection in your pants.

Heads you win, tails you win . . .

Natasha eyes you curiously as you knock back the bubbling brew and drink more circumspectly. As she wets her lips the bubbles fizz and explode, hitting soft pouting skin. You hope to God you've guessed right. Whatever happens this evening, a permanent erection is an absolute certainty.

Go to Scene 147

Scene 4

"No, Will, we can't."

You push him away and your heart cracks anew as you see the pain on his face.

"Barbarella, I . . ." He trails off, unable to look you in the eye. You stand, straighten your dress, and go to leave.

Barbie, that was either the most sensible thing you've ever done, or the most idiotic. Rejoin the party.

Go to Scene 116

Scene 5

The plant will probably shrivel and die as soon as you leave. Astrid continues to babble; Will has no option but to instruct her to sniff out some more coke. When she has gone, his own anxiety takes center stage.

"That bloody chandelier hasn't been oiled since the Boer War; the noise is making my fillings vibrate."

Time to calm things down and get everyone to focus on what this is really about.

"Guys, this could be our one big chance to make it. People like Jenner and Newt win or lose our combined salaries every night of the week. Let's face it, no matter how much money we earn, we spend it. And in ten years' time we'll just be older, uglier, and more knackered. Only one thing will stay constant—our credit card debts."

Will nods vigorously, the others stare dumbly, horrified at your vision of their future.

"I'm not joking. This could be the only chance we ever get to make some serious money. We've got to go for one big hit. We've got to wait 'til Jenner gets overconfident, and then win huge—on one big hand."

Barbarella, with her very personal reasons for revenge, warms to the plan, but completely misses your point.

"Barnie's right, but we can't just win, we've got to humiliate that bastard. Don't forget, Catherine's got her Olympus minidigicam." She taps Catherine's Prada bag with a long finger. "Just wind him up so much that he does something stupid, and next weekend's tabloids can be full of the fat gimp."

Her voice shakes with emotion and you can't resist giving her hand a squeeze.

"Barbie, we'll make the fat slug crawl on his belly."

And so you enter the stud. Tintin, Haddock, Snowy, and Calculus, entering the secret hideout of Rastapopoulos.

Go to Scene 79

Scene 6

You make it back to St. John's Wood easily enough, and the cab swings to a halt opposite your small but elegant terrace. But this Midsummer Day is destined to be far from ordinary. Parked outside your front door is an ungainly group of paparazzi. Alert to your arrival, they gather their cameras and start to circle your taxi. The cabbie gives you a knowing wink, but your mind is too busy buzzing with possibilities to respond. Dave's not someone famous, surely? No, don't be ridiculous. Hurriedly, you pay the cabbie and, with head down, run up the steps to a heavy white front door. But they're not really interested in you, just your flatmate.

"How's Catherine feeling?" . . . "Is she pregnant?" . . . "Has she seen the papers?"

You smile as blandly as you can, fumble with the key, and dive inside. Your best friend, Catherine, a political journalist, has been bringing her work home with her—in the form of the minister without portfolio, Edward Bunger—and it looks like the shit has hit.

You grope for the light switch only to illuminate a dressing-gowned figure at the top of the basement stairs.

"Fuck. Astrid. What are you doing?"

Astrid, a well-built Belgian, inhabits your basement room—a room that no one else in London would take due to the lack of air, light, and kitchen facilities.

"Sorry, Barbie, I didn't mean to frighten you . . . I didn't put the light on as it costs money and . . ."

"Astrid, you don't pay for the electricity, it's all included."

"I know—that's why I don't like to use it."

In all her bovine simplicity, Astrid has a way of disarming you utterly. The fact that she pays you £160 a week for one room with a sink and a kettle also tweaks your guilt strings.

"Astrid, I can't chat, I need to talk to Catherine."

"*Ya*, I saw the newspapers, he sounds like a complete klootzak."

Whatever a klootzak is, something is very wrong; Cat's in big trouble.

"Look, we'll be drinking at the Admiral Boderington for most of the afternoon. If you've got nothing else going on come and join us . . ."

And with that, you leave the Belgian in the hall, watching your sandaled feet as they trip past the banister towards your apartment. Entering your eerily quiet flat, you throw the keys onto the kitchen table; it's covered with the Saturday papers and you stoop to examine one of the tabloids. The front page shows a photograph of a government minister and his family. The ingratiating minister, Edward Bunger, hugs up to his Labrador, two teenagers, and fat wife. The headline reads "Minister Admits Affair."

"Ooh dear. Poor Cat."

Heading from the kitchen through the sitting room, past the low cocaine table, and out into the hall, you scan for any signs of activity. Now outside Catherine's bedroom, you press an ear to the door, only to hear soft music—U2—she must be in a bad way.

"Cat, are you awake?" Silence. "I'm coming in . . ."

Catherine's head peeps out from under her covers, but only to sip more coffee and sneak another drag of a Marlboro Light. She wipes a tear away from a puffy right eye before crumpling into another sobbing fit.

"Cat, don't cry."

You rush to the side of her bed in time to give a comforting hug and catch a monologue of snivels, dribbles, and laments.

"I've been dumped for a varicose forty-eight-year-old."

And indeed she has—you can't deny it. Slightly uncomfortable with early morning levels of intimacy, you opt for "take her mind off it." It won't solve anything but it may stem the sobs for a while.

"Look, you're so much better off without him. He's twice your age. You know politicians never tell the truth."

"It's not Edward. His bitch wife is blackmailing him. I know it's not Ted."

Ineffectual. Talk about the weather.

"Catherine, it's great outside. Summer. Come on, get out of bed; you'll feel so much better."

Catherine mutters, resists your tug on her arm and winces as the curtains are whipped open.

"Come on, we have to be at the Admiral by twelve. Get in the shower. And turn that awful music off."

Go to Scene 8

Scene 7

"Visit London Zoo." You read it aloud.

She has completely misinterpreted your appeal to fantasy. You cringe to think of her reaction to your sordid, base request.

"Make love on a London rooftop beneath the midsummer stars."

She reads it with an uncertain voice.

Thank heaven you put "make love" and not "shag."

You look at her. Neither of you is smiling. You, Barnaby, are too nervous—desperate to ooze Ying sensitivity—and she is busy thinking. Maybe you should have gone for the Viagra.

Still thinking.

Finally, she answers, "I'm sure they have roofs at London Zoo. I don't see any reason why it won't work."

Clouds part and a shaft of heaven-sent moonbeam strikes you in the scrotum.

"Then what are we waiting for?"

Go to Scene 103

Scene 8

A few hours later, and your black cab swings into the King's Road. Despite the glut of traffic you wind your way westward with a silent, thoughtful Catherine and soon find yourselves entering the green calm of the Admiral Bod's pub garden. Barnaby, your ex-boyfriend, and his Asian sidekick Kamran are already reclined in the courtyard. They have reams of newspaper spread on the table.

"Welcome, ladies." Barnaby greets you with two kisses that belie his Romford Comprehensive roots. Kamran doesn't bother to stand or lift his sunglasses. "Hiya, girls." He holds up the newspaper and shows a photo of Catherine in a bust-enhancing dress. She's leaving a restaurant with the minister.

"At least it's a good photo, you might get some topless work."

Catherine looks at the picture and passes a hand through her hair with an embarrassed, strained frown. Her eyes are still puffy. You can never tell whether Kamran is being endearing or snide. You assume the latter—just in case.

"Don't be a dick, Kamran. Go and get us some drinks—we need them."

But you should know better than to insult one of Barnaby's friends.

"For Christ's sake, Barbie, Kamran was just trying to make a joke . . ."

"Yeah. That sort of twattish comment is really going to cheer Catherine up."

Scene 8

Kamran finds the whole thing vastly amusing, but that doesn't stop Barnaby being annoyed on his behalf.

"Barbie, it was a joke . . . a stupid little joke." He glowers at you with all the passion of a jilted lover—but sensitive, heart-on-his-sleeve Barnie is too nice not to notice Catherine's increasing discomfort. "Look, Catherine, we're really sorry about . . ." Barnaby trails off, looks down at the newspaper, then back up at Catherine. "Look, Kamran was just about to go to the bar. What d'you want?"

And so drinks are bought, sun-warmed seats found, and further awkward confrontation avoided. You have to expect these regular flare-ups with Barnaby—it's all par for the love–hate course. He's never really gotten over your breakup, and looking across at his wholesome face you can't help feeling that your split-up was a mistake, a jealous overreaction. He loved you, would have done anything for you, and even you can't help thinking that the chemistry is still there. If only you could learn to trust him again.

True to form, as the first couple of rounds fly by, Barnaby's hurt turns to gentle flirt. But there's no time to respond, or even enjoy, because at the first opportunity a prideless Catherine draws you aside and into a private girly chat.

"Barbie, I know you think I'm being pathetic." You don't know what to say. So you let her continue. "You just can't understand. We were so right together. Edward was the perfect gentleman. And he hates his wife . . . she's a complete witch."

She goes on, but you can't bear to listen. Catherine, your last ally in the battle against half-witted males, turned into a stereotype mistress. You daren't respond; to even try to have this conversation in your current mood would risk your friendship. Better bring the boys into the debate (they're listening anyway) and let *them* tell the truth.

"I know," you pat her hand, "what do you think, Barnie? Kam?"

They look at each other, obviously unsure whether you've

given them the cue to tell the blunt truth or whether you want them to fabricate some succoring fiction. Eventually, Kamran ruffles his overwaxed hair, and opts for blunt. "Catherine, no one ever leaves their wife because of a mistress." Catherine tuts, not realizing that in this one thing, men always know better than women. With Barnaby nodding support, Kamran explains, "Cat, the point when you had the most influence over Edward was the minute before you first slept with him. Since then, his motivation has gone down with every shag."

"That's crap, just because you two emotional retards—"

Barnaby interrupts, "Cat, we're just trying to help. Kam's right. Men only leave their wives because they're having an ego-crisis, the person they leave *for* is totally irrelevant. All you are to Edward is someone young and pretty enough to confirm that he isn't past it."

You glare at Barnie; he's gone too far. He looks at you with genuine bewilderment.

"What? That was a compliment."

Enough already, the afternoon is turning into a gender-insight manual. And worse, it looks like the great love of your life is from the dark side of Mars and your best friend is a wallowing Venusian shrew. But you don't have time to consider what this says about you, Barbarella. A screech of plastic and bearings, eclipsed in Lycra, announces the arrival of Astrid. She's managed to navigate her way on Rollerblades. Her arrival raises a few eyebrows, but you don't bother to explain, and soon another player is arriving.

The screech this time is of gleaming Michelin tires on the other side of the pub-garden wall. It's another, more historic ex-boyfriend, Will, in his red sports car. Will's presence further elates the table and you six, among the din of pleasant repartee, settle down comfortably to an afternoon of gossip. The gin flows, but it has little impact on your collective livers. Only Catherine, emotionally weakened, shows signs of getting messy. "Give her more" is the consensus of your caring circle . . .

Will is first to sense that she might be becoming good value. "So, tell us, Cat, are New Labour ministers as kinky as the old Tory ones?"

To everyone's amazement Catherine, well ginned-up and defiant, gives an answer. "Not quite. Definitely up there with High Court judges, though. I'll e-mail you the photos if you want. You'd be amazed how persuasive a politician can be."

Will smiles weakly, but Kamran starts spouting questions, his mind buzzing. In inverse proportion to Kamran's surgent mood you sense that the interrogation may flip Catherine into another depression. Time to pause the gin and make a tactical switch to some happy juice.

"Give it a break, Kamran. Go and get some Pimm's," and with that magic command he trots to the bar.

As the afternoon trundles its mint- and cucumber-garnished course, your conversation gets louder and more vulgar. People at neighboring tables start to look uneasy. Of course, that only encourages you all the more, and the afternoon skates on with urgency as your individually troubled friends outshine even the English midsummer sun with their energy. Only Will seems to be holding back, and as Kamran discusses JPEGs with Catherine, and Barnaby talks to Astrid's generous chest, you take the chance to ask Will "what news." For once, the one-time playboy really does have something to say. He's gone and mistaken lust for love.

"I've just got engaged," he whispers conspiratorially. But the lowered tone proves to be a mistake, because with unerring instinct the four turn as one. "To Annabel," he finishes timidly.

Barnaby laughs like the Hooded Claw, Astrid's Lycra deflates, Kamran's face turns a shade of English, and Catherine spills her drink down her chest. That's how you'll always remember it. Pure unabashed horror mixed with an acute, bowel-clenching terror.

How could he? Lovely, refined, delicately featured Will? Your lifetime playmate.

"That's . . . great."

You just about form the words; fighting nausea and the dread feeling that something is wholly wrong—nature out of kilter—as wrong and stomach-churningly depressing as Amazonian deforestation. And you, Barbie, are a dwindling resource, a lone, bachelor mahogany still standing proud among scarred acres of smoldering, smitten stumps. You're doing it again. Thinking of yourself. Will might be happy harnessed to the horsey, weak-chinned Annabel. So just make the most of your time together. He won't be able to spend many more decadent Saturday afternoons with you. Annabel is already disapproving of your relationship.

Barnaby, with unexpected compassion for his rival, breaks the silence. "So, Will, when's the big day?"

"Three months' time . . . September 21st, in the chapel near Annabel's parents' house. Invites are on their way."

"On their way? You only got engaged last night!"

"What can I say? Annabel's a bit of an administrative marvel."

Will's mobile rings a rescue and he stands to answer. "Hi, Pumpkin."

You all eagerly eavesdrop on the conversation.

"Flowers . . . uh, not sure, what do you think?"

He stands and walks to the far end of the garden for more privacy.

Barnaby mouths at you: "*Pumpkin??*"

Kamran, himself facing the imminent prospect of an arranged marriage (he says he's on death row), is the most affected of you all.

"This is totally not right. He might as well commit suicide. This is all your fault, Catherine. He's on the rebound because you dumped him for a fifty-year-old."

Oh God, raking up more friend-incest from the past. Catherine did have a brief fling with Will, back at Christmas—and she did indeed dump on his ego by leaving him for an old man (the minister)—but Catherine defends herself gamely.

"That has nothing to do with it, Kam. Will's just feeling his age . . . men do weird things when they get paunchy."

The mention of paunch could get the boys to close ranks. Time to throw some oil on the waters, Barbie.

"Guys, save it for Annabel. Look, if Will marries her, he'll be buggered for the rest of his life. I know what she's like, I went to school with her, and if she wants something she won't stop at *anything* to get it. And she wants Will. Whatever she's done for, or to, Will, we've got to get him out of it." You ignore Barnaby's snort and continue to outline the germ of a plan. "He just needs to remember how good it is to be single."

But Will is coming back, and the conversation must return to more anodyne felicitation. Kamran, keen to induce Catherine into a careless state, soon sets down a round of champagne tequilas in order to toast Will's news. Barbarella, you've known Will the longest, you should probably make the toast, but for some reason the words don't form. Will senses your hesitation and with the bravado that endeared him to you so long ago, he steps in and makes his own toast.

Hands placed over the glass, ready to slam, Will declares with faultless accent: *"En todos los bares hay alguien que te follaria."*

Barnaby pretends he understands, but Will doesn't wait before giving the English: "In every bar there is someone who will fuck you."

Possibly the best line you've ever heard. You wonder whether it's true. You have a terrible smile on your face. Come to think of it, everyone does, as if God just made an addendum to the commandments. The afternoon is past its bedtime and you'd better start making plans. This could be your last night of collective freedom, the last time the six can go on a bender before the marriage cancer claims you—one by one. Or maybe this is the night to get back with Barnaby.

What will you all do? Everyone has ideas, but, Barbarella, what would *you* like to do most? Catherine has an invitation to a political boat party, the culture minister is doing his bit for the country by having a party for young black musicians. It's really a shameless opportunity for some star-struck Labour MPs to rub shoulders with C-list celebs. Mind you, Barbie, you're a complete sucker for fame and power.

Will himself suggests a party at his brother-in-law's country estate. All are intent on an evening of hunting and fishing, but you are pack leader, just pick a scent and track it to a delicious consummation.

Barbarella. Time to make a first decision. Time to leave the cozy confines of a gossipy afternoon and begin to play. Just look around at your dear emotionally challenged friends: Will has been bewitched by a pony-riding banshee; Catherine looks set to sacrifice her ego; Kamran is straining at his CK seams, and Barnaby seems ripe for love. Astrid will watch on with Belgian misgiving, but you, dear Barbarella, will need Becky Sharp wits. For you are a player, and the game has begun.

The audience has been introduced to our rather troubled heroes and found them a little wanting, but don't be dismayed by their disparagement. Once true villainy rears its gruesome head your band of delinquents will positively hum with sympathy. The corrupt, the grotesque, and the downright wicked will all vie to drag you into their gutter. So ready yourself, there will be battles, sexual and pugilistic; fortunes, made and lost; elopements, seductions, corruptions, and betrayals—

all set against a glorious Technicolor backdrop of epic proportions.

But remember, you must steer the ship. Friends are diving overboard with self-destructive abandon and the sharks are circling. So keep all your wits: for success is the only goal.

One last sling from your glass. Everyone is waiting.

Do you want to go to Will's country house party? **Go to Scene 166**

Do you want to go to Catherine's political boat party? **Go to Scene 16**

Scene 9

"To the longboat, boys. To the river. We'll sail up her like ye pirates of old, Barnaby Filigree and his merry band of cutthroats."

You use your Long John Silver accent to general amusement and to stem Will's flow of objections.

"There be the dread pirate Barbarella, lusty queen of the South China seas; the firebrand Kamran the Damned with his deadly scimitar; William, privateer and adventurer; the beautiful Catherine Scarlet, devil-scourge of the Spanish Empire; and of course cabin boy Astrid. All bent on revenge and ravishment. Ready to sail up the Thames and into the heart of the English Empire—there to pillage, rape, and topple a government . . . or die in the attempt."

The evils of daytime drinking are clear.

Draining your glasses, the six split—boys and girls. Boys back to Will's discreet terrace in Thornton Place, girls back to Barbie's.

Go to Scene 65

Scene 10

Will takes credit cards from everyone and marches off with Barnaby to collect chips; Kamran sets off in hot pursuit of waitress Sally; Astrid pulls Catherine to one side, and you can't help but worry when you overhear, "So, Catherine, how does this stud poker work? Is it the same as strip?"

"Astrid, don't worry about the cards, tuck up your dress, play with your hair, and pout a lot, especially at Jenner. He has an ongoing bet with a well-known club owner on how many women they can sleep with before they die of gout. So it shouldn't be difficult to keep his attention."

Astrid, relying on the translation difference, takes this as flattery and swears to do the best she can.

Catherine and Astrid's other job is to be ready with a distraction, to save you when all else fails. You leave them to their plotting and wait for the boys to return. Will turns up first, all tense smile. "They don't use chips in the stud room. It's dollar bills or nothing." He waves a disappointingly small wedge of hundred dollar bills at you. "We're up against some big guns and this won't go far, so you need to keep a clear head. Play some black jack to get up mental speed. The stud resumes at two, that gives us half an hour."

But the real action is happening upstairs. Kam is in the bedroom above the cardroom with giggling Sally. Spotting the walk-in wardrobe isn't difficult, and, misty-voiced, he promises sensual and pecuniary riches—enough to have Sally in the "cubby," naked and yearning in under five minutes. With the door closed behind them, it's dark, stuffy, and cramped. But Kamran is a pro; he locates the small viewing glass, finds the twisting levers for rotating the chandelier, and discovers a new sexual position within sixty seconds. Happy to multitask, he then proceeds slowly with Sally's first tantric sex lesson. Settling to a gentle rhythm, Kam rests an eager eye on the room below . . .

Two o'clock and others begin to enter.

First comes a small Arab, middle-aged, dyed hair, expensive tailor, and shiny shoes. He is talking animatedly to a man of similar years but Caucasian, fat, and loud, both in dress and temperament. It's Jenner. Then comes a tall young brunette in a short black dress followed by a menacing-looking Arab—shockingly handsome but for a hooked nose that renders his countenance permanently sneering. Then a taller man, who can only be American and has all the class of an all-star Texan oil baron.

Where are you, Barbarella?

Wait, there you come now, with all the swagger of a high-rolling aristocrat approaching the scaffold in late-eighteenth-century Paris.

Go to Scene 62

Scene 11

"Wow, you weren't messing around . . ." Barbarella doesn't look shocked, just a bit disappointed. "I was kind of thinking it would be something a bit less . . ."

She doesn't finish, just stares at you in silence. The famous Barnaby gift of the gab shamed into submission.

"Look, I know I promised, but I don't really think we're going to be able to do anything like that tonight—even if we tried. To be honest I'm just completely knackered. Can you take me home?"

Well done, Barnaby. You spend your entire "social chameleon" life covering up the estuarian accent, and persuading Barbarella that you're "good enough," and then blow it all with that piece of muck. Your mind really does belong in the gutter. How do you even come up with this filth?

You're back at St. John's Wood in under fifteen minutes. Barbarella doesn't ask you in for coffee, and you settle for a tired peck on the cheek. The trip back to Clapham is a bit of a blur and by the time you get in the flat you're pretty done in. Grabbing a pint of tap water, you collapse on the sofa and promptly fall asleep in front of SkySports 3.

"Wow, you weren't messing around . . ." Barbarella places hands on her slender hips, juts out a proud

bosom, and looks down at her gorgeous body. "Is there a dress code?"

"Um . . . I'm sure you'll be fine."

Barbarella is clearly UP FOR IT. It takes twenty seconds for you to get Kamran on his mobile. He gives you the address of "The Lash" and with only the hint of a curious tone, wishes you fun. "Just mention my name at the door."

"The Lash" is an ordinary-looking house in King's Cross, next to some smart-looking offices. It takes bare minutes to get there.

The house seems like any other in the quiet little street—until you knock. A six-foot-four, bodiced vampiress answers with a polite smile.

"Hi." You desperately try to maintain a semblance of dignity as you stare into metal-spiked nipple guards.

"Kamran said we would have some fun here."

The magic "K" word invokes a smile and a welcome. You are beckoned into a small hall.

"If you wait here for a few moments, I'll call for a hostess. Would you like a drink first or do you want to go straight down to the dungeon?"

You hide a nervous gulp and are directed to the bar, a horrid little neon affair with a clustering of weirdos. You're amazed by the numbers of women and sheer acreage of PVC . . . You order two vodkas and wait.

Barbarella, sweet Barbarella, looks around with an expression of mild, quizzical amusement; her light summer dress utterly out of place among the heavy leather. Regret is slowly dawning as the sheer seediness of your fantasy dawns on you. Best get down to things quickly . . . only the thought of Barbarella, suspended for your pleasure, stops you from darting back on to the street. A spiky bleached blonde in rubber stockings greets you: "Friends of Kamran are friends of The Lash." She shakes your hand with rather inappropriate formality. "But . . . Barbarella . . . I didn't recognize you . . . are you here for the usual?"

"Yeah, but we're together . . . he's after a little fun as well."

You follow her down cold steps and into the "dungeon"—it turns out to be a cellar—surprisingly large considering the size of the house above, almost as though they've broken through into next door. You don't question, but hurry past assorted perverts to a changing room.

The small, curtained corner contains the most embarrassing array of clothing you have ever seen. Red PVC you reject as distasteful, anything with chain mail is obviously absurd. You put the gags to one side and finally opt for a leather "biker" jacket and a pair of leather trousers—only to be informed by a cruel draft that the trousers are crotchless. You look down, embarrassed by free-falling tackle.

Nothing for it, Barnie. Taking things firmly in hand, you stride forward and reenter the dim world of "the dungeon." The room is empty, but for Barbie, standing ready and waiting in a black PVC cat suit. Its tightness aches against her firm flesh and two zips run the length of each long leg, up over the hips and into the armpit before descending to a finish at delicate wrists. You can imagine the "zzzzzzzz" noise as you take a zip in each hand and see the outfit fall away . . . but that is all to come. Now she is turning and you can't help but return a smile as you notice sharp steel nipple-spikes on each seamed black breast.

Then you notice it. In the murky light it's difficult to

be sure, but as she turns the silhouette is unmistakable . . . built into her marvelous outfit is a proudly jutting dildo. It puts you to shame with its perky trajectory and bulk.

Barbarella follows your gaze, then looks you calmly in the eye . . .

. . . "My usual . . ."

The (Disturbed) End

Reader, you might try to disguise your more depraved leanings next time. Why not return to the start and go for a more subtle approach?

Scene 12

The garden, though demonstrating the same absurd formality as the house, possesses more charm. The hedges may be a little crisp and the patio terrace a little regimented, but with the addition of a hundred assorted guests they possess a warm inviting air. The addition of half a dozen champagne waiters adds to the welcoming ambience and your homing instinct takes you to one immediately.

Glass in hand, you spy Barnaby lying on the grass surrounded by a group of young girls, half of them looking concerned, the others tittering innocently. Will's "stepniece" Charlotte (bear in mind the frequently confused lineage of the family) clutches his head and holds a bag of ice to his eye. You can't have nineteen-year-old Charlotte pawing over Barnaby without a little competition.

"Barnie, what the hell have you been doing?"

You step in, pour champagne down his gullet, and the fizz forces him to sit upright and splutter a cough. Charlotte withdraws gracefully, probably relieved to get away from a frenzied Barnaby.

"That mad old bastard, he could have fucking blinded me, I'll kil—"

You pour more Veuve down his throat to keep him quiet. Apparently, the "mad old bastard" is the ancient family friend holding court to a bunch of young girls over by the makeshift champagne bar. It looks like Barnaby got into a fight with him, but you don't dare speculate . . . Sometimes you just wish you could get into Barnie's head for a while . . .

"God, you're a fool. What happened? Come and sit down and stop acting like you're back in school."

You lead him to a garden seat, safely out of sight, nestled by a tall hedge and by a relaxing water feature. Barnie doesn't want to talk about it, and he sits staring at the ground. Obviously the social chameleon is embarrassed that his "white trash" roots are showing. But no matter, this is a perfect vantage point to eye the field. You sit by Barnaby's side, and, as his pain subsides, you slip into companionable people-watching. The gaggle of humanity, chirruping and laughing, consists, you note, of disappointingly little youth. The bulk consists of the plump middle-aged and the sagged fully aged. All are tittering with that peculiar resonance unique to upper-middle-class, late-middle-aged dinner parties—one of your principal reasons for leaving home.

"What's Kamran up to?" Barnaby, clutching the ice to his head, is still feeling competitive. You scan.

"Can't see him. Have you seen Catherine?"

"Yeah, she's on the patio, talking to my lovely Charlotte."

Barnaby's obviously trying to make you jealous. It's pathetic. But he points, and, to your horror, you notice Charlotte's dress for the first time. God, you must have been blinded by concern for Barnaby. It's exactly the same as yours. No hope that it's a cheaper replica. *Exactly* the same. Except that an obliging summer breeze confirms that she regrettably possesses a flatter stomach, longer legs, and DD breasts. The antique mirror was taunting you.

Bugger.

When will you learn to stop playing the "who's the most attractive woman in the room" game. Barnaby's voice breaks into your thoughts. "She does look amazing in it."

Oh God, even he's realized, that means *everyone* will notice. How utterly humiliating.

Scene 12

"I need a drink." You mumble the excuse, get to your feet, and beat a retreat. Barnie has shown his true colors. He's either genuinely lusting after Charlotte or just playing games. Whichever it is, he's best avoided. Heading away from the house, you search for some solace in the lush verdant beauty of the garden.

Go to Scene 14

Scene 13

You take some time to survey the state of play. The crowds are already starting to thin now that the speeches are over. Worryingly, even the C-list is beginning to leave. At this rate you'll be left talking to Harriet Harman—which is hardly going to have Barbie running back in outraged jealousy.

And so you morosely head over to the bar and contemplate life. The evening has taken its toll and, standing alone with your unhealthy thoughts of life-failure, you feel the gnawing self-doubt rise like bile. Your ego was never particularly robust, but with a shortness of breath, you realize that this is about much more than that.

It's about Barbie. She sees you with other women and she doesn't care. You see her even look at another man and you're smashing furniture. Barbie always leaves you wanting more, feeling you have something to prove. Oh hell, you might as well admit it; you love her.

And the stupid bitch couldn't care less.

That's been your trouble for the last two years. You love her insecurities, fears, and failings; the way she refuses to ever acknowledge that she cared about you; the way she sometimes cried after making love. She needs you, and together, you were invincible. It's not about settling down, but teaming up—you could take on the world with Barbie by your side.

But what's this? You must have been lost in self-reflection for longer than you realized because Barbarella is bearing down upon you, helloing and smiling.

"Barnie, what have you been up to? . . . Terrible, isn't it . . . we should have gone to Will's party."

You barely get a chance to interject, and Barbie doesn't seem to mind. In fact, she's so convincingly normal that you have to double-check whether your recent voyeurism wasn't just the imagining of a febrile mind. With no little acting talent you manage, "Barbie, is that a seam? Is your dress inside out?"

Mortified, Barbarella rubs frantic hands up each side of her dress before realizing the joke. She concedes your point with a bashful smile. But before you can plague her with guilt, she is staring over your shoulder and mouthing in disbelief: "Oh, my *God.*"

Go to Scene 133

Scene 14

Popping through a hedge at the far end of the croquet lawn, you come across some boys throwing a rugby ball around. They must be Charlotte's age. Deep in your thoughts, you miss Olympia's shrill dinner call and instead decide to spectate awhile.

You feel drawn to join the *ad hoc* game, but deep down you know that girls only slow things down when they get involved in boys' fun. Never mind, to your left, sitting and inspecting his ankle, is a Prince William clone, presumably a victim of earlier scrimmaging. In your current state of mind you know you shouldn't, but can't resist an introduction.

"Hi there, what've you done to yourself?"

His double-cuffed shirt is untucked, flapping out of a divinely fitting pair of jeans. He stands to introduce himself and it's suddenly too late, your heart is thrust into a vacuum of teenage whim . . . the smell of his sunned skin, the pale, clear eyes, the schoolboy hair, the "I've been sailing in the Caribbean" Oakley marks.

"I think I've sprained it."

Time to goad his masculinity, Barbie. You're well aware of the requisite steps to land this beautiful specimen.

"Oh dear, have the big boys hurt you?" You smile to soften the gibe, but he imperceptibly draws himself to full height before replying.

Scene 14

"It's nothing, twisted it on a fucking rock," he predictably swears to affirm his masculinity. This is just too easy.

"You need to strap it up." Your expression is one of genuine concern. There are few enough boys like this to let them get damaged. Kneeling down on the grass, he lifts his trouser leg to show you the sprain, but all you can see is tanned, tight flesh, encasing swimmer's legs, just bursting with masculinity and power, and crying to be wrapped around you. The psychology is scary but clear. Make love with Oedipal abandon. He brushes the hair out of his eyes and squints in the sunlight. "I'm Nicholas."

"I'm knicker-less," you growl inwardly. Your heart breaks anew.

"I'd better take you inside and clean you up a bit." You smile with an obvious lack of innocence and he smiles back with false casualness, eager to hide his lack of years. You lead him with motherly tenderness up the steps, through the conservatory, and into the gothic monstrosity, him limping and you tottering. It turns out that Nicholas is also sleeping in the east wing, but is sharing with four friends. He insists you go to his room where he can change his muddied trousers.

And the room just smells of boys, delicious adolescent boys, brimming with fresh testosterone. It's almost dripping off the walls. You drink it in like a glass of 1975 Cheval Blanc. With slightly nervous and unseemly haste, Nicholas unbuttons his trousers.

You're obviously just reacting badly to the taunts of Charlotte's youth. But compromising yourself for a quick ego-fix is hardly the answer. Just how insecure and amoral are you?

Do you match his schoolboy lust with your schoolboy desire? **Go to Scene 122**

Or do you bury your corrupting intentions and make for dinner? **Go to Scene 178**

Scene 15

You pass the drink to Kamran, who shrugs and downs it in one. "All the more fun for me." He belches and gives a glazed grin. "That's my second."

But Will is urging you into action. No time to delay . . .

Any regrets? Kamran calls it the Shangri-la Smoothie—and you've truly missed out. Still, God alone knows what's in it. So perhaps better safe than sorry. When the time comes, remember, you were the dullard who didn't touch a drop of the stuff . . .

Go to Scene 99

Scene 16

So be it, to the boat party. A marvelous chance to see politics and showbiz combine in a vomit of insincerity and tokenism. Should be great fun.

But, oh, oh, don't forget—there'll be a huge press presence. With even the remotest chance of being a girl on film, you'll have to repair the increasingly obvious damage of an afternoon's drinking. Touche Éclat and Beauty Flash Balm won't save you now. A quick trip back to St. John's Wood is in order. Dress for sexcess—every detail from the Nars Nails to the pick-me-up powdered nose.

Catherine and Astrid join you. Catherine needs help preparing for the paparazzi, and Astrid just needs help. When Astrid first arrived in London she was intriguing and fun. You got drunk together, flirted together, and shared crude stories. But then she demanded too much attention—not just from you, but also your men. She's started to look like you, talk like you, dress like you, and you don't know how much longer you can stand it. So you leave her with Catherine and escape to your room.

Now then, Barbarella, forget about Astrid, she's not that bad, and anyway, she'll cling on, no matter what you do. So concentrate on more important matters. First up, what to wear? Black cool or white trash?

Black: the last-season Stella McCartney. Class is permanent. **Go to Scene 130**

White: the barely-room-for-knickers number. Coarse is perfect. **Go to Scene 126**

Scene 17

With Catherine's media connections, you were secretly optimistic at the prospect of a party on Rosling Street. But Barbarella's reluctance to reveal who is holding the party should have given you some clue—that this is not going to be just any party. It's at the ill-gotten home of Godfrey Thomson, friend and former colleague of none other than the Minister Without Portfolio himself, Edward Bunger. The man's omnipresence is beginning to get annoying

It takes times like this to make you realize that you really do not have the faintest understanding of how women think. Catherine was publicly humiliated in the morning papers and now seems ready for a second helping. This is emotional suicide. What is she thinking? And why doesn't her so-called best friend Barbarella stop her? This is going to get messy; you can feel it.

The cab pulls up with a squeal. You leave Will to pay and walk along a short gravel drive, through an imposing front door and into the party from hell. You are greeted in a large hallway by the sight of a gaggle of rather junior members of government and a small snatch of TV nonentities who think they are mixing in high and powerful circles.

Kamran, although keen to make a discreet entrance, errs fatally. He stumbles over a thick rug and bumps into Carol, the host's wife.

"Well, hello there. I didn't realize we'd invited some youngsters to come and play."

With a thick smile that has a reputation for being ghastly, Carol touches Kamran's elbow to provide unneeded support. She leads him away and into a minimalist drawing room; as he becomes submerged within the middle-aged morass, you realize he is lost to you. You await Will and Barbarella and can't help a masochistic smile as they arrive in your corner with looks of horror.

Will is muttering under his breath. "Nightmare." He looks accusingly at you. "Whose bloody idea was—"

Barbie interrupts him. "Oh Christ, look at Catherine."

You peer into the sitting room and sure enough, Catherine is now sitting on Edward's knee. She already seems to have lost his interest. Edward, with an enviable eye, has caught the attention of an anorexic researcher. He has obviously decided Cat is disposable, for he feeds the young blonde low-calorie canapés and flirts outrageously. Catherine is forced to watch with mounting humiliation. You all creep nearer, the better to eavesdrop.

"So how do you manage to keep yourself so wonderfully slim?" Edward smiles at the blonde waif as he ungallantly shifts his thighs under Catherine's weight.

Cat avoids your stare, aware of how ridiculous she looks. She excuses herself from Edward's lap (which allows him to resuscitate his thigh with a vigorous rub), and goes into the hall. Edward barely looks up from his new conquest.

Catherine reeks of distress as she storms past; you consider following, but Will is raising a meaningful eyebrow.

"Leave her to it, Barnie. Don't get involved."

Damsels in distress, Barnaby—your forte. And what better way to make Barbarella jealous than to have her best friend clinging to you? Besides, Catherine has had a rough time of it today; you really should see if she's OK.

But then, maybe Will's right. No one is ever thanked for getting involved in other people's business. Especially their love life. Catherine is acting like a complete moron. If you try telling her the truth, she'll just hate you for it.

It's the age-old boy's own dilemma. How do you treat your friends? Are you a rock, someone they can always rely on, or do you just try to avoid all that messy emotion stuff?

You're a brick, Barnie. Follow Catherine and make sure she's OK. **Go to Scene 137**

You're a selfish prick, Barnie. Go and get yourself a nice glass of punch. **Go to Scene 251**

Scene 18

It's a tight squeeze in the closet. Not wishing to hurt Will's feelings, but still needing to breathe, you hiss in desperation, "Christ, Will," and jab him with an elbow. He tries his hardest to move up, but the closet is restricting and you have no option but to remain firmly pressed. Flatteringly, a proud piece of manhood nudges your left thigh.

The voices near are quiet and muffled and you both peer through the angled slats, intrigued to see who the mystery intruders are. All you can see are the waists and legs of a man and woman. She appears to be bending over the desk, while he lifts her skirt and prods her in a curiously asexual manner. It might almost be described as medical. You struggle with Will to get a better view.

You have been placed in an unusual situation. Voyeurism is not really your thing, or at least not with someone at your side. Yet here you are, standing in silence, sipping champagne and gaping through slats reminiscent of a peep show. The only difference from that place in Tokyo is that you haven't been provided with tissues.

The silence makes you incredibly aware of every sound, every breath, and every embarrassing moan. There is nothing to do but watch. Perhaps it's the drink, or even the emotional strain of the night's events, but you are feeling distinctly turned on. Ridiculous really. More predictably, Will is sharing your emotion.

Scene 18

And so the two headless bodies begin to perform, the man has amazing wrist speed, and the woman a spine of spaghetti. If there was room to turn on Will (for cathartic purposes) you would, but there isn't. So you wait and you watch, and you watch and you wait. Christ, you need to do something. Divine intervention allows Will to somehow maneuver his hand up your dress (the double-jointed arm that made him so splendid at leg spin for his school eleven). Don't allow yourself to stop and consider how sordid this is.

A well-trained man can be taught to please you in exactly the way you know best—but every now and then, his mind must waiver, the concentration goes and the overriding sensation is one of "door slams on clitoris." Will causes you to jolt, and with a loss of balance you both come crashing out of the closet, knocking the brass desk lamp on to the floor. You are left, four individuals fumbling in complete darkness and (two of them in particular) wondering what the hell is going on.

Before your eyes have time to adjust to the newly blackened room, you become lost in acres of bare smooth skin, tingling and caressing as it rubs vigorously against your own. Will's hand doesn't seem to want to stop, and you're happily distracted by it. All you can imagine is eels writhing together in a confined tank.

But you don't have time to consider the absurdity, because with a sudden flare, a flaming light illuminates the scene.

Go to Scene 84

Scene 19

Before leaving the conspiracy, Catherine sets the plan rolling. Pulling out her mobile, she dials up the paper: "Hi, Charlie, it's Catherine. Listen, I've got a great scoop. It'll break outside Godfrey Thomson's house in the next hour or so . . . yeah, Holland Park . . . OK, just make sure they're in position in the next thirty minutes . . . OK . . . no problem."

Flipping the phone cover shut, Catherine flashes a smile more wicked than a Sacher torte. Turning to Barbarella and Astrid, she takes control. "OK, girls, it's time to get frisky. A couple of lines to get us all in the mood. Then, Barbie, you go downstairs and tell Edward that we need to see him for a private briefing in the study. That's our usual code for a quickie. He *won't* believe his luck. Trust me . . . Edward Bunger will come."

Slightly perturbed by Catherine's appalling but unintended innuendo, you grimace briefly before heading for the study with Astrid and Cat. The girls chat to each other awkwardly, but soon lapse into silence. You take up your position, hidden behind a thick velvet curtain, and the next few minutes pass in silence.

You congratulate yourself on such a brilliant plan. In a few moments you'll be treated to the most wonderfully comic display of erotica by people thinking you are doing *them* a favor. You imagine Barbarella's heart pounding as she leads Edward up the stairs, wondering how far she will have to go before you call a halt and bring in the heavies. You watch as Catherine talks to Astrid, obviously caught between the horror of her predicament and the lust to obtain revenge—or maybe there's a hint of excitement at the prospect of communal love. You stand in silent wonder as Catherine taps tense fingers on the desk. Then she does something so unexpected it gives you an instant erection. She slides out of her dress to reveal pert brown breasts and a small satin G-string. Before Astrid can move, Catherine dashes over to the door, conceals all beneath a black bathrobe, and lights up a big fat cigar.

It doesn't take a sex therapist to see the thinking behind this act. When Edward and Barbarella finally enter the room, the minister stares, dumbfounded. He puts up no resistance as Barbarella helps him shuffle out of his trousers.

Catherine begins the verbal seduction. "I thought you might enjoy some more company. After all, you're such a popular man and I'm *very* keen to keep you interested. Barbarella and Astrid mentioned how attractive they thought you were, so I thought, let's have some fun together."

Edward is unable to answer, dumbstruck by the mind-blowing possibility of three women (or possibly appalled at the porn-standard dialogue).

Catherine continues in the tone of a schoolmistress. "Just remember I'm the one in charge here and I'll give the orders, so get undressed and go over to the desk by Astrid."

Yikes. You stand peering, waiting for Catherine's next command.

"Oh, and leave your socks on." This from Barbie, ever keen to take up the dominatrix mantle.

Eager to get the party going, Edward walks, nay, virtually staggers, towards Barbarella. "You look amazing, Barbarella. Can I help you take off your dress?" This is crunch time. Will she be able to go through with it?

Edward's undersized head is bulging with eyes, his orange

chest hair is positively screaming "run away," and he's wearing holed gray socks and a pencil erection. What will Barbie do?

"My, I thought you'd never ask—I'm roasting."

Bingo.

As the minister gets to work on Barbie's dress, Catherine sits back pensively, barely noticing as the flushed Astrid playfully strokes her hair. Barbie's dress has now been removed and flung, to reveal a distinct lack of underwear and surgically enhanced breasts. You strain to see more. Edward prostrates himself, kneeling before Barbie, the celestial goddess. Far from showing further signs of embarrassment, she's clearly enjoying the attentions of the minister—holding hands aloft, eyes closed, basking in the limelight.

It doesn't take long for the mood (and possibly the coke) to affect Astrid uncontrollably. She begins to work on Edward with amazing thespian talent, assuming she is still acting. Catherine, still unsure, pats Edward on the head and looks desperately towards your curtain, willing you to take a photograph.

But Astrid has a hand between her thighs before she can escape.

And you, Barnie?

You watch.

The scene unfolds and you can't help but laugh at everyone's enthusiasm. Edward is practically salivating as Astrid batters him with her chest. Catherine and Barbarella both have their eyes shut and you can't resist a quick ogle at Barbie's gym-worked bottom.

But that is all.

Edward, temporarily unsighted by Astrid's body, comes up for air. He notices you, and with the others fumbling, you stare at each other across the room—uncertain, silver-backed rivals, ready to take charge of the harem. Then he notices the camera.

With lightning reflex, you capture Astrid's attempt at self-induced orgasm forever on film. More critically, for the future of

English politics, you capture the end of Edward's political career. He manages to look shocked, confused, and lustful all in the same expression.

But the frozen horror doesn't last long: "You bastards. Catherine, you bitch. I'll kill you."

Raised voices are a signal for Will and Kamran to burst in and frog march Edward towards the front door. You run after them, eager to hear his cries of desperation. Edward struggles at the top of the stairs, but only succeeds in looking more ridiculous. Will and Kamran are too powerful. Will hisses into Edward's ear: "Like a fox to the hounds."

"For God's sake put me down. Let me go . . . please . . . not outside!"

By now, the guys have Edward at the front door. Kamran turns to Will: "Don't you hate desperate people?"

And with relative ease the front door is opened and Edward is pushed down the front step.

Naked.

Good morning, Great Britain.

MINISTER COCKS UP
TEDDY BARE

The (Exposed) End

A nice snap for Barnie's collection, but our hero didn't get much action. That's what happens when you put vengeance before libido. Give it another go, Reader, and try to get in the thick of things.

Scene 20

You're off. With no time to lose you sprint inelegantly to the door, and barely have time to see Astrid trip Annabel with a well-positioned and solid ankle.

You remember the house well enough to locate the dog pantry almost immediately. The dogs are sitting sleepily just as you remember them from over a year ago. Two wily springer spaniels, a Jack Russell, and the true object of your search—a rather fat, "retired" beagle called Finbar.

You bend down and pet the old beagle. "Hello there, old fella." You pull out the handkerchief provided by Oswald and see the dog's eyes dilate.

"Three drops of this scent can attract the Indonesian musk vole from up to a mile away. I assure you, it works just as effectively on *Homo sapiens*," Oswald had explained earlier. "I'm afraid I carry this small vial more from habit these days."

No time to allow Finbar to slump into pheromone-induced torpor, Oswald cunningly shook hands with Will and he now reeks of the stuff. Time to set Finbar on the trail. Whoever gets to Will first may not be able to control themselves . . .

Neglecting to find a leash, you set Finbar off with a curt "Seek," and the arthritic hound stumbles off, nose firmly to the floor, in search of the scent.

Finbar may be fourteen in dog years, but he hasn't lost his "nose." Like an aging Elvis, he waddles on shaking back legs, but with a sudden yelp generates a tremendous turn of speed and shoots into the garden. He's probably smelled a fox. Will wouldn't have gone into the garden, he hates the dark.

With a curse you realize that your cunning plan is beginning to unravel. When Snuffy stalked her man sixty-odd years ago she had one of the nation's finest pedigree bloodhounds on her team. You have a pheromone-addled nonagenarian beagle. Time to get real. Time to rely on your own instincts. Will would have almost certainly gone up to one of the far bedrooms. You know his style. But Finbar has returned from the garden and is looking at you with the intelligence of Lassie, his big appealing eyes seem to be talking to you.

What to do? Your future happiness dangles over the abyss.

Do you follow Finbar's unerring nose and traipse into the gloomy garden? **Go to Scene 208**

Do you trust your own instincts and head straight to the bedrooms? **Go to Scene 261**

Scene 21

Back at the party you catch your breath and grab a large whisky. You don't have long to mull yourself into a depression, because Kamran, stuck with Astrid, is compromised and desperate for help.

"I keep introducing her to people I don't know, just to be rid of her. And she keeps coming back. People might think she's my girlfriend."

You don't hesitate; sending Kamran for drinks, you make a brilliant double play: "Astrid, I've got to talk to you . . . privately," looking nervously over your shoulder, "it's about Barbie and Will, but we have got to talk privately, go down those steps to the far right cabin. I'll meet you there in five minutes."

If Barnaby is not having fun, then no one will. And besides, now Kamran owes you a favor.

Go to Scene 13

Scene 22

You note with mixed feelings that the formal gallery has been chosen as the site of the evening's dining experience. It is less imposing, more windowed, and generally less miserable than the rest of the house, but you can't help remembering that the last time you were here, all those years ago, was the culmination of a happy night of drunken lovemaking with the now soon-to-be departed Will. Mind you, that week you christened just about every room with your passion—it was Will's idea of fun. You wave distantly at Will as he sits politely at the far end of the table, and wonder if he, too, is reliving the memories. But back to the present, Will is history, time to concentrate on the future—and so you slip into the chair on Barnaby's left.

First check out the identities of your dining companions. The old boy responsible for Barnaby's black eye earlier has joined the foot of the table and introduces himself to you as "Uncle Oswald." To the other side of you is a decaying dowager, who refers to herself as Snuffy, and Kamran and Astrid make up the opposite side. Catherine has been separated from Charlotte by a seemingly dull banking couple from London.

Despite possessing ears old enough to have heard Queen Victoria, Oswald seems to be alarmingly alert and is already trying to impress you and Charlotte's friends with his seventeenth-century walking cane. Oswald thrusts the cane alarmingly at you:

"Just put the palm of your hand on it, there, that's right. Grip it, girl. Now imagine where that has been."

Not wishing to upset this screamingly senile relic, you reluctantly place your hand on the knob, not remotely pausing to contemplate where it's been.

"It's very warm," is all you can offer, but Oswald isn't to be put off. "Yes that's right—did you feel a tingle?"

You half nod, but fail to form a sentence. Oswald whips it away and proffers it to Astrid. "You look a game sort. Put your lips to it and tell me if you feel a tingle."

And so Astrid has the peculiar privilege of putting it to her mouth. Now you know exactly where that cane's been. You covertly rub a napkin between your hands, below the table line.

"Tell me, do you feel it?"

Astrid is slightly more vivacious in her response. "Yes, yes. I did. Wow, it's like electricity."

God, you just hope that Astrid isn't about to confuse friendliness with sexual allure. Oswald beams and pats her hand. "That, my dear, is the sexual energy of Peter the Great, Imperial Ruler of Muscovy. I purchased it in Uzbekistan before the collapse of the Union."

Astrid beams back.

Fortunately, this rather odd social interplay is squashed beneath the personality of a late arrival. Slumping between Astrid and Charlotte in the previously empty space is, frankly, a Mediterranean god. The accent and tan are unmistakably Cannes.

"Amazing, I made it in time for the starter. Unbelievable. To think, seven hours ago I was playing polo in Rhode Island."

Ding, ding, ding, jackpot. And he has barely turned the ignition on his Rolls-Royce charm. Turning to you with a buffed denture smile, he urges you into the web of his conversation. "My name is Marc, Marc-Pacaud." He doesn't ask for yours, but continues, "To be honest wiz you, I don't actually know anyone here. My father asked me to come. He is the Comte de Villefort and waz at 'arrow with 'is Lordship."

With this last gorgeous piece of self-inflation, he plucks a butter-dripped spear of asparagus from his plate and nibbles delicately. You dream of lapping up his butter with a rough tongue. No doubt about it, looking around the table at your potential competition, all females within the vicinity of Marc's aftershave are thinking as one.

Barnaby engages Marc in conversation, eager for some lime-light. "So were you at Harrow as well? Your English is certainly very good." The gibe would normally make you laugh, but somehow it just makes Barnaby look bitter. Marc pauses, contemplates another spear of asparagus, then continues before anyone can change the subject.

"No, I spent my youth in Polynesia, my father, he waz governor of an island there for a time. My youth," he pauses dramatically, "waz one long dive for the pearls. No equipment, just zese arms and zese lungs. Of all the divers, I could stay under longest. I am champion of France in this sport. That is what I do."

Oh God. Record-breaking cunnilingus. You can't help but adjust yourself, training your cleavage on the Frenchman. Charlotte's eyes twinkle, Astrid twists awkwardly close, and Catherine strains to hear the conversation. Even the dowager, Snuffy, is disengaging herself from a conversation to lend an ear.

Marc is on a roll. He is a living cliché, and the diving speech is meaningless gibberish, but that is irrelevant. Tonight is for fun, nothing else. You notice that your body is way ahead of you—"shoulders back, chest out," as your mum used to say. You turn and notice that Barnaby is visibly upset by Charlotte's rapt attention to the Frenchman. Morosely you feel that the two of you are suddenly second rate. And with a vicious reaction you decide to goad Barnie with a whisper: "That man is such an arse, but I can't help thinking he will be magnificent in bed." Barnaby draws breath at the word "will"—typical ex-boyfriend, perfectly happy to forget you until you show signs of interest in another man. Maybe Barnaby does hold intentions towards you after all, but this is no time to relish your discovery. You turn back to the conversation only to notice a mutual twinkle in Marc and Charlotte's eyes. The girl is positively ruining your evening.

"You see, Charlotte, my sport requires you to address all your fears, your inadequacies, your doubts. Each time I go down it is to the utmost of human endurance. A slight panic, an extra heart beat 'ere, an unnecessary flap of ze leg, and the oxygen in my brain will run out, and I" . . . dramatic pause . . . "will remain forever at the bottom of the sea."

By now, Charlotte is monopolizing him with eager questions. You'll have to do something quick, this isn't just about fun anymore—your femininity is on the line. Fortunately, Barnie, with mutual interest, has a plan.

Go to Scene 26

Scene 23

Grins all round. But before you can dwell on sordid thoughts, the shadow from a dark plump cloud descends upon you. Barbarella notices it first.

"Oh Christ, not that wanker."

You turn, but your vision is blinded by a gilded glare, brighter than any jeweler's window. Only one man you know insists on wearing so much gold jewelry. Only one man can disgust you quite this much. That bastard.

Nigel Jenner.

Your face reddens with rage. A slug of brandy does little to dull it.

"Well, you youngsters. Come to play with the big boys?"

"Tosser," you cough behind your hand.

Barnie—not funny, not restrained—just bitter.

"However do you get by with such manners, Mr. Wilson? Still, there's really no disguising your lowly Romford roots. Be proud and loud, that's what I say. After all, there aren't that many third-world cities in the South of England. You have a unique social heritage."

You mull, your usual razor mind temporarily paralyzed by hate. Nigel moves on to Barbie.

"Barbarella, you are looking so much better—lost that other

chin. I shouldn't think you'll have to stick with "Romford Man" much longer now."

Barbie makes a fist of verbal self-defense. "Nigel, you young blade, you're not offering yourself to little-old-me, are you? I feel humbled, I'm not worthy. And, besides, I don't think I've got the upper body strength to stay breathing under such a mountain of a man."

You love her.

But Nigel is rousing himself.

"Barbarella, I'm so sorry. You must have misunderstood me. How embarrassing. I wasn't referring to myself, I was thinking of someone altogether more suitable. A brick maker, or a fish and chip shop owner, perhaps. You've got to work your way up the social scale more gradually—you've sunk right to the bottom, you know. I fear that by the time you're up to the likes of anyone here you'll be too old. After all, you may look ravishing in this light, but I saw those shots of you at Henry's reception . . . time's running out, dear girl."

Time to unsheathe that rapier wit, Barnaby. You've verbally trussed this turkey before, time to do it in defense of Barbie's honor. Slash a verbal zed on his sweating forehead; no, better still, carve "toad" on his blubbery neck; or "flatulence" on his chubby backside; or . . .

. . . Too late

. . . he has gone.

Gone to harass Catherine with intrusive questions and gloating benevolence.

But Barbie is chastising. "My hero," she bats eyelids in mock worship, "you saved me from that hideous man. You're so brave."

"Barbie, you know what happened the last time I verbally humiliated him. He published and we were damned."

Barbie's venom is temporarily abated. She remembers the photograph, as well as you remember the caption:

Scene 23

"Carrington Heiress, and the Slime"

Below, a picture of the two of you staggering from a reception party at the end of a long night. Needless to say it was four o'clock in the morning. Barbie *had* drunk five pints of champagne, and she *had* slipped on the lawn. But nonetheless, if you'd spent the equivalent of Ghana's national debt on facial beauty treatment you would never expect, in any circumstances, to display quite so many chins in any one photograph.

You didn't see her for over four months. Rumor has it she spent every night for sixteen weeks in the gym.

For you, if anything, the consequences of verbally assaulting Nigel Jenner were more damaging. At the time you were indestructible, Barbie on your arm, a queue of eligible girls waiting to take her place, and your first real bonus in the bank. Barnaby, social climbing chameleon, had well and truly climbed out of the council house gutter and was playing with the stars.

Little did you think that the fat blimp, who seemed the perfect victim for your infamous cutting humor, would turn out to be a newspaper columnist with a strong sense of vengeance. Your ItBoy career was over before it had begun, killed by a few column inches. "Barbie's bit of rough" with his "pretied bow-tie" was caricatured as "Mr. Cro-Magnon"; a prehistoric figure bemused and dazzled by such dizzying social advances as cutlery and vowels.

The phone calls from eligible girls dried up. They forgot to return your calls and, worse, you hit a sexual trough. And all because of Jenner and his poisoned quill.

But wait, Will has returned with a wad of dollars and some news to break your mutual silence.

"It's in the bag, chaps. Two o'clock restart, that gives us half an hour to prepare." With all the tenderness of a boxing second, Will takes you into his care. "This isn't the ordinary crowd. The dicks don't swing any lower. There are two Arabs, one is the worst poker player I have ever seen, and the other is a professional gambler. One American whom I have never met and finally—the real treat—a certain Mr. Jenner, social columnist, and multi-millionaire. Just remember the chandelier goes anticlockwise to raise, clockwise to fold. Oh, Barnie, there's just one thing I have to tell you. Can we, uh, have a private chat?"

Will looks to Barbarella as he speaks this last, and with only a small huff she leaves.

He puts his arm around your shoulder, and lowers his voice: "You're not going to like this."

Go to Scene 246

Scene 24

It doesn't take long to find the others. They are idling by the exit, eagerly debating the age-old question—what to do next? One party might be drawing to a close, but the night is barely flowering into pubescence. The day's extensive alcohol consumption fuels the friendly rivalry between Will and Barnaby.

"What's wrong with the West India? It's perfect," Will gibes at Barnie, "or does it make you feel inadequate?"

The exclusive casino always exposes the differences between the two of them. Will is in his element at the West India—he knows virtually every member. Then again, Barnie has the cash to throw around. He enjoys outbetting Will and thinks losing a lot of money impresses the girls.

As for the others, Catherine seems distracted, Kamran seems distracted by Catherine, and Astrid looks like she's been rolling on the floor.

"Hello, Barbarella. Good news, Annabel has gone home with a migraine." You wince at her indiscretion, but Will is too busy arguing with Barnaby to have heard anything.

"That's great, Astrid." You turn to Catherine, eager for some sanity, but are disappointed.

"Barbie, have you seen Edward? He's invited us all on to another party over in Holland Park, but he's disappeared."

Will breaks off from arguing with Barnaby. "Barbie, it'll be the party from the Black Lagoon—let's go to the casino and make some cash." He nods eagerly, but Catherine is adamant.

"Look, I don't care what you all do. I'm going to Edward's party whether you join me or not." She looks at you. "Are you coming, or do I have to go on my own?"

Oh dear. Catherine's still in a bad way. The cause, you suspect, may be more to do with the novelty of rejection than true love. Edward and his nasty world of politics and peccadilloes have proved too much. Catherine may have your sympathies, but the West India *is* full of high-rolling idiots. With a bit of luck you could win enough to pay off your credit card.

Decisions, decisions.

Time to invest some time in your friendship. Catherine needs support, and support she shall have. **Go to Scene 196**

Your credit card needs help more than she does. The party is bound to be a disaster and, besides, you're not sure that you can stomach running back into Edward Bunger. **Go to Scene 186**

Scene 25

The slab of clay stares back at you. It taunts you with memories of an ashtray you made in school—the year, aged thirteen, that you gave up art.

What to do?

Your mind wrestles, but your eyes are happy to spectate. Carmen looks tranquil, almost asleep. Her long firm calves send your eyes roving up to tightly muscled thighs. There you sight small fine hairs as they catch the light and urge you to stroke. The perfect curve of her stomach, the delicate ribs pressing out against her tanned skin and the swelling of her breasts. Breasts covered in damp clay, the nipples hardening at its coldness.

"*Barnie,* what are you doing?"

She jumps at the first feel of wet clay and looks down at her coated breasts in horror. But it would take a hard woman to deny pleasure to a man with such a look of enthusiasm.

"Barnie, no wonder you had to retire." Carmen smiles. She can't put her dress back on now that she's covered in mud. For five long seconds she looks through thickly mascaraed lashes at your imploring face. Then, closing her eyes she languishes back, arms raised above her head in submission . . . ready for you to complete your masterpiece.

The (Mud Glorious Mud) End

Lying through your back teeth got you far, Reader. But if you want to go all the way, a more sophisticated approach might be better. If you're smart, and ignore your conscience, you can have whatever you want . . .

Scene 26

Marc continues.

"So, you see, in France, I am, how you say, a 'pinup.'"

Barnie feigns confusion and interjects. "Ah you mean like a pop star or footballer. In England we say a 'prick up' or just 'a prick.'"

"Yes that is it, I am a 'big prick.' My father, le Comte, he gets very embarrassed with all the television attention, but for me it is OK."

You let out a snort and Catherine can't make eye contact. Astrid doesn't get it. Marc smiles glibly around the table. And sure enough, Charlotte is suddenly looking less interested than before. Ah, fickle youth. Only Uncle Oswald can respond with decorum: "But, surely, your father must be very proud that you can sit about holding your breath."

"*Non*, *non*, you do not understand. It is more than that. It's not just sitting around with your mouth shut."

Barnie pipes in. "I don't suppose you'd be very good at that."

But before Barnie can push home his advantage, Olympia booms shrilly from the far end of the room: "WHAT DO YOU MEAN STUCK?"

The poor kitchen-hand fails to register any sound at your far end, but the gist is clear from Olympia's strident tones: "It can't be stuck. George, do something about it."

And George, Sixth Lord Ravenshaw, trots off obediently to sort out the domestic crisis. Olympia calms herself and addresses the hungry throng.

"My apologies everybody," she sighs theatrically. "Half the main course appears to be stuck in the lift from the kitchens. They probably haven't been serviced since the First World War."

This with a glower at her husband's empty seat. She effects a twittering gaggle of conversation from the ninety-odd guests, no less so than at your, far end.

"God, I'm starving," booms Astrid.

You wince at Astrid's latest shibboleth, but before you have an opportunity to chastise her, Lord Ravenshaw returns and announces that the main course will be some while. A man called Frank is coming from the village with his tool kit etc., but tuck into the wine and try to drink through the hunger is the general advice. And so you do.

Baroness Snuffy shouts, "More gin, boy," to a nearby, middle-aged waiter, who quickly returns with a bottle of Bombay Sapphire. Snuffy relieves him of it with the skill of a Parisian pick-pocket, sloshes out seven generous glasses, and pops the bottle in her handbag. "Bombay Sapphire is a wonderful appetite suppressant, but it must be drunk neat."

The gin does wonders for the conversation, but before you can tempt the risqué Snuffy into any juicy prewar confessions, Lord George, your host, is back with some more bad news: "I AM DEEPLY SORRY EVERYBODY. FRANK, FROM THE VILLAGE, HAS GOT HIMSELF WEDGED."

With British restraint, all refrain from groaning, but the misery is clear, no more food for at least another half-hour. More wine is circulated and the babble reaches a higher pitch.

Then you suddenly notice that Charlotte and Marc are standing. "We're just going into the garden so Marc can have a look at the sculpture," Charlotte announces casually.

Scene 26

God, she doesn't hang about. With a panging fear you realize that this evening you risk coming a pitiful second while the beautiful people dazzle you with their perfection. Fortunately Barnie is thinking for both of you.

"Astrid, I had forgotten, you're a huge Henry Moore fan, you must go with them," he splurts out.

Astrid blinks at you. And so you kick her under the table and nod imperceptibly. Astrid comes good: "I would love to meet Henry Moore, yes," and so she joins Marc and Charlotte as they leave for the garden—and you buy yourself time.

While the others discuss the Frenchman, and plot and scheme, you become lost in your thoughts. Charlotte, mocking you in her identical dress (she hasn't even mentioned it), is drawing the eye of every male from Oswald to your own dear doting Barnaby. She has all the charms of youth, but seems to possess none of the hang-ups. She can't be as perfect as she seems. God, if only she had a spot on her back, your jealousy would be abated a little, but she doesn't, just a small, dark, alluring mole between her shoulder blades. You bite a lip at the thought of Marc ignoring you and vow that you won't let the "beautiful couple" make you feel inadequate. Marc may be a tosser, but you'll master his arrogance. You bite your lip with renewed vigor at the thought of his hard body. But Barnie is talking to you. "That's all you have to do, Barbie. Just sit there, look longingly at Marc, and bite your lip like professional. Just don't forget to stand up as soon as Astrid does."

Barnie has long since ceased to make sense, so you smile warmly and nod in agreement. It is only when Marc, Astrid, and Charlotte return that you realize some serious plotting has taken place. With somewhat obvious acting, Barnaby begins with a carefully thought-out opening: "Marc, we've just been trying to hold our breaths. I can't believe how hard it is. How on earth do you hold your breath for over a minute?"

This is sufficient to prize further dialogue from the puffed Marc.

"One minute? That is nothing. Here and now, I could probably keep my breath for five minutes, maybe longer."

The French demigod loosens his bow-tie with thespian ease. Oswald borrows Marc's Patek Philippe and with a final gasp from the Frenchman, Oswald starts the clock.

Thirty seconds gone, it strikes you anew how impressive this is going to look. Five minutes is a long time. One hour's oral sex on twelve breaths. You can't forget your rival as Charlotte renews her interested gaze. Something has to be done, and, judging by the desperate look on Barnie's face, you can't rely on him to do anything. One minute thirty and Charlotte is looking *very* interested. Time to act. Maybe just a kick to the shin or a stiletto to the foot. You draw yourself down and extend a leg, ready to lash out, but it would seem that someone has a better idea. Beneath the tablecloth, a serious game is afoot. You look around. Kamran is smiling his normal thoughtful smile. Surely not. The dowager looks as though she has nodded off, but Astrid has fire in her eyes—Bingo—must be.

With sinuous intent, Astrid coils her foot up the inside of Marc's leg, turning it at the knee junction before driving it towards the happily awaiting groin. There, with skill known only to a few back in Antwerp, her supple toes tinkle the glockenspiel of desire.

Above, she continues to smile. And to those who fail to notice her subtle lip licking, nothing appears untoward. Certainly Charlotte, bless her, can't understand her failure to maintain Marc's attention.

Marc smiles gently. And holds his breath.

With ninety seconds gone, Oswald instills a sense of drama. "An entire minute everybody, an entire minute."

This is met with a gentle ripple of polite applause from the British reserve. Few notice Oswald's inaccurate timekeeping. And so the minutes pass. Charlotte's with increasing interest, Marc's with increasing pleasure, Barnie's with increasing spite, and Oswald's with increasing timekeeping confusion.

"Two minutes," he cries with false astonishment after three minutes thirty-eight have elapsed.

More foot artistry and the blood is draining from other vital organs. Marc stops smiling and starts to concentrate. You remember guiltily that you should be biting your lip and realize that it must be part of this convoluted plan. If only Marc can get to four minutes he will save face and blame the Concorde flight for his underperformance. You can see Marc's concentration, but with gibbon dexterity, Astrid's foot unzips Marc's fly, finds little resistance from tight, thonged briefs and . . . enters the forbidden domain. Marc lets out a whimper of precious air.

The Patek Philippe registers five minutes.

"Three minutes, ladies and gentlemen, three minutes."

Marc's erection is sucking away his life. Astrid's foot continues to knead, it's everywhere and, teasingly, nowhere. Like a she-panther in heat, she sits and gnaws her lip. And then . . . she stands.

But someone still kneads.

It wasn't Astrid at all.

Obeying Barnaby's instructions you stand, utterly confused, and in turn excuse yourself.

And yet the foot still burrows.

And yet, and yet, the dowager, she is smiling, and biting her lip.

Marc-Pacaud slumps across the table.

A gasp goes up from the collective. Charlotte jumps up, eager to check for a pulse. But Kamran is mouthing wisdom: "Barbarella, someone needs to take Marc upstairs and make sure he's all right." He adds unnecessarily, "Give him a once-over."

Frenchie has well and truly conked. A victory of sorts . . . except that all you're left with is the game-playing child, Barnaby. It's a bit of a long shot, but Marc may just be revivable. If anyone can do it, surely you can. But then, he might just be a waste of time and resources. I guess the real question is, how keen are you to get a little private time with Marc-Pacaud?

Which is it to be?

Tend to the poor broken Frenchman immediately.
Go to Scene 66

Do Not Resuscitate, let him wait. **Go to Scene 180**

Scene 27

It doesn't take long for Astrid to return to her normal equine state.

"God, Barbie, how long have you had Astrid on this stuff?"

"Don't lecture, Barnie. You try living next to her for six months. It doesn't do any harm, just calms her down a bit."

And with Astrid temporarily subdued, Will's paranoia takes center stage.

"That bloody chandelier hasn't been oiled since the Boer War; the noise was making my fillings vibrate."

Time to calm things down and get everyone to focus on what this is really about.

"Guys, this could be our one big chance to make it. People like Jenner and Newt win or lose our combined salaries every night of the week. Let's face it, no matter how much money we earn, we spend it. And in ten years' time we'll just be older, uglier, and more knackered. Only one thing will stay constant—we still won't have paid off our credit cards."

Will nods vigorously, the others stare dumbly, horrified at your vision of their future.

"I'm not joking. This could be the one chance we ever get to make some serious money. We've got to go for one big hit. We've got to wait 'til Jenner gets overconfident and then win huge—on one big hand."

Barbarella, with her very personal reasons for revenge, warms to the theme, but completely misses your point.

"Barnie's right, but we can't just win, we've got to humiliate that bastard. Don't forget Catherine's got her Olympus minidigicam." She taps Catherine's Prada bag with a long finger. "Just wind him up so much that he does something stupid—and next weekend's tabloids can be full of the fat gimp."

Her voice shakes with emotion and you can't resist giving her hand a squeeze.

"Barbie, we'll make the fat slug crawl on his belly."

And so you enter the stud. Dorothy, Tinman, Scarecrow, and Lion heading west, to the castle of the witch. **Go to Scene 89**

Scene 28

"Sorry, Martin, I'm so ditzy. I completely forgot. I'm supposed to be going to another party with my friend. We're supposed to meet up at," you check your watch, "ten. She'll be waiting for me. It was lovely meeting you."

Well done, Barbarella. He sure was trouble; a man who drinks slimline tonic, listens to Ella Fitzgerald, and plucks his eyebrows. Your ego was almost sacrificed on the rocks of homosexuality. Why are the nice ones always gay?

Tripping off to the loo you thank your lucky stars. Nothing is more humiliating than throwing yourself at a man who's more interested in your shoes than breasts. Lovely Martin would have become your best friend, and then he'd have slowly driven you crazy.

Go to Scene 92

Scene 29

The hardest part about making riches at the West India is getting in. Tonight is no exception. Fortunately, Catherine is having the same trouble, and you meet her on the doorstep negotiating with a discreet doorman. There's no time to ask her how she's been separated from the others, because she seems to be in a spot of trouble.

"Just get Will down here and he'll explain . . . no I'm not press, I just want to speak to Mr. William Burton, he knows who I am."

"Oh, I know who you are. It's just that Mr. Burton specified you would be with a Mr. Barnaby Wilson." He looks over his glasses at Cat's obviously absent companion, and smoothes down his Barney's tie.

"That's right," you interject, running up the steps and eager to put the heavy front door between you and an avenging policeman, "here I am . . ."

"Can I see some ID then, sir?"

"Um, I've got credit cards, will that do?"

"Sorry, sir, I'll have to insist on photo ID. A driving license or passport, something like that."

The doorman has obviously decided to enjoy himself. Power corrupts, and absolute power seems to corrupt bouncers no matter how shitty or expensive the club. It's the same the world over. Well, Barnie, all your short, miserable life you've been turning tail at the first resistance from a doorman (mind you, they do actually kill troublemakers at nightclubs in Southend), how about you show some backbone for a change. Come on, you're dressed in a tuxedo, on the run from the police, you're going into an illegal casino with some top totty on your arm, the bow-tie is flapping about your neck. What would James Bond do in this situation?

And besides, the doorman may look quite tough, but at the end of the day, he's only five foot six.

You Only Live Once. To hell with it—show the little shit some manners. **Go to Scene 165**

Live and Let Live. "Look, I'm really sorry, but I don't have any photo-ID on me. If you could please just get Will, he'll be able to sort all this out." **Go to Scene 43**

Scene 30

You burst out of the cubicle just in time to catch Astrid.

"Astrid, what did she say?"

Astrid turns like a startled ox. "Barbarella, what are . . ." She trails off, terrified at your intensity.

"Astrid, I heard everything. Now tell me, who is it?"

Astrid is suffering contortions of the soul. Some split loyalty, some dislike of conflict—for rumor and gossip—stays her tongue. Eventually she steps forward, and, casting a furtive glance over her shoulder, whispers softly.

Go to Scene 32

Scene 31

You gulp the glass in one. If you must drink of the poisoned chalice then do it swiftly, and live not in doubt. In half an hour you will venture forth, either with a beautiful and aroused young woman on your arm or a permanent erection in your pants.

Heads you win, tails you win.

Natasha eyes you curiously as you knock back the bubbling brew. She drinks more circumspectly and, as she wets her lips, the bubbles fizz and blow, hitting soft pouting skin. You hope to God you guessed right. Whatever happens this evening, a permanent erection is an absolute certainty.

It takes just under twenty minutes of trite conversation for you to feel the first effects. It starts as an itch then turns into a burn. And finally, like a phoenix rising majestically from the flames of desire, a magnificent banana burgeons into life.

Normally you'd be proud to display such an object of desire. But at this exact moment in the conversation—she is still talking about her childhood pets—it seems slightly out of place. You bend slightly to try concealment, but after ten minutes the agony of the unnatural desire causes a flash of pain across your face. She notices.

"Are you OK? What's wrong? Is there something wrong with your stomach? Oh my God, are you . . . !?!? . . . You're the same as all the rest."

She runs, leaving you alone with your erection, and as you

watch her recede into the crowds, you can't help but feel limp (with the one notable exception). There is only one thing left to do.

In your condition, pulling a woman is out of the question.

Ignoring the wise words of Lord Baden-Powell in his seminal work *Rovering to Success* you shuffle off ashamedly to the little boys' room and make yourself at home.

"Self abuse is a very dreadful thing leading to insanity and, at any rate, causing permanent and severe damage to the system." *(Lord Powell,* Rovering to Success, *5th Edition, 1947)*

Baden-Powell *must* have been misinformed.

The (Sticky) End

Not exactly the Perfect Ending, Reader. You don't seem to be the most socially sophisticated of lovers—but why not start over and try to get whatever you can?

Scene 32

"She said it was Kamran—that he's gay—and that he tells Barnaby bad things about you because he loves Barnaby himself."

The shock of revelation bursts your anger. You stand, slack-jawed (until you catch sight of your three-quarters profile in the mirror—mental note, Barbarella, watch the double chin). Kamran? the bum-squeezing, tit-groping pulling-machine?

Barbarella, stop this madness. Annabel is the only one spreading poison here. Kamran reads lingerie catalogues, for heaven's sake. He can't be gay.

Don't be played for a sucker; ignore this rubbish; rise above it. Forget the whole thing and concentrate on having a good time. OK, to be more realistic, store up the information for use later on. Remember, Barbie—softly softly catchy monkey . . . **Go to Scene 226**

Suck on this, Kamran Jazeer; I will strike down upon thee with great vengeance and furious anger those who would attempt to poison and destroy my brothers. **Go to Scene 218**

Scene 33

Carmen enthusiastically gulps down the proffered champagne cocktail.

"I feel like dancing," she laughs, the Geordie accent now resonating where before it was barely noticeable.

That should be a warning, but obligingly you follow her on to the dance floor. After all, dancing is the best foreplay there is—and she's a professional.

But even professionals can lose coordination after two bottles of champagne . . .

Carmen looks fantastic for the first thirty seconds. Then she slips, midspin, concusses herself on the hard floor, and lies at your feet, motionless.

Do you rue the missed opportunity, and let the barman call an ambulance, or do you put your daytime TV skills into action?

George Clooney—who needs medical knowledge when you look this good? **Go to Scene 117**

Doogie Howser—do you need it spelled out? Order another scotch and stand back. **Go to Scene 115**

Scene 34

Defeat and retreat never sit well and so you don't dally once your mind is made up.

Catherine rustles up a cab with her usual aplomb and with a little encouragement (and a minor miracle) the cabbie accepts six in the back.

The mood in the cab is a little slow—the sense of retreat all too strong. Kamran even requests that you drop him off, but Catherine refuses. "We stay together—that's the rule."

"Right, stay together until Edward smiles a gold-toothed smile and you'll trot off like a child."

Fortunately the journey doesn't last long.

Go to Scene 78

Scene 35

First impressions in the casino's stud room are good. You look around the table after friendly introductions and realize the opposition are all clichés.

Barbie sits reassuringly to your right. Newt, an oversized American from somewhere down south—where marrying your cousin is the norm and gambling recklessly impresses girls—sits to your left. You smile inwardly as Daisy from the black jack table joins him. She stands behind him with an arm draped casually over his broad shoulders. What a gal—sights aimed on hard cash and not ashamed to speculate.

Will sits opposite; Astrid and Catherine have gravitated to the spot behind him and stand, comfortably loitering. Next over is Bodi, a middle-aged Arab in an immaculately tailored suit and the shiniest shoes you have ever seen. Then Wasim, the danger man. Darkly handsome but for a nose so hooked it renders his face into a permanent sneer. And then Jenner. He sits, filling a vast chunk of space with his bloated body. He sneers across at you like a James Bond baddy.

"Well, everyone, pleasantries over, shall we let Jacob break the seal on a new deck?"

The croupier obeys.

"Minimum stake $100—no maximum. Any objections? Then let us begin."

Scene 35

"One moment please," interjects Bodi. "Can I interest anyone in a little mental refreshment?"

He clicks manicured fingers and a discreet Arab manservant steps forward with a silver tray covered in thick lines of what looks like coke but could be anything.

"Ladies first."

He politely offers the tray to Barbarella, who snorts greedily at two lines. She looks up at you with a grin, pupils dilated, brain bubbled, and totally closeted from reality. Nigel Jenner accepts the tray with a podgy hand and sucks up the powder greedily. The tray does its round and finally returns to Bodi, who hoovers the remaining lines. Only you and Wasim reject the kind offer.

"Shall we begin?"

Bodi smiles and the cards come sliding forward.

Barbarella is giggling with Will, and is, frankly, acting like a child. But the sight of the first card transforms Jenner, Wasim, and Newt. They display a hard poker edge. It's obvious that this isn't just a game; it's a battle of egos. This is the reality of life or death to people whose wealth shields them from the real world. Nigel's eyes smile at you across the table as he licks a canine tooth.

Be afraid, Barnaby. Barbarella is too far done by drugs, drink, and debauchery. Her cash is as good as lost. These guys will cheat, lie, and kill—not for money, but for their pride. Even harmless little Bodi, the smiley Arab, will have "something arranged" if he catches you cheating. The vengeance of Jenner would be horrible. You picture him stroking a soft white cat as he watches the piranha chew on your flesh . . .

Go to Scene 91

Scene 36

With a few skips, you're well inside the club and quickly get high on the atmosphere. The club is currently fifteen men to every woman. You can't help but smile. Will, it would appear, is more interested in quick, easy money than quick, easy girls.

You take your time as you meander through this veritable lair of eligibles. As you'd expect, the West India reeks of money, but as with all casinos, an acrid whiff of desperation also hangs in the air. You stroll by the green-baize tables and can't help but notice that behind the façade of casual sociability the air hums with concentrated activity. A hand grabs your waist—it belongs to Will.

"Bloody good standard in tonight. We'll have to sharpen up if we're to stand a chance of financing our next night out."

Will thrives in this place. His cheeks glow with the fire of illicit gaming. His great-grandfather was a founding member and Will has been coming here since he was a kid. You recall his childhood tales; young William turning up with his father when the drunken mother required her "darling" to be looked after for the evening. Together with a school chum, they'd run the length and depth of the building while Father gambled away the cars, stables, and stolen Russian icons.

The club itself is stunningly fitted in deep oak and mahogany. The austerity of the wood is calmed with silk Persian rugs and *chaises longues* draped in rich fabrics and rich women. You've only been here once before, and your favorite part was the superbly stocked bar. That includes its choice in barmen. You recognize Marcus immediately, a law student supplementing his studies.

"Hello, Marcus, are you still soliciting?"

"Hi there, what can I get you? Barbarella, isn't it?"

Time for some free booze. You pull a pout, take hold of his warm hands, and in a squeaky child voice, "I got no money . . . has Marcus got anything for less than a penny?"

He smiles. "Complimentary olives?" but lets you stroke his wrist.

"Marcus, you know how frisky I got last time on Armagnac."

And with a raise of an eyebrow you point to a bottle of the 1968. Marcus starts to pour a healthy measure before you intercept.

"The bottle, Marcus, the bottle."

Game over. Obediently he pushes the newly opened Armagnac towards you.

"Will that be one glass?"

Hmmm, better share it with your friends. The turbulent events of this evening are causing you all to flag. Even Kamran's roving eye is looking slightly glazed.

"Six please, Marcus." You ambiguously pronounce the first word, and give of your most lascivious smile. "Thanks. I owe you one."

Go to Scene 40

Scene 37

The first few hands pass with little to note. Daisy squeals intelligently each time you win and no one seems to notice the chandelier's minuscule turns. Daisy's long brown legs, exposed by a long slit in her cream dress, distract you enormously, but you manage to stay on top of the game. Men can think about two things at once, but only through constant practice—so one of the thoughts has to be about sex.

By now, you are beginning to enjoy yourself again. Barbie has won another ridiculous amount of money, and you're nearing the early retirement mark. Daisy is blatantly blowing on your ear, and Newt is playing so rabidly that his once massive pile of dollar bills looks sadly lackluster.

With no thought that you may be being set up, a dream hand turns up—four aces.

To be fair, 200 million of your neural links are devoted to an image of Daisy's naked body covered in crisp green notes. You shouldn't be blamed for everything. The old ticker beats a little faster as the chandelier begins to creak—anticlockwise.

Soon Newt and Bodi are out of the game. Barbie folds, to leave you staring across the table at your sweaty nemesis.

He raises $30,000. You match it and raise by another $30,000. (It's just like Monopoly.)

Nigel, with no sign of doubt, raises by $50,000 (or is it Go for Broke?). Catherine cranes her neck for a better look. Will's jaw begins to twitch with tension. Even Astrid looks vaguely alert. Daisy, oozing hormones, quivers against you. This is no time for an erection, Barnie—concentrate.

The chandelier turns anticlockwise; you match Jenner and raise by even more.

This ridiculous battle swings to and fro, with the chandelier waltzing imperceptibly anticlockwise all the while. You borrow Barbie's funds, and continue to raise. Until, finally, you push forward the last of your money.

"And I raise you another," quick mental arithmetic, "five, ten . . . fifteen thousand four hundred and twenty-six dollars."

Nigel contemplates your smiling face.

"Mr. Wilson, I see you are temporarily fundless. I assure you, I will lend any monies you require to end the game."

You nod in agreement and accept dumbly. Nigel continues the absurdity. "Your fifteen, and I raise one hundred thousand dollars."

Gasp, shock, horror, etc.

It's toy money now. You ignore Will's apoplexy and sign a small slip of paper. Nigel hands you the necessary stack of cash.

"I call you, Nigel."

Jenner smiles. Jenner knocks his cards together on the table and looks you in the eye. He fans the five cards in an enormous fist . . . and smiles.

Nothing disconcerting in that, but the reaction on the chandelier is terrifying. It begins to turn, at first slowly, but then with a speed to make a draft. But far worse. *It's spinning clockwise.*

Time to run.

But Jenner is placing his cards on the table and all you can do is stare like an open-mouthed moron as he places each down in turn.

Nine spade . . .
Ten spade . . .
Jack spade . . .
Queen spade . . .
King spade.

Dead.

Your limbs are numb. Your brain fizzes and your mouth is so dry you can barely swallow. Luckily, your instinct for self-preservation sparks to the rescue. With creaking willpower, you lift both hands on to the green baize. You feel like a drowning man lying at the bottom of an icy lake. Somehow you manage one last act: barely noticing the spinning chandelier, you make two small fists with each hand, and with the last twitching energy of a corpse you look Jenner in the eye, smile to gain some time, and wait for "disaster recovery" to kick in.

Nothing happens. You made the double fisting signal and nothing happened. You look casually up at Catherine and realize she's too absorbed with the game to react to anything. She is staring at your down-turned cards, oblivious of the fanning chandelier, oblivious of your fists, and oblivious of the fact that you are all about to be rendered bankrupt—names dragged through the gutter, homes gone, bike gone, no sex ever again. Just do something, Catherine, you stupid, stupid bitch.

Cat stands transfixed and you have no option but to turn over your first card.

Ace of diamonds.

Your hand returns to a fist in one last silent cry . . . Nothing.

You go to your second card. To reveal it will be to admit defeat. You finger it slowly, feeling its crisp edge cut into your fingertip. Nothing matters now.

And then she comes. Astrid comes to your rescue.

It starts as a muffled cry, then through bitten lips comes a moan. Her face is the color of a plum and it's hard to tell from her expression whether she is feeling pain or rapture. Astrid staggers forward, clutches at the table, and cries thanks to the gods with a long deep guttural groan.

It could be the odd drug combination—never mix Rohypnol and coke; she could be faking; to be frank you don't care. Buxom, bounteous Astrid rolls her eyes theatrically and falls, with all her heavy-boned weight, on to the priceless Louis XIV table. Needless to say, it shatters into a thousand shards of joy.

You stoop to scoop the cash; pat Astrid's motionless backside, smile heroically at Barbarella, and whisk her away before anyone can react. You even manage a quick adieu to Jenner and a wink at Will as you fly out of the stud.

"Just keep walking and smiling," you instruct.

"But what about Astrid? We can't just leave her there!"

"Barbie, go out the front door and we'll be doing ninety down the Embankment with fifty grand in ten minutes. Just keep smiling. Will can get Astrid home."

Taking your advice, Barbie is not slow to take advantage of the Belgium-sent salvation. Jenner, sluggish oaf that he is, manages to sidestep Will and is out of the stud and shouting after you. But, pressing a ludicrously large note into the doorman's hand, you skip out of the front door and fly down short steps to motorized safety.

Go to Scene 45

Scene 38

Heads? You won!

Are you sure you didn't cheat? OK, suppose you'll have to be trusted. Well, if it is heads, then you get your (wicked) way first.

Barnaby unfolds your note carefully, and, squinting under the dim streetlight, reads aloud.

Only question is, what did you write?

"I want you to play the Devil with me while a stranger plays the Angel. I won't be able to choose so must have both. Chastise and surprise." Gosh, how embarrassing. **Go to Scene 74**

"I want to have your babies." Gosh. **Go to Scene 72**

Scene 39

"Are you OK?"

The little-boy look doesn't seem to make an immediate impression. The blonde turns back to the spotty barman to make small talk—an insult and a challenge . . .

You order a scotch and try a second time.

"Will you at least accept a drink as a small token of my eternal regret?"

"No . . . Thank you."

She makes a good impression of being bored—not just angry. The barman is beginning to enjoy himself as he waits for your next move.

Do you: beat a hasty retreat and try your luck gazumping Will's Australian actress? **Go to Scene 49**

Risk another slap? **Go to Scene 59**

Scene 40

Barnaby has managed both to stay on his bike and get into the club by the time you rejoin the others. You fill glasses, and, with grins all round, eagerly anticipate the night's events. But there's no time to make a toast, or even take a sip, because a dark, plump cloud is approaching. Barnaby notices it first.

"Oh Christ, not that wanker."

The shoes give it away. Only one man you know insists on wearing gray Pierre Cardin slip-ons without socks. Only one man can repulse you quite this much.

Millionaire and part-time newspaper columnist, Nigel Jenner.

Grotesque.

"Well, you youngsters. Come to play with the big boys? Or just here to watch?"

"Tosser," you mutter under your breath.

"My dear Barbarella, I don't think I've ever seen you looking so cross. Not even my Sunday feature ["Jenner's Winners"] got you this angry . . . or did it?"

This man temporarily, if not permanently, destroyed your public image. He forced you to spend two months in the gym. Confidence knocked, friends avoided; all because of one photograph.

Yes, that photograph. The party. You, Barnaby, that dress. Paparazzi. *Chins*.

The photo destroyed you and the narrative below it killed off

Barnaby's ItBoy pretensions. Defamatory references rendered Barnie a social pariah, while you were dubbed as yet another burned-out socialite. Friends assured you that the double chin was just unfortunate. Anyone would exhibit a similar number when turning at that particular angle, at that particular speed, in that particular light. The photographer was obviously very skilled.

"Barbarella, you've lost so much weight from your face—you look fantastic. What have you done with all the extra skin?"

You snort, voraciously cocained laughter.

This is going to be painful. If you hang around any longer Barnaby is going to open his fool mouth. The last time that happened, Jenner published and you were damned.

But a cowardly retreat never sits well. You'll never get over Jenner if you run at the first sign of his enormous shadow.

What to do?

Do you face your demons? Stay and talk to malicious columnist. **Go to Scene 42**

Do you run for it? **Go to Scene 44**

Scene 41

Disgraceful, still, it should be interesting. You hand Barbie your note and she tucks it into her ample cleavage.

Go to Scene 67

Scene 42

The six of you stare in disgust at the produce of a sick and vicious womb. How could forty-six fragile, well-intended chromosomes be responsible for such a monster? Will steps in.

"Well actually, we were rather in the mood for celebration. And what better way to celebrate than to gamble our respective bonuses? I think we've all done rather well this year."

Will is clearly lying. He hasn't shifted a case of plonk all year. Astrid looks flustered. "But I won't get a bonus 'til next year."

"It's OK, Astrid, you can have some of mine. It's so big I wouldn't know what to do with it."

How generous, Barbarella, and how liberal with the truth. Nigel continues: "Well, perhaps you might like to be my guests. The table will be ready in an hour. Meet me by the library and we'll try to reduce your overdrafts."

And, with a smirk, he returns to his equally tanned friends. They appear to be hailing from somewhere Arabian.

No avoiding it—a gauntlet has been tossed in your direction.
Go to Scene 46

Scene 43

The doorman looks down at you.

"I really am very sorry, sir." He shuts the door on you. Breathlessly you knock loudly, in anger. The doorman returns, this time more conciliatory. "Sir, if you have a message for Mr. Burton I will gladly see that he receives it."

You hastily swallow pride and scribble a cry for help: "HELP—they won't let us in."

Five minutes you wait on the doorstep.

But then with a rush, the door opens and gale-force Barbarella comes flying on to the street followed by the rest of the gang. "I didn't touch him—stupid old bastard. You're supposed to be a gentleman, Will; you're supposed to defend my honor."

Will is pink with annoyance. "Barbie, I saw you put your hand in his pocket. What were you looking for? Loose change?"

Barbie turns away from Will, visibly upset. She catches your eye and winks before theatrically huffing. Kamran explains: "Barbarella was caught trying to bribe the croupier with her prestidigitation."

You look confused. Kamran holds up a hand and wiggles his fingers: "Ball juggling. She was trying to influence the roulette ball by manipulating the croupier's. In my view a legitimate gambling technique—much more fun than card counting."

You can't help but laugh. "Barbie, you were thrown out of a casino for touching up the staff—fantastic!"

But Will is genuinely annoyed; after all, his grandfather was a member here. "And what do you bloody propose we do now? Go to the bloody zoo?"

"Will, I'll make it up to you, promise. Catherine's been invited back to a party on Rosling Street. I'm sure we'd all be welcome."

Without any discussion, the matter is settled. A cab is hailed and the six of you pile in.

Go to Scene 17

Scene 44

Judging by your cheek-clenched tension, and Barnaby's clenched fists, it might be wise to end the conversation.

"Well, it really was lovely to see you again, Mr. Jenner," then turn your back on him and talk to the others. "So what shall we do?"

He insists on the last word and to your back says, "Well, if you have the class and money to join us, we'll be starting a game in the back room in an hour. It really would be wonderful to see you there."

You hear Jenner's bulk recede before Catherine sparks up with a suggestion. "Look, why don't we just go over to Holland Park? The party'll be really kicking off by now. If we stay here, we'll just end up broke."

She looks at you all hopefully and you sense the enthusiasm in her voice. It's probably derived more from lovelorn desperation than any genuine desire to go to a good party. You turn to see that Jenner has sloped back to his equally bloated companions, ready to gamble away the equivalent of Chad's national debt. Admittedly, you would be somewhat out of your depth. But what if you won?

Barnaby is ready for a fight. "Come on, guys. We can't slink away just because we're scared. We could make some serious money . . . Don't listen to Catherine, she just wants to sit on Edward's Bunger."

Scene 44

Crass perhaps, but you can't help laughing. Catherine huffs an exasperated sigh.

Time to make a decision, Barbarella, do you run or stay? Are you heroic Hector or pathetic Paris? Roobarb or Custard? What shall it be?

Dunkirk. Skulk off to Holland Park. **Go to Scene 34**

Thermopylae. Battle onwards to glory (and/or financial ruin). **Go to Scene 46**

Scene 45

The bike whines up the road and you clench Barbie's thigh. The fresh air of freedom rushes into your lungs and you whoop a "Yeehaaa."

You have thousands of dollars stuffed in your jacket pockets, the ravishing (and excitable) Barbie clenched to your back. But best of all, burning a hole in your trouser pocket, scorching your manly loins, is a fantasy so sordid, that even Barbie dare not speak its name.

Your imagination runs riot as you zigzag your way to the river. What sexual pleasure do you give the girl who's done everything/one? What sexual mountains can be left to conquer?

Let's just hope they involve lots of leather.

You cross the river at Waterloo Bridge. Unable to resist any longer you pull over and dismount. The slowly flowing Thames, the Houses of Westminster, the London Eye, HMS *Belfast* all form a backdrop to this moment of truth. Barbie, brazen as ever, but a little confused, stands impassively, hands on hips.

Barnaby, you've come a long way tonight. But a great need is still torturing your troubled soul. Barbarella is within your grasp at last. Remember, never be afraid of failure and rejection. "THEY CAN, BECAUSE THEY THINK THEY CAN." Hesitate not, for now is the time to push on—onwards to the Elysian Fields.

Scene 45

How do you explain your discomfiture?

"Barbie, we need to talk . . . I need to tell you something . . . I love you." **Go to Scene 262**

"Barbie, I don't even know where we're going—and this bit of paper in my trouser pocket is giving me an erection." **Go to Scene 240**

Scene 46

All right then, Barbarella, reassemble the troops. You have been challenged. It is time to remember why you are here. It is time to reawaken the smoldering fire, started so many hours ago in Fulham. There you were, six suffering souls, burdened by late-twenties London life. You all drank to sex and valor, determined to cast aside your woes. A steady measure of Armagnac could provide the tonic needed. Go for a large serving just in case. Six glasses are filled, then raised. This time, Barnie makes the toast (relying on holiday Spanish): "*En todos los casinos siempre hay alguien* mas idiota *que tu*." Savor. Slam.

The venom and vehemence has returned to your eyes. You resemble the valiant knights who crossed forth into a night of frivolity because, damn you, they needed it. Barnaby signals for another round of galvanizing drinks, and Astrid laughs with glee, while a gorgeous smile creeps back onto the lips of Catherine. Even Barnaby and Will are smiling at each other. What a good idea it was to stay.

However, the issue of rather intense gambling must be resolved. Can you all really be so frivolous with your bonuses? Of course you can—if you ever bothered to open a bank statement you'd probably find you've spent it already—but there is the principle of losing. Never again do you wish to be at the mercy of Jenner.

Beneath the conversation, you hide for a moment with your thoughts. While you're a capable gambler, it's normally with other people's money. Time to take this game seriously.

Go to Scene 52

Scene 47

The combination of champagne and Natasha's tight grip leaves you feeling heady. You flash along the embankment up Cheyne Walk and onto the King's Road. There you screech to a halt at some traffic lights. The night is cooler and Natasha's bare legs are covered in goose bumps.

You barely notice the policeman until he is standing in front of your bike. With a sudden sickening sensation, you realize you are ten times over the limit and have been caught speeding by a policeman on foot.

He smiles, and over the roar of the engine he signals for you to get off the bike.

Standing in the road, head pounding with frenzied panic, you desperately try to think. But your mind is caught in a dizzying whirl. Through the inebriation you try to judge the situation (will this mean prison . . . a Shawshank shower?). The officer can't help grinning now, and you know to fear the worst. He is going to enjoy this.

"Would you turn the engine off, please."

You look at him still in a daze, and then you look at Natasha. She is sobered and cold, her arms crossed defensively against her chest. The short cream dress hitched tantalizing high. With painful regret you turn finally to the bike.

Then comes the voice. The devil voice. Strangely similar to

Kamran's, but with a touch of the child catcher from *Chitty Chitty Bang Bang*. Pure evil.

"Distract him, leave the girl, and run. The idiot's on foot, you'll be parked in Bayswater before he can signal for help. That's assuming he does signal for help with a naked Viagra-filled girl in his arms . . ."

You grab the girl. Upordownupordownupordown? DOWN.

The dress rips down and you manage to collect a G-string on the way. Fortunately the dress didn't allow for a bra and the result is maximum impact as she is pushed, tripping on her knickers, into the arms of the policeman.

You hop aboard the bike before the policeman can say, "Are those breast stickers for added uplift?"

And before she can reply, "Yes, they look horrid, but do the job," you are away, wind screaming through your hair and into your streaming eyes.

Go to Scene 159

Scene 48

La Traviata II
(Return of the Wayward Woman)

Opera in three acts,
first performed at the Teatro la Fenice, Vienna

Dramatis Personae
Barbioletta (*Prima donna soprano*)—Barbarella Carrington
Barnedo (*Primo tenore*)—Barnaby Wilson
Capitano Kamuzzi (*Primo baritono*)—Kamran Jazeer
Il Marchesi de Willigny (*Baritono comprimario*)—Will Burton
Mademoiselle Catalina (*Seconda donna*)—Catherine Henderson
Barone Déjeuner (*Falsetto*)—Nigel Jenner
Sally Serving Wench (*Contralto*)—Sally (West India barmaid)
Belgiotto (*Silent*)—Astrid Van Staveren

Act 1 An opening preview finds our wayward Barbioletta destitute and abandoned, her belongings being carted off to pay her bills—a glimpse of the past?—or perhaps of the future . . .

We join the present with our heroine at a party with her gay friends. The scene opens with a drinking song, "*Libiamo ne' lieti colici*" ("Let's Drink"). But the evil Barone Déjeuner enters and threatens their livelihood and morals. The companions plot and swear to overcome the dark tyranny that has borne upon their once happy lives.

A memorable aria lays down the ultimate challenge from the evil Barone. The young nobility must take up the gauntlet in the local gambling house, against the cheating yet wealthy company of the Barone.

Act 2 The poet, Barnedo, declares his love for Barbioletta ("*È strano! È strano! . . . Ha! fors' è lui . . .*") and swears to help her in the fight against the Barone.

Il Marchesi unveils a secret plan to the gentle fellows; the local gambling house conceals a room within which to frolic and pass a beady eye upon the gaming activities below. The amorous Capitano Kamuzzi valiantly volunteers to seduce Sally Serving Wench, thus gaining entry to a concealed room where he may spy.

Act 3 The companions enter the gaming room, Il Stud, dressed as matadors (*Di Madride noi siamo mattadori*) and the game commences. In a stunning aria "*Voi lo sapete*" ("Now you shall know"), Barbioletta relies upon her beauty, charm, and wit to distract the Barone Déjeuner and his companions. Then, Barbioletta, relying on signals from the Capitano upstairs (using an unusually advanced mechanical system), wins several hands, commenting that being unlucky in love is compensated by being lucky in games. Barone Déjeuner challenges her to higher stakes. Barbioletta continues winning. The Barone becomes suspicious.

Act 4 The game continues with a gypsy fight and building tension. Belgiotto, while not served with an integral role, is of imperative importance in the final scene. Barnedo signals Belgiotto (Aria: "*Largo al quadrupede*") to cause a diversion by collapsing on the gaming table, thus concluding the dominant theme of intrigue.

The contemporary version of this fabulously engineered opera has Barbioletta skip from the gaming house with Barbedo singing an endearing duet, "*Follie! Sempre libre*" ("Ever free, flitting from joy to joy"). However, the original tragedy provides, instead, a chastening finale—Barbioletta dying in poverty, and of consumption—"*Oh mio rimorso! Oh infamia!*"

Calm down, Barbie. Leave the grand circle and return to the reality of the West India Club. **Go to Scene 10**

Scene 49

"William, howthedevilareyou?" *(Kp–Kp4)*

Will glares back at you with ill-disguised annoyance, but his voice carries all its usual sincerity. "Very well, mate, I was just considering a bit of a dance." He turns his back on you and offers a smile and a hand to the diminutive girl. *(QKnP–QKnP3)*

But nothing will stop you now; your blood is up.

"And who's this lovely lady?" You manage to avoid sounding hideously smarmy by applying a disarming ironic smile. *(KB–QB4)*

Will, with the enthusiasm of one reminded of his manners, introduces you to Natasha.

Olive skin, dark sulking features delightfully offset by overlarge pouting lips. All atop a body you remember seeing underwear-clad in Maxim. Not that you need to exercise too much imagination . . . The more skin showing the more publicity received. A basic tenet of marketing. And since dear little Natasha's last single bombed, she needs all the publicity she can get.

"So, Natasha, how did they persuade you to attend this hideous self-publicizing marketing event of a party?" You sense that after Will's arrogance a little down-to-earth honest cynicism might go down well. *(KKn–KB3)*

"I am a hideous self-publicist—that's my job." She warms to your theme; sure enough, cynicism is the right tack. Now, don't blow it, just show her how downright clever you are and the title will be yours. First, pretend you've no idea who she is—it drives celebrities nuts . . .

"I'm sure you are very good at it. So why are you after attention? Politics, music, or were you just unloved as a child?"

"I was overloved as a child, which explains why pop industry sycophancy and adoration bore me."

She answers honestly—the combination of the party's general nauseous insincerity and Will's self-obsessed prattling has obviously turned her blue. Quicken to the theme, Barnie . . .

"The price you pay for success. You must enjoy an upside?"

"Of course I do, I'm just feeling bored . . . every now and then I stop and look around," she pauses and pointedly looks at Will, "and just feel how futile it all is . . . I wanted to be a doctor once . . ."

Will's rant must have depressed her more than even you realized. Time to end this.

"Look, I'm great at bursting emotional bubbles. Let me get you a drink and I'll share my patent-pending cure for ennui."

And with the confidence of a German army invading Belgium, you take her hand and lead her to the bar. *(QB4–KB4 xmate)*

Will looks on in wonder as you slip away.

Go to Scene 57

Scene 50

Nonetheless, Joey is your favorite character and that line just set you thinking along a series of hot Italian thoughts. Now that you clearly have this sexy boy on your arm, why delay the inevitable? Which sounds more appealing—a reptile house, or the comfort of your bed,. reputedly with the best sprung mattress in North London? No contest really.

The whole point of this weekend was to remind yourself how much there is to play for. Through the invariably depressing haze of work and nasty boys, it's good to know that you're still on track. And who cares if Jay has a girlfriend, that's his responsibility. Plus, he's on holiday, and what goes on tour stays on tour. Take a slight detour and you could be home in ten minutes. Starbucks is open already for your Frappuccinos and the Sunday papers have long been written. They might even have your picture in there somewhere.

"Jay, lets go back to my place instead. I'm cold."

"No problem, baby." Jay doesn't seem to have any willpower of his own. A quick pull of his hand and you're steering him back the way you came. Regent's Park Zoo is deceptively large, but eventually you lead him back to the tall perimeter railings.

You turn to Jay for assistance . . . but he is gone.

"Jay? JAY? Don't muck about . . . this isn't funny . . ."

You're alone. And suddenly the zoo doesn't seem such a

friendly place. Feral odors and latent growlings permeate the air, a sharp snarl makes you jump, and a splosh sounds in the distance as a waking otter dives into its greasy pool.

"Jay, where are you? If you don't show yourself in ten seconds then I'm going."

Maybe one of the animals is loose, maybe Jay's being eaten. And what about Kamran? He just seemed to disappear, as well. Oh, Barbie, you should never have been allowed to stay up to watch *American Werewolf in London*; you were just a child. The terrifying memories come flooding back and you can almost hear wolf breath as the creature stalks through the undergrowth.

"OK, Jay . . . I'm going now . . . hope you have fun."

And for the first time you contemplate the eight-foot railings. Slipping between the bars isn't an option (no, you don't have a fat bum—even a well-oiled Calista Flockhart would struggle); its up and over or nothing. You pathetically grip the cold cast iron, scrabble with stilettoed feet on slippery metal, and soon give up. It can't be done, not by you, Barbarella. Girls like you don't have upper body strength; you can just about open a jam jar.

The only choice is to stand with your back to the railings, try not to look edible, and wait for day. If there is some predatory animal stalking the zoo, then dawn should give you a better chance. Look up and left and you'll see the sky in the east taking a borage hue; the sun isn't far away. And there must be people who come in early to feed the animals, even on a Sunday.

Barbarella, don't trust a man not to play silly buggers, and never turn your back on Kamran. Didn't your grandma teach you any homespun wisdom? If you carry on like this you'll never get it together with a nice young man.

The (Silly Bugger) End

This wasn't the Perfect Ending you had in mind, Reader. You made some pretty dodgy choices along the way. If Barbarella is to be fulfilled it looks like you'll have to play harder . . .

Scene 51

The groan rate is rising. Despite yourself, you can't help but peer round the edge of the desk. At first, all you see is a long slender foot, thrust high into the air. You strain to see more . . . the perfect leg, two actually, flung high and wide. Then you recognize her—or rather the mole in the middle of her thigh. It's Barbarella. With a stomach-acid pang, you look at her companion for the first time and recognize Will's fine-boned profile.

Time to run. Orpheus leading Persephone from Hades, you don't turn back. They won't recognize you from one rear view. In your haste you leave the cabin door swinging on its hinge.

Oh poor, unrequited Barnabus. With one crushing loss after another, this evening is turning into a Greek tragedy. There's only one thing you can do. Forget all you've seen and suppress this monstrous memory. Rush back to the anonymity of the party, have a stiff drink, and take some time out to think . . .

Go to Scene 21

Scene 52

Considering the rest of your team one by one, your thoughts finally rest on Barnaby. You're glad he's onside, always so full of himself, so confident . . . your mind starts to drift to the past. When you were together he cherished you so much; he was so happy to have you around. Not in a "grateful" way or anything hideous like that. He just enjoyed being with you—like a four-year-old enjoys being with his favorite uncle. You ponder whether money should be your only motivation this evening. Barnie's endorphin-flushed face is smiling at you and an inner voice gently coaxes, "Sex, Barbarella. Come on . . . oh go on, be a cupcake."

Let's face it, if you want him so badly, all you have to do is say so. But where would the fun be in that? Make a few flattering remarks and test whether Barnaby has other plans. Drawing him to one side for privacy, you ask, "Barnie, you're great at cards, aren't you?" He nods, you smile. ". . . Is there anything you aren't great at?" (smooth your hands over your hips, smile some more). "What will we do when we win?"

He seems to be buying in—responding teasingly, "Dearest Barbarella, if we win tonight we can do anything you want . . . Tell me your greatest fantasy, and I will grant it."

Hmmm, he obviously is feeling confident. Laughing at his nerve, you reply, "I'll do better than that."

Slipping into Lauren Bacall mode (with such ease it's almost plagiarism), you close your eyes to mere slits and eye Barnaby speculatively up and down. In the back of your mind you're thinking desperately of something so erotic, so lustful, so not already done by Barnaby that it'll blow his mind. You're crap when it comes to imaginative sex, despite what others might think (or you might *like* others to think). Placing trust in the written word, and taking advantage of a few moments more to think, you decide to write your fantasy down (easily identifiable as adapted from *Sex and the City*, but you're pretty sure that Barnaby doesn't watch it). Taking a page from your diary's "To Do" section, you compose a sizzling request. The burgundy ink from your pen almost ignites the paper with the intensity of your thoughts. Only question is, what do you write?

"I want you to play the Devil with me while a stranger plays the Angel. I won't be able to choose so I must have both. Chastise and surprise." **Go to Scene 54**

Or, "I want to have your babies." **Go to Scene 56**

Scene 53

Disgusting . . . is that legal? Still, neither of you can stop smiling as she tucks the note into the front of her dress.

Go to Scene 67

Scene 54

Interesting choice—didn't think you were the type. Can't wait to see how that one turns out.

But suppose we'll have to . . . patience, patience, when the time comes—remember what you wrote.

First, you have a game of cards to play.

Go to Scene 58

Scene 55

Once Barbie has got over the shock she warms to her challenge. She strolls out of earshot and makes a few swift calls. You will never cease to be amazed by her capacity to deal with any situation. Maybe you should have made it three women . . . or more.

But Barbie is back, so pay attention. It's lucky dip time.

"We go to St. John's Wood . . ."

And with the power of 100 horses you speed north, towards the plow.

Go to Scene 163

Scene 56

You serious? Can't wait to see where that one ends up.

But suppose we'll have to. When the time comes—patience is a virtue—remember what you wrote.

First, some five-card stud.

Go to Scene 58

Scene 57

At the bar you establish (with great surprise and enthusiasm) that Natasha is, after all, a pop star. You begin to weave your vicious web, suspecting that she might just succumb to a sentimental tale that proves life needn't be futile. So, armed with an astounding capacity for fiction, you spin a story that would melt even the toughest cynic's heart.

"Everything has an upside," you begin as if you do have a patent-pending formula for curing depression. "And everything has a cost—you've just got to concentrate on the upside."

"I have no idea what you're talking about." She smiles to soften the rebuke.

Come on, Barnie, think. DO NOT BLOW THIS ONE.

"I need to give you an example. At the risk of sounding like Will, forgive me if I use my own life to demonstrate." Wry smile. "My job in the city used to earn me more money than I knew what to do with. But I lacked a sense of purpose" . . . you pause for effect and desperately to think of something . . .

. . . the big lie . . .

no one ever thinks to question the big lie . . .

"But that changed totally when I went on holiday to Borneo. I went to an orangutan orphanage that was about to close because of money—all it needed was a small annuity to stay afloat. That's what gave me the idea, and so now, I work for three days a week in the city, and for the other four I'm a social entrepreneur, advising and helping voluntary projects to stay afloat using charity marketing and stuff. I can now *enjoy* screwing people in the city, just because I know it's helping towards paying for my upside. I know it all sounds a bit naff, but it keeps me sane."

You try to look a bit embarrassed—typical Brit—unable to reveal anything truly important without feeling the need to apologize . . . and with an awkward smile you finish. "An upside, that's all you need to . . . to never feel totally miserable."

Emotionally vulnerable or not, few drunk women would be able to resist such a plea from the heart. Now is the time to shut your gob and listen. If you can manage that, it'll be game over.

And so she talks and you listen and inwardly smile as she pours out her heart. She tells of a glossy, glamorous but essentially empty life. And you nod, and whimper, and laugh in understanding. And after forty minutes you know she is yours to harvest . . . as easy to gather as a windfallen apple in September.

Go to Scene 101

Scene 58

You fold the scrap of paper tightly to make sure Barnaby can't read it, and then hand it over. He puts it in his trouser pocket.

"But that's not fair, I should get a request as well."

You pout and hand him the pen and another sheet from your diary. He hides his scribbling from view and with alarming speed completes a wish. It's Barnaby's turn to fold his note for secrecy, and he hands it over with a beaming smile. Only Beelzebub could guess what he's written. You tuck the note into the top of your dress, where it fixes snugly against your left breast.

Shocking, but neither of you can wipe the grin from your face.

Go to Scene 60

Scene 59

"Look, I'm not trying to make a cheap move on you just because you're not wearing knickers."

The mortified barman tries to hide in his ice bucket.

"It's just that I don't like body-checking a woman to the ground and not making sure that she is OK. You're not exactly a prop forward, you know."

Simple, blunt, Barnaby. Heart in the right place, awkwardly expressing his deep-felt concern about accidentally abusing a waif of a girl with his masculine physical presence.

She thaws slightly.

"Look, I'm more embarrassed than injured, thank you for your concern, but really, I'm fine."

Time to tactically withdraw, good impression made, groundwork done, foundations laid, etc., etc. After two more champagne-hours, you can renew your acquaintance. Except that through alcohol-befuddlement, she will remember you as a friend . . . virtually.

Except Barbarella has a different plan.

"Barnaby, you big oaf, what have you done to this poor girl?" Then to the blonde, "God, poor you . . . Barnie is so clumsy and he doesn't realize how overpowering he can be . . . It's sometimes hard to remember that he has the most wonderfully talented hands."

She almost growls with innuendo, and beams expectantly, monologue over.

If the massed Labour hierarchy could have heard her, they would be clamoring. The government spin-doctors are not worthy to kiss the straps of her Manolo sandals. She could get Iain Duncan Smith reelected as party leader.

The blonde is suddenly interested.

"So what do you do with your hands?" she queries with warming interest.

And Barbie, bless her, with the efficiency of a German army invading Poland, spies an old acquaintance across the room and disappears in a puff of Chanel. But before you can take advantage, a thought slaps you. You pause, transfixed, and wonder why Barbarella should go so far out of her way to help you. There's only one conclusion: Barbarella is over you; *it* is over; all your dreams and hopes . . . must die.

Closure, Barnie, yes, that utterly naff Americanism, you've got to get over Barbie—and now's the perfect time to do it. The girl's blonde, knickerless, and she's asked you a question (about yourself!) . . . the ball has bounced and is sitting up, firmly in the middle of the court. Your opponent has moved from her baseline, and is stranded—halfway to the net . . . Do you:

Lob—tell her that you are a sculptor. **Go to Scene 105**

Make the killer pass down the line—tell her that you are a doctor. **Go to Scene 69**

Tell the truth—spank the ball into the net. **Call 999**

Scene 60

Shit. The game—better concentrate. Will is talking to the others,

"Ra ra, ra ra ra, cheat ra ra make an absolute fortune ra ra, ha ha ha." . . . Better rejoin them and find out what he's going on about. Your delicious thoughts are forgotten as you try to follow a typical Will ramble: "The old man was a tremendous cheat, you see, he introduced the 'cubby'—fantastic fun. Giles and I used to hide in there and watch them play in the stud . . ."

The cubby, it turns out, is a cupboard-cum-walk-in-wardrobe in a bedroom above the "stud room."

The "stud room" is overlooked from the "cubby" via a small periscope installed by the late Lord Wrotham's father (Will's grandfather's godfather). He set up a system whereby a footman could overlook the game and signal to the peer using specially designed levers to rotate the chandelier. Sounds ingenious and sounds ridiculous, but his Lordship was shot dead one night in mysterious circumstances in St. James's Park, so who knows?

Will finishes his tale to universal silence. You look from Barnaby to Astrid to Kamran to Catherine and everyone is smiling as if you've just been handed the final golden ticket to Willy Wonka's chocolate factory. Go forth, Veruca Salt.

Scene 60

If you can't win the game honestly, then cheat. Your minds plot individually on how the cubby can best be used to your advantage. While the boys opt for more military strategies, you prefer a more operatic plan.

Go to Scene 48

Scene 61

Will almost kisses you when you accept his suggestion. He rescues Barbie from a celebrity chef, and wins her over quickly. You get Astrid and Kamran to extract Catherine from the upstairs loo, while you sneak out and find a cab. Within ten minutes you're piled in a taxi and being whisked east to the freedom of William's discreet little club, the West India.

The West India Club is one of Will's favorite haunts, full of poor sophisticates and rich trash, symbiotically feeding off each other. Will adores the place because he can strut his pedigree and supplement his income at the same time (there's only so much money an alcoholic can make from selling wine). Barbarella is pretty indifferent. The place is packed with filthy rich males, but most will be fat, ugly, or just generally filthy. You despise it on principle, but at the same time can never quite resist.

Take a breather. In the game of love, you've been a poor loser all evening, but luck must change. Courage! And shuffle the cards. If you don't turn up the queen of hearts, you might just deal yourself a running flush and walk away with lots of lovely cash. So steel your frayed nerves, for gambling is not for the weak, and this club is swilling with cash. It's not often you get the chance, so nose to the trough, and scoff your fill . . .

Go to Scene 135

Scene 62

In the stud room, everything is eerily quiet and equally serious. The room is a little less lavish than the rest of the club; the furniture, primarily a large green-topped circular table and eight gilt chairs, oozes *ancien régime* grandeur, but the carpeting is plain navy and the walls are sparingly filled with somber, military oils.

Four men are already seated and waiting in silence. One look tells you that guys like these don't just play for money. Monumental egos are at stake. To be discovered cheating would definitely be a bad idea. Newt, a big Texan slick, looks harmless enough, but Bodi, the middle-aged Arab, could probably have something "arranged" if you got on his wrong side. The younger Arab, Wasim, would probably do the job himself. As for Nigel Jenner, he licks already wet lips and comes to greet you with a firm handshake and a nasal drone.

"Ready to sell your house and move back in with Mum and Dad?"

"We'll have to see how things turn out, Nigel." You settle for a bland response and a blander smile. There'll be time enough for revenge.

Settling into a high-backed chair, you peer around the room in a vain attempt to spot Kamran's eyehole, but his view will inevitably be well concealed—so instead you try a brief glance up at the chandelier, half expecting it to be moving.

Stop looking at the ceiling, Barbarella—time for tactics. You can either play Bond girl or blonde girl, sharp or dumb. Sharp to annoy and rile, or dumb to generate false confidence. No contest, sharp is much more fun—time to offend some people. Newt is like a sitting duck.

"So, Newt, where are you from? Dallas? . . . Or *Dynasty*?"

Obviously Texas doesn't produce girls quite like you; he seems to have problems understanding.

"What d'you say, girl?"

"I was just thinking, does anyone take you seriously when you're dressed like Cliff Barnes from an early episode of *Dallas*."

"Maybe you wanna get those goddam marbles outta your mouth, girl." He laughs at his own joke, but only Jenner joins him. "Listen, people take me plenty serious when I tell them I sold my business for one hundred million dollars last year."

Time to cause some mischief.

"A hundred million?" You pointedly look down your nose at Bodi, the middle-aged Arab sitting to your right. "You could probably buy this guy's whole country for that."

Sure enough, Bodi's ego kicks awake; he feigns a laugh. "One hundred million, that *is* a lot of money. Tell you what . . . Newt . . . I'll toss you for it."

Newt laughs, but halfheartedly. He takes a gulp of bourbon and can't look you in the eye. Barbie, that was perfect. Divide and conquer. Nothing like a bit of tension and animosity to give you the edge. Newt and Bodi will continue to verbally circle each other as they vie for alpha male; Will nods a silent "well done."

Resting in your seat and knocking your drink back, you sneak another peek at the chandelier. Nothing doing, but you start to imagine what Kamran might be up to. It seems somewhat unjust that here you are, surrounded by an international forum of imbeciles, while Kam is indulging in deliciously gross carnal misconduct. If only you could swap places with Sally for an hour . . .

Go to Scene 64

Scene 63

The silver coin sparkles in the air before Barbie clamps it between her slapping hands . . . a girl catch.

She looks at it, and then at you.

You blurt a guess, desperate for haste . . . Barbie looks you squarely in the face. "I knew I wouldn't win." With no shade of disappointment, Barbarella unfolds your scribbled note. "Never mind. I'm dying to know what you wrote."

Barbie squints against the weak light to read your scrawl . . .

Time for some more honesty. You made your decision a few hours back, and it's too late to change your mind now. What deviance did your sweaty imagination conjure back at the West India?

"I want you to seduce a girl, bind and blindfold her . . . then let me join in." Golly, how embarrassing; Barbarella's not that kind of girl—surely? **Go to Scene 55**

"I want to visit an S&M club . . . you'll have to do anything I request." Gosh—she'll probably run a mile. **Go to Scene 11**

"I love you, Barbarella. Will you marry me?" Golly gosh. **Go to Scene 262**

Scene 64

. . . Two swarthy arms caress your back, placing delicate pressure on the shoulder blades. His voice stirs you from your state of ecstasy-induced reverie.

"Can you feel my hands releasing negative energy?"

You can only moan.

"The back symbolizes stability and dictates how much pressure you can take. I must unload you of that pressure. To do that I must soothe the surface and penetrate to the root of that pressure, starting at your feet."

He runs his tongue up your calf, crossing to the inner thigh as his hands massage your sides. You are turned over onto your back so that the pressure root can be reached. He places his weight upon you, pulling himself towards your lips. You wait expectantly, but he pauses.

"The secret is to wait," he whispers, "then when it comes, enjoyment and release are heightened."

But you can't wait. Taking control, you grip his left buttock with one hand while firmly holding the back of his neck with the other.

"Don't you know that Barbarella never waits for anything?"

Go to Scene 188

Scene 65

Back at the apartment, William cracks open some Laurent-Perrier, *Tosca* blasts from the CD player, and the three of you—warriors bonded by the prospect of coming battle—prepare . . .

Kamran busies himself in the kitchen with a melon ("for zinc," he explains); bananas ("potassium"); egg-white ("texture"); and a beetroot ("for luck"). And while the "Smoothie of Testicular Rejuvenation" froths in the blender, he pumps the veins on his biceps with one-handed press-ups. You have to cringe. Meanwhile, William showers and applies Clinique turnaround cream.

You take the next bathroom slot and sit smoking one of William's hand-rolled Cervante cigars in a full tub, focusing on your sexual goals for the night. Yes, have fun, yes, try to pull whatever randoms come your way, but tonight's number one objective, your overriding *raison d'être*, is to win back Barbarella. You recapture the image of her pink bottom as she gets out of a hot bath—it's the only testicular rejuvenation you need.

"Barnie, remember, don't use soap—pheromones are your best friend."

You hear Kamran's advice from the kitchen. But you can't quite bring yourself not to—to each his own. Lightning wit, boyish smiles, and massive alcohol tolerance are all the friends you need. And if that doesn't work, a quick speed on your throbbing bike should loosen things up.

By the time you emerge from your mind-clearing sauna of a

bath, William is checking his bow-tie in the mirror; Kamran has found Beverly Hills Formula whitening toothpaste, and Tosca is in mid-death-anguish.

But you don't have time to lament. Kamran is offering you a pint glass of smoothie. "You've got to try this, matie—it'll blow your mind."

A taxi hoots from the street. You don't have much time to decide, better just get this over with.

Careful. Kamran is known for his sense of experimentation—there could be anything in that glass. It is upon such trivial matters that impassive Providence performs her inscrutable work. What you decide now could rewrite your fate. Do you:

Take the smoothie down in one, and risk Kamran's voodoo? **Go to Scene 223**

Tell Kamran he needs it more than you do? **Go to Scene 15**

Scene 66

You consent to Kamran's suggestion eagerly and, with soaring pleasure, note that Charlotte puts up little resistance. Before anyone has even attempted to lift Marc out of his place setting, Will appears, looking rather flustered.

"Sorry, guys, looks like the food's gonna be awhile."

"Will, stop worrying about your stomach. Can't you see Marc's sick." Will looks puzzled as he spots Marc whimpering. "Just help me get him upstairs."

Will obliges and the two of you take leave of the gallery. Will slumps Marc on to a bed and leaves, preoccupied with his sister's kitchen-lift fiasco. You start to wonder if the Frenchman is going to be all right, but he does, eventually, regain consciousness. The color returns to his cheeks, but Marc retains an expression of alarming serenity, eyes staring up to the ceiling. Fortunately he utters your name, so memory loss is not going to be an issue.

"Barbarella, what happened?"

"Don't worry, Marc," you dog-pat his head, "everything is going to be fine. Just rest."

After further minutes' convalescence Marc inhales deeply, then he instructs you, with Gallic incoherence but immeasurable seduction, to place a hand on his forehead. With physician-manner, you oblige, and its cool restorative effect is nothing short of wondrous, because Marc doesn't hesitate to pull it down, and slide it through his still-unzipped trousers.

"You zee . . . it beats like a fish, like a whale."

Slightly disturbed at the analogy, you still manage to force a smile.

"Barbeee, what you did to me downstairs waz very, very bad, but very, very good. I am still hot for you. You see zat I have great stamina. Come to me."

And with that, two strong diver arms lift you onto the Muff King. He pulls at your G-string, it offers little resistance, and smothers his face with the odor. The speed of the next events tumbles before your wine and gin-fuddled brain. As if sent from heaven, *he* asks *you* to sit on his face. Your dress is now hitched becomingly and Marc is removing his clothes, only leaving on a pair of silk black socks. A little spooky, but who cares; you have found a man offering unprecedented head. But then he ties his legs to the bedposts and asks you to secure his arms. OK, very spooky, but you can't possibly care when he tries to nibble your nipples as you lean over him, and fixes you with his deep brown Mediterranean eyes.

So there you are before him, knees slightly bent, quivering, trying not to buckle.

"Dive, dive, dive, Barbarella."

With as much grace as possible, you plunge a ripe bottom on to Marc's gesticulating face, then hold on for dear life. And you, eager to stock up as much as possible, wonder how long your thighs can possibly keep this position.

But your pleasure must be postponed. The door creaks behind you and before you know it, Barnaby is grabbing your hand, pulling you off Marc's face like a gas nozzle from an unfilled tank. You try to resist, but Barnaby is urging you with desperation, "Barbie, there's been a disaster, we've got to go . . . *now*."

Go to Scene 182

Scene 67

Midgrin, a thought strikes you. "What would Barbie's fantasy be, given an unlimited choice?"

You can't resist asking.

"Barbie, this isn't fair. I'd feel terrible if I didn't offer you a similar deal. Write down your own wish and I'll see what I can do."

Barbie doesn't hesitate . . . obviously it's some festering need. She writes swiftly with a clear hand, and tucks the folded paper into your trouser pocket.

Go to Scene 23

Scene 68

But up in the cubby dear Kamran is finding it increasingly hard to concentrate. He strains his neck desperately, but can't quite see beyond a plump breast. Taking control, the eagerly impatient Sally engages in a position forgotten even to Kam (that page of his illustrated *Kama Sutra* has been stuck shut since '92). For once Kamran has something new to learn and frankly, he is captivated. With skill and dexterity beyond her nineteen years, Sally maneuvers herself into the "cascading oyster." Never has a woman shown Kamran Jazeer the way with such invention. This woman is a true Messiah; his spirit absorbs all and the game below is forgotten. For balance, Kamran clutches on to a lever . . .

Downstairs, the game continues, but your success begins to wane. It is Barnaby who first suspects something may be wrong. For three games in a row, the chandelier turns left—dictating that you play higher. All of you play with faltering belief as your winnings begin to shrink. Wasim becomes suspicious, assuming that you're trying to frighten him off. In response he raises the stakes even higher. A lump sticks in your throat.

Catherine laughs nervously; Will mops his brow; Barnaby stares fixedly at his five cards. You check that your lipstick hasn't faded; no one speaks. The croupier continues to deal and you all continue to sign your lives away. Lady Luck no longer appears to be smiling. Lady Luck is too busy—rutting with a pink-faced waitress in the bedroom above.

Scene 68

What is Kam playing at? The swindle was working perfectly, so what's the problem? Will tries to catch your eye, but you ignore him in favor of your cards. Victory is so close you can smell its sweet perfume. And you want it bad. Scam or no scam, bloody-minded panic is driving you to play on—and for lack of an alternative resource you continue to rely on the chandelier.

Stop, stop. This is madness, Barbarella, are you nuts? Quit while you're ahead. **Go to Scene 237**

No way. What's wrong with going a little crazy? If you want to get a hat get a head. **Go to Scene 233**

Scene 69

"I'm actually a doctor, but am working with a developmental chiropractic unit at the Middlesex." The lie trips from your tongue with the ease of practice. "I'm more used to healing people than hurting them. That's why I feel bad . . ." The puppy dog eyes start their magic. "Are you sure I didn't hurt you?"

You dredge the depths of your anatomy knowledge (you were once beaten up at school and spent eight weeks in the hospital).

"You landed directly onto your sacroiliac. If you're not careful the tendons will overstrengthen to accommodate the soft tissue damage and cause a long-term misalignment."

Then the killer . . . "I'm just trying to impress you now." Cute nervous laugh. "But seriously, you should take it easy for a few minutes just until you can tell the extent of the damage."

She responds quickly. "Let me guess. I should accept a drink and wait for your diagnosis." But the quip has no venom. Carmen has bought the doctor story, she is assured of your good intentions and, and most importantly, she has accepted your doctor–patient relationship.

Stage 1 completed successfully. Time for stage 2—more to drink.

Carmen turns out to be a dancer for Four-ploy, a slightly naff boy band. You've never heard of them. (No, you're not getting old, even teenage girls get boy bands mixed up these days.) Carmen turns out to be from Newcastle. Carmen turns out to be more drunk than she first appeared. Carmen turns out to have bruised something in her lower back, though God knows what. Carmen starts to stretch her bruised spine like someone in need of a massage. Carmen needs another drink.

Stage 3—try to maintain a witty and interesting conversation while scanning your Top Forty for a fantasy involving a nubile (and very flexible) dancer who is wearing no underwear and has drunk too much champagne for her frail figure to accommodate.

Surely, Barnie, there must be something . . . oh, yes . . . Kamran was bragging about it the other day . . .

Carmen is looking at you with an expectant look. She has just finished saying something.

Do you:

Offer to give a clinical opinion? **Go to Scene 119**

Offer another drink? **Go to Scene 111**

Scene 70

STRAIN, CREAK, STRAIN, CREAK. The screech of the chandelier is loud, but it can't eclipse Astrid. She valiantly piles dollar bills down the front of her ripped dress. "Come and get it, Jenner. If you can."

Shaking her chest provocatively, the half-stunned Nigel Jenner lunges across the table. "Give me that money you—" A decade of dinners and drink beach him halfway. He can't move. Grounded.

STRAIN, CREAK, STRAIN, CREAK . . . CRASH.

. . . Pause . . .

. . . Scream . . .

. . . Silence . . .

You'll always remember the blurred horror of those moments. Empirically, Nigel Jenner lies crushed by a chandelier, thick blood seeps onto the green felt. You look at Astrid, then Barnaby, then Will. No remorse, no regret. In fact it's vaguely amusing. You cover your mouth in case you should emit a giggle. Barnaby grabs your arm.

"Christ, let's get out of here *now*."

Picking up any evidence that might trace you to the scene, and some spare dollars (to cover next month's minimum payment), you run. Through the lounge, through the bar, people staring, through the corridor, people staring, into the hall, people staring, towards the door. One last dash, push hard. Free.

Outside in the cool night air, you gasp to catch your breath and steady yourself on the hood of a parked Lexus, which sets off a sensitive alarm. Barnaby grips your shoulder and pushes you forward. "The bike's just round the corner . . . *quickly.*" By now, treasured bills are spilling from your clutch, fluttering onto the street. You grasp at them, laughing with hilarity as they float away on the late night breeze.

Disposable society.

Around the corner and onto Barnie's bike. As the bike races away from the crime scene, your head spins with success, endorphins, alcohol, and speed.

Go to Scene 241

Scene 71

Denying all knowledge, you take the "device" out of her hands. If she accidentally figures out how to turn the bloody thing on she could be in for a shock.

"I really think I could sculpt you, but only if you really don't mind."

She smiles, maternal instincts returning, "How do you want me?"

"Naked." Before your mental filter has time to work you've said it. ". . . Uhh . . . and lying on the rug."

Crunch time.

She raises one eyebrow, but doesn't flinch. Maintaining eye contact, she contorts a hand behind her back and releases the zipper. She shrugs out of the dress and, wriggling, lets it fall to the floor. You gasp. There, before you, gilded bronze in the dim light, is the most perfect body you have ever seen. Steffi Graf's Grand Slam legs, a Kylie butt, the waist of Grace Kelly in *Rear Window*, breasts from— She interrupts: "How do you want me?"

You can barely think, the loss of blood is so rapid.

"I'll get the clay," you mumble like a teenager on a first date.

As you scrabble around for a bag of modeling clay, Carmen makes herself at home. She lies, arms draped above her head, eyes shut peacefully.

"Perfect," you murmur with a vaguely French accent, "don't move from that position. You are . . . perfection."

Scene 71

So she lies there and you throw a slab of damp clay onto the wooden floor. And suddenly, with mounting horror, you realize you haven't the faintest idea how to begin.

Go to Scene 25

Scene 72

Barnaby stares at the crumpled paper in terror.

"Barbie. I don't know what to say . . . are you serious?"

You weren't when you wrote it. But now, looking over the lights of the Thames, standing with Barnaby, so caring and considerate—so *perfect*—you realize that it's what you want more than anything in the world.

"Barnie, I want to try again. Get out of London, away from all this crap, and start a new life together." You pause to let Barnaby respond, but he just stands in shock. "We don't have to have kids straight away . . ."

Even you can hear the desperation in that last sentence and you trail off. Barnaby hugs you. "Barbie, let's take you home."

You ride back to Barbarella Towers, holding onto Barnaby as though your life depended on it. Once in the flat, Barnie looks distinctly uncomfortable.

"I think I should go."

You twitch a nod. "Fine. Thanks for the ride home."

He turns to leave, but you can't bear it. "*Barnie*." Grabbing a shoulder you turn him and plant a passion-rich kiss on unresponsive lips. Pressing your lithe body against his, you kiss again—still no response. You rub a slender hand up the front of his trousers, nothing. You might as well be seducing a cadaver. The prospect of a baby is more potent than a bottle of bromide.

Barnaby is dead to your desire and you pull away.

Scene 72

"Barbie, this is a bad idea. Look, I'll call you tomorrow . . . I promise."

Yet more folly. All this talk of babies may have damaged Barnaby's sex drive forever. You know it's pointless trying to run before you can walk. Getting Barnaby to the maternity ward would be a five-year project, a project that will tax your powers of manipulation and seduction (in that order) to the utmost. These days, if you want to be a twenties mother, the only real option is the accidental route.

Shut the front door and go to bed, Barbarella. Barnaby has gone, but the damage needn't be permanent, there'll be time enough to sort this mess out on the morrow.

The (Dead) End

Sort it out, Reader. Things will get better—but you'll need to show a little more social cunning. Why not play again?

Scene 73

You gather in a small anteroom, everyone desperate to talk. Catherine is glowing from within, and not for the first time this evening you remember why she is such a dear friend.

"You are a genius, Barnie," she kisses.

Astrid, flushed and flustered, is gabbling loudly in half-Flemish. Barbie shows signs of strain.

"Barnaby, for God's sake shut that Eurotrash up. She'll give the bloody game away."

Oblivious to the fact that Eurotrash is only a yard to her right.

"Slip some more of this into her drink. Just a bit, she's already had enough to dope a Thoroughbred. And I don't think you're strong enough to carry her all the way home."

You pinch a little of the proffered powder.

Hold on. Rohypnol? Barbie, you can't be serious. That's for date rapists (and very bored students), isn't it? We've been through this before; you can't go round spiking people's drinks—it's not legal. And it's not as if drugging Astrid will help you win the poker game. Will it?

Give the drugged drink to the hapless Belgian. **Go to Scene 27**

Avoid criminal charges and pour the glass into a convenient pot plant. **Go to Scene 5**

Scene 74

It is nearing five in the morning and you are tiring fast. But word is bond. Barnaby smirks as he reads your note. "Sounds a bit kinky, but I'll give it a go." Barnie is eagerly efficient and you silently regret being quite so forward.

"Look, Barbie, I need to put your helmet back so I can make a quick phone call." Barnie takes his bow-tie (undone *à la* Connery hours ago) and neatly covers your eyes. The crash helmet does the rest, and you stand, unseeing and unhearing, in the cold of early morning.

Within a few minutes, Barnaby helps you on to the back of the Ducatti, and you can do nothing but hold on to his stout midriff for dear life.

"Don't go too fast. I'm still feeling giddy after that game of cardsssssss."

Too late. Either Barnaby doesn't hear or he's ignoring you. The bike screeches away with wondrous acceleration. Unable to see, you try to imagine which direction you might be taking. If you go north, you could end up not far from home. If south, well, you've no idea what's down there. As for the west, there's the vague hope that you might be going to Heathrow. Finally, to go east, well, twice in one day would be an outright crime.

Clutching to Barnaby with all four limbs, you feel a thrill of anticipation. The regret of sharing such an outlandish fantasy begins to fade with the exhilaration. In order for it to work, it is imperative that you put your friendship aside, forget all that has happened in the past, and effectively pretend that you have just met. You love sex with strangers—it's so candid. There is the freedom to reinvent yourself, to be as nefarious as you like.

The bike comes to a halt. You've only been on the back for five minutes, therefore not too far from the river. But again, you have no idea in which direction you traveled. You could be anywhere in Central London. Barnie helps you off the bike, but insists you keep the helmet on. You can barely hear him.

"No way, you have to keep it on. You'll ruin the surprise."

Had you removed the helmet, you might have caught a telltale glimpse of the Thames. Not that it matters terribly. It would satisfy your immediate curiosity. But you are in safe hands—there's no need to worry with good old Barnie.

With as much grace as anyone can display when wearing an oversized helmet with no view, you take Barnaby's lead and follow him blindly; up some steps and over something that feels like a wooden plank.

Go to Scene 200

Scene 75

Barbarella's face. And a scrawny white bum next to it. Not that you can recognize all your friends by their arse . . . but it's undoubtedly Will. Acid rises to the back of your throat with a wave of nausea. And with quelching stomach, you realize your left hand is still perched on his thigh. Oh, the indignity of it all.

Only the smell of burning carpet can break into such horror. All is a blur. Clutching random clothing, you burst to your feet and out into the passageway. You don't even think to put out the flaming curtain or unplug the smashed lamp or exchange postcoital pleasantries. No afterplay, you're sprinting. You don't stop to vomit at the rail, but hurl yourself into the purifying Thames. It cleanses and cools your tortured homophobic soul . . .

You tread water and look back at the boat with alarm. Smoke is already billowing and naked figures are following your lead . . . Will the white, holding his nose; Barbie, diving with a smile, and finally Carmen, panic-stricken, windmilling arms as she hurtles to the water.

They join you in a grinning huddle, ten meters from the boat. By now, the boat is really beginning to burn and flames are roaring out of your dear little porthole. Carmen's body rubs against you. Barbarella grins a wicked smile. Even Will's quiet face has a look of devilment as reflected flames dance on his corneas.

But Carmen's chilled nipples are stabbing you. With united thought, the four of you swim downriver, and to the far bank.

The (Soggy) End

Reader, you sniffed out a little fun for Barnie. But there is more to life than a few feverish fumblings. The Perfect Ending could be just around the corner. Play again and see where you'll take Barnie next . . .

Scene 76

As he draws you away from the central bustle of the party, Edward opens the conversation. "I just wanted to ask you how Catherine is. I'm worried sick about her."

He has obviously established the important place you hold in Catherine's life and needs to pump you for information. You get ready to play the insidious minx. Catherine is out of view, something the minister will have considered. Here he is, asking for an insight into Catherine's state of mind. Obviously he's paranoid. Time to make him pay for all the grief he's caused.

"She's fine. Honestly. You know Catherine—she's a tough cookie. You don't need to worry about *her* . . ."

You leave the last word, emphasized and dangling. But Edward is a cool customer, he barely twitches at your implied threat, signals to a waiter to bring you both fresh drinks, and says, in a low voice, "I think we need to talk properly. Can we discuss this somewhere more private?"

He points an open hand towards some downward steps and, despite a love for public scenes, you consent to follow his lead.

Putting aside his years and the genetic warning shouted by his amber hair, you can't help but notice the confidence with which the minister carries himself. Thinking back to a previous conversation with Catherine, you start to understand what she meant about "paternal attraction." Having never spoken to him, you'd naturally built him up to be an obdurate, ruthless bastard. Pleasantly surprised?

He leads you into a low-ceilinged cabin. It starts to feel ridiculously reminiscent of a James Bond scene; the plush red décor fitted with brass, a crystal decanter and cigar case resting on the desk.

"Take a seat, Barbarella." Edward sits comfortably on the requisite brown leather armchair, while you opt for the low sofa. Not wishing to appear intimidated, you decide to recline nonchalantly, only to realize that you've misjudged the distance behind you. You fall back in what seems a screaming invitation. Without awkwardly reshuffling, all you can do is pretend to be comfortable and point to the drink sitting on the desk.

"Could you hand me my glass, please?"

The minister obliges, pausing to admire the stretch of thigh preceding you. He passes your drink and resumes his position opposite.

Something strange is going on here. Barbie, do you get the feeling that he doesn't want to discuss Catherine? The man is positively salivating. Oh well, looks like you chose the right dress.

The only question is, what are you wearing under it? If you can't recollect, then from the view Edward got when you fell back on the sofa, he can sure as hell tell you.

Be honest now, for good or ill remember, are you wearing knickers or not?

Knickers. **Go to Scene 220**

Or not. **Go to Scene 230**

Scene 77

You excuse yourself and locate Kamran on the dance floor. He spins Catherine with gay abandon and you stop to admire her disciplined physique for a few moments before remembering the urgency of your mission. Dancing up behind Cat, you sandwich her against Kamran in a Romford-teenager move. It would normally earn you a slap from the hard-bitten newshound, but Cat is careering out of control. She barely registers your presence as you fumble in Kamran's front trouser pocket.

With a frisson of homophobic horror, you negotiate past the inevitable obstacle and bag the powder. Kamran smiles and gives a thumbs up. Above the music, he shouts something indecipherable and no doubt libelous. Kamran's infamous powder is a unique blend of Pfizer's finest; herbal remedies known only to the ancients (and a pharmacy just off Tottenham Court Road), bound together with a liberal lacing of coke.

Dancing backwards you bump your way through shuffling dance steps, grab two fresh glasses of champagne, and empty the entire packet. You stir with a finger and head back to little Natasha. You approach, admiring her small trim figure—and imagine her naked, the oversized breasts bouncing before you . . .

Time for the kill. Hand her the drink. Get on with it, Barnie. Nothing will happen for thirty minutes and by then your sex drive might be bored into submission. Maybe you should have saved some for yourself.

Oh, God.
You idiot.
Which glass is which?

Schoolboy error—you must never take your eye off the ball. Now you'll just have to guess. There's really only one thing to say— PRIAPISM.

You're right-handed, so you would probably have poured using your right hand. In that case it'll probably be in the glass in your left hand. Probably. **Go to Scene 3**

Or maybe not, maybe the right hand. **Go to Scene 31**

Scene 78

By the time you arrive at the Holland Park address, it's starting to get late. The cabbie stops in a leafy side street and the sound of an old Oasis album leads you to the correct address. Godfrey has certainly avoided tax to good purpose. The high-financed house, set slightly off the road and secluded by tall rhododendrons, could fit your flat in it ten times over. You crunch up a short gravel drive and pull an old-fashioned doorbell.

The door is opened to reveal a mixed gaggle and a blast of music. The majority seems to be made up of party wallahs, researchers, and assorted Millbank hangers-on, but the occasional TV-familiar face lends an air of quality. The overriding timbre of the party chatter is one of conceit.

Kamran, though keen to make a discreet entrance, errs fatally. He stumbles over a thick rug and trips against Carol, the host's wife.

"Well, hello there. I didn't realize we'd invited some youngsters to come and play."

With a loose smile, which has a habit of being ghastly, Carol touches Kamran's elbow to provide unneeded support. She leads him from the large hall and into a minimalist drawing room. You follow, but as he becomes submerged within the middle-aged morass, you realize he is lost to you . . .

*

Tread carefully, Barbarella. Remember, politics is just showbiz for ugly people, so beware of lofty vanity and heightened pomposity. If you get stuck with a wrong-un you could be talking about NHS waiting lists for hours. So stay close to Will and Barnaby. And don't forget, your sole purpose here is to sort out Catherine, and deliver her from the wicked Edward Bunger.

Oh God, there they are. Catherine's sitting on his knee. Despite Edward's betrayal, she seems lapdog-loyal. Lord, what fools these mistresses be . . .

Peering over Astrid's shoulder, you see into the drawing room and watch Edward run his hand through Catherine's hair. She sits on his lap . . . "Daddy's lap," you think with a shiver.

Will is muttering under his breath, obviously trying to get your attention, "This is a bloody nightmare, what are we doing here?"

"Saving Catherine from herself." You nod towards Cat. She is still sitting on Edward's knee, but seems to have lost his attention. Edward, with an enviable eye, has caught the attention of an anorexic political researcher. He's obviously decided Catherine is disposable, for he feeds the young blonde low-calorie canapés and flirts outrageously. Catherine is forced to watch on with mounting humiliation. You casually edge nearer, all the better to eavesdrop.

"So how do you manage to keep yourself in such good trim?" Edward smiles at the blonde waif as he ungallantly shifts his thigh under the weight of Catherine.

Catherine avoids your stare, aware of how ridiculous she looks. You know how much time she spends on the scales and in front of the mirror. She excuses herself from Edward's lap (this allows him to resuscitate his thigh with an ostentatiously vigorous rub) and goes into the hall. Edward barely looks up from his new conquest.

Scene 78

Following Catherine to the door, Astrid blocks your path. Grabbing your arm, she roars with laughter and insists you meet Alan.

"Ho, ho, he's so funny. I can't understand a word he says, but he makes me laugh, ho, ho."

You realize that she's referring to one of the last bastions of socialism, Alan Smith. With the alacrity of a stand-up comic, he entertains Astrid with his favorite working club anecdotes.

". . . So I told the silly bugger to leave the dripping on the doorstep and fuck off down the mines. And he bloody did, and with his Woodbines."

Astrid shrieks with laughter, despite the fact she has no idea what "bugger" or "dripping" or "woodbines" are. It's all too much for your delicate sensibilities. Must escape . . . must get to the door . . . must get out now.

Go to Scene 80

Scene 79

"I was worried you'd run to share the chips with your welfare chums," gibes Nigel.

No one seems put out by his obvious lack of manners and you greet this latest display of rudeness with only a simple honest smile.

Nigel is still smiling, but he does little to conceal the venom in his eyes. You meet his stare confidently only to find stark truth glowering back at you. It shouts, *"I know you are cheating."*

You can't help looking across at Will in panic. Jenner sees all and you realize he is reading you as easily as one of his tabloid headlines. Will rescues with a distraction. Grabbing Daisy by the elbow, he guides her over to you.

"Daisy, why don't you go and give Barnie some luck. I think he's bled his own dry."

She looks confused at first, but then seems to make up her mind and sashays round the table with swinging hip. You immediately manage to evade Jenner's gaze and concentrate on smiling at Newt's obvious jealousy. Daisy, of the Body, slips a pert cheek onto your narrow chair and joins the team.

The distraction also gives you time to think. Jenner knows you are cheating—but does he know how? Is Kamran still tupping the lovely Sally in the cubby, or is his numb body sinking to the bottom of the Thames? Nigel exudes bloated confidence as he dries a damp forehead with yet another new kerchief. The cards are dealt and you squeeze Daisy's rump for luck.

Time to play.

Go to Scene 85

Scene 80

You escape to the hall, but Catherine has already gone. She's probably crying in a bathroom upstairs, better go and see if she's OK. Climbing the stairs, you don't stop to admire the framed photographs aligning the wall. Most of them are of political legends, but the odd celebrity has crept in. Godfrey with Sting; Godfrey with Elton; Godfrey with Queen.

Finally you reach the bathroom,. only to find it empty. Catherine has vanished, and so with the skill of a Côte d'Azur cat burglar, only drunker, you decide to explore. Checking that no one is coming up the stairs, you creep across the landing and notice a door slightly ajar. You suspect that Catherine may have been overcome by professional curiosity—and sure enough, there she is, standing in what turns out to be a large study, holding a file full of receipts.

"Cat, I've been looking ever—" You stop short, surprised by the sudden sight of Barnaby (what is he doing sniffing around Catherine?), and Cat takes the opportunity to get a word in.

"Christ, Barbie, what is it with you two? How am I supposed to be an investigative journalist with you both barging around?"

Barnaby shrugs at you. "Cat thinks she might be able to find some dirt on Edward."

You shut the door, turn, and address Catherine, "Cat, if you want revenge on Edward then for God's sake be careful." Catherine sighs histrionically, she doesn't want to hear negatives, so you change tack. "But if you *do* want to make an ex-lover suffer, then you've come to the right people." You drop a smile at Barnaby. "We've been making each other suffer for months." Barnie nods.

"You just need a plan."

Catherine looks at you both, grinning like morons, and shakes her head. "I don't know, Barbie, this is between me and Ted . . ."

Choices, choices. Barbarella, tread carefully. What you decide now could bring down the British government. Edward Bunger is a well-respected minister, and this Cabinet has enough skeletons to hide without you rattling any bones. The sensible thing would be to take Catherine home and let her get a good night's sleep.

Two wrongs don't make a right. Take Catherine home and leave well alone. **Go to Scene 228**

Two wrongs don't make a right, but they make a good excuse. Make Edward suffer. **Go to Scene 94**

Scene 81

With a freshly informed Barbie, you exit the thinned party and join Kamran at your agreed rendezvous on dry land. You find him humming an old Shirley Bassey number, amiably sitting against Cleopatra's Needle on the Embankment. He greets you with an enthusiastic wave and holds up a small Nokia. It's been stolen from Will, and the screen is filled with recently written text. You read:

Hi rabbit, I MUST c u. Go down steps by main bar. Wait 4 me in far right cabin. Await further instruction . . .

"She'll be there by now, you idiot," you reprimand. "Send the second message." And with blurring finger speed, Kam taps out,

U in? Turn out the light.

Seconds go by and then with a loud beep that makes you all jump, Will's phone registers "message received." You laugh with the realization of how tense you are . . . Kam opens the message.

"It's from her," he shouts in boyish excitement. "It says light off—what now??"

Kam flashes back:

Scene 81

Clothes off and before he can send you make him add don't worry my luv. I hve the dor covred

The three of you wait impatiently. The beautiful stillness of the Thames ignored, the drone of late night traffic all but unheard. This is crunch time. Once Annabel is naked the battle is half won.

The phone beeps its receipt.

Clothes off it says simply.

And with feverish excitement you picture darling skinny Annabel, with her perky little Daryl Hannah nose and flat chest, and long slender legs, all seen with the light of a crescent moon.

But Kamran is busy and you must stay prescient to curb his wilder tendencies . . . too late. It's sent: lie bck on desk and spread legs apart —wide.

And while you use your own phone to text Astrid and Cat their starting orders, Kamran becomes lost in his own fantasies. Sht yr eyes, mbate and thnk of me. I am comng in—DON'T OPEN YR EYES.

It's done. Your directorial debut will now unfold like a theatrical farce. In years to come, literary scholars may comment on your mature sense of comic timing and will debate the inspirational source of your comedy of errors. But for now, you must wait backstage, and let the players act their scenes.

And so with a certain sense of anticlimax, the three of you walk the short distance back to the boat, secure a taxi, and sit parked, engine running idly, imaginations running wildly.

Go to Scene 131

Scene 82

Well done, Barbie. Annabel is full of tricks, but she'll have to get up a hell of lot earlier to catch you out. Lying bitch. Lie low for a few minutes, have another (small) line, and when the coast is clear go rejoin the gang.

Go to Scene 24

Scene 83

She laughs at your dreadful honesty and you squeeze her hand. She makes no move to withdraw it.

"I'm sure you can control yourself for a while longer." She glows as she speaks. "Besides, better the devil you know . . . At least with the 'Barnaby Beast' I'll have an interesting conversation before he succumbs to his hideous base instincts."

She drains the last of her glass and the thought of her succumbing arouses your hideous base instincts immediately. You strain against your Calvins.

"The way I'm feeling I'll end up chasing you around the boat. I'd feel terrible if I forced you to jump in the Thames."

"I'm sure it wouldn't come to that . . . even if I had to use some form of restraint."

Her laugh tinkles as she slips off to powder her nose.

And you feared a night of dull melancholic conversation. How could you have underestimated her? After all she's an Australian. They come with a sexual guarantee—never to disappoint (at least never from lack of enthusiasm).

You subtly check for signs of unnatural rigidity and realize that with her exit the pressure valve has been released. That can only mean one thing . . . *She* took the Viagra and it should be kicking in right about now.

Go to Scene 151

Scene 84

The sight before you is reminiscent of a crass canvas by Pollock. The darkness deceived you into imaging beautiful flesh; the light reveals a scene infinitely more ungainly and shamed. The woman, kneeling against the desk, has her dress pulled up over her head, and with a shock you see Barnaby staring wildly from between her dangling breasts. Will looks near to a heart attack. They are both utterly compromised—legs entwined.

You'd be more sympathetic, but are currently lying directly between the girl's legs with your head dangerously close to the sharp end. It's not a view you're familiar with and precious moments are lost making mental notes for your waxing woman. You neglect to consider the source of light until the crackling sound of flammable upholstery becomes unmistakable.

"Fuck."

You finally notice the fire, spreading with ferocious speed. In desperation, Will tries to douse it with champagne, but his efforts are futile. Barnaby fumbles with his trousers and the girl shrieks hysterically in Geordie. You drag her in a scramble for the cabin door.

Go to Scene 86

Scene 85

The first few hands pass with little to note. Daisy squeals intelligently each time you win and no one seems to notice the chandelier's minuscule turns. Daisy's long brown legs, exposed by a long slit in her cream dress, distract you enormously, but you manage to stay on top of the game. Men can think about two things at once, but only if they are money and sex.

By now, you are beginning to enjoy yourself again. Barbie has won another ridiculous amount of money, and you're nearing the early-retirement mark. Daisy is blatantly blowing on your ear and Newt is playing so rabidly that his once massive pile of notes looks sadly lackluster. Time for the kill.

And with no thought that you may be being set up, a dream hand turns up—four aces.

To be fair, 200 million of your neural links were devoted to thinking about Daisy's naked body, covered in crisp dollar bills. You can't be blamed for everything. The old ticker beats a little faster as the chandelier begins to creak . . . anticlockwise.

Soon Newt and Bodi are out of the game. Barbie folds, to leave you staring across the table at your sweaty nemesis.

He raises $30,000. You match it and raise by another $30,000. (It's just like Monopoly.)

Nigel, with no sign of doubt, raises by $50,000 (or is it Go for Broke?). Catherine cranes her neck for a better look. Will's jaw begins to twitch with tension. Even Astrid looks vaguely alert.

Daisy, oozing hormones, quivers against you. This is no time for an erection, Barnie—concentrate.

The chandelier turns anticlockwise; you match Jenner and raise by even more.

This ridiculous battle swings back and forth, with the chandelier waltzing imperceptibly anticlockwise all the while. You borrow Barbie's funds, and continue to raise. Until, finally, you push forward the last of your cash.

"And I raise you another," quick mental arithmetic, "five, ten . . . fifteen thousand four hundred and twenty-six dollars."

Nigel contemplates your smiling face.

"Mr. Wilson, I see you are temporarily fundless. I assure you I will lend any monies you require to end the game."

You nod agreement and accept dumbly. Nigel continues the absurdity. "Your fifteen, and I raise one hundred thousand dollars."

Gasp, shock, horror, etc.

It's toy money now. You ignore Will's apoplexy and sign a small slip of paper.

"I call you, Nigel."

Jenner smiles. Jenner knocks his cards together on the table and looks you in the eye. He fans the five cards in an enormous fist . . . and smiles.

Nothing disconcerting in that, but the reaction on the chandelier is terrifying. It begins to turn, at first slowly, but then with a speed to make a draft. But far worse, *it's spinning clockwise.*

Time to get the fuck out o' here.

But Jenner is placing his cards on the table and all you can do is stare like an open-mouthed moron as he places each down in turn.

Scene 85

Nine spade . . .
Ten spade . . .
Jack spade . . .
Queen spade . . . .
King spade.

Dead.

Go to Scene 167

Scene 86

With dramatics that would bring the Palme d'Or Committee to protest, you run to the nearest man.

"Please help, someone's started a fire, it's out of control."

The giant and the lamb spring to mind as you are manfully whisked away. The chivalrous rush to put out the inferno, an alarm siren wails, and mass hysteria grips the boat. Lights plunge into darkness and the music drones to a halt; a mad stampede inevitably follows . . .

Caught in the crush, swept up and out of the boat, with a surge you are spilled onto the Embankment and ushered away from the blaze. Kamran is beside you and has his jacket about your shoulders.

"Are you OK?" he shouts above the din.

He stares at your face, through heavy-lashed eyes, trying to diagnose your state of mind and health. "I'm fine," you stutter.

"Is Barnaby still on the boat?"

"I don't know," and suddenly Kamran is gone. You pull down your dress to a more modest level and, realizing arson to be a criminal offense, make your way swiftly up onto the Strand and into a cab. You're a little fazed because hormonal Kamran left you in a becomingly disheveled state, but you stare pathetically from the back of the taxi and realize that for once in his life Kamran has acted gallantly.

Scene 86

Back home to St. John's Wood, Barbarella—alone.

The (Forlorn) End

Reader, you can do better than that! Why don't you go back to the beginning and start again—just think about what you could be missing out on.

Scene 87

Quite right. You can't go round drugging every girl you fancy. Trouble is, after another half-hour of her wittering you can barely stand it.

"There's just no excitement left, nothing seems fresh," she whines.

Time to turn this baby around. Do or die.

"Natasha, you can't expect to resolve your problems in a flash. You can't go from miserable to blissful in a single night. But you can make a start." You pause for a breath, knowing that this is make or break. "This is what I propose. Let your hair down, do something ridiculous. Remember that life, at the end of the day, is just a big game—except you can't win or lose. You can just have more, or less, fun."

You leave it there, tantalizing.

By now she is all curiosity.

"What do you mean? How do you propose I 'let my hair down'?"

She shakes it provocatively, not realizing the profound effect she is having on your blood pressure.

"OK, this is the game. You haven't been in London long; and after all, if you are tired of London you really are tired of life. Write down something you would really like to do in London on a piece of paper. I will do the same. We combine the two, jump in a cab, . . . and do it . . . simple."

Scene 87

She laughs at your stupidity, but nonetheless writes down her idea on a paper napkin. And so do you.

Now, how to make the carnal act sound romantic?

Go to Scene 7

Scene 88

Before leaving the conspiracy, Catherine sets the plan rolling. Pulling out her mobile, she dials the office: "Hi, Charlie, it's Catherine. Listen, I've got a great scoop. It'll be breaking at Godfrey Thomson's house in the next hour or so . . . yeah, Holland Park . . . OK . . . just make sure they're in position in the next thirty minutes."

Flipping the phone cover shut, Catherine flashes a smile more wicked than a Sacher torte. Turning to you and Astrid, she takes control.

"OK, girls, it's time to get frisky. Barbie, go downstairs and tell Edward that I need to see him for a private briefing in the study. That's our usual code for a quick screw. He'll get the picture, especially if you tell him you want to join in. Trust me, Edward Bunger will come."

Slightly disturbed by Catherine's appalling innuendo, you head back down to the party. Meanwhile, Astrid and Catherine head for the study while thinking of their top ten men. They have to be feeling frisky, ready for Edward.

"Russell Crowe, Russell Crowe, Russell Crowe, OK, I'm ready."

Didn't take Catherine long. Astrid is almost there, but her choice of man is worrying.

"Jean-Claude Van Damme, Jean-Claude, Jean-Claude, Jean-Claude."

Scene 88

"Astrid, you can't seriously get turned on at the thought of him, can you? He must be smaller than your leg!"

She shrugs. Catherine decides to ignore her. "My name is Maximus and I shall have my vengeance. In this life or the next."

Go to Scene 104

Scene 89

"I was worried you'd run to share the winnings with your welfare chums," gibes Nigel.

No one seems put out by his obvious lack of manners, and you greet this latest display of rudeness with only a simple, honest smile.

Nigel is still grinning, but he does little to conceal the venom in his eyes. You meet his stare confidently, only to find stark truth glowering back at you. It shouts, "*I know you are cheating.*"

With rising horror, you can't help looking across at Will in panic. Jenner sees all and you realize he is reading you as easily as one of his tabloid headlines. Will rescues with a distraction. Grabbing Daisy by the elbow, he guides her over to you. "Daisy, why don't you go and give Barnie some luck. I think he's bled his own dry."

She looks confused at first, but then seems to make up her mind and sashays around the table with swinging hip. You immediately manage to evade Jenner's gaze and concentrate on smiling at Newt's obvious jealousy. Daisy, "the body," slips a pert cheek onto your narrow chair and joins the team.

The distraction also gives you time to think. Jenner knows you are cheating, but does he know how? Is Kamran still tupping the lovely Sally in the cubby, or is his numb body sinking to the bottom of the Thames? Nigel exudes bloated confidence as he dries a damp forehead with yet another new kerchief. The cards are dealt and you squeeze Daisy's rump for luck.

Time to play.

Go to Scene 37

Scene 90

Interesting decision.

Snuffy is still reminiscing, but you interrupt with a plea, "Snuffy, I need some advice." And so you detail your plight. Annabel you taint with a description fit for Catherine de' Medici; you gloss over the way you split up with Will (he stood you up at the theater so you slept with his cousin), and instead paint a sorrowful picture of star-crossed lovers kept apart by fickle fate.

Snuffy is suitably impressed. "My dear girl, how dreadful. You must do something." She takes a deep breath as if deciding to let you in on a secret. "I know how important it is. You see, when I first met Horace, he was about to get engaged—to Barbara Cartland, you know, the romanticist."

You're not sure whether senility isn't creeping into her recollection, but her eyes retain a vibrant glint as she tells of a world long beyond common memory, a time when biplanes ruled the skies and motor cars came with a handle.

"Of course I was much younger than Barbara, and she didn't have my looks, but she did have rather trim ankles *and* a long head start. The Cartlands had been entertaining in St. Lucia over the winter and Horace spent his time sailing and laying a suit at young Barbara. Her grandfather was filthy rich, you see, and Horace always had a weakness for money. So by the time they came back for the season, the whole affair was pretty much settled. Then I met Horace—and fell in love."

Scene 90

You smile encouragingly, eager for her to cut to the chase. She duly obliges. "She knew I was after him, but I wouldn't be put off. Barbara was always good with words; she could always make one feel, well, stupid, but at heart she just didn't have any style. She was just a scared bully with no sense of fun."

Snuffy could be describing Annabel, and with a sense of destiny, you listen on. "Of course that was when I had the idea. Terribly simple. I organized a game of sardines. I cheated, of course, and we had ten blissful minutes in a broom cupboard." The old lady smiles with nostalgic warmth. "I do think it was the most passionate kiss of my life. Of course, you'd need to know how to cheat at sardines . . ."

Suddenly Barnaby is sitting beside you. He has a fake angry look about him, obviously not happy at being left alone with Annabel. His arrival brings Snuffy out of her reverie. In a different tone she ends abruptly: "The whole thing was very underhand. Forget all about it. I'm sure all you need to do is shake your tootsies at this Will fellow and he'll come running."

"Who'll come running?" Barnaby blusters in rudely. Before you can form an answer, though, the others are jostling to their seats. To Snuffy's right sits Kamran. He introduces himself to the old girl as though she were still in her prime. Kamran always did have the ability to make any woman feel special. You can't bemoan his gift even when it distracts Snuffy from confiding her secrets. To Kamran's left sits Catherine, who is animatedly arguing with a rather chipper, white-dinner-jacketed octogenarian at the end of the table, who oddly introduces himself as "Uncle Oswald." Next to him sits Astrid, then dear darling Will, and next along and opposite you, rather inevitably (given Olympia's twisted sense of humor), sits the delightful Annabel. After Annabel things rather peter out with a humorless-looking middle-aged banking couple.

But you've got to concentrate. Introductions are over and the conversation is kicking off. If you can show Annabel up as the bitch she is then Snuffy might help you prize Will away.

"Annabel, Will. I think we should have a toast," this from Barnaby, obviously trying to bait you. And with a strong sense of irony he raises his champagne flute. "Annabel—Will. May their love always be as strong as it is today." You raise your glass with the others, pausing only to share a sly grin with Catherine.

Barnie's irony isn't lost on Will, and he eagerly tries to move things onto neutral ground. "Lady Fotherington, you're looking well. Have you been to India again this Easter?" He turns to Annabel in explanation. "Snuffy has a home near Pondicherry."

"Yes, I was able to get out there this year. I went with my grand-niece, and we had a lovely time."

You spot the opportunity to lay an ambush for Annabel. She's always had an irrational hatred for people who care for the environment ("weirdy beardy swampy types") and despises their "pathetic attempts to do something—just to salve their consciences," so you set a trap.

"I'd love to go out to India. I quite fancy going on some sort of 'green' holiday. You know, a holiday where you get to do something for the environment." You deliberately sound a little hesitant, inviting the inevitable rebuke.

"God, Barbarella, how wet. Just because you drive around for fifty weeks of the year in a three-liter sports car doesn't mean that you have to spend the other two planting trees in chapati-land."

Perfect. Time to push home your advantage.

"No, but unless we do something, in ten years' time there won't be a single tiger left in the wild."

"For God's sake, Barbie. What's got into you? That's what zoos are for. God, if I could shoot the lot, just to stop everyone's whining on, I would."

Bingo. You spy Snuffy working her mouth in readiness for a riposte. Time to sit back and watch the fireworks.

"YOUNG LADY, in my time it was considered very agreeable for a woman to appear stupid in society, but I like to think the world has moved on." Snuffy pauses to let the rebuke sink in. "Tigers are interesting, intelligent, and beautiful creatures," she pointedly looks over her half-moon spectacles at Annabel, "which makes them very rare indeed."

There is a deliciously awkward pause. That worked better than you could have ever expected.

But the silence doesn't last long because Barnaby is obviously in the mood for fun. "I still can't believe you two are getting married. Tell me, Annabel, how did Will propose? Did he do it properly?"

Annabel looks shyly at Will, who confirms what you suspected. "Actually, Annabel proposed to me," he says a little bashfully.

You can't resist. "Oh how exciting. Did *you* do it properly, Annabel?" You pause for effect. "Of course, that explains all those carpet-burn knees." The last cryptic insult isn't lost on Annabel, but she ignores it effectively.

"We were walking in the garden at sunset, and the idea popped into my mind out of the blue," she smiles, as if butter wouldn't melt. "I suggested it almost as a joke. I couldn't believe it when Will suggested we do it straight away."

You pause to think. It's scarcely credible that Will wants to marry this coat hanger of a woman, but for him to want to rush through the engagement is even weirder. Something is eluding you, some nugget of information that would answer the riddle.

Then, as you glance across at Will's elegant, but rather feminine, hands, you understand with a rushing clarity. The frayed cuff on his shirtsleeve, silky cuff links instead of the usual gold. God, he's not wearing his grandfather's watch. And then you remember. Will used his Capital One card for every purchase he made today. The answer is obvious—Will is broke.

You smile at your previous wild theories. As you look at

Annabel talking, you inwardly wince at the thought of her bony frame dressed in a rubber fetish suit. Annabel was always too dull for that idea to be really credible. But she does have money, and Will knows it. God, he must be desperate to marry Annabel for cash. She may look OK scrubbed and dressed up, but surely Will can't ignore the receding chin and horse profile.

You mentally tot up your financial situation. You're never particularly liquid, but you could maybe get some cash out on your credit cards. Barbie, you're not seriously considering *buying* a husband? How marvelous. No time to think, the conversation is drawing you in. Snuffy is recalling some of her own proposals.

"Of course women have never played a completely passive role when it comes to marriage proposals. A lady must give out clear signals that she is receptive. Men are such cowards, you see."

Annabel interrupts to go on the offensive. "Barbie, surely you've thought of proposing. You must have the patience of a saint, waiting around all this time."

Snuffy comes to your aid. "I'm sure Barbarella is having lots of fun turning men down." She smiles at you and pats your hand like a kindly great-aunt. "Aren't you, dear?"

You smile politely. Annabel can't help giving out a snort of derision as she rather unattractively laughs into her champagne. You look across at her with renewed hatred.

"Lady Fotherington, Barbarella doesn't really suit relationships —do you, Barbie?"

You mumble to Snuffy some sort of explanation. "I don't seem to have much luck with men."

She smiles at you, and bless her, says, "Really? How odd. I could understand that you, Annabel, might want to propose, but I can't believe Barbarella doesn't have her pick of young men."She inspects you through her strong glasses. "Barbarella, you must scare them away with your good looks." She saves the best 'til last—obviously Snuffy has taken a firm dislike to Annabel:

"Honestly, men are such cowards. You should try to look, well, a little plainer," and with a magnificently subtle gesture she waves a hand, casually, in the direction of Annabel.

But before you can fully admire the old lady's marvelous bitching, Olympia booms shrilly from the far end of the room: "WHAT DO YOU MEAN STUCK?"

The poor kitchen-hand fails to register a sound at your far end, but the gist is clear from Olympia's strident tones: "IT CAN'T BE STUCK. George, do something about it."

And George, Sixth Lord Ravenshaw, trots off obediently to sort out the domestic crisis. Olympia calms herself and addresses the hungry throng. "My apologies everybody," she sighs theatrically, "half the main course appears to be stuck in the lift from the kitchens. It probably hasn't been serviced since the First World War."

This with a glower at her husband's empty seat. She effects a twittering gaggle of conversation from the ninety-odd guests, no less so than at your, far end.

"God, but I'm starving," booms Astrid.

You wince at Astrid's latest shibboleth, but before you have an opportunity to chastise her, Lord George returns and announces that the main course will be some while. A man called Frank is coming from the village with his tool kit, etc., but tuck into the wine and try to drink through the hunger is the general advice. And so you do.

Baroness Snuffy barks, "More gin, boy," to a nearby, middle-aged waiter, who quickly returns with a bottle of Bombay Sapphire. Snuffy relieves him of it with the quick-fingered skill of Martin Daniels, sloshes out seven generous glasses, and pops the bottle in her handbag. "Bombay Sapphire is a wonderful appetite suppressant, but it must be drunk neat."

The gin does wonders for the conversation, but before you can draw Snuffy into any sardines confessions his Lordship is back with some more bad news: "I AM DEEPLY SORRY, EVERYBODY—FRANK, FROM THE VILLAGE, HAS GOT HIMSELF WEDGED." With British restraint, all refrain from groaning, but the misery is clear; no food for at least another half-hour. More wine is circulated and the babble reaches a higher pitch.

Soon people begin to circulate more freely. Barnaby goes off in search of Will's niece, Catherine becomes wrapped up in another older man, and to your relief Annabel and Will excuse themselves to step into the garden. No doubt Annabel wishes to beat a retreat and moan to Will about his horrid friends. Uncle Oswald misunderstands their motives. "You two run along and have some fun," he winks at Will.

So, as the blushing lovebirds exit, you take the chance to air your theory. Gathering round at one end of the table, you spill your beans.

"It's so obvious. Will's broke. He's marrying Annabel for her trust fund." Oswald's not convinced, but Snuffy and Kamran are in firm agreement.

"I knew it. He still owes me fifty quid." Kamran provides fresh evidence.

But Snuffy seems quite concerned. "How sad. You know you have to do something. She reminds me of a young Barbara Cartland oozing round my Horace like an anaconda."

But you are way ahead of them. "Snuffy. How do you cheat at sardines?"

Snuffy transcends the decades and draws on treasured memories of a more innocent age. "Well, it's quite complicated. You need a dog really."

Go to Scene 198

Scene 91

The sharp realization of impending disaster clears your brain. You are on your own. These guys may be good—you just have to be better, match every bluff, counter every cheat, and find every weakness.

Nigel Jenner—grotesque loathsome egomaniac.

Newt—dumb rich and out to impress Daisy the bimbo.

Bodi—muscle in jaw twitches if he has a good hand.

But Wasim has just called Newt. Time to observe.

Newt reveals a running flush, six to ten, and wins twenty-four thou. Wasim concedes without a flicker, and his cards are absorbed into the pack.

Was he bluffing? Probing for weakness? Probably. And he dropped twenty-odd thousand without a qualm.

Wasim is a pro.

The next few rounds flash by. You make a half-hearted play on a double pair, but get nowhere. Surprisingly, Barbie, you think, is playing like a maestro. "You boys are far too serious, it's only a game," she opines after winning $2,000 on a pair of eights. "I knew that was a good hand."

She can't actually be that stupid, but has almost everyone convinced. After an hour she has made an impression as a random, but lucky poker player and is up fifteen Gs.

Bodi's tray continues to do its rounds and you consent to one thin line, in the interests of research, but maintain mental alertness.

Then, long after you had given up on the cavalry, and with a creak to wake the Cincinnati Kid (famed heavy sleeper and dead eighty-nine years), the chandelier comes to life.

Anticlockwise—raise. You look at your hand—three threes, nothing special. Only Wasim is still in the game. You raise to $5,000, ignoring an internal squeal of panic. Wasim follows.

The chandelier creaks anticlockwise. Still no one notices. You nervously raise another $15,000.

Wasim pensively follows. The chandelier turns once more.

"Barbie, would you lend me all of your money?"

It's time for the kill.

Jenner is suddenly alert; Bodi, the ever polite, keeps smiling; Newt, at the prospect of some real financial damage, can't help rubbing his hands in glee.

Barbie, almost absentmindedly, hands you twenty-six grand. You add your remaining wealth and push the lot into the center. You stop for a quick glance towards Will, smile with a confidence you don't possess, and, "I raise $56,000."

You're broke, the gold card was on the limit, you spent this year's bonus two months before the check cleared, and with the recession coming you probably won't get another. Forget any plans of leaving London for the country, and pray to Zoroaster that Kamran's alibi isn't proving too distracting.

Wasim . . .

. . . thinks.

He is searching you for psychological distress, probing at your thoughts, looking at your hands for signs of tension, at your face, reading you.

If he sees how confident you are, he'll fold . . .

Barnie, you've got to distract him . . .

"Da da da dat da da dat, dadadadada dat dat;
Da da da dat da da dat, dadadadada dat dat;
Da da dat da da dat, dadadadada dat da dat dat."

Scene 91

Under your breath at first, but then with a vigorous warbling whistle. The Red Hand Gang. It never fails. You manage to smile as you blow. No man could stand it for long. Wasim manages thirty seconds before pushing forward a mountain of cash. He foolishly matches your boldness.

"I call you."

Time to stop whistling, time to see if Kamran knows how to play poker, time to pray.

You turn your cards, one at a time. Three threes, nothing special.

Wasim smiles; such is his self-restraint that you barely know whether you've won or lost until he stands, collects his few remaining dollar bills, and leaves with a curt nod.

And so you scream into six figures, Barbie screams with clapping delight, and above you, Sally suppresses a muffled cry as Kamran picks up speed.

"Perhaps we could all do with a break," suggests Nigel, and with a hubble of chatter the little party adjourns for twenty minutes.

Go to Scene 73

Scene 92

Fatigued by the evening's events, you retire quietly to the powder room. It's empty and you sneak into an end cubicle. Once safely locked inside, you withdraw a small compact mirror and something to sprinkle on it. You have been cutting back, especially now that work is threatening spot drug checks, but this evening you need some assistance. Sniff, cadabra.

It's only when you are about to flush and go that you notice two familiar voices. There are few who can crucify the English language quite so brutally: Belgian waffle & horsey-drawl. With scant thought for dignity, you kneel in order to get a better view.

Perched on a sink and with enough *derrière* to block it, Astrid seems to be getting along famously with Annabel. This much is clear; Annabel is trying to infiltrate the gang—the long way round. But no time to speculate, Barbarella. Clandestine conversations are afoot, so lend an ear . . .

"So what's Barbarella like to live with?"

"Oh she's been very kind to me. I don't know how I'd have survived London without Barbarella."

Behind the locked cubicle door you smile at Astrid's ingenuous simplicity. You need more friends like her.

"But I imagine she can be quite moody. She used to be an absolute nightmare at school. I can see why Barnaby dumped her."

You restrain yourself from talking out, but only just. Luckily,

Scene 92

Astrid is familiar with your version of events.

"No. You've mixed up. Barbarella left Barnaby."

"Yeah right, then why is she so desperate to get him back?" Annabel leaves her poison hanging in the air, then she hits you with napalm. "I tell you, Barbarella hasn't got a chance in hell of getting back with Barnaby. She has a rival for Barnaby's intimate affections," she pauses to emphasize the point, ". . . someone who spends their entire life telling lies to Barnaby at Barbarella's expense."

"Who? But why?"

Annabel laughs maniacally.

"I'll give you a clue. You've spent the whole day with them and they're here tonight . . ."

Barbarella restrain yourself—discretion over valor—Astrid is asking the questions for you. "Who? Who would do that? That's horrible."

And cupping her hand for privacy, Annabel, on tiptoes, whispers in Astrid's ear. You virtually wedge your head in the gap under the loo door.

"Oh, my good God. But that's bang out of order." Bless her—you've no idea where she learnt her English, but Astrid does look physically shaken at the revelation.

Annabel finishes applying lipstick and makes a final pout in the mirror. God, how you hate her weak chin.

"I know . . . but what can you do? If you told Barbie she wouldn't believe you." And, raising her eyebrows to Astrid, Annabel turns and leaves. Leaves Astrid dumbfounded and sitting in a damp patch on the sink unit, and you with a cricked neck.

Barbarella, this is serious. You have a traitor in your midst, a jealous and poisonous rival for Barnaby's affections. Annabel distinctly said, "You've spent the whole day with them and they're here tonight" . . . but who could fancy Barnie so much that they'd want to split you two up? You'd trust Catherine with your life, and besides no one could be that good at acting—she's been drizzling for twelve solid hours about Edward bloody Bunger. But that only leaves the boys! Will and Kamran. Kamran has slept with more women than Mick Jagger, and you can vouch for Will personally—men can't fake. Can they?

Whoa whoa there, hang on a minute. Duhha. This is Annabel talking. Christ, Barbie, those drugs are making you paranoid-delusional. She must have seen you go into the loo ahead of her. She's been playing you like a sucker. Really, Barbarella, pull yourself together, you're acting like a prep-school novice.

But then again, the existence of a traitor would explain why you don't seem to be getting anywhere with Barnaby. And you only have to ask Astrid.

Which are you?

Hawk. Let's roll. Interrogate Astrid and then hunt down this social assassin like the traitorous dog they are. **Go to Scene 30**

Dove (or is it ostrich?). Let it go. If you lose any more friends you'll have to become a hermit. **Go to Scene 82**

Scene 93

As she goes to leave, you wince more dramatically than ever, clutch at your side, and make to stumble. Using Kamran's unique "martial love art," you manage to crook a foot on the back of Charlotte's knee. She falls as you fall, two lovers tumbling through the barriers of age and etiquette . . . and onto the bed.

You grasp at her bottom with one hand, feel the silk of her thigh with the other. Rather heroically, you resist the urge to grasp (fact-findingly) at her groin to check for metal attachments. Instead, you push her away as if horrified by the thought of physical contact. Then, with an expression of puzzlement you jump to your feet, trying to look sexually nervous (for the first time in sixteen years), and imperceptibly back away, clutching at your injured side.

"Are you OK?" She's young and confused. "Did I hurt you?"

"Honestly I'm fine, it's just a bruise."

"Sorry. I didn't . . ."

Awkwardly, she leaves, wanting to stay, unsure who is the hunter and who is the prey.

You've tried this ploy in the past—and that was perfect. She'll be well and truly confused—unsure whether she couldn't resist you, or you couldn't resist her—. Either way up for some more . . . just in time for Barbarella to arrive.

But now it's time to get ready; tie your bow, ruffle your hair, brush teeth, and remedy the worst of the mud stains on your trousers. Fortunately nothing is ripped, other, rather oddly, than your underwear. And so you discard your ribbed Moschino briefs and set forth commando across the length of the somber house and into its contrastingly pleasant garden.

Go to Scene 177

Scene 94

"Catherine, leave it to us. We'll go and get the others. Better get out of here—we can meet up in the bathroom."

Barnie comes with you as you return to the party below. It has revved up a bit in your absence. Even Will has been swept up by the party atmosphere—deeply involved in a rather vocal argument with Edward Bunger and Dicky, a celebrity hairdresser. They're re-running the hunting debate, again, and Will's voice shows signs of exasperation. "Do you know how small a fox's brain is?"

"About the same size as yours from the sound of you." Edward laughs at his own joke, the researcher by his side smiles, and Dicky bursts into claps and giggles.

Will is obviously rattled by Edward's savvy, his rather blunt ripostes, the silent derision of the slender researcher, Kate, and the flamboyance of Dicky. You decide to help Will out, and strike a first blow in the struggle with Edward Bunger. Barnie obviously has the same idea, but he isn't quick enough—you talk over him. "Hunting is a perfectly natural thing to do," you look across at Kate, "like sleeping with a partner of the same age," and then down at Edward's bulging belly, "or only eating as much food as you need."

You smile at your own stultifying wit (always a mistake) and wait for Edward to splutter his annoyance. Instead he laughs, before taking a deliberate puff at his cigar.

"From what Catherine tells me you prefer things far from

natural, Barbarella." He looks at your chest. "I'm sure we can *all* think of ways of improving on nature . . . It's very rare indeed for Mother Nature to achieve perfection." With this last he gives Kate a squeeze and a smile. She whimpers.

You're livid; Will is perplexed (bless him, he thought they were real); Barnaby smiles, appreciating the wit (and reminiscing about your post-op boobs); you curse Catherine for an untrustworthy bitch. But in his bewilderment Will mistakes an Alcopop for beer, and in saccharine horror, he spits a mouthful over Dicky. The NutraSweet has an unfortunate effect on Dicky's hair bodifier. It develops unprecedented adhesive qualities, and as he squeals people rush to help.

Fearing an unruly scrum you opt for retreat. Firmly leading Will, Barnaby signals to Astrid and Kam, and together you head upstairs to the bathroom.

Go to Scene 96

Scene 95

You tell her the truth.

"Really?" She giggles inanely and you inwardly groan. Your chin dips and you struggle to retain enthusiasm. She really is thick. Best get on with things before the conversation sends you into a trance. Be direct. "Would you like to try it?"

She stares at you open-mouthed, suddenly unsure what she is doing in this seedy houseboat with a complete stranger. You smile as innocuously as you can, praying that you haven't blown it.

But the damage is done.

"I think I'd better be going."

Your left engine is hit, it's going up in flames. You fight the throttle stick, but it's no use—the plane refuses to respond. All power gone, the plane begins to spiral into a downward spin. Carmen shuts the hatch door on her way out.

The (Crash 'n' Burn) End

Success in life is all about knowing when to lie and when to tell the truth. Why don't you play again and try a better strategy?

Scene 96

Up in the bathroom, and it's time to plot. Everyone understands why Edward must be stopped. Kamran comforts Catherine, who remains visibly upset. You concentrate on turning hurt to hate. Think, Barbarella, think.

"Cat, was he sleeping with Kate when he was with you?"

Catherine winces.

"Did he ever call out someone else's name during sex?"

Cat grimaces. He once called out his wife's name, which has to be the most humiliating experience of her life. Your plan is working. Catherine is infuriated with shame and anger. One more question should fire her up sufficiently.

"Is it true that he used to shower straight after having sex with you?"

Cat looks at you with daggers. Serves her right for telling Edward about your breast op. Before any of your flabbergasted friends can interrupt, you take the helm in formulating a strategy. Due to your lack of military knowledge, you opt to present your plan as a classical tragedy.

The Fall of Edwardus Phallus

In a remote Londinium township, Barabareda hears the news of her lifetime companion, maiden Catharsis. The maiden has been spurned by the powerful and esteemed public figure, Edwardus Phallus. Adhering to the fine qualities of democracy,

Barabareda urges Catharsis to voice her anger. Together they shall seek revenge on the power-hungry Edwardus. Accompanied by the renowned gladiators Barnabus, Wiltus, and Kamreates, they hunt down Edwardus to a protected Londinium home.

Barabareda: *Knowing Edwardus' fond feelings for fair maidens, I trust that we shall be able to lure him into a state of submission. Catharsis, you shall accompany me, and Astrida shall conceal herself in a water carrier. Together we seduce Edwardus while taking care to conceal our own feelings of nonarousal. We must fight, as a gladiator would tend to his sword.*

Catharsis: *But pray why do we need three famed gladiators? For what purpose shall they serve?*

Barabareda: *Human morals can only transport us so far. We require Brutus' strength. Once Edwardus has been undressed and compromised into a state of submission, the people of Londinium shall see what kind of man Edwardus really is. The gladiators shall assist in removing Edwardus from his safe abode out into the harsh reality of life.*

Astrida: *Indeed, in a country where the values of democracy and liberty are so carefully guarded, transcending one's political position in such disgrace shall surely infuriate the good people of this city.*

Barabareda: *Yes, fair maiden. Edwardus will fall. His soul shall perish.*

The End

Everyone is staring at you, expressions marked by puzzlement. Cat speaks first.

"Barbarella, what are you talking about?"

"Look, don't insult my classical skills. I won a prize at school for my Greek translations."

That was a blatant lie. You couldn't cope with French, never mind Greek. The only prizes you won at school were button badges for turning up on Sports Day. Pretending to patronize their inability to interpret the classics, you repeat the plan, but in a more understandable form.

"Look, the girls seduce Edward. We get him naked while Barnaby captures the moment on Polaroid. Then you boys barge in," you point to Will and Kam, "pick up Edward, and throw him out onto the street where the waiting press get photos for tomorrow's tabloids. Is that clear enough?"

Will has a query. "So how come Barnaby has the best job?"

"Because he has a steady hand." You flash a smile at dear old Barnaby.

Kamran chimes in with another flaw. "But what about the researcher, Kate? A bird in the hand is worth three stripped to the bush . . ."

Kamran never was the greatest wit but he does have a point. He continues rather cryptically, "She's a pop star to your tennis player." Barnaby laughs boyishly—obviously some "in" joke (if only you could get inside his head for a while . . .). You ignore them. No time for adolescents.

"Don't worry about Kate, she won't have a chance."

Go to Scene 88

Scene 97

"You owe me big time," Barbarella says with meaningful looks at the thinning throng. "I've got us all invites—we're going to a proper party."

"Yeah, like *this* was supposed to be a proper party . . . Where is it then?"

"OK. If you want the truth, it's at Godfrey's fat-cat mansion. You know, *offshore* Godfrey, the dodgy ex-politician. Catherine's been invited by Edward B., and I want everyone to come and show Cat some solidarity. Come on, at least it won't be dull."

It doesn't take long to round up the others. Kamran has been silently busy and is swapping business cards with a woman twice his age (a sculpting client, you hope). Astrid is equine-sweaty after an hour of solid dancing, but her monumental energy seems undiminished as she bounds after you. And as for Catherine, she is way ahead of you—organizing cabs, ushering the others off the boat, and generally arranging things so that she can sit next to her former/future lover, the infamous Edward Bunger. It obviously didn't take them long to patch things up. A whole day spent sleaze-free was obviously too much for the politician to bear.

You leave your motorbike behind for safety reasons and instead decide to go by cab with the others. Kamran forces you to join him in playing gooseberry to Catherine and Edward and you both sit with silent tongue, watching Catherine simper over the minister in the back of the cab. Edward himself doesn't deign to talk to you, but he gives a victorious look as Cat nuzzles into the fat of his neck. If only you could understand women.

But soon the cab is pulling up with a screech of hackneyed brake-pads. Kamran, obviously as nauseated as you, jumps out first. You both race along a short gravel drive, through an imposing front door and into the party from hell. You are greeted in a large hallway by the sight of a gaggle of rather junior members of government and a small snatch of TV nonentities who think they are mixing in high and powerful circles.

Kamran, although keen to make a discreet entrance, errors fatally. He stumbles over a thick rug and bumps into Carol, the host's wife.

"Well hello there. I didn't realize we'd invited some youngsters to come and play."

With a thick smile that has a reputation for being ghastly, Carol touches Kamran's elbow to provide unneeded support. She leads him into a rather minimalist drawing room and, as he becomes submerged within the middle-aged morass, you realize he is lost to you. You await Will and Barbarella, and can't help a masochistic smile as they arrive in your corner with looks of horror.

Will is muttering under his breath, "Nightmare." He looks accusingly at you. "Whose bloody idea was—"

Barbie interrupts him. "Oh Christ, look. Catherine's turning into a bloody lemming."

You peer into the sitting-room and sure enough, Catherine is now sitting on Edward's knee. She already seems to have lost his interest—Edward, with an enviable eye, has caught the attention of an anorexic researcher. He has obviously decided Catherine is disposable, for he feeds the young blonde low-calorie canapés and flirts outrageously. Cat is forced to watch with mounting humiliation. You all creep nearer, the better to eavesdrop.

"So how do you manage to keep yourself so wonderfully slim?"

Scene 97

Edward smiles at the blonde waif as he ungallantly shifts his thigh under Catherine's weight.

Cat avoids your stare, aware of how ridiculous she looks. She excuses herself from Edward's lap (this allows him to resuscitate his thigh with a vigorous rub), and exits into the hall. Edward barely looks up from his new conquest. Catherine reeks of distress as she storms past; you consider following, but Will is raising a meaningful eyebrow.

"Barnie, let's get out of here. We can go to the West India Casino—loads of totty and if we don't score some, we can make some money at roulette and blow it on whores," he says, only half joking.

Damsels in distress, Barnaby—your forte. And what better way to make Barbarella jealous than to have her best friend clinging to you? Besides, Catherine has had a rough time of it today; you really should see that she's OK. But then, Will's casino is packed with rich-but-dims. They'll be bursting to give away cash, and you don't often get an invite.

I suppose at the end of the day, it comes down to this—how good of a friend are you to Catherine?

Very close (and by the end of the evening hopefully a lot closer). Follow Catherine and make sure she's OK. **Go to Scene 137**

You can buy her a consolation drink out of your winnings. Avoid a tear-drenched shirt and follow Will to his friend's private casino. **Go to Scene 61**

Scene 98

Harvey smiles down at you.

"Bet you've never come across anyone like me before. Have you?"

You don't offer an answer, but just lie there, breathless and uncomfortable. Eventually Harvey offers an explanation.

"Self-love is all you need, Barbarella."

There's no real answer to that. As a wise bunny once said, "Masturbation: the primary sexual activity of mankind. At the start of last century it was a disease, by the end a cure. In the twenty-first it will become a leisure activity."

The (Self-love) End

Scene 99

Will opens the front door on to a balmy summer evening. The heat of the sun has gone but the paved streets radiate warmth. This is your London, this is your time, be ready to enjoy . . .

You follow the taxi on your bike and make the short trip to the river. The girls pull up in another cab. Barbarella is looking as polished as a guardsman's boot, and before Will has time to pay the cabby you leap to her side, arm and smile proffered. Kamran, eager for attention, has Cat by the hand and leads her into the braying press pack. Will, with charm and good grace, accepts his booby prize.

Up and across the gangway. Will steadies Astrid to keep her from toppling into the river. Cat walks tall through flashing bulbs and manages a comfortable smile. Kamran steals a friendly squeeze in all the confusion.

Cat produces your invites and is waved through. She has already spotted Edward Bunger, adjusting his cuffs nervously and desperately seeking to avoid the expectant gazes from other guests. Barbie steers you through the throng, pausing only to eye him up and down. Will greets him Cuban style. A well-directed cloud of Cohiba smoke envelops the minister's face, providing the smoke screen he has been dreaming of.

You only have to look around to see you chose the right party. The government, it would seem, knows how to enjoy itself.

The celebration is a gimmick to celebrate and emphasize the

burgeoning success of Britain's cultural sector. The black music industry seems to be on the end of this latest piece of government benevolence. For the government to successfully govern it is obviously necessary for the cabinet to mix and be seen to mix with the cultural icons of the day. Everyone has turned up for the free champagne and free publicity. You can feel the throb of insincerity as politics and showbiz combine. An ad hoc stage in one corner hosts speeches from the great and good, but you manage to blot out the noise.

The six split up, each prospecting at a separate river. Catherine is daggering looks across the boat towards the minister while simultaneously chatting to a black, bemuscled dancer. Barbarella is obviously at the bar, and you see that Kamran has sought out the high ground in order to survey. And that reminds you . . .

You have your own agenda, Barnaby. No time to enjoy the quality of the champagne or take in décor fit for a Lord Chancellor. It is time to play.

Catherine hasn't exaggerated the guest list and there are one or two prime joints on display. At last you spot Will. With the instinct of a hunter-gatherer, he has homed in immediately on his berry. The Aussie soap-cum-pop star is looking a tad uncomfortable, but is still drinking—a good sign. You can never work out whether Will does a lot of research (the girl in question has just split from her record-producer boyfriend) or just possesses a nose for detecting emotional vulnerability. Well, he'd better enjoy it while he can. Now that he's engaged this may turn out to be a rare night off "bird-duty."

But this is not the time to speculate or spectate. Let Will gather his berries; you will hunt more honorable prey. You down the last of your fizz and with a rolling wrist collect another. With the sweep of forward-facing eyes, you scan the room.

Scene 99

A politician's wife, rendered presentable by intense beauty and fashion consultancy since the last election, is obviously the worse for drink. She is dancing by the far rail, head down and pristinely cut bob swinging—alone.

Go to Scene 125

Scene 100

Your thighs tingle and Harvey gives you a final slap on your towel-covered behind.

"Just do that once a fortnight and I guarantee you'll never get cellulite."

"Harvey, if this works so well then why hasn't everyone heard of it?"

You turn and can't help laughing at the sight of him licking out the bowl. He picks a bit of the Weetabix from his teeth and smiles.

"I dunno. All I know is that Elle Mcpherson swears by it—and she hasn't got an inch of cellulite on her."

It looks like you've just discovered the holy grail of beauty treatment. This book does have an educational element after all. And to think that almost all the ingredients can be found at your local pharmacy.

The (Elixir of Youth) End

Scene 101

The trouble with depressed people is that they're generally quite dull. Finebonestructured-curvybodied-almondeyed-poutylipped Natasha is no exception.

And this is no night for an emotionally charged meeting of minds topped with angst-ridden love. This is not a night for pretending to make love. This is a night for sex—hard, fast, and preferably with a dash of idiosyncrasy.

Natasha, bless her, is warming to her theme, animated at meeting someone so emotionally intelligent. As you listen to her drone, you anticipate the dangers of a six-hour conversational ordeal culminating in a deep and heartfelt hug. And so, in the troubled mire of your scheming brain you formulate a plan.

Kamran always carries a small plastic bag of ground Viagra (he gets it from somewhere in Soho). He swears by it as a fallback option.

"When all else fails take one tablet's worth for yourself and slip the other two in her drink. Never failed yet."

You hear his voice whispering in your ear and imagine Kamran, the red-faced, horned demon, sitting on your shoulder and urging you on.

You can't. It might kill her. Imagine the headlines. Imagine the prison showers . . .

"Do you know where I really want to be right now?" she

chunters on. "Back in Queensland on my father's farm, riding round the fruit orchard, and doing something real."

Time to decide.

You're not seriously considering this, are you? There's a maximum sentence of five years for this sort of thing. Not to mention the risk of PRIAPISM. *If you haven't heard of that then learn fast. There is a risk, in healthy young men (and Barnaby almost fits that description), of Viagra inducing a two-day erection, after which nothing . . . yes* NOTHING*—not a sausage—for the rest of your life . . .*

Better safe than sorry, trust in your natural charms. **Go to Scene 87**

But what a way to spend the next forty-eight hours. Call for Kamran's narcotic assistance. **Go to Scene 77**

Scene 102

On entering you are overwhelmed by the eerie silence. Jay points to the darkened glass where sets of eyes sit flickering, watching, and waiting. He pushes you up against a pane and kisses deeply. Pressing closer, ensnaring you in a celestial embrace, you feel the warm glass through your dress. A zip hisses undone—there's a new reptile in town.

Hands run everywhere, but, making a valiant effort for his belt, you are startled by a heavy thud. A recently woken rattlesnake, disturbed and irate, throws itself at the glass by your head. The pane separates you from bared fangs and with a scream you stagger back, only to crash into a metal sign. It wobbles noisily.

But Jay has his arms round you, eagerly caressing your bruised elbow, your possibly hurt bottom . . . and breasts . . . With fluid movement, he turns you round, lifts your dress, pulls your knickers to one side . . . and with knee-trembling vigor all you can do is hold on to the sign for balance (and dear life).

Do Not Approach or Excite the Alligators

Oh, Barbarella, you rule breaker . . . But time to take control. You've banged your head on the sign twice, it's creaking in protest, and your knees aren't far behind.

Slipping from your Italian *rampante*'s eager thrustings, you turn and bend. This time it's Jay's turn to stagger back, overcome with the force of your generosity—and Barbarella's special brand of fellatio. Developed and perfected over many years, mastery of this art has rewarded you with enough free dinners to feed Mozambique.

"Oh God. Oh my God. I love you."

Men are so predictable. You'd like to answer, but can't. Instead, you finale with the "corkscrew flick."

Jay cries out uncontrollably and crashes his fist against a glass pane. It crunches with the sound of shattering glass and Jay rips his flesh. You scramble to your feet to help him. Blood is pulsing from his hand, and in the half-light a small snake drops from the smashed glass and writhes viciously on the floor. The sight transfixes you both in horror. The snake coils up, ready to strike. Jay stares, petrified.

Just as well the snake's only a baby; you're more than capable of handling anything under nine inches. Swift footwork and the baby mamba meets an untimely death at the expense of a Manolo heel. The price of fashion, eh?

Jay is speechless, and stares at you in disbelief as he continues to drip on the floor. With perfect nonchalance, you brush glass splinters from Jay's shirt, and kiss him on the cheek.

"I think we should go."

Taking his arm, you lead Jay out into the early morning sun, leaving behind a dead snake and a happy security camera. In the clear light of day, the cut turns out to be quite bad. You insist that he should go to the hospital. He insists on going home with you.

"Well, I must have some plasters at home somewhere. If not, there's always the nicotine patches."

Scene 102

Don't fret, Barbarella, he'll live—just go easy on him for a bit. Congratulations, by the way, that was some cool-headed thinking. If you hadn't switched to fellatio at the key moment who knows what head injuries you could have sustained?

Now, collect your prize, go home, and welcome in Sunday morning with coffee, papers, and a supremely large double bed, big enough for two.

The (Sexually Charged) End

Scene 103

It takes less than fifty seconds for the two of you, giggling insanely, to flee the party and hail a cab.

She is passionate now that her mind is made up. You are the perfect beau, and she is committed to you and you to her. The prospect of sex in the outdoors has banished any sense of ennui. As your cousin, Mary, used to say, "It's not easy to be miserable with your legs in the air."

Natasha sucks at your lips, hands everywhere. Her small dress is hitched above her waist now, and you cup a perfect buttock in your left hand and curse the speed of the cab driver. He has you by Regent's Park in less than eight pounds. You pay the dear cockney fellow with a smile and a tip. Natasha readjusts clothing and you run down the street, together, hand in hand, both high on the prospect of sex.

Regent's Park Zoo, with its quaint Victorian railings, appears to have less security than a Third World prostitute. With a little help, you carefully ease Natasha over an imposing metal gate and then vault it with manful energy. Once inside, the zoo becomes ominously eerie; you creep past the bird enclosure, stopping only briefly to look at the mad bears on "Bear Mountain." Natasha clings as you approach the wolves. They are awake and active, eager eyes glinting yellow and red in the moonlight. The whole place, with its time-warped nineteenth-century architecture, takes on a surreal edge in the bright night. Finally you approach a suitable building for your rooftop frolic.

"The Reptile House," a plaque reads in old-fashioned stenciling. The building is large, with a colonnaded front entrance and many doors along its fifty-yard length. The roof, a lichen-blotched slate, starts some three yards up, and then slants steeply upwards to a proud apex. There, in the center, some fifteen feet above the ground, is an iron-clad skylight.

"Danger is the greatest aphrodisiac of all." *(The Diaries of Casanova,* Volume II*)*

If she's not terrified of heights, she'll be scared witless by the sight of an anaconda below. Natasha will cling to you like a sex-rationed nymphomaniac.

You look at her, smiling up at the imposing building. Her profile, with its cute nose, can't help but induce affection. Maybe this could be long-term. There must be thousands of roofs in London. She needn't find out about the orangutan orphanage lie for months, and by then you could have covered more ground than Mary Poppins. Natasha's cries of pleasure will be heard from St. James's Palace, the Houses of Parliament . . .

"How do we get up there?"

The practical Aussie interrupts your thoughts.

In your ridiculous mood there is really only one answer.

"I will climb, but you, my fair sweet princess, you shall fly."

It takes only seconds to scale a heavy iron drainpipe, clasping to some guttering, before flopping, exhausted, onto the slanting roof. You cry with pleasure as Natasha joins you, her body panting at the strain. Five tentative steps and you are lying together; face to the skies, hoping friction proves stronger than gravity.

If anything, the zoo looks even more absurd from your new vantage point. The animal pens merge into Regent's Park, traffic flows, and London hums, all blissfully unaware of your existence. Natasha tentatively turns onto her front . . . and clambers on top of you. She kisses lingeringly and holds onto your warmth. You hug her back, eager for reassuring softness. She strains to look through the green dirtied glass, but can't make anything out of the murk.

A wolf howls, a lion roars, a beaver dives into its chill little pool; a she-panther rubs against her mate. Natasha pulls her dress, up and over her head. It tugs her breasts upward into a parabolic wave. They continue to undulate as she hangs it from the skylight. Then she begins to undress you, kissing and licking all the way. Shoes slide the length of the roof and free fall into a bush far below. She flings your dinner jacket over her head and finally pings your Calvins to a multilingual signpost somewhere in the gloom behind your head.

You are both naked now—apart from her G-string—and with a frenzy born of vertigo, you desperately ease it over her curved bottom.

The nineteenth-century ironwork creaks in protest as you re-adjust your weight and turn her onto her back. The moon illuminates the curve of her thigh and sends your starved eyes up their length—to your eagerly waiting new home . . .

Forgetting condoms, danger, and CCTV cameras (and foreplay), you thrust against and into her. The gods of love cry out in your honor, but you don't hear them over the disapproving shriek of the skylight. It gives way in a splintering cacophony—and you crash, like dear little Icarus, back to earth . . .

Go to Scene 145

Scene 104

You walk back down to the party and find it as noisy and busy as before. Edward is talking softly to Kate, the researcher, by the French windows. With a sudden loss of nerve you stop, midway into the room. What if he tells you to bugger off, you've just told him you think he's an old licentious pervert, for God's sake. This needs thinking through. The idea of having to go back upstairs and tell the others that you offered yourself to Edward and he said "no thanks" is unthinkable. You cogitate tactics and approach tentatively. "Edward, could I have a word . . . privately . . ." He looks doubtful. "It won't take a minute—it's very important."

You smile at Kate. "Sorry, do you mind?"

She concedes and slinks off in search of a fresh drink. Base Camp reached.

"What is it?" Edward says bluntly. Tread carefully, Barbarella. Too obvious and he'll smell a rat, too shy and he won't bite.

"Edward, Catherine asks if you could meet us in the study for a private briefing." You breathe harshly, desperately trying to look nervously aroused.

It obviously works. A wicked smiles flashes across Edward's mouth. Necking his drink, and loosening his tie, he turns across to Kate and shouts, "I'll be back in two minutes. Something important has come up."

Two minutes? Just a figure of speech surely. No time to dwell—just think of Daddy and how proud he'll be that his daughter helped destroy socialism. Actually, don't think of Daddy. There are times and places and this isn't one of them. Remember, you're supposed to be feeling turned on by the promise of a foursome with Edward.

You lead Edward out into the hall, and slowly up the stairs.

Entering the study, you find Astrid reclined on the desk. Cat is nowhere to be seen. The sight of Astrid takes Edward by surprise.

"I think there's some mistake. I was looking for Catherine."

The door slams behind you.

You turn and swallow back a giggle as you see Catherine dressed in a silk robe (where the hell did she find it?), puffing on a cigar.

"No mistake, darling. I thought you might enjoy some more company. After all, you're such a popular man and I'm just desperate to keep you interested. Then Barbarella and Astrid mentioned how gorgeous they thought you were. So I thought, what better than for us all to have some fun together."

Edward is unable to answer, dumbstruck by the mind-blowing prospect of three women. Two perhaps, but three? Can he cope? Probably—their combined weight will be significantly less than his wife's.

Catherine continues with the tone of Anne Robinson. "Just remember, I'm in charge here, and I'll give the orders, so get undressed and go over to the desk by Astrid."

Desperately wishing that Catherine forgets your presence, you stand, uncomfortably waiting for your command. Perhaps of gravest concern is the fact that you now feel desperately sober. A hand taps your thigh. You remember that Barnaby is concealed behind the curtain.

"Slip some of this down, it'll help. Make sure you pass some to Edward."

Barnaby passes you the erotic equivalent of hemlock (where did it come from? Probably Kamran). In desperation, you take a mouthful of liquid and pray that whatever it is, it takes effect promptly. So thoughtful of Barnaby to help you out.

Edward is shuffling out of his trousers. Time to grasp the nettle, Barbie. "Oh baby, leave your golfing socks. They really turn me on."

Catherine stares at you in annoyance as you sweep the dominatrix mantle from her, exchanging it for the remainder of the liquid supplied by Barnaby.

"Cat, have a sip of this."

Without even asking what it is, Catherine takes a mouthful, then seizes Edward. A lingering kiss ensures that Edward gets a share of the hemlock too. Don't forget Astrid. You offer the phial and she finishes it with a gulp.

Eager to get the party going, Edward walks towards you and offers to help you undress.

"My, I thought you'd never ask." (And was hoping you wouldn't.)

The prospect of your body being revealed by the cold glare of light is a mortifying thought. You stall Edward as long as possible, flattering his physique while you dim the lights, but the minister is intent on getting to work. He lunges for your dress. Catherine, trying not to appear jealous, sits back with Astrid, who playfully strokes her hair. Barbie, you must relax. Better lose that expression—you're not using a public toilet in Marseilles.

You are now the center of attention. You must perform, and perform well. Your dress is lifted away and Edward smiles appreciatively. Thank God you completed the course of sunbeds; nothing like a healthy tan to make all seem toned. Fortunately, the only remaining light in the room is one flickering candle on the fireplace; it provides ample shadow to give you cover. Out of the corner of your eye, Cat and Astrid seem to be getting carried away on their own which leaves you pretty much alone with Edward. There are certain things about your friends that you'd rather not know. Latent female desires fit snugly into that category. Your head begins to feel dizzy.

You lick at Edward's ginger chest. He's not quite so unattractive with your eyes and his mouth shut. But before you can work up any momentum, a third party breaks into your fun. Someone's hand (and you can't work out whose) is working its way up your leg. Edward is moaning (you'd like to put it down to your efforts, but suspect third party assistance). Frankly it's hard to work out what is going on. You can see Cat's dolphin tattoo, but that's only one piece of the jigsaw. Whatever Barnaby has given you seems to distort as well as intensify. You decide to subscribe to Adam Smith's theory in a manner that would have him making metal tacks faster than a production line. "*Laissez-faire*," you murmur out loud. God, your mind's wandering . . . concentrate, Barbarella, there'll be a camera flash in a second and you can't look like a Reader's Wife. Think tight abs, chest out, and look as though you're enjoying yourself, but not too much; run against that hand between your thighs (you'll figure out whose it is eventually). Maybe you're not a complete prude after all. Just as long as you don't have to think too much.

With slight horror, you sense that Astrid is getting too close for comfort. You can tell by the perfume; it makes you sneeze. Time to disentwine and take stock of the situation.

Yep, as you suspected—three forwards are most definitely scoring. Perhaps a little prematurely, you reach for a cigarette. A slit of light cuts across the floor as the door is eased quietly open. Will, undoubtedly desperate for a peek, peers in and signals at his Rolex. Barnaby is delaying badly on his David Bailey role and you suspect that his attention may have wavered. Grabbing the robe, you check that Edward still has eyes closed and creep over to the curtain.

"Christ, Barnaby—shoot," you whisper harshly.

He nods dumbly, transfixed by the wrestling match.

Scene 104

"*Now.*"

A better response—he springs into action and takes a career-finishing bum shot of Astrid and a career-finishing face shot of Edward. He also skillfully manages to get Catherine's cookie for Kam.

"You bastards." Edward isn't slow to the point. "I'll fucking kill you."

Raised voices are a signal for Will and Kamran to burst in and frogmarch Edward in the direction of the front door. With a squeal of laughter, you dress hurriedly and manage to get to the top of the stairs in time to see a struggle at the front door.

But Will and Kam are too powerful. Will hisses into Edward's ear:

"Like a fox to the hounds."

Edward protests: "You can't do this. My wife . . . I'm a government minister . . . No . . ."

The door is open. Will turns to Kamran. "Don't you hate desperate politicians?"

And with relative ease the minister is pushed down the front step and onto the exposed gravel drive.

The naked truth of Edward Bunger is revealed to the nation.

NakEd'

COCKSURE MINISTER TAKES A TUMBLE

Go to Scene 108

Scene 105

"I'm actually an artist," you lie with an ease even Kamran would admire. You cast your mind back to recall Kamran's basic routine and all the while imagine the blonde in the dimly lit confines of the *Anomie*. You try to look cutely uncomfortable. "I sculpt."

Then, as if to explain Barbie's outburst, "Barbarella . . ." you point in the general direction of Barbie's departure, "has filled her house with my pieces. She is on a constant mission to end my enforced retirement . . . but that's all very dull." The puppy dog eyes start their magic. "Are you sure I didn't hurt you?"

"Barnaby, I'm fine, honestly, just bruised pride. I'm more worried about you. Why have you stopped sculpting?"

She's hooked. Just get her into the net and you'll have fish for supper.

"I used to sculpt anything and everything. Then," you hesitate coyly, "usual story, I fell in love. Francesca. She was the most beautiful woman in the world. I sculpted her and nobody else for months. And then . . ." you pause dramatically, desperately trying to think, ". . . she drowned . . . in her bath."

In her bath? Are you trying to blow this one? Hold on, she may have bought it.

"I understand." She looks at you through glistening eyes. "It must have been hard."

"I haven't sculpted since. I don't think I could."

Perfect. Stage 1 complete. Time for Stage 2—lots more to drink.

Carmen turns out to be a dancer for Four-ploy, a slightly naff boy band. You've never heard of them. (No, you're not getting old, even teenagers get boy bands mixed up these days.) Carmen turns out to be more drunk than she first appeared. Carmen turns out to have bruised something in her lower back, though God knows what. Carmen starts to cat-stretch her bruised spine like someone in need of a massage. Carmen needs another white wine spritzer.

Stage 3—try to maintain a witty and interesting conversation while scanning your Top Forty for a fantasy involving a nubile (and very flexible) dancer who is wearing no underwear and has taken too much of the vine. Surely, Barnie, there must be something . . . something involving artists' clay . . . oh, yes . . . Kamran was bragging about it the other day . . .

Carmen is looking at you with an expectant look. She has just finished saying something.

How do you respond?

"Carmen, will you help me? I think I could sculpt you. There's something special in your face. Just looking at you makes me feel like Prometheus, the Titan, who fashioned the human form from clay." **Go to Scene 113**

"Do you want another drink?" **Go to Scene 33**

Scene 106

One look at the Breathalyzer, and the officer plays rough. He has you up against the car and handcuffed. Sadly this is no role-play. Astrid and Cat sit very quietly, perhaps worried about guilt by association.

"Look here," you pathetically try to intimidate the officer, "I hope you realize you're committing a section twenty assault. I don't take threats lightly. And I want to make a phone call. NOW."

Obviously, Catherine and Astrid haven't seen the film you're referring to. "NOW" was supposed to be their cue to run, allowing you the distraction to make a classy getaway. But the girls sit there dumbly.

"It'll be possible to make a phone call at the station, madam. Oh, and perhaps you might hand over the car keys, please."

Barbarella, you are going to jail—somewhere to think about the 520 needless deaths caused last year by drunk drivers. Andover police station turns out to have an attractive south-facing cell with minimalist design based on self-catering student accommodation at Exeter campus.

If you are lucky you'll share it with Astrid. And yes, she probably will make every attempt to keep you warm.

Scene 106

The (Banged Up the Wrong Way) End

Reader, Reader . . . this is about as far from the Perfect Ending as you can get. Please, play again, and show some better sense . . .

Scene 107

You lost . . . but you won.

Barbie's most intimate desire, the fantasy she couldn't bring herself to reveal in fifteen years of depravity. And you hold it in a trembling hand.

"I want to bed a devil and an angel."

You smile across at her . . . but she looks you straight back, unashamed and challenging.

"I'll have to make a quick call to heaven to enroll an angel," you banter weakly, hastily speed-dialing.

You stroll, back turned, and whisper urgently into your mobile. "Kamran, where are you . . . good . . . alone? . . . Get rid of her . . . I don't care . . . just wait right there. I've got a present. You're not going to believe this."

The next few moments pass in a blur of anticipation. You begin by planting a kiss on Barbie's pert little nose, before blindfolding her with a combination of handkerchief and bow-tie ("Always be resourceful, daily objects can have a multitude of alternative uses . . ."—Lord Baden-Powell, *Rovering to Success,* 5th Edition).

You slip a helmet over her head and guide her to the bike. Suddenly she's just so helpless and delicate, you can't help but enjoy the sudden pump of adrenaline as you think of what's to come. An image of Barbie naked and on all fours pops, uninvited, into your head. You stall the bike.

But barely ten minutes pass before you are finally at the

Anomie. You lead Barbarella (still helmeted to prevent perception of the Thames giving the game away) up and along a plank, then down into the belly of the little barge.

Kamran greets you with an enquiring smile, but knows enough not to talk. And so you remove the helmet at last. Barbie stands in the middle of the low-ceilinged cabin and waits, eyes still blindfolded but every other sense straining for information.

"Barbarella, this is the devil speaking" (you speak as deeply as you can without sounding ridiculous). "Take off your dress."

And with little difficulty she lets it drop to the floor to reveal her personal trainer-nurtured, "mother-was-a-model" natured perfection.

The light is never bright on the *Anomie*, but yellow streetlight, from flickering lamps, bounces off her curving (but surely cosmetically enhanced) breasts.

Time for some fun.

Go to Scene 141

Scene 108

The sexual gladiators have scored. A fantastic triumph over Edward Bunger and the self-serving British government. But while you might like to carry on and celebrate with great jollity, you are all currently ensnared in the lion's den. Once this story breaks, people will be looking for scapegoats and the six of you are currently hot favorites.

You hear the breaking of glass and the heavy thud of Carol's footsteps. Too late. The news is out. Flying down the stairs you run like Persephone from Hades. Will and Kamran are in hot pursuit, but within three minutes you're all shamefully breathless and stagger to a halt by someone's driveway.

Leaning windblown on the hood of a car, Kamran peers nervously back down the street. "Barnaby and Catherine must still be in there."

Will looks at you nervously, then at Kamran. "I think I saw Barnie chasing Catherine into the bathroom. I guess her performance was a bit too good."

Normally those words would leave you frozen in jealous horror, but perhaps it's the elation or the adrenaline—all you can do is smile. "So where did Astrid end up?"

The three of you break into collective hysterics . . .

Scene 108

Game won, Barbarella. Well done, you've demonstrated exceptional political mastery. The only question now is whether to quit while you're ahead. Which will it be:

Game over—return to the safety of St. John's Wood? **Go to Scene 112**

Game on—finish off your winning streak and carry on reveling? **Go to Scene 110**

Scene 109

You knock and enter in one move, oblivious of the fact that someone may have already beaten you to the cabin. Quickly, you find a brass lamp and turn on a subdued bulb. The cabin is empty. Carmen shuts the door behind her and the music, the chattering, the platitudes, and the lies subside to a low murmur.

The reality of impending activity slows your mind, and the sharp details of the cabin furnishings burn onto your visual neurones. But as you smile and look down at Carmen, it is the smell of her warm, silken skin that captivates you.

Your heart is pounding so heavily that you barely hear her speak: "It feels funny down there."

She leans over the broad oak desk, posterior jutting, hand rubbing her lower back. And as she rubs, the hemline of her skin-tight red dress rises imperceptibly higher. And she rubs. And it rises. And she rubs.

Come on, Barnie, no time to freeze.

You warm your hands and remember the anatomy from biology class . . .

Do you:

Boldly go straight for bare skin? **Go to Scene 121**

Maintain the pretense of professional decency? **Go to Scene 123**

Scene 110

Eventually, lungs filled, you manage a sentence. "What shall we do? We can't stop now."

But Will has had enough. "Look, I'd better be going—I promised Annabel I'd stop by and make sure she was all right."

"Oh come on, Will, don't be such a coward. *Pumpkin's* not allowed to make your life hell until *after* you're married."

But not to be deterred by transparent peer pressure, he kisses you on the cheek and bids you both goodnight. He heads south in search of a cab and his departure grates away some of your happiness. You look at Kamran and smile; this is alien territory. You've never been on your own with him before. "I might pack it in as we . . ." you start to speak, but the sentence calcifies on your tongue as a darkly attractive man rushes up the street. You recognize him vaguely from the party.

"Guys, you wanna get movin' like now. It's going off back there."

Oh yeah, you've only managed to put two hundred yards between you and the party, time to get going. But as you jog briskly, who is this ambrosial blend of all things good and male?

"I'm Jay. I dunno what happened back there, but it was some major shit."

You lap up his *Sopranos* accent. Jay, under casual interrogation, turns out to be a model, hot out of Armani Exchange. His girlfriend is home safe in New York and he claims to be from

Milan. You suspect he's more likely Venezuelan, but who gives a fuck as you admire his finical tailoring, sculpted looks, and finely toned muscles. Oh and that smile . . . the Ice Queen is melting.

"So, where we going to? You guys gonna show me some fun?"

Kamran looks from you to Jay and says, "I'm up for it, but I think Barbie wants to go home."

You give Kamran a stare. "No way. I'm on a second wind. Jay, you're in very safe hands. London is ours for the taking."

Jay chuckles deliciously. The Italo-Venezuelan looks do it perfectly for Miss Carrington.

"I was reading about Regent's Park Zoo. I read it's the oldest in the world."

Kamran raises an eyebrow and suppresses a grin. "Well if that's where you want to go, Jay, I'm sure Barbie would love it," and waves down a black cab.

"Regent's Park, please, the inner circle, just by the zoo."

Go to Scene 120

Scene 111

Carmen enthusiastically gulps down the proffered champagne cocktail. "I feel like dancing."

She laughs, the Geordie accent now resonating where before it was virtually unnoticeable.

That should be a warning, but obligingly you follow her onto the dance floor. After all, dancing is the best foreplay there is—and she is a professional . . .

. . . But even professionals can lose coordination after two liters of champagne.

Carmen looks fantastic for the first thirty seconds. Then she slips, midspin, concusses herself on the hard floor, and lies at your feet, motionless.

Do you:

Rue the missed opportunity, turn and go back to the bar, and have another scotch? **Go to Scene 115**

Try to help, using your limited medical skills? **Go to Scene 117**

Scene 112

Trying to conceal a yawn, you realize that your work is done and it might be a good time to call it quits. The flame that first sparked so long ago in Chelsea has been burning too long. Looking around you, the others are also starting to flag. You know the boys will never admit they are tired—you've had enough experience with Barnaby to know how his ridiculous ego works.

Unfortunately in life, there are times when you have to accept that you are no longer a spry, well-slept student. Despite your valiant efforts this evening, late twenties require rest. Bid William to head for St. John's Wood, and escape back to the comfort of your bed.

Yet again, you failed to bag Mr. Right, but at least you can now categorically write Barnaby off as an inconstant, immature idiot. And anyway that wasn't the only point of this evening; you tossed aside your problems and had some fun. But real life carries on, and nothing emphasizes that more than a large double bed in which to lose yourself.

Scene 112

Good night, Barbarella.
Sleep well.

The (Disappointingly Dull) End

Come on, Reader, reality might be dull, but with enough vodka and Red Bull it needn't ever be as bad as this. Why don't you take a deep breath and have another crack?

Scene 113

Well done. You've judged it spot on. Carmen, of limited intelligence, requires fewer than average drinks before she believes that kind of rubbish.

If you needed proof, she supplies it now. Shielding your somber face in her hands, she kisses you. "Barnaby, if I can do anything to help, I will. Just tell me what to do."

Anything? Did you hear that? She'll do anything.

Time to get out of here. Call a cab before she sobers up.

Go to Scene 139

Scene 114

OK, Barbie, give up. Close your eyes, "let love lift you up where you belong," and then call a taxi. After all, there's nothing you like better than a serious licking to start the weekend.

Well, at least your hangover is starting to lift, but the fact is you have committed a gross professional misdemeanor by sleeping with Dave. So why the hell did you do it? To prove that you can still seduce a twenty-one-year-old? Since your mother signed you up for those "Knowing Yourself through Asthanga Yoga" classes, you've become obsessed with waning youth and eligibility . . . but to sleep with a graduate, Mrs. Robinson?

Fine, at twenty-eight you have no prospect of marriage, but it's not as if you want to get married—it's just that you don't want to turn into a Candace Bushnell caricature either. Your yogi suggested that you should be more proactive in seeking a partner and become penetrable to commitment. Well, you get the penetrating bit right and Dave soothes your sensitive ego for a while—but the comforting intimacy must end. Time to get back to reality. The stagger back.

You painfully squeeze into the excuse of a dress, not quite sure whether Dave is smirking or smiling as he watches you struggle. With biting realization you see that Dave's conquest will be all over the office by nine o'clock on Monday morning, and your typecast status as a nymphomaniac will now spread to working life.

But no time to consider the effect on your associate directorship chances. A cab is waiting downstairs and your knickers are still nowhere to be found. Well, it would be a nice way of thanking Dave for having you.

Just pray to God they don't wind up in the internal mail. **Go to Scene 6**

Scene 115

That line between helpless with lust and just helpless is a fine one, two or three drinks at most. Carmen got it wrong. You got it wrong. You had the opportunity and you blew it. Even with Barbarella doing all the hard work you still failed. One thing is certain, Barbarella has moved on, and so must you. A gulp of Lagavulin lifts some of your Presbyterian gloom. Time to start over—and scan the room.

Take your time to survey the state of play, but not too long. The place is already starting to thin now that the speeches are over. Worryingly, even some C-list are beginning to leave.

And there is Will, still banging away. You can tell from the girl's body language that he's crashing. Time to save him from himself. Tomorrow, he'll thank you for the demonstration.

But before you make a move, a small voice warns you away. You shake your head to eject the verbal tinnitus. Was it a higher force trying to guide you? Perhaps the gods have a greater purpose for you this evening. Or is it some runt of conscience steering you from Will's path? After all, the girl is just a passing temptation to you, but to Will she could be a marriage-wrecking lifesaver. A wave of indecision glues you to the bar.

Time to act, Barnaby:
Do you reassert your faith in reason, ignore Jiminy Cricket's chirruping and lock onto the Aussie temptress? **Go to Scene 49**

Do you succumb to "the voices" and wait by the bar to see what Fortune brings? **Go to Scene 149**

Scene 116

With a pink glow (of virtue) you head back up to the bustling party-deck. Barnaby's nowhere to be seen, and you suppress a flash of annoyance. No need to dwell. You grab a drink and knock back two-thirds. "*En todos los bares*" and all that. Scan the room—there must be someone. Oh yeah, almost forgot, that yummy guy is still talking to the sports minister. He's standing among the rather somber group, hand casually in trouser pocket, chiseled face furrowed into a frown. Probably bored out of his mind.

You stride over purposefully and take the time to think how you should play it. The party is going downhill fast so this could be your last chance. Should you wow them with your political savvy? . . . Or just have some fun?

Do you act naturally intelligent? **Go to Scene 154**
Do you act naturally blonde? **Go to Scene 156**

Scene 117

You stare dumbly at the limp Carmen for long moments; torn between the realization of failure (if you can only get women on the verge of alcohol-induced collapse, what's the point?) and the realization that you should do something.

This last obligation is compounded by the reaction of the spotty barman. First at the scene, the young barman is practicing some basic first aid (obviously inspired by his inside knowledge of Carmen's underwear habits). Even you can tell he is failing miserably to achieve the recovery position.

Without considering the implications, and perhaps half believing your ridiculous lie, you step forward. "Allow me . . . I'm a doctor."

You say it with calm sincerity and the barman falls back. It doesn't matter what you do, as long as you do it with sureness and with demonstrable intent. Your theory on lying, bluffing and dissembling—if you believe it, then everyone else will. The hastily gathered crowd sighs with relief as you take the helm.

And besides, the recovery position isn't exactly difficult, even when you've got a knicker deficit to conceal. A crowd has gathered and one or two of the uglier politicians are blatantly trying to peer.

Carmen's head lolls to one side, and you cup a cute little cheek and bravely resist the urge to kiss her. You lift a closed lid to reveal rolled eyes. Yep, she's out cold, you think lamely. You check her pulse, make sure she hasn't swallowed her tongue, feel her left tit for luck, and thank God as two green-clad ambulance men arrive in blistering efficiency.

"She's unconscious," you state authoritatively, and then to the gawking crowd, "she'll be fine . . ."

And in the mêlée you take the chance to recede, back to the bar, and ready to fight again. For the night is young and you, Barnaby, you are Mercutio, you are Barabus of Malta, and the play must go on. So pipe up, minstrel, scan the stage, Barabus . . . Hark, what's that over yonder? 'Tis Will banging away like a besieging cannon, and that poor damsel, look, verily she is yawning—at nine forty-five? Save her, Barnie.

Go to Scene 49

Scene 118

You hadn't exactly planned to make love next to a python, but the wanton night must end soon and this will be your final jolly.

You came to the zoo every summer as a child because of your love for wild animals, but now it's your turn to be feral. Who would have thought all those years ago that you'd come back to this site of innocent memory and corrupt it with a public display of obscene sexual gratification? Well, your mother might. She was always concerned about your behavior. That's why you ended up at a convent school.

On the way to the reptile house, and just to enter into the spirit of things, you swap favorite sex stories with Jay. He tells you about the time he stimulated a girl using an aubergine then put it back in the refrigerator before his mom noticed it had gone. The family had moussaka for lunch the next day.

Well, there was the time that you . . . or was it . . . or who was it . . . ? You thought you had so many tales to tell, but can only think of Catherine's conquests instead. They tend to be funnier and definitely more slutty. Desperately not wanting to let your side down, you recount the time when you (aka Catherine) ended up having sex on the set of a kid's TV program, using nationally recognized hand puppets as sexual aids.

Once you've got the first off your chest, the rest start to come out in a tumble. But there's no time for the story about the weekend in Wales, or the Svelto toilet cleaner incident, because there before you, resplendently redbrick, stands the Reptile House.

Jay, like any good New Yorker, isn't fazed by a locked door. His penknife comes out, three twiddles, and you're in. The door swings open onto blackness, and a puff of musty air billows out to greet you.

Go to Scene 102

Scene 119

"I could probably make a quick diagnosis in one of the cabins."

You hear your voice before you've fully decided to make the move. Just as well, you never did have enough bottle for this sort of thing.

Waiting waiting waiting waiting.

Eventually she speaks: "Would you mind? I think I feel something."

BarbiethankyouBarbiethankyouthankyouthankyouthankyou.

And with that you take Carmen by the hand, lead her through the mass and down into the furthest cabin.

Go to Scene 109

Scene 120

Within fifteen minutes, you are all three standing outside Regent's Park Zoo. Kamran sizes up the iron railings.

"It can't be that difficult, just about everybody I know has broken into this place."

By now, you've become so hexed by Jay that Kamran's presence is becoming an irritation. Fortunately Jay isn't put off, and remains blatantly eager.

"Barbie, how about I lift you over the fence and look up your dress?"

You blush. You like his tone a lot. If it weren't for bloody Kamran you could be growling obscenities on Bear Mountain within five minutes. Still, once inside you can lose Kamran easily. London Zoo is like a maze—a subtle nudge and the wolves will take care of him . . .

But first you have to get in. Kamran gives Jay a bunk up, and with expected elegance Jay lands lightly on the other side of the eight-foot railings.

"Come on, Barbie." Kamran locks his hands together, licks his lips, and smiles eagerly up at you.

Oh dear, Kamran is after an eyeful. The only question is how much of an eyeful will you give him?

Barbie, are you wearing any underwear? Can you remember that far back? Of course you can, be honest now, for good or ill. Are you wearing knickers or not?

Have you a sensibly covered bott? **Go to Scene 224**

Or would you expose the lot? **Go to Scene 222**

Scene 121

"I'm afraid I'll need to move your dress," you say in a calm, British Airways pilot voice. And shamelessly you hoik up the Lycra-imbued cotton.

The lights on the Embankment shimmer off the Thames, shout through the porthole, and scream off the perfect curve of her bottom.

And as the visual image emblazons, you hear her shriek.

"You pervert. You're not interested in my back at all."

And for the second time that evening, you feel a stinging slap. Carmen adjusts her dress and slams the door behind her.

Go to Scene 129

Scene 122

The beautiful, adorable Nicholas sits on the bed as you help him remove his trousers. As suspected, his legs are every bit the swimmer—tanned and muscular, and just yearning to be touched. His right hand fails to conceal a budding erection, which is your cue to take decisive action. You mount the bed, then Nicholas, the pale blue dress riding up your thighs. With the innocence of a middle-aged prostitute, you slip your cool slender fingers down the front of his underwear and around his attentive manhood. You giggle at your naughtiness, before stripping tenderly but expertly. The dress floats off with a skill that Charlotte can only dream of. The ease of your conquest slows your wits. His eager beauty stuns you. So tanned, so toned, so young, it makes you groan. Easily, you push him back on to the soft innocent white duvet, kissing tenderly and gnawing at his flesh.

He stares with disbelief into your eyes; the "I've been to Africa" necklace dangles from his neck and you use it to pull him towards you. But no time to linger. He turns you over and, kicking off your heels, you can only dream of what's to come. His hands move over your edible buttocks, and bottom-bare he thrusts . . .

. . . and comes.

Scene 122

Oh, so, so desperately disappointing.

The myth of youth, puissance, and duration shattered so tragically. You can barely contain your disappointment.

But if you're quick, maybe you'll still be in time for the starter.

Go to Scene 22

Scene 123

All you know about human anatomy has come from the art of sexual massage. You've never massaged anyone without sexual intent and it's too late to start now. Kamran read a book once. An ancient Zoroastrian erotic text. All meridians and pathways and pleasure nodes. You never really listened.

Remember, Barnie . . .

You cast your mind back to the illustration on the back page and try to recall Kamran's febrile explanations.

Think, Barnie.

There was a node just around where she was rubbing . . . and as you stare at the waiting buttocks you begin to remember . . .

. . . just below the bit where spine meets hip . . .

. . . and it was on a pathway . . .

. . . a pathway that directly linked the brain . . .

. . . to the clitoris.

Bingo.

Go to Scene 127

Scene 124

He smiles candidly. Not offering an answer. Your five-minute clock is running down and you decide to reveal a flash of intent.

"I like funny men. Tell me, have you ever made someone laugh and come at the same time."

"Not yet," he rises to your challenge.

Thirty seconds left.

"Look, my friends are about to leave. Can I give you my phone number?" You offer a business card and he accepts it gladly.

With a guaranteed date sometime next week, you skip back to your buddies.

You could give lessons. **Go to Scene 24**

Scene 125

You begin to close. Crossing through the throng you notice younger prey. But they can wait. You begin a mantra in the quiet calm of your mind. "Quick Kill Quick Kill Quick Kill."

Closing in. The hair is dyed. "Quick Kill."

Closer still. Double chin. Crow's feet. "Quick Kill." "Quick Kill."

You move for the final swoop. Smile ready.

Then you notice them.

Ankles.

Ankles as thick as your knee.

Fat ankles—peasant stock—Hoover bag legs—pull out, Barnie—pull out—boobytrap.

With the grace of a dancer, you pirouette without spilling a drop of alcohol. Not a drop that is until you collide with the blonde—she drops to the floor like a shot pheasant.

"The direct approach. I like it." You can already hear Kamran laughing tomorrow at lunch. "Maybe a small cosh would be more subtle. . ."

You glance down to see what you have bagged.

The microdress probably did little to soften her fall, and it certainly does nothing to preserve her dignity.

Dumb from drink you can only stare as, arms and legs akimbo, you realize Barbarella isn't the only girl to forsake underwear tonight.

With a planted smile, you belatedly lend a gentlemanly hand

and profuse apologies. The smile has secured fixed grin status, but you can't shift the lecherously contorted face any more than you can resist blurting out the inevitable witticism.

Fight it, Barnie. Don't say it. She's gorgeous and feeling a little absurd and emotionally vulnerable. Miss Right—your ideal—say something gentlemanly, apologetic, and genuine. Suppress that evil thought, suppress . . .

"You're not a natural blonde, are you?"

Idiot.

The slap surprises you more than it hurts. But as she walks away to the bar with barely mustered dignity, you retain your inane grin.

When will you learn, Barnie? Are your Essex roots so implanted? This will be a long night if you don't act with more prescience. Kamran is probably on number two by now. You survey the deck and realize your indiscretion has gone largely unnoticed. The blonde is by the bar, hastily ordering a drink. You recognize her from somewhere.

It's time for action, Barnie. Perhaps if you apologize to the blonde she might let you have another look. Hate can turn to love, but more often it turns to lust. You could do with a fortifying scotch anyway.

Your mind is all but decided when, out of the corner of your eye, you see the Aussie pop-star yawn. Yawn at 9:45? You spot an opportunity for self-ego-inflation. Will wouldn't stand a chance . . .

It's just this sort of minor, seemingly inconsequential decision that changes lives forever. You could end up marrying one of these girls . . . or better still, Barbarella may get so jealous that she begs you to come back. Oh, the pressure. What'll you do? Think Blonde. Trust in your predatory instincts and go for the easy kill by the bar? **Go to Scene 39**

Think Brunette. Joust with Will in a battle for Antipodean gold? **Go to Scene 49**

Scene 126

Are you still breathing? The dress is pure frippery and somewhat restrictive, but you look stunning. It does beg a supplementary question: Underwear—yeah or nay?

Of course not, even the skimpiest would bulge under this asphyxiating number, and anyway it's a warm midsummer night. Deodorant is the only underwear you need.

You join the others. Catherine looks relieved that her shift with Astrid is over. "Come on, we need to be going. The boys'll be waiting."

Time to go. Just remember, you've made your decision—no knickers—and only the devil can foresee how that will change your fate. When the time comes, good or ill, you've made your bed (and wearing no knickers there's a good chance you'll get to lie in it).

Go to Scene 144

Scene 127

And so it begins.

"Tell me how this feels," you manage to say with medical sincerity.

And with strong thumbs, you begin to probe the top of her buttock.

She lets out a small breath as you begin and you thank God for Kamran and his dedicated research. And as you continue, you're pretty certain that she enjoys it. But it's hard to tell in the dim light.

"Is that painful?"

"No it's . . ."

Her voice trails off and you know she is ready. Now or never, the close, the try-line in sight, just one last dive . . . You trail your hand down the curve of her bottom, over impossibly smooth skin; and down the thigh, the tickle of fine blond hairs; and then up between her legs. She shudders silently as you fumble.

Then you hear a groan.

At first, you assume it's your own. But then, from the gloom, you hear it again, slightly louder. It's coming from inside the closet.

You ignore it, and focus everything upon the gentle sensation on your right hand, the short bristling hairs—then suddenly, everything happens at once.

Carmen, affected by your machinations, lets out a breathless whimper, her arms, quivering under the strain of supporting her upper body, give out and she slumps forward onto her chest. The brass desk lamp crashes to the floor and plunges the room into blackness . . . just as the closet door flies open in a swirling mass of writhing bodies.

Before your eyes have time to adjust to the darkness, you find yourself lifting the prostrate body of Carmen onto the floor. Hard, fast, and fun, with a dash of idiosyncrasy—the perfect midsummer's dream. And as you tend to Carmen, ripping the thin dress up and over her head, the pumping alcohol-fueled blood dizzies your mind and soon there are three women before you, and above you, and below you. And there are hands, many hands and mouths and legs and breasts, so many perfect breasts, but most of all you will remember the skin, the acres of bare, smooth skin—tingling and caressing as it rubs against you.

Just as you begin to think you'll go mad with sheer desire, a glowing light illuminates the scene. And for the first time you see faces.

Go to Scene 75

Scene 128

You can hear people crossing the passage outside the cabin door. Hopefully your absence hasn't been noticed. Everyone seemed to be fairly wrapped up in the party atmosphere, but then again, the minister was very much under scrutiny.

Edward slides his hand up over your hips, intent on verifying by just how much you have grown over the years. You close your eyes, enjoying the sensation as it sets your thighs tingling. He pulls you down onto his lap and teasingly kisses you, judging if his gamble has paid off.

Barbie, you've made no moves to resist. Is this entirely wise? Catherine, your father, the government? This could bring them all down.

"Barbarella never gets caught, does she?" he murmurs, as if reading your thoughts.

All right, if you are certain, but bear in mind, you need to pace yourself. It has been little more than an hour since you boarded the boat. This is a pretty quick turnaround, even for you. There's a long night ahead. Edward feels in his jacket pocket and pulls out a rather large cigar tube.

"Barbie, can I tempt you?" he asks.

Of course, you're always open to temptation. The speeches will shield any noise you may wish to make.

*

Scene 128

Barbie, what are you doing? Not a Bill C.? How are you going to explain this to Catherine? Well, at least keep the noise down and hurry up about it. And for God's sake keep your eyes shut—haven't you noticed he's ginger? When you're quite finished, everyone will be waiting back at the party . . .

Go to Scene 140

Scene 129

Nothing for it but to reenter the fray. Take heart, Barnie, the night is not over 'til there are only fat ladies left. Will's little filly must be well and truly ready for a change of conversation by now.

You check your face for signs of failure in a convenient wall mirror. You still look presentable, if a little worn. Your face never used to show tiredness, just part and parcel of the gallop towards thirty. You don't mind so much, you just dread the time when you start looking forty. But no time to dwell; it's time for a comeback. And so, turning off the lamp, you take your leave of the little cabin. But before you shut the door behind you, an unmistakable noise emanates from within—a groan. Like any good voyeur, you duck back inside, shutting the door behind you.

It takes a few seconds to adjust to the light, but even blind you could figure out what is going on; a wardrobe door pings open and two tumbling, writhing bodies drop to the thickly carpeted floor. You dive behind the desk.

What to do?

Make a run for it. **Go to Scene 250**

Stay awhile. **Go to Scene 51**

Scene 130

You remove the price label from the dress. It's yet another that you *could not live without,* but haven't actually worn. Serves you right for underestimating your size; it's taken six months of fiber supplements to make it fit. Well, if you are successful tonight, the digestive deprivation will have been worth it. With that thought in mind, you rummage at length for a suitably stylish pair of knickers.

Eventually your two pieces of clothing are smoothed into place, and fresh makeup restores you to alcoholic virginity. Catherine peers tentatively around your bedroom door and distracts you from the finishing touches.

"Can I hide in here for five minutes? Astrid's driving me nuts." She proceeds to use your bed like a couch. "What should I do if I bump into Edward? Should I just ignore him? Or should I smile as if nothing has happened? His wife won't be there, she never supports him in anything."

Fortunately you're not expected to answer any of this; unfortunately Catherine spots a flashing red light on the answer machine by your bed. She presses it automatically.

"Beep . . . Barbarella, Michael here [your boss]. We need to talk about last night. David's a bloody trainee *and* the son of a critical client. Rupert [the chairman] isn't impressed. Better come and see me first thing Monday and we can talk damage limitation."

Oh dear. You weren't going to tell anyone about last night. You attempt an expression spanning shock, puzzlement, and affected nonchalance.

"Shall we order a cab?" You breeze out the room and avoid an inquisition from Cat.

Go to Scene 144

Scene 131

As per the plan, Astrid charges off the boat first. In broken English (the result of too much excitement and drink), she relates the farcical events.

"I found man, like you said, Barnaby. He was small and old and had funny tongue and big eyes."

Normally you would be hurrying Astrid to get to the point, but now you sit back and relish her every description.

"When I told him I wanted to go some places, his eyes got even bigger," she laughs at her European humor. "I told him to go to cabin room, like you said. I bet him eyes got biggest when he in."

Much as you would love a full discourse, there isn't time. Catherine is running off the boat. She spots Barbie waving from the cab and joins you.

"It worked, it worked! I kept Will up on deck and he didn't even get suspicious. Mind you, I didn't think he'd go down to the cabin to look for my earring." She gives you a big kiss and hug. "Barnie you are *so* clever; I couldn't keep a straight face when I heard your text came through. Poor Will. Oh, here he is now."

You all look up to see Will storming off the boat with a face of thunder. Regardless of how he really felt for Annabel, there's nothing more humiliating than finding your *Daily Telegraph*–announced fiancée lying naked in the wake of a bug-eyed pensioner.

"I guess it worked," Kamran interjects unnecessarily. But Barbie is calling from the cab.

"*Will,* over here."

Will sees you through blooded irises. He storms over to the cab and flings open the door. You greet him with five broad grins.

Only a complete misery could compete with the gust of bonhomie that greets Will as he tries to form a sentence. His tongue freezes. He looks with cold angry eyes, from Barbie's twinkling teeth to Kamran's Pan-sent grin. But you offer a hand.

"Jump in, mate. We want to go to your casino—the West India," and with a sigh, Will's mouth quivers at the edges into a smile.

He has no idea how you did it, and at this precise moment in time, he doesn't want to know. The horror of what he's witnessed—and perhaps the relief at what he's escaped—has broken his curiosity. For now, he jumps in beside Catherine, squeezes her thigh and politely barks to the cabbie, "If you can head toward Bayswater Road please." He turns back to you. "My darling fiancée can find her own way home."

"I'm not 'avin' six in the back of my cab, mister."

Of course not. More than his job's worth.

"Barnie, you'll be OK on your bike, won't you?"

Barbarella has no idea how terrifying it is to ride on two wheels when you've just had a skinful. But you can't undo all your good work, you're the hero of the hour. And you may well be back in with a sniff. In that case, Barnaby, now might be the time to strike . . .

Barnaby, a life-changing decision may be coming up. OK, Barbarella may be a bit of a snob, and you may argue all the time, but facts are facts, you love the girl. She's your north, south, east, west, working week, Sunday rest, etc. And this is probably as good a time as any to stop all clocks and offer up a juicy bone.

Scene 131

There comes a time in every man's life when he has to look to his soul and decide once and for all whether he wants to scurry around the fringes of life, to idle in the wings, or whether he is willing to brave the hot lights and take center stage (and risk making a complete arse of himself). The time to look into your soul is (possibly) NOW:

"I don't really know how to get there. Will you come with me, Barbie?" **Go to Scene 252**

"No problem, I'll see you all there." **Go to Scene 244**

Scene 132

"I'm in advertising."

"I thought so. Thought I recognized your name in today's paper. Didn't you get lucky last night?"

Unsure of what he's referring to you can only presume he means the advertising award—not the nubile twenty-two-year-old.

"Yeah, best internet link."

For the first time since last night you feel a flush of pride at your achievement. You take a long, leisurely sip from your glass, fixing your gaze on Edward. In this light he appears less affected by age and the pressure of a political career; he does indeed have some appeal. Perhaps Catherine isn't as foolish as you originally thought.

Now come on, Barbie, you're a clever girl. You need to work out this man's strategy before you can develop your own. He is unashamedly coming on to you, but why? It's imperative that you establish if he's playing you—so that you can play him:

1. Is it a cheap attempt to make Cat jealous? If so, avoid like faux Cartier.
2. He finds you genuinely attractive? If so, he's got to try harder than this.
3. Unknown agenda? If so, establish immediately.

Scene 132

Time to show some prickle (older men love it). "Look, I'd really like to know why you are keeping me from my friends and a moderately good party?"

"Well, to be completely honest, the political speeches are about to begin. I'm doing you a big favor—promise."

You maintain a noncommittal expression.

"I can't believe your father would be very pleased if he knew you were here, would he?"

Oh, God. He knows your father. More than that, he has known him for some time. Edward starts to recount tales of summers in Gibraltar, spent at your parents' second home. That period of your life when your parents could escape the taxman and you could escape St. Mary's Convent and flourish in the heady climate. He remembers you well, and asks you to stand up.

"My, how you've grown."

Normally that would sound ridiculously perverse, but, Barbie, you can't help but break into a small smile. Edward exhales before laying his cigar to rest. You perch yourself on the end of his desk and steal a final puff from his stub before viciously crushing it in a glass ashtray.

You bend, then kneel down, mesmerizing Edward with your assertive chest. You pause and studiedly share a smile before cupping his hand in your palm. Edward, with the confidence of age, reciprocates by taking gentle hold of a breast.

You could, with an in-your-face billow of smoke, state simply, "I'll pass your regards on to Dad," and exit swiftly. **Go to Scene 140**

Or do you remember your manners and be polite to Daddy's friend? **Go to Scene 128**

Scene 133

Barbarella can barely articulate but you don't need her explanation. Turning around you see Annabel elegantly striding towards you. Her tall bony frame almost makes even Barbarella look dumpy, and, although her flat chest does little for *your* libido, Barbarella has always been intimidated by Annabel's aristocratic physique.

Annabel, stealer of friends and wrecker of lives (well, Will's anyway). Be careful, Barnie. Keep your mouth shut and see what the Gorgon has to say.

After a flurry of insincere greeting, Annabel grabs the initiative with an opening, "Barnaby, Barbarella, *so* good to see you two together. You always deserved each other."

Never openly rude, never open to confrontation, Annabel has a knack of insulting without insults. But Barbie is her equal . . . almost. "Annabel, how are you? Oh, God, I almost forgot, congratulations! I didn't know you were coming along tonight. I thought Will said you were celebrating with friends."

Lightly insinuating, perfect. Barbie truly is a master of the hidden gibe. But Annabel knows every weakness of your dear friend. They were at school together, in the days when Barbarella was far from the seaweed-wrapped perfection of today. Although Annabel was an Alice-band monster, she did have a certain knack for popularity with her own sex, a knack that Barbarella has always lacked. Annabel made Barbie's life hell at school . . . and even now, she has the power to transport Barbarella back ten years with a well-barbed quip.

Against the odds, Barbarella maintains the offensive: "So tell me, how did you propose?" Barbie laughs musically to soften the insult but you notice Annabel's abdomen stiffen. Barbarella, fueled up, foolishly continues. "Did you go down on one knee?"

"Barbie, one really shouldn't imagine everyone spends as much time on their knees as you. I see they are a little pink already . . . my you are a busy little worker."

Sure enough Barbie's knees are already a little carpet rouged from her night's activities. She looks at you with a bashful flutter; your heart breaks anew. Barbie loses her perfect posture and half an inch in height. But no time to dwell, time for you to step in and switch the conversation to a more neutral track.

"William hasn't been able to keep the smile off his face all night, have you got big plans for the wedding?"

And so Annabel is off, bragging and waxing. She has spent the entire day locked up with her mother, rabidly drawing up lists and now all she wants to do is talk out the steam. And while she whines about the "horrible press" (only *Tatler* will have the faintest interest), and the "darling vicar" (no doubt some pedophilic old fool), and the dangers of an autumn wedding (yep, Will only has three months before the garrote descends). *You* have time to think . . .

This wedding already has more momentum than a must elephant. The longer it's allowed to live the harder and bloodier will be the kill. You must act with the ruthlessness of Herod and kill this infant child. William must be rescued, and rescued tonight. Not only for his sake. This is your big chance to impress Barbie, to show her just how splendidly superior and downright clever you actually are.

But Annabel will be no easy opponent. She has her talons

deep within Will's flesh and they won't be easy to dislodge. As she blathers with Barbarella about her insistence on formal dress, it would be easy to dismiss her as a simpering female. But you know better. Annabel was forged in Cheltenham Ladies and finished top of her class for social cunning; she's forewarned of your collective hate, and worst of all, she knows you will try to pry Will from her grip . . . and is looking forward to the fight.

This will take Prospero-scheming Barnaby—and so, with a murmured half apology, you excuse yourself from the unhappy conversation in search of Kamran and a plan.

Go to Scene 238

Scene 134

Back in the house the diners are well beyond decorum. You rejoin Snuffy and although pudding eventually makes an appearance, everyone is too drunk to know what to do with it. As you turn to top off Snuffy's glass, there is a commotion at the other end of the dining-room. Polly, one of Charlotte's friends, is clambering onto the table, clad in a gentleman's coat and bowler hat. She steps on a chair, totters on cheap-looking stilettos, then back on to the table.

I saw the light on the night that I passed by her window
I saw the flickering shadows of love on her blind
Sheeeeee was my woman
As she deceived me I watched and went out of my mind

The hat spins off, the coat falls . . . *Polly* . . . an ill-fitting bra digs tightly into her unfeasibly large bubbies.

My, my, my, Delilahhhhhhh

Then the moment the front row have been aching for. The bra pings off with a sigh of relief.

Why, why, why, Delilah

But before Kamran has time to get on the table, and as Polly hums the trumpet solo, Olympia returns. She cuffs her grinning husband with a look.

GET DOWN FROM THERE YOU . . . YOU HARLOT.

Polly's finale is, if anything, even more dramatic than her entrance.

Forgive me, Delilah, I just couldn't take any more

She slips indecorously and lands facedown in a crème brûlée, before finally slumping to the floor in a drugged faint.

You suspect this has something, nay a lot, to do with Barnaby and Kamran, but you don't have time to find out; Will has the same idea. "Shit. Get Barnie and Kamran. We need to get the hell out of here before Olympia finds out. I'll have the car running out front . . . *quickly*."

Go to Scene 182

Scene 135

The hardest part about making money out of the West India is getting in. Tonight, with Will, you have no trouble. You fly through open doors and are whisked courteously to the inner sanctum.

The club itself is stunningly fitted in deep oaks and mahoganies. The austerity of the wood is calmed with silk Persian rugs and *chaises longues* draped in rich fabrics and rich women. Your favorite part has always been the superbly stocked bar, including its choice in barmaids. All are bright students desperate to pay off loans, and all are willing to flirt outrageously with the clientele. You spot a little brunette, on tiptoes, reaching for a bottle. Perfect for making Barbie jealous. You decide to introduce yourself.

But before you can get anywhere, Barbarella is presenting a trayful of brandy glasses and Will is lighting you a cigar.

"Bit of an odd crowd in tonight—no Americans. We'll have to sharpen up to stand any chance of minting it. Now, I've been thinking about how we can make a killing and . . ."

You feign interest in Will's rant, but are really more interested in Barbarella. The day's events are obviously taking their toll because she's staring into space, daydreaming. Kamran is equally uninterested, hawking at the rich elderly and poor young, caught between two desires. *And then you catch him.*

Blatantly he clocks Barbarella up and down—ogling every

detail, every curve of flesh and dip of bone, sucking up the mental image. And all with a passion so powerfully etched on his face that he almost looks angry.

Kamran is in love with Barbarella. Of course he is, any man with a pulse would be, and Kam is most certainly a man. He reads lingerie catalogues, for heaven's sake. That explains why he's always getting in between you and Barbie. But before you can dwell on your discovery, Will's drawl ignites a flicker of distraction: "Ra Ra Ra Ra Ra Ra Ra cheat Ra Ra Ra made a fortune Ra Ra Ra Ra, Ha Ha Ha."

Desperately your brain and ears focus. Thoughts of Barbie and Kamran can wait. This is about money, and for once Will has something important to say.

"The old bloke was a tremendous cheat, you see. He introduced the 'cubby.' Fantastic fun. Giles and I used to hide in there and watch them play in the stud . . ."

"Hold on." Will's diatribe is meaningless code, but if you can translate into English, the potential of the cubby seems interesting. "Start at the beginning, who is Giles and what is the 'cubby'?"

And so Will takes a deep breath. Patronizingly at first, but then with youthful enthusiasm, he takes you through his childhood tale.

Go to Scene 161

Scene 136

"I'm a criminal barrister."

Edward splutters on his drink, and half the contents wash across the desk. He starts to mop up, clearly flustered. You can't help but be bemused at this man's extraordinary behavior. If you knew a career could generate such a response, you might have used the line earlier.

"Eddie, do you require some legal advice or something?" you ask, unabashed.

"Sorry . . . I just need to clean my shirt." Edward heads straight out the door.

Go to Scene 140

Scene 137

With a sigh of relief, you leave the room and rest your reeling head against a stair banister, tempted to bash away. This party is like some sort of nightmare. So much for a night to remember. This could prove to be the most miserably unrewarding night of your life. The joy of the afternoon has long since set and, with a pang, you realize that at barely midnight, you are already knackered.

Take heart, Barnie, it's not (just) age; have a swig of cheap champagne and find Catherine. The sight of her cleavage quivering as she cries on your shoulder will revive flagging spirits. Now where did she go?

Presuming that she is sobbing her heart out discreetly in the bathroom, you ascend thickly carpeted stairs. You locate the bathroom, but Cat is nowhere to be found. And so with the skill of a Côte d'Azur cat burglar (learned as a teenager in your first girlfriend's house) you creep along the upstairs landing in search of your sobbing friend. At the far end of a long hall, you detect a faint noise, and, with eager cunning, steal up to the bedroom door. It's slightly ajar. Peering in, you see a bedroom converted into a study. Cat is rifling through desk drawers, clutching a small camera. She is far from tears.

"Cat, what the hell are you doing?"

Catherine jumps guiltily, "Christ, Barnie, you scared the life out of me. How am I supposed to be an investigative journalist with you barging around?"

Scene 137

Catherine, instead of crumpling under the humiliation of a second rejection from Edward, is displaying enormous pluck by immersing herself in her work.

"So what exactly are you looking for, Catherine? I thought you were a legit journalist."

Cat smiles at your innocence. "If I can, I'll bring the whole bloody government down, but mainly I just want to nail Edward."

So far, it would seem, she's found nothing and continues to rummage.

"Cat, this is crazy. Look, I know Edward has made you look like a prat, but if you get caught stealing your career will be finished."

Cat stiffens at the word "prat" but she seems to take your point. As much as you adore Catherine, the word "stupid" has crossed your mind in reference to her handling of Edward. He never made any effort to conceal his libertine ways. He made a fool of her openly. Yet she remained faithful to him. At a party only two months ago, she told you how she intended to handle this relationship like a man. She would have sex like a man—do it then walk away, no feelings, no regrets. But Catherine clearly didn't stick to her code; men do not cry themselves to sleep. Men do not wait for phone calls. Men do not remain faithful. Or at least you don't know any men who have admitted such qualities.

But tonight something has snapped. Cat's eyes burn with suppressed tears, there is a bitterness that could decimate armies or, if properly harnessed, burn Edward to a crisp. You could show her how. She steps towards you, her emotional cupboard stripped bare, and takes your hand with a squeeze that almost makes you wince.

"I just don't know what to do . . . Will you just hold me, Barnie?" As she presses her small frame against you for comfort, you hold her tightly, murmuring solace. One overriding thought repeats itself: "I'm in."

Choices, choices. Tread carefully, Barnaby. What you decide now could bring down the British government. Edward Bunger is a well-respected minister and this cabinet has enough skeletons to hide without you rattling any bones. The healthy and sensible thing would be to take Catherine back to your place and (just) let her try to get a good night's sleep.

Or is retreat not your style? It wouldn't take much to cajole Catherine into the most evil and sadistic revenge. You could make Edward Bunger suffer most horribly.

Either way it's "time to go to the mattresses." But literally or literarily? In the godfather sense or the how's your father? Only you can decide. Remember, this isn't just about the fate of the government and British democracy—the very future of your sex life is on the line.

Which will win out?

Vengeance. Challenge Edward Bunger to a most deadly duel. **Go to Scene 143**

Lust. Catherine will have forgotten all about him by dawn. **Go to Scene 185**

Scene 138

"I'll do it. One hand—all or nothing. Deal the cards."

No one can quite believe this is happening—least of all you. Will rests his head on the table, unable to watch; Barnaby looks paralyzed; Catherine walks out. Jenner pushes a mountain of green notes into the middle of the table. You add your meager pile.

The cards are dealt.

You look down at a pair of eights and then up at the ceiling. The chandelier turns left in encouragement. Will loses his nerve.

"You don't have to do this, Barbie. You can still just walk away."

"Shut up, Will. I know what I'm doing."

Jenner smiles at both of you, and tosses five upturned cards on to the table.

"Three queens," he looks at you pointedly, "and some dross."

Bugger.

You look imploringly at Astrid. You need the sort of distraction that only an eighty-five-kilo Belgian can provide. Whether she understands your plea, or whether something snaps in her narcotic-riddled mind, you can't guess: "No No No No," she wails and flings herself on to the table, desperately clutching at the piled cash. Jenner responds first, wrestling with her like a boar in a pit.

"You stupid cow, get off the table before you break it."

But the strain on her dress is too much. Threads of Lycra groan then snap. Astrid's chest crashes out, and catches Jenner on the side of his head. Will runs to help Astrid back into her dress, but is tripped by Newt who thinks he's trying to steal the cash. The oil baron strides forward instead, but a chair is pushed into his groin by the Arab team. Bodi and Wasim dash like Tintin and Haddock at the cry of the Castafiore.

The tragedy of the situation is that Astrid remains shrilly unaware, screaming above the commotion: THERE'S ONLY TWO QUEENS AND A KING. LOOK, YOU'VE MADE A MISTAKE. LOOK, BARBIE, IT'S A MISTAKE.

But you can't answer. You can only feebly motion at her and squeeze out a sympathetic smile. And as the croupier runs to get a floor manager and Kamran holds on for dear life, the chandelier screeches a chilling warning. Strain, creak, strain, creak—the sound of a light shaft slowly disengaging from a two-hundred-year-old set of bolts. A chandelier can only go so far to the left before it protests.

Go to Scene 70

Scene 139

It takes barely a minute to organize a cab to shuttle you down to Chelsea. Kamran's houseboat rocks its greeting and you plunge a hand into the end pot plant to find the ill-hidden hatch key.

Carmen is shivering against the cool night air and you look up to see her silhouette, the long blond hair shimmering in the moonlight like a mane. Your groin urges you to hurry.

"My home," you lie pleasantly once inside the little cabin. "Can I get you a drink?"

She investigates the various artistic junk, as you uncork a bottle of prechilled Chablis. You fumble with the foil in a frenzy.

"What does this do?" she queries, unearthing what you recognize to be Kamran's latest investment, an antique electrostimulator used by suppressed Victorian gentlefolk to stimulate their privates. According to the brass plate on the top, it's called the "Chattanooga" and has a patent pending. You cringe at Kamran's hideousness.

What to say?

"I've no idea, I bought it at an antique shop in Camden, but no one knew what it was." **Go to Scene 71**

"It's an antique electrostimulator used by suppressed Victorian gentlefolk to stimulate their privates." **Go to Scene 95**

Scene 140

Applause breaks out as you slide back into the throng of the party, almost as if two hundred people are well aware of your recent action. Actually, the attention is very much directed towards a makeshift podium at the bow of the boat. The culture minister is in the middle of a groundbreaking speech on booming black Britain. He attempts some rap to the utter dismay of all, and then proceeds to present a series of checks to a stream of grinning recipients.

The palaver seems to go on forever, but eventually the minister stands down and allows you to beat a retreat to the bar. A martini, and the astringency of a plump queen olive, reawakens your sensibilities. Relax. Shoulders back and survey the field.

Go for the one who looks as though he's having the most fun. The next man to laugh gets you. There, that's him, looks like something out of a J. Crew catalogue, talking to the sports minister. Make sure your drink is near replacing, think goddess, and go forth . . . A familiar voice catches you unaware: "Weren't the speeches magnificent? How uplifting. I feel almost buoyant."

You turn to find Catherine and Edward behind you, hands clasped secretly. Almost as if a Philly Blunt had been jarred between your teeth, you answer with the coolness of a downtown poker player.

"Quite."

Edward winks enigmatically, then leads Catherine away.

Scene 140

Confused, Barbarella?

The man's a bastard, no mistake. You stand dumbfounded, and try to figure out what game he's up to. As ever, nerves always make you reach to play with the sapphire ring on your right ring finger, but with mounting horror you realize the ring is missing. Thoughts of the manipulating Edward Bunger fly out your head. Oh, Christ, don't say you've lost the ring down in the cabin? If you have, you can hardly ask for help finding it. How the hell will you explain what you were doing there? Think where else it might be. You definitely had it when you arrived, at the bar, talking to Edward. Shit, the cabin marks the spot. Grab a drink from a passing tray. Just one will do, Barbie.

Do you hunt for the ring? It is a sapphire after all. **Go to Scene 142**

Diamonds are a girl's best friend. Forget about it, join the minister's circle and hunt down a solitaire for your wedding finger. **Go to Scene 150**

Scene 141

You tie her hands roughly (remembering you are the devil), but can't resist a quick kiss on her ever-pouting lips. You lie her on her back, on a thick, specifically put-there-for-this-purpose rug. With a quickening heart you realize the full implication of being Satan, Lucifer, to hell with it . . .

The first thrust takes her by surprise. She gasps in shock at the intrusion, but this must be a long night and so you withdraw.

"The angel," you invite and inform.

Kamran sets to with the passion of a convert performing the Lord's work. And with biblical prowess, he creates the Kingdom of Heaven, here, on earth. With subtle pressure, and considered use of nail and tooth, he writhes Barbarella's body up into an eddy of pleasure. His hands are everywhere, and where his hands are not, he is biting or licking or kissing as gently as only a seraph could. After bare minutes, Barbarella, tied and unable to fully respond, is thrusting her head up at her angel.

You don't waste time spectating. Kamran keeps a wicker carpet beater neatly propped in a little umbrella stand by the entrance steps. You whisk a practice stroke through the air and listen to the satisfying whoosh. Time for old *el diablo*.

Barbie's naked body still quivers for sensation long after Kamran has stopped. Finally, she settles and begins to regulate her discordant breathing. But you don't allow much respite before turning her on all fours and slipping a towel in her mouth.

Scene 141

You barely need to say the words: "The devil."

And with the final syllable, you whisk the cane beater into her gorgeously bent bottom. It stings crisply, but the surprise-fueled reaction couldn't be more pleasant. She bucks a quivering cheek and struggles vainly with her hand ties. The gag stops anything more than "Bbnneee bbneee! Stoppp!!" and you set to it again, and again, and again.

You can't help kissing her pinkened little cheeks before passing the baton to the angel.

This time Kamran goes into overdrive. He keeps Barbie on all fours and slips like a car mechanic into position. Five minutes of choreographed tongue waggling barely dents his enthusiasm or stamina but before an orgasm can mount, you pull him away.

"The devil."

Kamran's artistic junk has proved to be a goldmine. You've found and mixed a bucket of Kamran's quick-dry plaster and now you begin to apply. With gentle hands, you circle each nipple. The cold makes Barbie wince and you can almost hear her nervous anticipation. But Kamran knows what you intend, after all he perfected the technique . . .

And so together, you cover Barbie's golden flesh with dead gray. Finally, with a prod from your mentor you fall back and watch in awe at the sight of Barbarella the living statue, her body preserved—on all fours, breasts dangling, legs spread in desperate invitation, and head drooped in sheer sensory overload. And then finally Kamran himself leaves off massaging with wet, plaster-clumped fingers and the whole begins to set . . . Barbarella tries to slump forward but can't.

You look at Kamran and smile at the man's sheer dedication to his art. He smiles back and nods towards the hatch. You understand—time for breakfast. And with plaster-sodden hands, you creep quietly away to a bright new day. The Thames still smells and your eyes glow yellow with the brightness of the morning sun in a clear blue sky. You shut the hatch on your still setting goddess and head towards a café in Pimlico. It's 7:30—time for coffee, croissant, and a paper.

The (Boys' Own) End

There's more where that came from, Reader. And don't forget you could still find Barnaby the Perfect Ending—if you play again.

Scene 142

Despite the fact that lovers are disposable, rings are not.

By now the passageway leading to your cabin is beginning to fill with couples embracing, or otherwise engaged in deep discussion. Discussions that should be whispered are clearly audible, but you squeeze past discreetly and quickly come up to the cabin. Slipping inside, you close the door firmly; the cabin is empty. You get down on your hands and knees and hunt for the ring. It can't have gone far. The door clicks behind you.

"Looking for this?"

Will holds up your ring, with two glasses and an unopened bottle of Dom under his arm.

"Actually, don't move. You look rather delicious from here."

You playfully roll onto your side, asserting every asset you have.

"Well, don't just stand there, Will. Pour me a drink. I'm gasping."

Go to Scene 152

Scene 143

Thinking above the loins for once, well done. If you're going to go up against Edward then you'd better gather the troops. You return to the party below and note with relief that your absence hasn't been noticed. Will, as it happens, is deeply involved in a rather vocal argument with Edward.

"Do you know how small a fox's brain is?"

"About the same size as yours from the sound of you." Edward laughs before taking a long puff on his cigar.

Will is obviously rattled by Edward's savvy but rather blunt ripostes and the weak titters of the slender researcher still glued to his side. It doesn't help that both minister and researcher are slightly taller than Will's usually adequate five-eleven frame. You decide to help Will out and strike a first blow in the struggle with Edward Bunger. Stepping into the argument uninvited, you land a kidney punch.

"Riding to hounds is a bit like shagging dumb blondes. Once you have tried it, the call of the horn will have even an old git running for another go." The blonde looks as though she must have misheard, so you pause to smile before finishing. "No matter how immoral and disgusting the practice."

Not pretty but you were small for your age and at Romford Comp that meant you learned to get verbal, or get kicked. Leading Will gently by the elbow, you excuse yourself with a grin. Edward knows enough not to attempt an immediate reply. He manages to return a smile but the thin-lidded eyes absorb your image, and you know that you have made an enemy. Somehow you doubt that Edward Bunger got to high office by neglecting to punish his enemies.

The stakes are a little higher but the game continues. Grabbing Barbie, Kamran, and Astrid, all huddled by the far wall for protection, you head upstairs to the bathroom. And so with Barbarella sitting on the loo, Kamran lying in an empty bath, and the rest of you standing, you call for order, and a little quiet, while Astrid comforts Cat.

You take the helm in formulating a strategy; describing your vision in terms everyone, even Astrid, can understand. *News of the World*–style.

Imagine the headlines, guys:

TEDDY BARE

Junior Minister Edward Bunger resigned today amid rumors surrounding his bizarre appearance outside a Holland Park address in the early hours of Saturday morning, wearing only a pair of socks.

Undenied rumors leaked by a government insider state that he became disorientated after a four-in-a-bed sex romp.

Your compatriots look unsure.

But Barbarella appears ready to grasp the nettle, and with an eye-twinkling nod, she takes control. "Barnie's right, we need to do this. It's not just about Cat's broken heart anymore, this is about Edward Bunger, one of life's bullies, getting some natural justice. And, besides, how successful do you think Cat's journalism career will ever be with Edward in government?"

You decide to outline the plan in monosyllables. "Right, we're all agreed. The girls seduce Edward. They all get naked and frolic while I capture the moment on Polaroid. Then you, Will, and Kam, barge in, pick him up, and throw him out onto the street. All clear on our positions?"

Barbarella looks nervously at Astrid, and then suspiciously at you. "Why does it take all three of us to 'get naked,' as you so Essexly put it. Surely one person could do it on their own?"

"Edward is sitting downstairs, as we speak, chatting to a twenty-two-year-old Oxford graduate with longer legs than Astrid's dad and less fat than a Linda McCartney sausage. If any of you fancy your chances, then by all means . . . but I think you'd stand more chance working as a team."

You take the silence as consent. Astrid doesn't know who Linda McCartney is and Catherine is in no mood for a second bout with the bulimic blonde. You expected further argument from Barbarella. With a pang you catch a rare insight into her insecurity as she looks silently down at the floor.

But Will has another query. "So how come you have the best job?"

"Because I've a steady hand."

You flash a smile at dear Barbarella. She nods wistfully in acknowledgment.

You'd better know what you're doing, Barnaby. Edward Bunger is big league. Cock this one up and your future won't be worth a button.

Go to Scene 19

Scene 144

A taxi arrives to take you down to the Thames. Time for a final inspection before leaving. Your bag contains enough plastic and cosmetics to perform surgery, and enough mood stimulants to induce surgery. One last drink and a mood-priming boogie to an old Beastie Boys CD and you're ready.

North London smells beautiful tonight, almost as if the wind that blew from Primrose Hill was carrying the primroses with it. Soon enough the lights coruscating on the Thames draw you from the Strand and onto an Embankment teeming with lightly dressed, alcohol-laced, fun-seekers. Summer evenings like this must be cherished. You're feeling elated and can't help but squeeze Catherine's hand. She's starting to look tense, only too aware of the public statement she'll be making this evening. A few words of whispered encouragement might help: "Fuck the bastard, he's a politician anyway."

Not perfect but nice try, Barbie.

Your shining knights, abandoned in Chelsea, have caught up with you. Sadly, so has evil Annabel. Ever since your schooldays she has displayed a remarkable skill for turning up where she's not wanted. You suspect she may be distrustful of leaving Will on his own for too long. She knows what you're all like.

Arms linked with a well-scrubbed-up Barnaby, you go forth. Across the gangway, fun awaits. If only Astrid could cross it with a bit more grace—entrances are everything. Light bulbs flash from preying photographers but thankfully Catherine is walking tall—helped by Kam's strategically placed hand on her pelvis. She produces your invites and is waved through.

With a murmured groan, Catherine spots Edward Bunger immediately, adjusting his cuffs and desperately seeking to avoid expectant gazes from the other guests. The orange hair may be turning mercifully gray, but jowly and baggy-eyed, he really looks all his fifty-odd years. You steer her right by him, pausing briefly to give him a look of disinterest and insouciance. Will chooses to greet him Cuban style. A well-directed cloud of Cohiba smoke envelops the minister's face—and provides the smoke screen he has been dreaming of.

Finally, Kamran passes Edward. With the maturity of a teenage boy, he ill disguises an insult with a flamboyant cough: "Tosser."

Jesus, Catherine must be mortified with embarrassment. Better leave them all to it for a bit. Time to disappear into the morass.

Laughter and the sound of chinking glasses fill the boat as the party really gets underway. Catherine hasn't understated the alphabetic level of the guest list, more Hugh G. than Sean C. Nonetheless, there are some cherries to be picked and you enter the throng with a quickening pulse. Your right hand feels uncharacteristically light—of course, you don't have a drink. Tactically leaving the others, you make for the bar.

The correct drink is crucial. For a start, what you drink tells a lot about you. What's more, if you get it right, you'll dance 'til dawn; get it wrong and you'll sleep by a bucket, so choose carefully.

"What'll it be, madam?"

It's free, so why not a champagne cocktail? **Go to Scene 146**

Because the beautiful drink martinis. **Go to Scene 148**

Scene 145

BLACK MAMBA
(Dendroaspis angusticeps)

The black mamba is Africa's deadliest snake. The venom of an adult snake will kill a grown man in ten seconds. The poison of the infant black mamba will kill in less than half that time.

So tells the legend on the outside of your glass cage. Fortunately, you can't read it—winded, and lying on your bruised back among thickly matted, mildewed straw. The plumped grass of a nest broke your fall and you in turn cushioned Natasha from any serious injury. She screamed with the fury of a thousand orgasms, but now lies ominously silent. Her heavy breathing reassures you that she is still alive . . . for the moment. But a broken spine and an instant death would probably be a godsend.

Snakes. There could be thousands of the little bastards in this dingy glass cube. Or there could be one, fat anaconda . . . waiting to ease out of the murk and slowly twist its length around you. Gentle as a lover at first, then with the vicelike intensity of a cabaret dancer's thighs (after a long sea cruise), and finally with the killing suffocation of a hydraulic wine press. Such is the rambling of your Indiana Jones–fed imagination until Natasha squirms you to your senses. She tentatively points above your head.

There, languorously draped over a thick bamboo pole dangles a medium-sized dull-colored snake. It barely seems to have registered your dramatic, fretful entry. Natasha moves gently to lie by your side and you both stare up from paralyzed bodies in unspoken understanding . . . it probably won't wake up 'til opening time . . . only seven hours to sit out.

You maintain your snake-watching vigil for unbearable minutes, as if the act of watching will render the snake impotent, or keep it from falling onto your soft vulnerable bodies. Then, as you begin to grow bored of the staring, your eyes glaze and your mental defense-mechanism asserts itself. Your razor mind, sharpened on the strop of danger, drifts gently into a sexual reminiscence.

. . . the first time you tried to make love . . . a camping holiday in the New Forest . . . Joanne Tubber . . . she found a worm in the tent and went crazy . . . that Inter-railing holiday with the mad Danish girl and her fluorescent blue mirkin: "You no like blue? Well, I hate you" . . . the villa in Italy where you used toilet cleaner as an anal lubricant . . .

A life of sexual disaster flashes before you—fate drew you here, you know that now. Those minor misadventures were just rehearsals; you can see your naked gray intertwined bodies on the front page of Monday's tabloids. The embarrassment of your family, the posthumous infamy. Beautiful corpses never aging, never the humiliating restrictions and failings of old age . . .

Cool, gently probing fingers distract you from your thoughts. Long fingers slide the length of your taut torso and into the pit of your hip. She cups your exposed jewels and you both feel your cremasteric contraction as blood pumps away from your mind.

She absently strokes, and as you remember the sight of her naked skin, the serpent recedes to an Eden caricature. You return her comforting caresses . . .

The (Would You Adam and Eve It) End

Scene 146

Good choice. The barman fails to include the essential slither of orange peel, without which you really feel you can't accept the drink. He apologizes unconvincingly and disappears to find an orange. It gives you a chance to look around. First of all, locate your five friends. It's vital that you know where they are—in a social emergency you might need immediate rescue. Then locate Annabel—never lose sight of an enemy.

Kamran already appears to be surrounded by a hive of politicians' wives. His hand movements suggest that he is talking about sculpting. He came up with a ridiculously successful scheme of sculpting elderly women's busts—quite literally. He gives the clay more lift than is biologically accurate and they love him for it.

Catherine is trying to maintain a low profile, but still has Astrid in tow. You can see the Belgian eagerly seeking male attention. As for Barnaby he seems to be successfully entertaining what looks like a girl-only group of political researchers. You feel a stomach clench of jealousy, but decide to bury it. Men are so simple, if you can out-ignore Barnaby now, he'll come running back to you by the end of the evening.

Finally, Will. Never losing sight of financial self-improvement; he's attempting to close a deal to supply Commons Claret (re-labeled Bulgarian Pinot Noir). Annabel is by his side, lapping up marital congratulations.

But, Barbarella, forget them all for a while, especially Annabel. It's not healthy to mull over that misery. Instead you should be taking stock of the field. Sift between the media, pop, and film stars, and then apply the five-step plan:

Step 1
Discount anyone who laughs at his own jokes—they'll be crap in bed.
Step 2
Discount anyone who talks too much—they'll be crap in bed.
Step 3
Discount anyone dancing while still sober—they're gay.
Step 4
Discount anyone who's too good-looking—if they're not gay they'll be crap in bed.
Step 5
If there's anyone left, grab him before someone else does.

A champagne cocktail is placed near your hand by the returning barman. You take a sip while eyeing the room, but before you can spot anything promising a black-tied gentleman blocks your view.

"Hello, Barbarella. I must say, Catherine's description didn't do you justice."

Christ, it's Edward, Catherine's betrayer.

You can't think of an interesting response, and, being female, decide not to make one. Taking your arm, the minister steers you away and to the nearest porthole.

Go to Scene 76

Scene 147

It takes just under twenty minutes of trite conversation for you to feel the first effects.

For twenty more minutes, she talks and you listen. You hold her hand to make a point, eager to reach for the next level of intimacy. And as she poignantly witters, you hold her hand and absentmindedly stroke the soft skin of her inner arm.

The fine hairs on her forearm begin to stand erect and you know the time is right. Time to talk about sex . . . your favorite subject.

But where to start? Subtle or bold?

Does it even matter? There was enough Viagra in the plastic bag to save the white rhino from extinction. If you were lucky with glass selection, you could probably say anything and get away with it. Her skin beneath your hand is tingling with electricity. You are sure it was the left glass . . .

How to begin?

"Natasha, can I be honest with you? These last few minutes I've not heard a word you've said. All I can do is watch your eyes twinkle with excitement as you talk. I think I need to give you my number, walk away, and have a cold shower before I make a beast of myself." **Go to Scene 83**

"My body is a hot plate in the kitchen of desire. Can I boil your eggs?" **Go to Scene 155**

Scene 148

A stiff drink is needed to kick-start your senses. You take a gulp and take stock of the gathering. The party is the launch of a new "International Centre for Performing Arts." Fortunately for the politicians, the lottery-funded building in Tottenham hasn't been finished—hence the convenient riverside venue. It's a bloody odd mix; the politicians, lured by the prospect of celebrity, have turned out in droves, and with them is every civil servant, public relations spin-doctor, and other hanger-on who could scrape an invite. In addition there's a respectable smattering of the relatively famous and then a minority of bemused black musicians. Bemused presumably because they can think of a thousand better ways of supporting the black music industry. Nonetheless, without admitting it, you quite like this government atmosphere. Dull comfortable men and pinched ambitious women don't generally appeal to you, but the sense of power in the discreet murmur of conversation arouses curiosity if nothing else.

But you are here to have fun, so concentrate your thoughts on more pressing matters—*who* are you going to have fun with tonight? Why not join your friends? It is always easier to scan talent from the security of your own circle. Except that Annabel is hanging off Will, so maybe avoid him. Nonetheless, be sure to have one of the boys nearby so that any potential suitors will understand the work they'll have to put in. And Barnaby will have to be fairly close by or he won't be able to get jealous.

Don't forget though, you'll have to offer some moral support to Catherine, it is clear that half the talk in the room is concerned with what she and the minister have been up to. The general pitch of conversation is certainly heightening; faces are visibly relaxing as the alcohol inspirits cheeks and the odd double chin. But not you, Barbarella. Makeup is to perfection—not a shine or line in sight—which reminds you, you can always stand next to Astrid if your allure needs emphasis.

After a brief scan of the room you note half a dozen or so men who fit your strict criteria. Three of them you know, two are fresh. *What to do?*

Be a passive wallflower. Stay at the bar, get another drink in, and wait for the drones to circle. **Go to Scene 214**

Imitate the action of the tigress and stalk your prey. **Go to Scene 216**

Scene 149

After doing what you have to do, you morosely head over to the bar and contemplate life. The evening so far is proving to be a bit of a travesty. The successive fuck-ups are beginning to take their toll. Standing alone with your unhealthy thoughts of life-failure, you feel the gnawing self-doubt rise like bile. Your ego was never particularly robust, but with a shortness of breath, you realize that this is about much more than that.

It's about Barbie. She sees you with other women and she doesn't care. You see her even look at another man and you're smashing furniture. Barbie always leaves you wanting more, feeling you have something to prove. Oh hell, you might as well admit it; you love her.

And the stupid bitch couldn't care less.

That's been the trouble for the last two years. You love her insecurities, fears, and failings. The way she refuses to ever acknowledge that she cared about you; the way she sometimes cried after making love. She needs you, and together, you were invincible. It's not about settling down but teaming up. You could take on the world with Barbie by your side. Oh, Barnaby, you wise fool. Stop wasting time chasing cheap thrills, and get down to getting down with the one true and only love of your emotionally timid life.

But what's this? You must have been lost in self-reflection for longer than you realized for Barbarella is bearing down upon you, waving and smiling.

Scene 149

"Barnie, what have you been up to? Terrible, isn't it, we should have gone to Will's party."

You bite into the soft flesh of your tongue, and steel yourself to announce your true feelings. When Cupid is playing the mandolin there's no time to hesitate, no time to delay, no time to even think.

"Barbie, there's something I've got to say to you. I should have said it long ago."

But with no sense of the appropriate, Barbarella is staring over your shoulder and mouthing in disbelief, "Oh, my *God.*"

Somehow you lose your train of thought . . .

Go to Scene 133

Scene 150

Drink in hand (two-thirds empty), you are about to make your way towards the sports minister's circle when you spot Barnaby in a pitiful situation. He accidentally bumps into a girl, knocking her to the floor. Like a puppy he follows her to the bar and is making heavy weather.

She's no stunner. In fact, now that you look at her she's quite familiar. You recognize her as a backup dancer from an unfortunate night in the IN–OUT club where you lost your bag and dignity (the bouncers ejected you from the gents). Her career has taken a slight upturn following a greatly publicized affair with three-quarters of a boy band.

Normally you'd leave Barnaby to his own devices, but a cunning thought grips you. *You will help him pull.* What better way to demonstrate to Barnie that you're completely over him, and therefore what better way to win him back. You don't hesitate.

"Barnaby, you big oaf. What have you done to this poor girl?"

Without even waiting for his response you start one of your infamous monologues.

"Barnie is so clumsy and he doesn't realize how overpowering he can be. It's sometimes hard to remember that he has the most wonderfully talented hands."

You almost growl the implication, and, in a puff of Chanel, are gone. Favor granted. If that doesn't arouse her curiosity nothing will. Barnaby owes you, big time.

Scene 150

Now back to the minister and his circle. Your chosen man is standing, hand casually in trouser pocket, chiseled face concentrated into a frown. Don't be afraid to admit that you are excited about mixing with cabinet ministers. As you approach, you hear the low murmur of deep discussion.

How to play it, Barbie? A chance like this to mix with the great statesmen of the age doesn't happen often. Should you wow them with your political savvy?... or just have some fun?

Do you act naturally intelligent? **Go to Scene 154**

Do you act naturally blonde? **Go to Scene 156**

Scene 151

Natasha returns, walking a little uncertainly.

"I feel a bit fuzzy-headed."

"Sit down for a minute." All concern. She sits, face slightly flushed.

"I don't know what's wrong. I'm not even that drunk."

"Why don't I take you home. I think we've done our duty by the party."

You both look around and indeed the party is beginning to thin. On the far side, Barbarella is beckoning madly. You try to ignore her.

"BARNABY!"

Barbarella comes bounding over with all her usual grace and lack of subtlety. "What are you up to? We're thinking of making a move quite soon. Bring your friend. Oh—is she OK?"

You both look down at Natasha. She's bent over, eyes shut. Maybe giving her the whole bag was a tad ambitious.

"Look, we'll give you a shout before we leave," and with ill-disguised contempt for your catch, Barbie saunters off.

She's right; Natasha doesn't look fit for much. Maybe you should call her a cab. One last glance at Natasha . . . *What to do?*

Scene 151

Live and learn, and cut your losses. Call Natasha a cab, head back to the bar, and pray you don't end up guilty of manslaughter. **Go to Scene 149**

Never say die. Stick around and hope for a revival.
Go to Scene 153

Scene 152

Will kneels by your side, taking your left hand. He eases the sapphire onto your ring finger.

"But, Will, it goes on the other hand."

"I know, just testing."

You slowly realize what he is trying to do. It would seem that the lifelong playboy is not so keen on the idea of marriage after all, or at least not to Annabel.

"Will, she's just such a nightm . . . Well, she's not what . . . I thought you'd end up with someone better . . ."

"Why are you so jealous? You had more than a fair chance to say yes."

He looks peeved, but plays with your hair, ruffled from the evening's adventures.

"Barbie, you don't understand. I'm broke. The wine business is fucked; I owe a fortune. If I don't marry Annabel I'm well and truly shafted."

Your mind is a blur.

"You can't let Annabel *buy* you, Will. She won't just give you a fat check—she'll drip-feed money, just enough to pay interest but not enough to sort you out . . . and you'll never be able to leave her and . . ."

Delicately, Will caresses your face, pausing briefly to kiss your lips. He tastes heavenly. You always had an Epicurean partiality for champagne kisses. Your mind is swept up in demulcent limestone tunnels and cellars, deep in Rheims. Dark, humid sophistication. Blends being mastered then laid horizontally. Slowly, contact is made and the pressure starts to mount; the fizz is being created. An unguent bond of the traditional and the precious.

Barbie, he's getting married. Have you no moral standards at all? Will only got engaged yesterday. An engagement ring must count as one of your off-limits categories? And what about Barnaby? Are you giving up on him already? OK, it's obviously tempting to have a snog for the sake of auld lang syne, but the Old Testament's pretty clear on the seventh commandment. God seems pretty vengeful on this one—conflagration, floods, cities wiped clean before the wrath of the Lord. You have been warned . . .

Annabel is Will's lookout. She obviously isn't right for him or he wouldn't be ready to schmooze. And anyway, what's in a kiss? (Judas.) Get down to it, Barbie. **Go to Scene 164**

How would you feel if it were the other way round? Annabel may be Satan's daughter but "do unto others" and all that. And besides, you're supposed to be getting back with Barnie—and you know how jealous he is of Will already. Get out of it, Barbie.
Go to Scene 4

Scene 153

With a bit of cajoling you get Natasha to her feet. She just feels dizzy. A few glasses of water and she'll be roaring—but first get her home.

It takes a few minutes to bundle her off the boat and onto your waiting bike. Fortunately, you always carry a spare helmet for just such occasions. Before you set off, you look into her eyes for signs of conscious awareness and gratifyingly the eyes smile back at you. Maybe you made the right decision . . .

She hitches up her already short dress and clamps you between dancer's thighs. With an internal cry of triumph, you open up the throttle and hurtle into the night.

Go to Scene 47

Scene 154

"Gerald, you're looking very well. How are you?"

Gerald Laithwaite, the sports minister, doesn't know you from Eve, but he's not near the top of the greasy pole for nothing. His sallow face lights up in recognition.

"What a lovely surprise. I didn't realize you were here."

"Wouldn't have missed it for the world. Wonderful speeches." Turning to the small circle you introduce yourself. "Barbarella, pleased to meet you."

And you shake hands in turn. To your dismay, catalogue boy has used your entrance to escape. So instead you meet the Welsh secretary, a rather sour-looking probable lesbian; David, a chartered accountant who can't avert his eyes from your feet; a handsome black stand-up comic, and a couple of nodders whose details you don't quite catch.

Without pausing, you place yourself at the center of attention. "So, what great public issue are we bringing our collective intellect to bear upon tonight, gentlemen?"

The men are bomb-shelled by your confidence and the Welsh secretary silently vows to bleach her upper lip. Gerald answers for the group. "We're rerunning the euro debate. For or against, Barbarella?"

Oh, God. You hadn't realized how unfortunate this was going to be. Do this quickly and painlessly—wow them with your knowledge, insult the Welsh secretary (you always hated her self-righteous, chip-on-shoulder blend of screeching politics), and bedazzle the attractive comedian standing stoically next to her.

With a gleaming smile, you go and claim your prize.

"I think we can learn a lot from the respective histories of Italy and Germany."

When you're depressed and can't sleep, you watch TV—BBC 2 Learning Zone has some marvelous programs for insomnia. You dredge some semisubliminal memories of "Introduction to Modern European History."

"Before the unification of Italy only 4 percent of the common people spoke Italian, in Germany the figure was 97 percent. The unification of Germany allowed Bismarck to create a world superpower, in Italy there followed seventy-five years of misrule and misery. I think the lesson is pretty clear—without cultural unity how can we expect to achieve proper democracy?"

OK, you made up the percentages, but it doesn't diminish the impact. With smug satisfaction you see that the comedian is gazing into your shining eyes.

Time to finish this off. You poke the minister for Wales on the shoulder with a firm finger. "How many euro-MPs can you name?"

She stiffens, eager to smash you with her political acumen. "Probably all of them. I used to be minister for Europe . . . and 64 percent of Eur—" But you don't give her time to continue (you've exhausted your entire thoughts on the EU).

You smile at the comedian. "Maybe you're right, there might be some benefits. I suppose eventually all of our politicians will be forced to emigrate to Brussels."

The comedian laughs generously. You smile and touch the Welsh secretary's crossed arm. "Only joking."

The comedian notices you drain your glass. Game over.

"Can I get you another drink, Barbarella?"

You smile demurely, offer an arm, and float back to the bar.

Go to Scene 168

Scene 155

She laughs a little awkwardly and excuses herself to go to the loo. You wait expectantly for five minutes. Then another five, and another. You begin to feel embarrassed, standing alone with two empty glasses. Then Barbarella comes to your rescue.

"Barnaby, what are you doing over here on your own? Not having a breather surely? It's not even midnight. What happened to that Aussie girl you were schmoozing over? She didn't blow you away?"

"Um no, she's just, um, just nipped in the loo. I gave her a full dose of Kamran's Viagra mix. I'm a bit worried . . . She's been in there quarter of an hour."

"Probably masturbating. Leave her; she'll be no use to anyone when she staggers out. We're all going to another party. Why don't you come along?"

You hesitate.

Barbarella, suddenly turning into Shirley Temple, pouts like a spoiled child.

"Oh, come on, it'll be fun. I haven't spoken to you all night and I'm getting withdrawal symptoms."

Hmmn. Barbarella is blatantly coming on to you. And there is an outside chance you blew it with the "boil your eggs" line. Maybe Natasha has made a bid for freedom. Or maybe she is strumming in the loo. Either way you've buggered it up. Perhaps it is better to walk away now with happy memories and no regrets—and with Barbarella.

"Don't pull faces, Barbie. The wind may change. Take me to your party. Where is it?"

Go to Scene 97

Scene 156

"Excuse me, do you know where I can find another drink? I just don't seem able to find the bar anywhere."

Excellent start. Four gentlemen make motions to help, but you determinedly hold onto your favored candidate's arm and tug him away. He receives some supportive looks from his colleagues of the "get in there" variety. You turn, look blankly into his square, handsome face, and ask: "Sorry, I didn't mean to interrupt you. You seemed to be having a very important conversation?"

"No, you saved me from a discussion about the euro," he says with a trace of Scots brogue.

"What's the euro?"

He looks at you curiously. You're overdoing it, Barbie—no one is that stupid, not even a weather girl doing the rounds. Aim for bubbly airhead, not imbecile.

He takes your hand, "My name's Martin," and leads you protectively towards the bar.

"My goodness, is the bar really here? I thought it was the cloakroom. How silly."

You giggle, suggesting genuine bewilderment, as if you've never been let out on your own before. Again, Martin gives you a sideways glance, still suspicious.

"Can I get you that drink?"

"I'll have a gin and slim, please."

Martin raises an elegant finger to the barman. "Two gin and

slimline tonics, please." The barman smiles enthusiastically and starts scuttling ice.

"Oh, I'm sorry, I haven't introduced myself. I'm Barbie."

He can't help laughing when he hears your name.

"Pleased to meet you, Barbie. So what are you doing at a party to celebrate the black music industry?"

"Oh really? Is that why there are so many famous people? I didn't know. My friend brought me because her boyfriend dumped her last night. How funny."

Martin starts gazing at the river through a Thameside porthole. Time to raise your IQ a few notches.

"So, are you a trendy record producer?"

"God no, I'm here to do a piece for *Heat* magazine . . . I'm a journo."

"Ooh, I bet you know lots of juicy gossip."

He laughs. "I haven't got a clue who anyone is. The only black singer I know is Ella Fitzgerald."

You smile. This is going better.

"So why are you here?" you ask.

"Favor for a friend." Martin bites his lip and the conversation trails off. Standing tall, no wedding ring, with a puzzled schoolboy look on his face—he really is yummy. Don't let this one slip, Barbarella.

"He must be a close friend for you to spend two hours listening to political speeches."

"Yeah, he is."

You can picture the two of you walking arm in arm across the Highlands, warmed only by whisky and body heat. He would be wearing a creamy sweater and hacker jacket. You would be attired entirely in Burberry, except for the Afghan-fur-trimmed hat bought for you by your mother. Two cocker spaniels would skip gaily by your side. The sun would set on your remote croft without having encountered another soul all day; you won't need anybody else, a log fire awaits . . .

Slowly, girl. You only met him five minutes ago.

And then, as he talks of journalism and you gaze adoringly up at his strong face, with his perfect brow and thick long lashes, you can't ignore a rumble of unease in your subconscious.

Some nagging thought is telling you something . . . that this man means trouble . . .

Do you trust to your feminine intuition—cut and run? **Go to Scene 28**

Do you trust in his male instincts—continue the dumb-blonde façade? **Go to Scene 160**

Scene 157

You manage to resist hurling your glass into the fireplace—but only barely—such is your renewed *bonhomie*. And so with the bravado of a Nazi general invading Russia you foretell of your great victory and explain the plan:

Operation Shylock

Our Respective Strengths:
Kamran Jazeer: Can seduce a dead nun
Will Burton: Smooth as a buttered bottom
Cat Henderson: Ruthless
Astrid Van Staveren: Shameless
Barbarella Carrington: Nerveless
Barnaby Wilson: Huge brain
Opponent's Weaknesses:
Rich
Stupid
Disaster Recovery:
Sergeant Henderson and Private Van Staveren will be responsible for disaster recovery. If the players require a diversion at any stage they will make a fist; this signal requires a prompt yet minor diversion, a thirty-second distraction. If things go seriously awry, I will give the double fisting signal. Then we'll require a towering inferno/biblical flood.

Stage 1

Captain Kamran befriends Sally, the waitress from Hackney, seduces and obtains access to her and the cubby via the upstairs bedrooms.

Stage 2

Colonel Burton gets Field Marshal Barbie and me a seat at the top table.

Stage 3

Kamran spies everything from the cubby and signals to the players below.

We clean up.

The five stare, in awe of your genius. You haven't seen Kamran looking so excited since *Basic Instinct* came out on DVD. Will injects a note of realism.

"And what do we do for capital? Sell Astrid's body?"

"From little acorns, William," you're on a roll, you have them in your palm. "It's credit card time, guys . . ."

You flick a gold card into an empty ashtray. The plastic clicks on marble unimpressively as you try to calculate when you last made a payment; Will is quick to trump—eager not to seem cheap. Barbie's corporate Amex follows, forcing a finesse from Kamran, Catherine, and finally Astrid's Capital One. Nestled together they make a happy collection—an orgy of credit.

"All for one and all that."

Will scoops up and is off to the cashier. Kamran follows, eager to receive his instructions and spot a suitable bar wench. Astrid and Cat pair off to hatch imaginative escape plans. And you are left alone with Barbie.

Left to your own devices for more than a few minutes, you always revert to the carnal. Tonight is no exception. Barbarella is blatantly flirting.

"Barnie, this is going to be great. I don't ever remember you being so clever . . . or so . . . commanding."

You laugh out loud.

"Barbie, you know you used to hate it whenever I took control—'Barbie the control freak,' remember? Demand, demand, take, take."

You didn't mean to be quite that harsh, but it doesn't matter, Barbie's not one to be bullied. Instead, she uses her charm to make you feel guilty.

"Barnie, you meanie, that's not fair. Tell you what, if that's how you feel, let me make it up to you," she pauses for added drama and pulls a pen and scrap of paper from her bag. "I present you with the greatest gift in my power. I grant you . . . a fantasy."

You take the proffering uncertainly. "What do you mean?"

"Oh, don't be so obtuse. Your dirty little mind is full of them. Just write one down, and when the night is over . . . I will perform."

"Anything?"

"Anything."

Time to exercise that eager mind, Barnie, for a free run of the sweet shop. This may be a once in a lifetime offer, so choose very, very carefully.

So much to do, so little time. Do you write:

"I want you to seduce a girl, bind and blindfold her . . . then let me join in." **Go to Scene 53**

"I want to visit an S&M club. You'll have to do anything I ask." **Go to Scene 41**

"I love you, Barbarella. Will you marry me?" **Go to Scene 253**

Scene 158

Up on deck, the gentle summer air fans your fervid desires. The sky is darkening with an intense blur of cerulean and navy blue. The Embankment is still crowded, the people only marginally less visible as the dark draws an easy close to the day. Martin's menswear catalogue jawline is silhouetted perfectly. For some time, you both remain silent, taking in the beautiful evening.

But time and Barbarella wait for no man. He brushes an invisible speck of lint from his cuff and you take the opportunity to take hold of his hand, cupping them in both of yours. Now that you've got his attention, you fix your eyes on his. One of your tests. A weak man will look away, flustered. A genuine player will hold your stare until you're a kissable distance away. But Martin doesn't even seem to be focusing on you; this is turning out to be a hard play. Maybe he just doesn't go for dumb blondes. As if to pull off an imaginary wig, you seek out an explanation with your normal voice.

"Martin, staring into space is supposed to be one of the five clinical signs of chronic depression. What exactly is so fascinating about the Thames? You seem completely detached. And don't tell me you're interested in rivers."

"So you've decided to drop the dumb-blonde bit. If it's any consolation, you're not very convincing." He smiles to show no hard feelings. "Sorry, I'm not very good value at the moment, am I? My boyfriend is in the Navy and I haven't seen him for over a month."

Oh, Barbie. Schoolgirl error.

Slimline tonic, Ella Fitzgerald, the poor guy couldn't have made it plainer if he'd hummed a Kylie song. The stunning ones are always gay. You must have been terrifying, not titillating him.

How utterly humiliating.

"I miss him so much. I just wish I could hug him."

Barbie, don't even think about it. The man is gay, GAY. He's more interested in your dress than what is in it. Don't you think you've humiliated yourself enough for one evening?

"Martin, you could always hug me as a substitute." Trust your charms. No man is 100 percent gay—surely? **Go to Scene 162**

Risk your Jourdain heels by sprinting a retreat? **Go to Scene 92**

Scene 159

You charge north, not caring where you end up. Twisting your way across London, imagining the "rozzers" on your tail, you eventually pull up opposite a McDonald's in Baker Street. You step away from the incriminating bike and pull out your mobile. "6 missed calls" it accuses, and so you dial Barbarella's number from memory. She picks up immediately and her comforting concern fills your ears. "Barnaby, where the hell are you? Nobody saw you leave, but we couldn't find you."

You cut her off, aware that your license number may be circulating the Metropolitan Police airwaves. "Barbie, just tell me where you are and I'll meet you there."

"We're in a cab. We're going to the West India. Mention Will's name on the door."

And so you head west, dreading the imminent sound of a police siren all the way. You stop once to check the address and soon find yourself parked in a discreet street. Dismounting, you leave your bike cunningly concealed behind a Range Rover, adjust your tie *à la* Sean Connery in *Goldfinger*, and hope to God that Natasha is doing her bit to keep you out of jail. Still, better report the bike stolen in the morning.

The West India Club is one of Will's favorite haunts. You fundamentally despise casinos but at the same time can't resist it. Full of poor sophisticates and rich trash, each symbiotically feeding off the other.

Will adores the place because he can strut his pedigree and supplement his income at the same time (there's only so much money an alcoholic can make from selling wine). Barbarella loves it because the place is packed with filthy rich males. Admittedly most will be fat, ugly, or generally filthy, but the odd dashing blade will crop up.

But never mind; in the game of love you have been a poor loser all evening. Luck must change, so deal the deck and play another hand. If you don't turn up the Queen of Hearts you may find a running flush and walk away with lots of lovely cash. Steel your frayed nerves, Barnie Baby, 'cause gambling is not for the weak. This club is swilling with cash and it's not often you get an invite, so nose to the trough and scoff your fill.

Go to Scene 29

Scene 160

He is stunning after all. As if possessed by some killer instinct, you rise to the challenge and become determined to make this man want you.

"Martin, your bow-tie's all crooked." He seems a bit perturbed as you invade his personal space in order to adjust and smarten, but before you step back you look up into his eyes, breathe him in deeply, and expose a hint of tongue.

It's usually a foolproof combination, but Martin's expression only registers alarm. This really is turning out to be a challenge. Perhaps he's shy and would prefer a bit more privacy.

"Martin, will you join me up on deck for some fresh air?"

He seems obsessed with looking out of portholes, so you may as well give him what he wants. He nods, places his hands on your waist, and eases you up the stairs.

Go to Scene 158

Scene 161

The Tale of William

Will's father lost much of his fortune at the West India—cars, stables, stolen Russian icons. When he came and Mrs. Burton was "entertaining," William Junior would be dragged along to the casino. Fortunately Will's mate, Giles, was the same age and they used to cause havoc trying to steal chips and look up women's skirts. They used to run amok that is, until the night they found the cubby.

The cubby is a cupboard in a bedroom above the stud room.

The stud room, it turns out, is the exclusive back room where the big boys play five-card stud for big money. The stud room is the place where men have been rumored to have lost $4 million-plus in a single night. The stud room is the room for gamblers with big, swinging dicks. The stud room is seriously scary.

Overlooking the cubby is a small periscope that was installed by the late Earl's grandfather. He set up a system whereby a footman could overlook the game and signal to the Earl using specially designed levers to rotate a chandelier in the stud. Sounds both ingenious and ridiculous but the Earl was shot dead one night in mysterious circumstances in St. James's Park, so who knows.

Will finishes his tale to universal silence. You look from Barbie to Astrid to Cat to Kamran and everyone is smiling. Each now possesses a small plumbeous nugget of information. Only you know how to turn it into gold . . .

The plan is still forming in your mind as you propose a new toast. You grab a tray full of drinks from a perky waitress called Sally; smile as she complains that they are for "sumwan ouse" in fluent Hackney; give her a twenty-quid tip, a pat on the bottom, and then ask for six glasses of brandy to be raised then tipped as you exclaim in perfect Spanish: "*En todos los casinos siempre hay alguien* más idiota *que tu*."

"In every casino there is someone more stupid than you."

Go to Scene 157

Scene 162

Martin grins at your suggestion, but condescends to give you a sisterly hug and a peck on the top of your head. Bursting with desperate vitality, you spend a wonderfully pleasant evening chatting about everyone and everything. You go back to his place in Hoxton, dance to Abba, and listen to Aretha Franklin's "If You Go Away" over and over. Eventually you both fall asleep on the sofa.

Congratulations, Barbie. In Martin you have a new best friend. A man who is articulate, sensitive, and interested in your bitching. If only "fag hag" weren't such an unpleasant expression.

The (Testosterone Free) End

Not the steamiest of endings. If that's the kind of man you're after you might have better luck as Barnaby. Remember, you can have whatever you want . . .

Scene 163

Back at HQ, Barbarella makes elaborate preparations. She mixes you a vodka martini and while you wait, showers, changes into a new (smaller???) dress, and sits smoking, nervously toying with a shoe on the end of her toe.

She occasionally smiles, but all conversation is superfluous. You desperately want to ask "*Who?*," but that seems a little pushy. So you content yourself with vodka and settle back in a deep armchair, conserving energy.

Then, as your pulse finally slows to its regular seventy-eight beats, the doorbell rings . . .

Barbarella, suddenly all fluster, rushes to her feet, slopping alcohol and "shitshitshit"ing all the way to door. Almost absent-mindedly she turns: "For Christ's sake get out of sight. Hide in the kitchen and don't stick your nose out until I come and get you."

Barbarella's kitchen, immaculately designed by the great lady herself and fitted with every item for a pleasant culinary experience, has no joy to offer you. Even in the first ten minutes you grow bored of its charming blue tiling. The cookery books offer no distraction bar the odd picture of Nigella, and after fifteen minutes you're ready to break the door down. The mere thought of the seduction tantalizes . . . On the other side of the thin internal wall there sits a glamorous and undoubtedly gorgeous acquaintance of Barbarella's; obviously straight but being lured to forbidden vice by the coke-laden temptress, Barbarella. You can see Barbarella now, leaning forward, lightly touching the victim's forearm, incrementally closing in, tongue tantalizingly touching at her top lip. You imagine the drug-ridden thought processes of the prey . . . the sight of Barbarella's long, tanned legs, the firm tight body . . . by now Barbarella's intentions will be obvious—the new girl will be thinking desperately . . . "Should I? . . . just for one night . . . no one need ever find out . . ."

Barbarella breaks rudely into your reverie, full of libidinous excitement. "I am a goddess . . . almost home and dry, just don't forget, you owe me big time. The cow has flown south, I repeat, the red cow has flown south. All systems go. All systems go . . ."

She starts up the empty microwave for a five-minute spin and, with the flushed cheeks of victory, whispers loudly in your ear, "The object is now bound to my four-poster with stockings and has an old sarong tied round her head. Give me five minutes to warm her up . . ." A quick pointed look at the microwave timer, ". . . and the little tigress is all yours."

And so she leaves, clutching a bottle of extra virgin and a fork.

The next five minutes age you by a decade. A beautiful mental image of a naked Catherine keeps you insanely feverish—her pert high-nippled breasts covered in olive oil . . . Or could it be Barbie's old school buddy, the blonde, snooty Caroline, with the lisp?

The microwave dings a summons.

You swallow from a dry mouth, take a deep breath, and venture into the bedroom. The lounge lights are already dimmed and your eyes are still maladjusted when you finally creep into the perfume-scented bedroom. Only a groan warns that you are not alone. Suddenly hands are holding you. They are Barbarella's. She whispers into your ear, "She's all yours, *chiquito*. Don't let me down, I've got a reputation to consider." And so she leaves you alone with a random woman spread-eagled for your pleasure and four hours left till the dawn . . .

You touch the soft flesh of a naked thigh and it twitches under your fingertip. And as you run along the oiled length of it you smell Greek salads and think of holidays in Eos and remember beach fumblings and the smell of the sea and . . . and then your eyes adjust. They adjust just in time to prevent gross indecency . . . for the thigh is bigger than expected, the body has a certain European stature—and no mistaking the head, for it is the head of Astrid . . .

Somewhere in the back of your saddened brain you hear Barbarella's front door slam shut. But it barely registers. She has sold you a lemon.

Astrid's generous body quivers at the lack of stimulation. You look to the ceiling for divine guidance but receive none.

Nothing for it, you must go to work . . .

The (Think of England) End

Oh dear, Reader. Barnie may be happy with second best but are you? Barbarella has treated you like a fool. Go back and get some revenge.

Scene 164

Here is the problem with you and Will: it's so easy to slip back into bad habits. Kissing turns to impassioned indulgence. There's a sense of desperation about your actions, almost like a prisoner's last request. No blindfold, cigarettes, or phone calls. God no. Just magnificent, intense sensations with the high-cheek-boned, light-featured, and floppy-haired William.

His fine hands run up your thighs, gently pushing them apart. They emanate a heat that could melt you. You rapidly reach the point where your surroundings descend into a fathomless blur. So much for Barnaby. The only thing on your mind is Will and five barely decipherable letters: S C R E W.

Looks like you've got some stamina, Barbie . . . but, nearing a disheveled state, you're both startled by a rattling door handle. Shit, you completely forgot that Annabel is on board. It's your motto, Barbie, "Don't get caught—ever."

"Barbie, *quickly.*"

Will breaks your thoughts. You have to do something fast. Well, there's either under the desk or in the closet. You'd normally have a choice but the fact is Will's increasingly portly build rules out the desk. You both run for cover in the closet and with seconds to spare pull the door behind you. Clever girl, you remembered the champagne.

Try not to breathe so loudly, have a sip of bubbly, and wait.

Go to Scene 18

Scene 165

And with no minor Tae Kwon Do talent (learned from Kamran, who uses it in extramarital self-defense) you apply slight pressure to the back of the doorman's knee, using your left foot, and prod him down the steps using only a thumb. It looks good and impresses girls but is a tad sneaky. You feel no pang of guilt as he crashes to the pavement, just jubilation. Tonight you're rewriting the rulebook. But you'd better get inside quickly, just in case. Shutting the door firmly, you find yourself in a warm, elegant hallway.

You spot Barbarella quickly; She's air kissing vibrantly, and, better still, Catherine now has her arm round you in thanks and admiration. The sound of money changing hands fills your ears.

Last time you were here you won $5,000-plus from an idiot inbred Russian, only to drop the lot on the roulette tables. You learned your lesson that night. At the West India, the house always wins. After all, the guy who owns this place (Will's godfather, just for the record) has just come through another messy and expensive divorce.

The club itself is stunningly fitted in deep oaks and mahoganies. The austerity of the wood is calmed with silk Persian rugs and *chaises longues* draped in rich fabrics and rich women. Your favorite part has always been the superbly stocked bar, including its choice in barmaids. All are bright students desperate to pay off loans, and willing to flirt outrageously with the clientele.

You spot a new little brunette, on tiptoes, reaching for a bottle. Perfect for making Barbie jealous. You decide to introduce yourself.

But before you get anywhere, Will is pumping your hand and placing a cigar in the other. Kamran is smiling wickedly as Catherine relays details of your heroic exploits on the doorstep (*Sun* headline style—"Sting like a Barnabee," you know the sort of thing) and Barbarella is "so proud."

And you, Barnie—"Lion of the Hour"—you smile nonchalantly, as any man of action would. You save the policeman story for later (when you're alone with the lads and you've perfected the exaggeration), because for now you're happy to bask in Catherine's embellishment and Barbarella's ebullience. Now that you're with Will, you'll be safe from any doorman vengeance—even if he does recover from the fall (Will's godfather *really* does own the place). And so, as the others laugh around you, the stress floats away.

Will does, eventually, manage to change the subject. "Bit of an odd crowd in tonight—no Americans. We'll have to sharpen up to stand any chance of minting it. Now, I've been thinking about how we can make a killing and . . ."

Will is ranting now, but snuggled beneath his drone you hide for a moment, safe with your thoughts . . . You commit the image of Natasha's tan-lined bottom to your long-term memory—safe for recall in your sexual dotage. And as you relish the vision of the pert little body and bouncing breasts—hardened by exposure to the cool night air—you consider whether she would have been worth a few nights in prison . . . perhaps.

But before you can slump into nostalgic sexual contemplation, something breaks your reverie. Kamran is equally uninterested in Will's chatter; he is busy hawking at the rich elderly and poor young, caught between two desires. *And then you catch him.*

Blatantly he clocks Barbarella up and down—ogling every

detail, every curve of flesh and dip of bone, sucking up the mental image. For a fleeting scintilla, the most overwhelming passion is etched on his face. He almost looks angry.

Kamran is in love with Barbarella. Of course he is—any man with a pulse would be—and Kam most certainly has a raging pulse (he has a collection of aerobics videos, for heaven's sake). That explains why he's always causing fights between you and Barbie.

"Ra Ra Ra Ra Ra Ra Ra cheat Ra Ra Ra Ra made a fortune Ra Ra Ra Ra Ha Ha Ha."

Desperately your brain and ears focus. Sexual longing can wait. For once, Will has something interesting to say . . .

"The old man was a tremendous cheat, you see. He introduced the 'Cubby'—fantastic fun. Giles and I used to hide in there and watch them play in the stud . . ."

"Hold on." Will's diatribe is meaningless code, but if you can translate into English the potential of the cubby seems interesting. "Start at the beginning. Who is Giles and what is the 'Cubby'?"

And so Will takes a deep breath and, patronizingly at first but then with childish enthusiasm, takes you through his childhood tale.

Go to Scene 161

Scene 166

Excellent choice. Some fresh country air is just what you need. Drain your drinks and head back to St. John's Wood. And so to Hampshire. The weekend-bag doesn't take long to pack and soon you are all down in the car, ready to go. Astrid buckles up in the back while you and Catherine don Chloé shades and turn on the CD player. The Mercedes SLK hood flattens with the smooth grace of a limbo dancer and, with the sun shining a light orange, you gently ease into the busy London traffic. Don't forget, Barbie, despite two liters of Evian and an industrial liver, you are probably still four times over the limit. So take it easy.

The city grime is soon replaced by motorway grime but with Travis tripping over the muffled sound of the engine, you don't care. As the sky begins to turn a vibrant navy, you turn off the M3 and are suddenly immersed in trees and hedgerows. The innocent country road requires significantly more skill to navigate and a few careless swings alert you to danger. An hour's driving has done little to sober you. Slow down, perhaps?

No way. "Who wants to live forever?" Speed on. **Go to Scene 190**

Not so flash. Slow down. **Go to Scene 170**

Scene 167

Your limbs are numb. The chandelier continues to creak mockingly, but your brain fizzes and your mouth is so dry you can barely speak. Luckily an instinct for self-preservation sparks to your rescue. With creaking willpower, you lift both hands onto the green baize. You feel like a drowning man floating to the dark bottom of an icy lake. Somehow you manage one last act; barely noticing the spinning chandelier you make a small fist with each hand and, with the last twitching energy of a corpse, you look Jenner in the eye, smile, and wait for "disaster recovery" to kick in.

Nothing happens. You made the double fisting signal and nothing happened. You look casually up at Catherine and realize she's too absorbed with the game to react to anything. She is staring at your down-turned cards, oblivious of the fanning chandelier, oblivious of your fists, and oblivious of the fact that you are all about to be rendered bankrupt—names dragged through the gutter, homes gone, bike gone, no sex, ever. Just do something, Cat, you stupid, stupid bitch.

Catherine stands transfixed and you have no option but to turn over your first card.

Ace of diamonds.

Your hand returns to a fist in one last, silent cry. Nothing.

You go to your second card. To reveal it will be to admit defeat. You finger it slowly, feeling its crisp edge cut into your fingertip.

The chandelier fans you gently, but does little to dry the sweat on your upper lip. Nothing matters now.

And then she comes to your rescue. Astrid, your beautiful, witty, European cousin.

"Mr. Jenner, please pass me the coke."

She leans across to reach the tray and, with dexterous use of muscles you didn't know women had, breaks out of her long-suffering dress. They bounce like sprung toys and in her panic, she contrives to slip and collapse onto the table with all her heavy-boned weight. The antique table, survivor of French revolution and German bombing, gives up its life to your cause. It cracks and shatters into a thousand shards of joy.

Everyone is mesmerized. Astrid, lying magnificently on a heap of cards and dollar bills, spills forth flesh from her ambitiously small dress. Jenner rages impotently and lunges forward to reclaim his cards.

The horror of the next few moments will forever stick in your mind.

The sight of Jenner scrabbling on all fours near the half-naked Astrid could be a cure for premature ejaculation. Jenner scrabbles like a blood-swollen tick; you dance in, and, pausing only to tweak his cheek, scoop up a handful of cash and drag Barbie out of the stud.

"Just keep walking and smiling, go out the front door, and we'll be doing ninety down the Embankment with a hundred grand in fifteen minutes. Just keep smiling . . ."

Taking your advice, Barbie is not slow to take advantage of the Belgium-sent salvation. Jenner, sluggish oaf though he is, manages to sidestep Will and is out of the stud and shouting after you. But by pressing a ludicrously large note into the doorman's hand, you skip out of the front door and fly down short steps to motorized safety.

Go to Scene 45

Scene 168

The comedian is familiar.

"So how come I recognize you?"

"George," he finishes for you before answering, "I'm on the late-night token Channel 4, black comic slot. I don't suppose you're an insomniac."

He flashes bright pearly teeth. You taste iron in the back of your mouth.

Remember, Barbie, five minutes only—then leave. Any longer and the inscrutable temptress will be stripped of her veil. Five minutes, then give him your business card and away. He'll call Monday (he won't want to look too eager). When he asks what you're up to on Wednesday, you'll be busy, but you'll offer Thursday. And if the free dinner's good, who knows what could happen?

But no time to dwell on the future, George has finished talking. Shit, you've no idea what he just asked you. What to say? You could just say yes—it usually works. Best not, you could be agreeing to anything . . . if in doubt fall back on fail-safe largesse—change the subject with bold flattery.

Which is it to be?

"Yeah, I agree." **Go to Scene 184**

"I love the way your mind works. Are you clever as well as funny?" **Go to Scene 124**

Scene 169

The pub is only seconds away by bike. You could have walked but no opportunity to cruise the King's Road on the red beast should ever be forsaken. Barbarella is late; it's part of her charm. You use the time to sit companionably and silently, and reorder some of your troubled thoughts.

"BarbieBarbieBarbie."

The closest thing to love you've ever experienced and the only woman to ever leave you for another man. You were never sure whether there was a causal connection. Still, that is history. You had nine months of Meg Ryan–Tom Hanks bliss and then suddenly, without warning, an e-mail brought proceedings to a crashing close.

"Superb," says Kamran as he thrusts a Saturday *Telegraph* into your face, shattering your introspection. "Looks like Ms. Catherine Henderson is back on the campaign trail."

"Minister Admits Affair" reads the headline. Below is printed an action photo of Catherine, Barbarella's flatmate and best friend. She's leaving a posh restaurant with the minister without portfolio, Edward Bunger. At the bottom of the page is printed a family album pic. The ingratiating minister hugs up to his dog, two teenagers, and fat wife.

"Catherine must be worried to have lost out to that," Kamran snorts with disgust. You can see his mind working. Catherine has toyed with Kamran ever since they first met over two years ago. Kamran sniffs opportunity.

"So much for the comfort and reassurance of a father figure. What she needs is a good . . ."

"Well, let's ask her, shall we," you interject as Barbarella saunters into the beer garden with trademark sanguinity and Catherine—the woman of the moment—in tow.

As Barbarella double kisses, Cat politely greets, strained but still smiling. Your eyes smile beneath your glasses as you contemplate the two girls. Barbarella is prettier and blonder, and fills rooms with her personality. Her legs make up at least two thirds of her sixty-eight inches. Catherine, darker-haired and paler-skinned, always looks as though her taller friend shades her from the full force of the sun. Kamran, still holding the newspaper, cracks a joke to break the ice and cheer her up.

"At least it's a good photo; you might get some topless work with the *News of the World*."

But Barbie is in one of her menstrual moods. "Don't be a dick, Kamran. Go and get us some drinks—we need them."

God, she can be a snotty bitch. For once, you decide not to let her get away with it.

"For Christ's sake, Barbie, Kamran was just trying to make a joke . . ."

"Yeah. That sort of twattish comment is really going to cheer Catherine up."

Kamran finds the whole thing vastly embarrassing; you're not going to let Barbarella throw a juvenile fit and get away with it.

"Barbie, it was a joke . . . a stupid little joke."

Then you notice Catherine's soulful eyes filling with tears. Her elfin frame shudders with suppressed emotion and a thought of genius strikes you: *be the one caring friend who understands.* You can guarantee Barbie will be utterly rubbish, and that leaves a major vacancy for the "compassionate-buddy" slot. Because when you and Catherine are well and truly buddied up, it will drive Barbarella absolutely nuts—*and she'll be sleeping with you in under a week.* The thought process takes barely a second.

"Look, Catherine, we're really sorry about . . ." You trail off, with the acting talent of Keanu Reeves, look down at the newspaper, and back up at Catherine. "Look, Kamran was just about to go to the bar—what d'you want?"

Kamran gets the drinks in, you get a bench for the girls, and Barbie is left with no doubt that you won't put up with her tantrums. The first few rounds fly by, beer flows, and Barbie becomes more animated with every gulp. She's in boisterous form, challenging you to flirt but slamming your every attempt. You satisfy yourself with giving Catherine more sympathy and some good advice.

But others are due to arrive and breach the close intimacy of your little foursome. First Astrid, Barbarella's latest hanger-on, swings in on Rollerblades. Normally the sight of 36 Fs stuffed into Lycra would provoke carnal desire, and indeed, a few weeks ago it did just that. But now you shudder with the wisdom of experience. Astrid is a beast. Then, finally, William arrives. He stands on the seat of his soft-top MGB, peers over the wall and down at you,

"Barbarella, my love mate, I have come to you," he flirts ostentatiously over a stiff rugby-shirt collar. "Barnie, pint of Guinness."

Will used to be a good friend; he even introduced you to Barbarella. But then you showed a bit too much interest in her—you, a Romford Comprehensive alumnus. It was almost as if you'd committed some gross breach of etiquette by sleeping with one of Will's exes—by stepping outside your own social limits and daring to play on William's turf. The friendship is still there but your pithy exchanges have dwindling warmth. You never really minded the Essex-boy gibes, but now you sense that the digs are meant to hurt not amuse. Deep down he's an insecure snob who's never forgiven his father for blowing the family fortune. Will boasts of his parents' Monaco retreat but fails to mention that they retreated there to avoid debts.

Will waves down at his car, "Just got to park the old madam," and disappears from sight. Unfortunately, he finds somewhere and is soon tucking into the afternoon's entertainment—gin, tonic, and Cat's disastrous news.

"Tell me, Cat," he asks with apparent concern, "what's it like sleeping with a minister? Was the power a huge turn-on?"

And to your amazement Catherine, well ginned-up by now, gives an answer.

"William, you're a wine merchant—you get women drunk to get them into bed. Edward is a politician; he talks for a living, so he uses his tongue . . . I'll e-mail you the photos if you want some pointers."

And with that offer, she leaves Will with a frozen half-smile and goes to the bar.

As the afternoon trundles its sun-dappled course your conversation gets louder and more vulgar. People on the neighboring tables are starting to look uneasy. Barbarella keeps avoiding your questions about last night; Kamran, with the clock ticking down to his arranged marriage, is looking twitchy as he jokingly interrogates Catherine about JPEGs; and Astrid is beginning to sense your collective lack of interest. You consider asking how her job hunting is going but a wobble as she crosses her legs brings back too many memories.

Will has been unusually mild today, almost back to his old friendly self. You decide to shake him out of his reflections.

"So what've you been up to, Will?"

"What've I been up to? Umm, good question. I'm getting married."

The clock above the bar twitches to a halt; a small dog in the corner looks up from a juicy bone. Kamran chokes to death on a pistachio nut; Cat drops a tray of gin and tonics, and Barbarella's breast implants explode. At least that's how you will always remember it.

Will, one time ItBoy, eligible bachelor and playboy—famous to *Hello* magazine readers for his wild party-going lifestyle. Admittedly he's thinner on top of late, but to have sunk to marriage? With a sudden overwhelming compassion you realize Will is giving up, accepting a slide into middle age.

Barbarella is the first to recover. "Great," is all she manages. And before you know it you're backslapping, drinking, and toasting. Gallows humor has always been your strength and it's sorely needed now.

"So, Will, when's the big day?"

"Three months' time . . . September 21st, in the chapel at Annabel's parents' house. Invites are on their way."

"On their way? You only got engaged last night!"

"What can I say? Annabel, she's a bit of an administrative marvel," answers Will with appropriate embarrassment.

His mobile rings a rescue and he stands to answer. "Hi, Pumpkin."

You all turn to eavesdrop on Will's conversation.

"Flowers . . . uh, not sure, what do you think?"

He stands and walks to the far end of the garden for more privacy.

You mouth to Kamran: "*Pumpkin??*"

But Kam is having a sense of humor failure.

"This is totally not right. He might as well commit suicide. This is all your fault, Catherine. He's on the rebound because you dumped him for a fifty-year-old."

Oh God, raking up more friend-incest from the past. Catherine did indeed have a brief fling with Will, back in the winter. And she did indeed dump on his ego by leaving him for an older man. But, with no sense of justice, Catherine defends herself.

"That has nothing to do with it, Kam. Will's just feeling his age . . . men do weird things when they get paunchy."

For once Barbie's is the voice of reason.

"Guys, save it for Annabel. Look, if Will marries her, he'll be buggered for the rest of his life. I know what she's like, I went to school with her, and if she wants something she won't stop at *anything* to get it. And she wants Will. Whatever she's done for, or to, Will, we've just got to get him out of it. He just needs to remember how good it is to be single."

You aren't exactly sure what she intends, and with a pang you suspect that she may be offering herself as a stalking horse. Stalker more like it. You knew she always wanted to get back with Will, and now she's probably out of her mind with jealousy. Why can't she just let Will get on with it? He's made his decision.

Calm it, Barnaby, this jealousy is eating you up. The thought of Barbarella's long legs wrapped around another man fills you with a sickening feeling. But Will is returning, and the conversation and your thoughts must return to anodyne felicitation.

The afternoon soon blurs into early evening, and for some ungodly reason Kamran decides that at a quarter past six it's time for a round of champagne tequila-slammers. Your stomach instinctively convulses at the first whiff. Kamran is obviously looking for a quick kill with Catherine.

Barnaby, you're the mouthy one; you usually make the toasts. But for some reason the words don't form. Will senses your collective hesitation and with self-inflation he steps in and makes his own toast.

Hands are over shot glasses, all look expectantly round, awaiting the signal, when Will declares in broken Spanish: "*En todos los bares hay alguien que te follaria*."

"What does that mean?" grins Astrid. Before you can translate, Will repeats, this time in English and with an unrepentant smile: "In every bar there is someone who will fuck you."

Bang, bang, bang. Tequila slips down and you can't help smiling. Too much mescal worm perhaps. The chilling disappointment of last night. The thought of Catherine's photographs. Even the sight of Astrid squirming in her absurd Lycra. Whichever, your thoughts are clear, and looking around at the fixated smiles, you realize you are all thinking as one: tonight will be a night to remember—your purity rating will take a hammering. It's midsummer's night, a night for fairy tales, a night for wishes, and a night for the bizarre.

Suddenly businesslike, everyone seems immediately sober.

"Where shall we go?" demands Barbarella, clapping her hands.

Catherine smiles genuinely for the first time all day.

"I've been invited to a boat party, and the culture minister is doing his bit for the country by having a party for young musicians. It's really just a shameless opportunity for star-struck Labour MPs to rub shoulders with some C-list."

Mind you, Barnie, you're a complete sucker for fame—and where there's musicians, there's usually dancers.

Catherine's ex will almost certainly be there. You could show him up as the complete twat he is and cure Cattie of her teenage moping.

Will has other ideas: "We could all go to a party at my brother-in-law's at Ravenshaw House. It's a joint birthday party. He's fifty, but his niece is twenty-one—lots of young corruptibles."

The squabbles break out, but you sit silently and stare. Imagination is in fifth gear. Tequila is pumping through your veins like adrenaline and you suddenly realize that anything is possible. It's time to put away childish things, young Barnaby, and put the bike back in the toy box. Tonight you will venture forth, armed only with lightning wit and easy good looks, ready for glorious self-fulfillment; you have only to pick and choose. The prospect of pure hedonism implants an unshakable grin on your slightly glazed face. You must look odd because suddenly everyone is staring at you.

Scene 169

"I think we should go to Catherine's party. Don't you, Barnie?" demands Barbarella. You realize that for once she's delegating responsibility to you.

Barnaby, time to make a decision. Time to leave the cozy confines of gossip among friends. Dark forces are ranged against you. Puck has blinded William with Oberon's flower, and only you are sufficiently scheming to tear him away from the Machiavellian mandrake, Annabel; Kamran needs the courage of conquest if he is ever to stand up to his parents—or maybe he just needs to find love; Catherine needs to forget before she does something stupid in the name of revenge; but Barbie, she needs to remember . . . remember the raptures of your lost love. Astrid will watch on with Flemish provinciality, but you, dear Barnaby, you will need the cunning of Chelsea Clinton's stylist, for you are a play-actor, and the first act has begun.

The evening holds much in store. There will be battles, sexual and pugilistic; fortunes, made and lost; elopements, seductions, corruptions, and betrayals. But as you look around at the rather soiled souls before you, pray do not disregard the enemy. Ranged against you are the corrupt, the grotesque, and the downright wicked who will all struggle to mark your tawdry lives with the sign of failure.

The checkerboard is set and Destiny is curling a bony finger about her king's pawn. She is ready to play, mate, and slay. One last slug from your glass—the fate of six hangs in the balance:

Do you go to Catherine's political boat party bash and keep delectable Barbarella sweet? **Go to Scene 9**

Or let Barbie go hang, it's time to move on . . . and Will's niece sounds interesting. Go to the country house party **Scene 171**

Scene 170

Prudence, a welcome arrival to our tale. Well done.

The freeway is refreshingly quiet and you have no problem spotting the boys in a Land Rover Discovery as they childishly overtake. Will honks the horn loud enough to wake up the sleeping Astrid. Kamran leans out of the window, his hair blown back to reveal Killer Loop glasses and a trademark smile. You look for Barnaby, but remember with a small pang that he was taking his motorbike; you hope he's safe, and involuntarily touch the walnut dashboard superstitiously. The Discovery accelerates. You'd like to follow, but Catherine is still looking mildly sick.

Still, within thirty minutes, you have arrived. A winding drive takes you past a line of cypresses. The fit-inducing strobe of the evening sun as it flickers through the passing trees quickens your pulse. Last time you were here you were Will's new paramour. How quickly times change. The formal front lawn ends at imposingly colonnaded steps. Kamran is at their foot, inspecting a damaged border of chrysanthemums that are suspiciously close to Barnie's bike. You dare not ask. And there, in the jaws of the nineteenth-century gothic folly of a house, as if about to be eaten by its hideous gargoyle frontage, stand Will and his elder sister Olympia.

Olympia is the nearest mortal equivalent to Nigella Lawson, both in looks and sheer culinary skill. When George, Lord Ravenshaw, tasted her cinnamon rack of lamb at a dinner party given back in her art school days, he fell for her immediately. And the timing was impeccable; that very season, William Burton Senior, "Daddy," was finally rumbled. Burton Investments was found to have invested in nothing but school fees and creative accountants for years. And so, while Will has been chasing financial rainbows ever since (you have three cases of barely touched Romanian Merlot bought from Will's Yaboowine.net to prove it), Olympia has had a plump marriage bed to fall back on. But Olympia is shouting, and it's always best to pay attention.

"Barbarella, how fabulous to see you again. It's been ages."

She rushes down the steps and throws her arms around you with a kiss. Then she sees Catherine.

"Oh, and little Catherine. I'm so sorry, I didn't recognize you. Have you been ill?"

Clearly she hasn't quite forgiven Catherine for the emotional scarring of her darling brother. Kamran obviously isn't alone in blaming Catherine for Will's rebound engagement. Speaking of Annabel, she doesn't seem to be around. You assumed that she'd probably want to tag along for the evening, but her car is nowhere to be seen.

"Will, isn't Annabel coming this evening?"

Olympia answers for him. "Well, she thought about it, but I told her tonight's menu and I think the calorie count scared her off. Annabel is so," she struggles to find the right word, "difficult."

Kamran lifts your bags out of the car, ready to take them to your rooms; Astrid plays gleefully with a nearby fountain, resulting in a hideous one-contestant wet T-shirt competition. Olympia turns to you: "A friend of yours?" You bite your lip and nod. "Well, I suppose she'll have to go in the west wing to be safe. I've put you in the east wing if that's OK. Will has already picked you out a room."

Inside, you creak up a flight of stairs to the east wing, while Catherine and Astrid, for their sins, are put in the west wing. The house is so monstrously big you have to call Catherine on her cell phone.

"Cat, I'll come and find you both in twenty minutes. I just want to freshen up first."

Will gaily accompanies you into your room, a stunning en suite that was once used by Merchant and Ivory for a Bonham-Carter bodice-ripping love scene. Kamran has already placed your bags by the colossal bed, and all that remains is to get changed, then get drinking. Will tells you to join everyone in the garden when you're ready and with a blown kiss he is gone.

Time for some serious preparation. You opt for a pale blue summer dress—socially acceptable coverage, but so gossamer light that it promises titillation with the slightest breeze. The dress slips on like a dream, but you can't quite reach the zip at the back. Normally your "wife" would be on hand to help, but Cat couldn't be further away. Never mind, Will is next door and he'll do perfectly. He positively enjoys this sort of sisterly interaction. But first you stop to peek into a rather warped antique mirror. It stretches your legs, giving them an extra couple of inches, and bulges benevolently at chest height. You spend long moments admiring your flat-stomached, long-legged, boulder-breasted loveliness. Tearing yourself away you slip into the hall, only to realize that you aren't sure whether Will is to the right or left of your room. It barely matters, Kamran is probably in the other.

Don't be so naïve. It is upon such seemingly inconsequential moments that your very future happiness may depend. Life is a pirate's island, filled with treasure troves and booby-traps. Pick very carefully, the clues are all here. Your bedroom is in the east wing and garden-facing (i.e. south); Will is a gentleman—would he have chosen you a room to his left or right?

Do you try the door on your left? **Go to Scene 172**

Or do you try the door on your right? **Go to Scene 174**

Scene 171

No contest really. Rich totty in the potting shed every time. And besides, Will's niece is supposed to be a nymphomaniac.

"I think some fresh country air would do us all a world of good."

Barbarella tries to look disappointed; Catherine tries not to look disappointed; and Will is full of importance.

"You can always trust Barnie to sniff out quality," he croaks.

You can't resist a gibe: "Good idea, Will. Double points for anyone who goes down on Will's niece."

Only Kamran laughs, the others turn their attentions to organizing transport, forewarning hosts, and finishing drinks. You, on the other hand, consider the evening's opportunities and, most importantly, Will's niece, Charlotte .

Pierced o' clit, famed, even at the tender age of eighteen, for her power over men, rumor has it she has a bizarre fascination with . . . no, that can wait for confirmation; after all, you shouldn't believe everything you hear.

The clear product of a broken home and too much pocket money; Charlotte turned too early to coke and sex as a substitute for parental love. You've only seen her once, in a bar, and then from afar, but the flitting moment was enough to crystallize a clear vision of oversized breasts on a tiny doll body. Yes, she was tiny, but with the easy grace of an athlete (well, a rider actually—but she competed at Goodwood and came in second in her class, so her pelvic floor must have cracking tone), and the wandering eye of . . .

The others are looking at you, waiting for you to finish your drink and so away.

Go to Scene 236

Scene 172

You knock on the door, and without waiting, barge in. Will is sitting in his underwear and shirtsleeves. He is talking quietly into a mobile, but you don't notice.

"Will, my zip is stuck." Will winces at you, looking meaningfully at his phone.

"No, darling, that was just someone in the next room . . . Yes it might be Barbarella . . . Yes the door is open . . . I'll shut it now." He pauses to give you another glare as you push the door to for him. "Well, of course, you're more than welcome to come . . . it's just that it's very late . . . you won't—"

He doesn't finish, instead, like a good little fiancé, he sits and listens and agrees and nods. Finally he manages a sentence. "Fine, I'll see you here in half an hour, Pumpkin." Disconnecting, he gives you a withering look. "Thanks, mate."

Not in the mood for guilt, you decide, instead, to address a few issues. "Will, she is going to be your wife—at some point you've got to get used to seeing her on a regular basis."

But Will isn't ready to discuss anything; he walks towards you, and, staring deeply into your eyes, exchanges a knowing look. "Forget about it." For a fleeting moment you sense him readying for a kiss, but instead he turns you deftly and with practiced ease zips your dress.

"Time we should be heading downstairs. I'll join you in a minute." And with a dismissive pat on your bottom he begins to dress.

Go to Scene 192

Scene 173

And so Charlotte turns to leave. You wince a last, silent gasp, but if she notices, she betrays no sign. There'll be plenty of time to impress on her your desirability. And by saving your performance until Barbarella arrives, you'll be killing two birds with the same chat.

Time to get ready for the party; the water coming out of the shower is brown, so instead you settle for a head dunk under the tap (to get rid of your crash helmet hair) and a quick tooth brushing. You remedy the worst of the mud stains on your trousers and with a certain relief, note that nothing is ripped—other, rather oddly, than your underwear. You discard the ribbed Moschino briefs and set forth, commando, across the somber length of the house and into its contrastingly pleasant garden.

Go to Scene 177

Scene 174

You knock on the door and without waiting, barge in. There is no one there. And judging by the tongue-scraper lying on the dressing table, you picked correctly. This is definitely Kamran's room. He must have gone down to the garden already, not wishing to waste a minute, especially with Barnaby half an hour ahead.

The room is invitingly empty and you can't resist having a rummage. You've always wanted to know what Kamran packs into his old worn-out duffel bag; he's always so protective of it. You spy the ex-army-issue bag hanging from a chair. Tentatively you lift it over to the bed, careful not to disturb the contents inside. Loosening the strap, you peer in and start to extract the contents one by one.

The first few objects are pretty standard. Toilet bag, Hom pants, a bag of marijuana, some tarot cards, but you're not prepared for what comes out next.

It's a magazine, but one that causes you to doubt everything you've ever known about Kamran—this month's edition of *Attitude*. Oh God, you had no idea about this. He's kept it so quiet. What about all the women he takes back to his Chelsea "love-boat," the *Anomie*? You can't wait to see Barnaby and Will.

No, Barbie, it's none of your business. God, what to do? Should you tell Barnaby? No, but, well, he'd love to know . . .

The sound of an uproar in the garden below startles you.

Scene 174

Better get out of here right now, in case Kamran comes back. You carefully stuff the other contents back into the duffel bag but, with a fumble, the magazine slides off the bed and onto the floor. It opens on page forty-eight, where, in the bottom left corner, is a circled advert:

BRONZE TORSOS ETC.
MADE TO SPECIFICATION
As seen in "Through the Keyhole"
Kamran Jazeer,
www.Sculpto.co.uk
P.O. Box 38, London SW7

All rather innocent, then. He came up with a ridiculously successful scheme of sculpting elderly women's busts—quite literally. He gives the clay more lift than is biologically accurate and they love him for it. But until now you had no idea that he dabbled with *male* sculpting. You can only wonder about the etcetera.

Barbie, store the thought in the "unfinished business" area of your hippocampus and guiltily sidle back out to the hall. There could be more to Kamran than meets the eye.

You've still failed to zip up your dress.

Do you head down to the garden regardless? It's almost zipped up anyway. **Go to Scene 12**

Do you go over to the west wing and get Catherine to help you? **Go to Scene 176**

Scene 175

Well done, you're back on course. Just pray that all the mooning over Charlotte hasn't irreparably damaged your chances of getting back with Barbie. First, you need to take time out to think, and so, making polite excuses to Snuffy and Uncle "O," you sidle off into the garden.

It's even lovelier empty of people. Not a chirrup of gossip breaks through the calm as you meander into its darker recesses. The cool air has its usual effect on your gin-filled bladder and you don't hesitate to pee into a large laurel. Halfway through, a subdued female voice startles you into skipping round the far side of the bush. With relief, you see that the female intruder hasn't noticed your latest act of impropriety (and that you've avoided pissing on your trousers).

"You're kidding?"

She's obviously talking into a mobile phone, and rather than scare the poor girl by stepping out from the bush, you decide to eavesdrop.

"So how'd you find out?"

Oh, Christ, it's Barbie. You can't spy on her, can you?

"Fucking Essex loser."

Hold on, she's talking about you.

"Barbie, who the hell are you talking to?" You step out from the bush and Barbie jumps at the sight of you.

It doesn't take her long to recover, talking to her mobile she says, "Look, I've got to go, Catherine—the loser's turned up. I'll see you in a minute . . . Thanks for letting me know."

She clicks the phone off and stands there, accusing you with her eyes. You crack first.

"*What?* What am I supposed to have done?"

Silence.

Your guilt-ridden conscience replays highlights from the last decade.

"Just tell me what I've done."

"You're such a twat. If you're going to have a ten-pound bet with Kamran that you can get me into bed, then you really should try and make sure I don't find out. Tosser."

She turns and walks back to the house. Leaving you slack-jaw stunned, and flying low.

Go to Scene 243

Scene 176

The house is deserted as you head over to find Catherine and Astrid. Clearly the other guests are all here, so there's no time to lose. It takes almost ten minutes before you manage to track the girls down. Their room is pretty poky, clearly reserved for the unfavored. Tiny windows render it murky even on this balmy evening, and the gloom of the décor contrasts strikingly with your fresh charm. Astrid has barely enough natural light to reapply her makeup, resulting in an inevitable orange tidemark. Catherine seems to have managed, though; she looks stunning in a diaphanous skimp of a dress. It sits well on her elfin frame as she perches on the window ledge finishing a cigarette.

"Cat, can you zip me in?"

Cigarette in mouth, she hops off the ledge and comes to your assistance. Now that you are all ready, it's time to make an entrance below. Before you do, Cat tries the door next to you. It's apparently where Barnie is sleeping. Not surprisingly, there's no sign of him. In fact, the only evidence that he's been there is a ripped pair of ribbed Moschino Tanga briefs. The three of you grimace in unison.

But take note, Barnaby has gone commando. And such information is invariably useful . . .

Go down to the garden in **Scene 12**

Scene 177

The garden, though demonstrating the same absurd formality as the house, possesses more charm. The hedges may be a little crisp and the patio terrace a little regimented, but with the addition of all but a hundred assorted guests the welcome has a warm, inviting air. The addition of half a dozen champagne-waiters also helps.

You spy the beautiful Charlotte some way off and edge cannily towards her; only for a doddering duffer, wearing a criminally cut, prewar dinner jacket, to interrupt your progress.

"You look like a game sort of chap, d'you mind me using you for a demonstration?"

Your initial reaction to the finely wrinkled old fool is pretty obvious. But, for fear of causing consternation and being acutely aware that you know no one yet present at the party, you attempt to recover the situation with some well-advised *bonhomie*.

"Certainly, sir," you quip formally, imitating his brigadier vowels. "How may I be of service?"

And for the first time you truly notice the other guests.

Far from being the expected mix of dowagers, colonels, and stuffy city types, you notice more than a smattering of vibrantly healthy young girls. Of course—you remember, *he's forty but his daughter is nineteen . . . lots of young corruptibles . . .*

Impress Charlotte's little buddies with the stamp of your good-natured desirability and the job is all but done. And so you oblige the old fart.

He is virtually surrounded by young girls, all smiling gamely and expectantly. You nod casually in their direction, noting that the old boy must have something still working up top as you survey the quality of the crowd he's pulled. A massive-chested brunette laughs with the hint of a Welsh accent as she complies with his instructions and holds a magnum of unopened champagne between her impressive thighs.

"Now, I must remember the order of things. You, Polly, you will play the role of Khrushchev, and you, sir, pardon me, I neglected to take your name."

"Barnaby," you trail lamely, like everyone else, held in the thrall of this madman.

"Yes, Barnaby, you will play the part of the American ambassador—Gregson. Right, Gregson, sorry, Barnaby, place this in your mouth, will you?" And so saying he stuffs a fat cigar deep into your throat. You try not to gag. "Rather unworthy, I'm afraid. Gregson, of course, never smoked anything other than Cuban dreadnoughts . . . Still, young Polly here is sure to have a steadier aim than Nikki, who was virtually dead by '62."

You would stop the mad old fool in his tracks, but note that he's gathering a sizable crowd—and among the new additions is Charlotte. You feebly comply as a gnarled but surprisingly firm hand twists your head so that it profiles the game Welsh girlie. Staring nervously forward you fail to see her hoik up an already perfectly short skirt in the interests of greater control.

"OSWALD, WHAT *ARE* YOU DOING?" the voice, possibly unique, belongs to Will's elder sister, Olympia, and the evening's hostess.

"I intercepted one of the waiters bringing you this old sword from the library. I can't believe you are wrecking the party already . . . and especially with the old 'Missile Crisis Routine.' Hello, Barnie, glad you could come."

She pecks you on the cheek allowing the ridiculous cigar to stay in place.

Scene 177

"Don't mind Uncle Oswald, he was British ambassador to Russia during the Cuban missile crisis and has been dining out on it ever since. Just don't hospitalize him, Oswald."

She departs, your last hope of salvation, and leaves you wondering only one thing—what the hell is the sword for? You raise a hand to extract the offending cigar, only to spot Charlotte looking on at your discomfort with a relaxed assurance. This is no time to wimp out, Barnie.

Barnaby, you have to expect this sort of thing with this sort of company. We're not just talking upper middle class here, the blood here is pretty blue. The elderly aristocracy spend their lives reliving glory days from the past, regardless of the consequences to life and limb. It might well expose your humble origins if you tried to cry off. And this is no time for Barnaby, "social chameleon," to let his mask slip—even if the old fool is brandishing a sword . . .

Bite the bullet. Chomp firmly on the cigar with a stiff upper lip. **Go to Scene 259**

Cry off for fear of maiming. **Go to Scene 179**

Scene 178

Unfortunately the collective surroundings of schoolboy paraphernalia are a little *too* much. Maybe you overinhaled testosterone. And you can't help but anticipate Nicholas's mother bursting in and catching you *in flagrante delicto* with her precious son. Anyway, the weekend already reeks of Mrs. Robinson.

With a reluctant sigh, you help him down to dinner.

Go to Scene 22

Scene 179

As casually as you are able, you extract the cigar and, looking Oswald in the glazed eye, attempt to fight your way out. You begin, of course, on the offensive (you have taken advanced history, remember).

"Are you sure you remember this all correctly? I don't remember this in A.J.P. Taylor's account of the crisis."

"Good God, man, Taylor was a blind ass who couldn't write about history he'd seen with his own eyes. The Cuban missile crisis would have ended in disaster, *Arrrmageddon,* sir, if it wasn't for my novel idea of diplomacy. Don't you see—no one could ever hit a cigar from that distance with a champagne cork? I knew that, Gregson knew it, and so did Khrushchev. So you see, the bet was all but won: the Ruskies would withdraw, Kennedy would be a hero, and the world would be safe again."

"Then why did Khrushchev agree to the bet?" you cross-examine gamely, but already know you're beaten.

Sure enough the old diplomat has an answer.

"Khrushchev knew he would have to withdraw eventually. This little ruse allowed him to do so with good grace and gave him the outside chance of hurting Gregson—whom he detested. That was the brilliance of my plan, you see . . . Nikki and Gregson absolutely hated each other. Gregson was man enough—so clamp your trembling mouth around that bloody cigar and think of the free world."

Not even a hint of a let-out. You know when you're beaten by a better man. Time to face the firing squad. You catch a sideways glance at "Uncle Oswald," carefully manipulating the lovely Polly's quivering thigh as she manfully wrestles with the champagne wire . . .

Go to Scene 183

Scene 180

You decide to leave Marc well alone. The dowager's well-directed attention is likely to keep him out of action for some time. Looking round it's obvious that the party is really beginning to break up. Kamran has disappeared, Uncle Oswald is bedazzling Astrid, and you can't help but notice that Will has gone off somewhere with Annabel. You opt to go and find Catherine, whom you've barely spoken to all night, and who's vanished too. She's probably escaped for a fresh-air smoke in the garden, so you make excuses and sidle off.

The garden is even more lovely empty of people. Not a sound breaks through the calm as you meander into its darker recesses. But, failing to find Catherine, you quickly get cold and head back towards the house.

Go to Scene 134

Scene 181

Oh dear—you may have just blown it.

"You're such an idiot, Barnie."

Catherine looks as though she could slap you; instead, she walks from the room, shaking her head. Barbarella doesn't even bother to say anything; she looks at you as though you've just farted in the soup, and follows her friend.

Kamran's easy smirk is back on his face.

"Don't worry, mate. Have another drink and forget about it." He finds a decanter of scotch and fills you a glass. "You've still got me."

And for the first time in your long friendship, Kamran gives you a hug.

The (Lads Together) End

You've a lot to learn, Reader. It's all *there for the taking. Play again, and remember, if you're smart—you can have* whatever *you want.*

Scene 182

"Quickly, you fuckwits," Will shouts, pushing you all into his Discovery. Catherine and Kamran are already in the back; Astrid soon appears half-naked, running down the steps, throwing herself in beside you.

You have no idea what is really going on, other than that you're fleeing before the wrath of Olympia. Will slams the doors shut and with wheels spinning in the gravel, a speedy exit is made from the scene of unknown crime. There's a general moody silence in the car; you break it.

"Is anyone going to explain to me what the fuck happened back there? I've left all my stuff behind."

Kamran looks at Barnaby, "Sorry," and they burst into giggles.

"Fine, if you want to act like stupid brats, fine."

But you're burning with curiosity, so you turn to Catherine. "What happened, Cat?"

She shrugs. "Sorry, missed it, I was in the loo. Just sounded like karaoke." Barnaby bursts into another fit of drunken giggles and with a huff you settle back in your seat. Boys. Sometimes you'd kill to get into Barnie's head for a while . . . But you can't lower yourself to ask him again, and Will still looks too angry to disturb.

The rest of the journey back to town is of little note. As you arrive before the grim city, fatigue begins to kick in.

Go to Scene 112

Scene 183

With a twirling but firm wrist, the retired ambassador runs the sword-blade up the underside of the magnum. A rather pretentious way of opening champagne and dangerously close it comes to slitting Polly's rather inadequate dress. But you don't see that; all you sense is the clatter of metal on glass, an almost orgasmic cry from the Welsh cannon, the pop, and a simultaneous stinging jab of pain as the cork tries to eject your eye from its socket.

For the second time today, you collapse to the floor.

Go to Scene 256

Scene 184

George looks at you as though you've just bled on his sheets. His jaw works, but for possibly the first time in his life the quick-fire comic is lost for words. You realize the size of your mistake when he eventually speaks.

"Jesus Christ! People like you, living smug worthless little lives, you wouldn't recognize suffering if it set light to the Saturday *Telegraph* and stuffed the business section up your arse."

He stalks off with crunching jaw.

Oh, well. These little *faux pas* moments are sent to make us stronger. You try to brush off the embarrassment with a laugh, but deep down you know your toes will curl every time you think back to this scene.

But not now. There'll be time enough to figure this out when you go to sleep tonight. Forget and move on, Barbie. Next time just remember to say "no."

You heave a destressing sigh. In the words of Snoop Doggy Dogg, you better lay low for a few minutes . . . then go find your friends.

Go to Scene 24

Scene 185

"Catherine, forget about Edward. He's bad news. Let's get you out of here—there's a spare bed at my place. We can go back and watch one of Kamran's old videos."

Catherine looks up at you, misty eyed. She really does have a cute nose.

"OK, then, let's just leave. I can't handle facing Barbie; we can text her from the cab."

Sometimes it's just that easy.

Catherine follows you down the stairs, but one step from the bottom, oh so close to freedom, you notice a strange rumbling . . . you clutch your stomach.

Time for a little honesty. Cast your mind back—it's a few hours ago now—to when Kamran offered you his hemlock smoothie. Were you dumb enough to drink it?

"Yep, swallowed it in one." **Go to Scene 201**

"Didn't touch it, guv'nor." **Go to Scene 255**

Scene 186

"Catherine, give it up. Edward's bad news. Come with us to the West India."

And with those words Catherine's defiance evaporates. Will doesn't hesitate, "Great, I'll sort out cabs," and rushes out to the Embankment.

Barnaby, you suspect, secretly wanted to go to the casino all along. He looks at you indulgently. "Well, this time we've got to win bloody big."

Go to Scene 232

Scene 187

"Barnie, what the hell have you been doing?" Barbie pours champagne down your gullet and the fizz forces you to sit upright and splutter a cough.

"The mad old bastard, he could have fucking blinded me, I'll kil—" Barbie pours more wine into your flapping mouth.

"God, you're a lout. What happened? Come and sit down and stop acting like you're back in Essex."

So you sit on a garden seat, safely out of harm's way, nestled by a beech hedge and next to a rather soothing water feature. With Barbarella by your side, you companionably people-watch from the comfort and security of your cozy spot. You dissipate the starred blindness in your left eye with a cold champagne glass and observe.

The gaggle of humanity, chirruping and laughing, consists, you note disappointingly, of fewer youngsters than first imagined. The bulk is made up of the plump middle-aged and the sagging fully aged. All are wittering at that peculiar resonance unique to these posh events.

Charlotte does have a few choice friends, though. The robust Polly with the firm thigh and firmer bust is probably the pick. Sure enough, Kamran has homed in. You smile grimly as you realize that he's working in tandem with your nemesis, Oswald Dryton-Gore. Joining Polly, and batting for the girls, is an attractive blonde. Tall, and with what Kamran would describe as "a figure blessed with a touch of anorexia," she stands with a wonderfully elongated body, bony hip and shuttlecock boobs jutting towards Kamran in invitation. Oswald, true to form, is making most of the running as he leans heavily on an old stick and flails his free arm in glorious arcs of anecdote relating.

"Have you seen Catherine?" Barbie interrupts your thoughts. It's time to kick off the jealous rivalry.

"Yeah, she's on the patio, talking to my lovely Charlotte."

Barbie stares, speechless with panicked jealousy. Time to push home the advantage.

"Charlotte's very pretty but she's a bit of a strange one. She came on to me big time when I first arrived, naïve teenager stuff but still pretty flattering. Kept asking me whether I liked her dress and would I feel the material and so on. Mind you, she does look amazing in it."

Barbarella sighs, and, claiming she needs another drink, huffs off.

Bingo, Barnie. You've hit the green light. Once she's got over the initial pang of jealousy, Barbarella will realize that she needs to put in a lot of hard work to win you back. This plan can't fail. So stop gaping at Charlotte and Catherine, rearrange your roaming erection, curse your lack of pants, and go join them.

Go to Scene 189

Scene 188

With a jolt you come to and flush crimson, quite unaware that you had such feelings for Kamran. It must be the tension. Catherine catches your eye, concerned. Looking down you see that cards have been dealt and the game is getting underway. Goodness. Pay attention, Barbarella.

The lights have unexpectedly dimmed. Hopefully that won't impede Kam's view of the game. Astrid is perfectly positioned in case you need a distraction, standing behind Will with heavy hands resting on his shoulders. She has followed Catherine's advice and is exhibiting an abundance of flesh and hair tossing. Barnaby has adopted an expression, which you take to be his "Five Card Stud" face, and Cat is playing the demure companion, perfected from her days as a hostess in Hong Kong.

Taking a healthy mouthful of Armagnac, it dawns on you that you are actually quite drunk. Heedless, you accept a line of the white stuff anyway (it was presented on a silver tray and it does usually perk you up). You ignore Barnaby's stare (he scrupulously declines the narcotic offer), because suddenly it's your turn to play and you're quite unprepared. Time to look at the chandelier. Fortunately the game has started at a gentle speed and nobody complains as you study your cards, bite a lip, and admire the ceiling. The chandelier moves, almost imperceptibly, to the right.

"I fold," and with casual poise you discard your cards on to the table.

Scene 188

So far so good—the plan seems to be working. You collect in the second round at the expense of Nigel Jenner and Newt. The third goes to Will and in the fourth you all fold early leaving Wasim to skin Bodi. A fifth round and you win big. Astrid claps her hands in glee, dreaming of new Astroglide Rollerblades. Will remains nervous. He has switched from cigars to cigarettes, dragging deeply and exhaling with a sigh. The cards are dealt for a sixth hand.

Success continues and eventually even Will begins to relax. Barnaby starts being cocky.

"Nigel, if you need to borrow, I don't mind. It's no problem, really."

For once Nigel doesn't have a response. He smiles a gold tooth and picks up a new hand. Trusty Kamran continues to work the levers and the winnings continue to mount—and as they mount, the stakes get higher . . .

Go to Scene 68

Scene 189

You never reach the chatting girls. Olympia's shrill cry calls everybody to the table and you allow yourself to be buffeted into the house by the gentle flow of people. The formal gallery, chosen as the site of the evening's dining experience, is less imposing, more windowed and generally less miserable than the rest of the house.

The irrepressible Olympia has incorporated you into her seating plans with her hallmark administrative expertise. Barbie is sitting to your left, but to your right is the rather curious-sounding Lady Fotherington.

You hear her before you see her.

"Just put them down there, boy. No, not like that. Give them here. And get me a proper glass. No, not a pint glass, a big glass . . . for gin. And ice." Without pausing for breath, she settles herself in that way peculiar to old people, looks you up and down and, "Well, well. Some young blood for a change, pleased to meet you. Lady Fotherington, but call me Snuffy, everybody does." She sees confusion. "Snuffy . . . as in the movies." And with a glinting eye she proffers a firm hand.

"Barnaby, but call me Barnie. As in the cartoon bear."

"Barnie, I remember a Barnaby, Tenth Hussars, Pokara, marvelous seat on a horse. Do you ride well, Mr. uh," she reads your place card, "Wilson?"

You've never ridden a horse in your life and this sort of upper-crust always makes you feel inadequate. Making doubly sure to hide any hint of council house estuarian, you answer with an accent that would do an Old Harrovian justice, "A mechanical horse only, and that not too well; I destroyed a border of chrysanths on my way up the drive this evening. I tend to go to pot when I see a pretty girl . . . My throttle wrist tenses."

Using the same line twice in one evening—tut tut, Barnie.

"Ah, much the same as a polo horse really, designed purely to titillate the opposite sex. You wear leathers instead of polo gear of course, much more sexually blatant. But a good polo player has the advantage of demonstrating his penetrative powers in mixed company. I sometimes wonder whether all sports were designed to allow men to practice penetration." She pauses, but only for a second. "What do you think?"

"Umm, well, possibly," you flounder.

Barnaby the wit, the funniest man in Romford, at a loss for words. You can't bear to disappoint this unique piece of British colonial heritage. You try to imagine her forty years younger . . .

"Well, there is snooker, that's all about penetration, oh and football, golf and basketball and netball . . . God, yeah, you might be right. The only one I struggle with is cricket—it's more like five days of foreplay."

Snuffy smiles, relieved that you're not the usual dinner party bore she has to put up with, but your nemesis, "Uncle" Oswald, has joined the foot of the table, and despite possessing ears old enough to have heard Queen Victoria, seems to be following your conversation.

"Absolute bloody rubbish. Cricket has given us a nation of sexual thoroughbreds. Thigh and buttock strength, sir. From all that crouching in the field. Compare football. It's given us a nation of poufs and yobs."

No time to wimp out of an argument. Even if it is as obscure and ridiculous as: "Sexual thoroughbreds? W.G. Grace? Michael Atherton? Geoff Boycott? I suspect the ladies may disagree. I suspect they may prefer a David Beckham, albeit with masking tape over his mouth."

You turn to Snuffy Fotherington for support. But by now, Barbie is joining you to your left, Kamran is sitting on the other side of Snuffy, and Astrid, who had slipped your mind, is sitting opposite Barbie on the other side of Oswald. They (even with Kamran's raised eyebrow exclamation that he has some news) do little to distract—but the last to be seated, Charlotte, blows your thoughts like a tea-leaf before a typhoon.

"Hello, Barnaby, are you feeling better?"

Snuffy doesn't fail to spot your ardor, Oswald has probably never missed a trick in his entire life, and, despite the acute need for blood elsewhere, for the first time in years, you blush.

Oh, Barnie, you poor sad fool. You really have fallen in love—you were supposed to just use Charlotte to win Barbarella back. This is a night for sorting out your love life (and failing that for a rough and ready sexual adventure), it's not a night for teenage angst. *You must try to get over her, she's young enough to be your daughter (well, in Essex anyway). If you really can't, then just get on with it, but stop mooning around.*

With saving grace, the starter is upon you. The asparagus tips, while showing a lack of imagination, do provide food for discussion. To one side, Kamran charms the baronet with talk of the impact of asparagus on urine odor while to your left Oswald busies himself by showing the girls his seventeenth-century walking cane. You scoff, and sit and watch Charlotte politely chatting to some tedious little banker as she delicately laps butter from her pouting top lip with a kitten-delicate tongue. Despite the strength of your adoration you can't help noticing, much further along the table, Polly, the fleshy Welsh wonder, deep-throating her tips with Celtic abandon. Her oral dexterity is not lost on Kamran.

Scene 189

But activity at the end of the table is demanding your attention. Oswald is speaking, and you can't quite believe . . .

"Just put the palm of your hand on it, there that's right. Grip it, girl. Now, imagine where that knob has been."

You look up to see Barbie, the shameless hussy, stretching over and below the end of the table. Astrid looks on in seeming wonder—Eurotrash. Oswald sees your incredulity and before you can turn a British blind eye, he is beckoning you closer to look. Social etiquette demands that you don't shy away. And so you lean over and peer to see a sight you had hoped to postpone for another fifty years.

Through squinted eyes you see a dark mahogany cane topped by an ebony black ball. Oswald presents it to you.

"Feel it, young man. Joseph Stalin used that cane after his first stroke. Before that, it was housed in the St. Petersburg museum, a relic from the reign of Peter the Great. Imagine the power possessed in the hands of perhaps two of the greatest statesmen in the history of the last millennium. Those very hands, which signed a million death warrants, the hand that created the world's largest empire, gripped that ebony knob. Think of that, young man."

Before you can think too much he has swiped the cane back and is presenting it to Astrid.

"Young lady, rest the ebony to your lips and tell me what you feel."

Dirty old bugger. He probably hasn't seen a girl's mouth in that position for decades.

"Tell me what you feel. The others may think it fanciful, but this cane contains the energy of two of the greatest personalities of our age. You can feel it, can't you? Like electricity jumping on to your lip."

This last is to Astrid and she duly agrees. The electricity must have short-wired some neurons because you can swear she is looking at Oswald in her peculiar calculating way. Astrid always did confuse friendliness with sexual allure . . . you fear for Oswald's feeble frame.

But suddenly peaceful social interplay is squashed beneath the personality of a newcomer. Slumping between Astrid and Charlotte in the previously empty space sits a Mediterranean hunk.

His name, he declares in a voice that carries to the kitchens, is Marc-Pacaud.

Coming from Romford, you instinctively suspect double-barreled surnames, but double-barreled *first* names belong to pimps and Mafiosi. Marc-Pacaud you suspect is both. And yet the accent (and tan) is unmistakably St. Tropez.

"*Mon dieu*. I made it in time for the starter. Unbelievable. To think twelve hours ago I was playing polo on Rhode Island."

Even you cringe at his hideousness. He grabs at a glass and downs it. Then, with the arrogance of one accustomed to being the center of attention, he interrupts Oswald's attempts to introduce everybody and, facing all with a fearsome smile, continues his one-man conversation: "To be honest with you I don't actually know anybody here. I am here at my father's request. My father, the Comte de Vichyssoise, he was at 'Arrow with 'is Lordship."

With this last hideous piece of self-inflation, he points a butter-dripped fork towards the head of the table. Then, turning his buffed incisors to your beloved Charlotte, he urges her into the web of his conversation: "Do you know his Lordship?"

"He is my father."

But, though the tan is yet to turn George Hamilton patent, his hide is as tough as leather. "Marc-Pacaud" has barely turned on the ignition of his Rolls-Royce charm.

"Then I must get to know 'im. For the father of one so beautiful must be very lucky. Tell me, iz your mother a unique beauty or are you the product of zum vanishingly improbable genetic mutation?"

Scene 189

The clatter of Oswald's cane hitting the floor tells a wordless tale. Even Oswald Dryton-Gore can't condone such appalling technique. Charlotte, so pure, unarmed against such a monster, can do nothing but blush. Marc touches a burning cheek with his filthy foreign hands and whispers something into Charlotte's ear. She laughs uncertainly, but blushes even more. Your teeth grind.

"So what do you do when you are not playing polo, Marc?" The baronet tries to disperse some tension.

"Polo is merely for joy, for fun," he oozes, even over the aging dowager. "My first love is the sea. I dive."

He pauses as though that is enough, contemplates some asparagus, and then continues before anyone can change the subject.

"I spent my youth in Polynesia. My father, he waz governor of an island zere for a time. My youth," another dramatic pause, as though anyone cared, "waz one long dive for the pearls. No equipment, just zese arms and zese lurngs. Of all the divers on our island, I could stay under the longest. While the others waited at zee zurface I would be in my world with ze fishes and ze turtles. That is nature's gift to me. I use that gift to push myself to the boundaries of human endurance, to go deeper than any other, to endure the pressure of the ocean, for longer than any other. I am champion of France in this sport. That is what I do."

There really is no answer to that sort of pomposity. But of course "Snuffy" is never lost for words.

"Barnaby here believes that all sport is a form of sexual role play. Does that hold for skin diving?"

Possibly for the first time in his overlong life Marc is nonplussed. Kamran can't resist explaining.

"She means are you a great muff diver?"

Marc-Pacaud snorts Gallically. "Oh, I see. Yes, quite. Certainly I have had no complaints. In many ways I see it as training for my sport."

He says this with a twinkled look at Charlotte. She smiles. Barbie, next to you, adjusts herself, training her cleavage on the Frenchman. Astrid twists awkwardly closer. Damn Kamran as a fool.

But Marc is now on a roll.

"Tell me, Barnabeee, can you think of a finer sport for the practice of better sex?"

But he is no longer addressing you; he has turned to Charlotte once more. "You see, Charlotte, my sport requires you to address all your fear, your inadequacies, your doubts. Each time I go down it is to the utmost of human endurance. A slight panic, an extra 'eart beat here, an unnecessary flap of ze leg and the oxygen in my brain will run out . . . and I will remain forever at the bottom of the zea."

The man is a living cliché. Good God, there's more. Charlotte, you idiot, stop asking him questions; he'll think you are interested. Oh no, surely not. She is interested! She's only nineteen. The thought of record-breaking cunnilingus has turned her innocent mind.

"So why do you do it?" she asks teenagerly.

"Because I have this gift. And because the ocean is my kingdom."

Meaningless gibberish of course, but if the agitation in Barbie by your side is anything to go by you have got to do something quickly; she is practically semaphoring him with her breasts. As your starter plate is efficiently removed, you decide something must be done to halt the *entente*.

Barbie whispers an aside, "That man is such an arse, but I can't help thinking he will be magnificent in bed," and it steels you into action.

Tread carefully, this man is not as big an idiot as you might think, and he certainly has the physical edge over you. You were warned that by chasing after both Barbie and Charlotte you could be spreading yourself too thinly . . . now it looks as though you might lose both.

What you decide now could influence the fate of everyone. How do you defeat this French cock?

Head-on, bull at a gate. **Go to Scene 215**

Or with subtlety, like a wily fox. **Go to Scene 193**

Scene 190

Slow down? No, of course not, silly suggestion.

Catherine is looking mildly green. What's wrong with her? It must be the drink catching up.

"Please, Barbie, slow down on the corners. I feel sick." But you mock her with driving exuberance. Cutting through a shallow bend you feel sporty tires grip and turn up the radio to aid your concentration. The rear tires skid slightly and you see Cat's right foot pressing hard into the floor. Maybe it might be an idea to slow down. Especially as a police car seems to be tailgating you. You didn't even notice.

As a last resort, the police car turns on the siren. Oh shit. You are going to have to think fast to get out of this one, Barbie. An obese policeman approaches; he taps on the window, heedless of the fact that you have the hood down. Idiot.

"Out of the car right now, young lady."

Well at least he called you young. That has to be a good sign. You trip out of the car due to the sheer height of your heels. That has to be bad. In an attempt to distract, you force chest forward and mentally will your nipples to protrude.

"Have you been drinking, madam?"

Oh dear, looks like this officer may not be playing ball. Desperately racking your mind for a way out, you vaguely remember something about sucking on a two-pence piece. Barnie swears that it scrambles the Breathalyzer—but you don't carry change.

Scene 190

There is always the get out of jail free card, but somehow you doubt even fellatio will work with this guy. Yikes, could be time to accept defeat. Your thoughts are interrupted . . .

"Could you blow into this, please?"

"Well, I could, but, Officer, I get terrible allergies this time of the year, and I'm prone to asthma. Perhaps one of my friends might help instead?"

"Just blow into the bag."

Accept defeat. Do what you are good at. Blow, Barbarella.
Go to Scene 106

Scene 191

You take the door on the right. It creaks as it opens, but not nearly loud enough to distract the occupants. The sight of Barbie with another man breaks your heart anew. She's sitting fully clothed (dress hitched becomingly), straddling a virtually naked man. With that physique (and those black silk socks) it can only be the Frenchman.

"Now you can breathe."

Barbie's order confirms your theory. From beneath her groin, where you presume his head to be, erupts a gasp, "Now. More."

She rides like a cross-country champion.

"Barbie, there's been a bit of a disaster. We've got to go . . . now."

Barbie looks at you with unfocused eyes. "Barnie, what the hell are you—"

There's no time to let her finish. Instead, you grab a hand and drag her, complaining, from the room. You barely hear the heavily accented cry for help as you race along the corridor, down, and out of the house.

Go to Scene 217

Scene 192

You can't quite face joining the party just yet, so you return to your room. Time to lie on the old-fashioned quilt and contemplate this unexpected event.

Will, head in the lion's mouth, refuses to admit that he's in deep trouble, just as he has always refused to admit that he loved you. There must be something behind Will's Stepford-dumb acceptance. It can't be pregnancy, he would have said something. Surely she hasn't bewitched him in the bedroom. Riding may be good for the pelvic floors, but Annabel just doesn't have the personality of a sexual temptress. She's bossy—but to the point of dominatrix?

Oh, God, surely Will hasn't fallen in lust with Annabel because she picked the lock to some unhealthy fetish. He never showed leanings toward that sort of thing when you were sleeping with him, but maybe he was in denial. God, how could he mistake love for something best purchased in King's Cross?

Time to gather forces. Annabel will be here in twenty minutes and you'll need to be prepared. Cat is still in her room getting ready, so one quick call to her mobile and she and Astrid are on their way. Likewise with Barnaby. Only someone as gauche as Barnie would carry their phone turned on at a party, but this time it proves useful in herding both him and Kamran up to your room.

Once gathered you explain stridently, "Look, Annabel is turning up after all. She got wind that I am here and is storming over in a protective frenzy. If we don't break them up tonight, we might not get another chance."

No one even considers that it might be inappropriate to split up a friend's engagement, instead all nod dumbly in consent. Eventually Barnaby offers some thoughts. "Yeah, that's great and everything, but he only proposed to her yesterday. Isn't it a bit soon to expect a change of heart."

"He doesn't love her, he can't."

You don't add "because he loves me," but Barnaby misreads it on your earnest expression.

"Fine, if you want to win back Prince Charming then we'll help."

"Barnie, this is nothing to do with me. Will's our friend, right?"

"Look, just tell us what you want to do. Charlotte's waiting downstairs and I think I'm in."

You can't quite disguise your jealous reaction, but Barnaby is a man and fails to notice it. And so you compose yourself and explain the theory. Astrid giggles at the thought of Will being beaten with a riding crop, but generally the four accept your logic. Annabel has ensnared Will with some deviant fetish. And so with cunning to terrify even the sternest foe, you collectively contemplate the downfall of Annabel.

Ten minutes more and you are casually descending to the garden.

Go to Scene 194

Scene 193

Softly softly catchy monkey . . .

"Marc, tell me, in your own country you must be a major figure. I seem to remember that 'holding of the breath' is a big thing in France up there with push-bike racing."

Subtlety was never your strong point. But then it seems Marc's ego doesn't allow for such sensitivity: "Ah yes, in France I am, how you zay . . . a 'pinup.' "

He has just enough sense to laugh self-deprecatingly. You look a little confused and interject; this is going better than you could have hoped, "Ah, you mean like a pop star or footballer. In England we say a 'prick up' or just '*un prick.*' "

"Yes, that is it, I am 'a prick.' My father, le Comte, he gets very embarrassed, but for me it is OK."

Barbarella lets out a snort; Charlotte can't make eye contact. Marc smiles glibly round the table and only Oswald can respond. "But surely your father must be very proud that you can sit about holding your breath."

"*Non*, *non*, you have not understood. There is more to eet than sitting about with your mouth shut."

"I don't suppose you'd be very good at that," you interject and elicit a shining giggle from Charlotte, 15–40 break point. "But could you show us how long you *can* manage to keep your mouth shut?"

"Here and now you mean? I could probably keep my mouth

shut for five minutes, maybe longer . . . allow me to demonstrate."

And with comical hyperventilation the French demigod loosens his bow, removes the Patek Philippe from his wrist, and with a final gasp starts the clock . . .

Thirty seconds gone. You suddenly realize how impressive this is going to look. Five minutes is a long time . . . one hour's cunnilingus on twelve breaths. On the minute mark, Charlotte has renewed her interested gaze.

Something has to be done. A kick to the shin. A stiletto to the foot. One minute thirty, and Charlotte is looking very interested. Time to act. You draw yourself down, extend a leg ready to lash out and then . . . but Oswald has beaten you to it. The stiff mahogany cane has all but broken the young Olympiad's webbed foot.

He cries out a splurt of air. Oswald nails the coffin. "One minute forty, well done . . . well done . . . the Olympics are a long way off. I'm sure you'll be up to five minutes before then."

But before you can really get patronizing, a loud shrill breaks the calm dinner party chatter.

"WHAT DO YOU MEAN STUCK?"

The poor kitchen-hand fails to register a sound at your far end, but the gist is clear from Olympia's strident tones: "IT CAN'T BE STUCK. George, *do* something about it."

And George, Sixth Lord Ravenshaw, trots off obediently to sort out the domestic crisis. Olympia calms herself and addresses the hungry throng.

"My apologies everybody," she sighs theatrically. "Half the main course appears to be stuck in the lift from the kitchen. They haven't been serviced since before the war."

This with a glower at her husband's empty seat. She effects a twittering gaggle of conversation from the ninety-odd guests, no less so than at your, far end.

"God, but I'm starving," booms Astrid.

Scene 193

You see Barbie recoil at this new demonstration of social ineptitude. Oswald launches into an appropriate anecdote, relating the time he spent stuck in a lift with an African princess, and Marc-Pacaud, champion breath holder, is all but forgotten.

Presently his Lordship returns and announces that the main course will be some while. A man called Frank is coming from the village with his tool kit, but tuck into the wine and try to drink through the hunger is the general advice. And so you do.

Baroness Snuffy shouts, "More gin, boy," to a nearby, middle-aged waiter, who quickly returns with a bottle of Bombay Sapphire. She sloshes out seven generous glasses, and pops the bottle in her handbag. "Bombay Sapphire is a wonderful appetite suppressant, but it must be drunk neat."

Like all athletes, and the French generally, Marc proves to be ill-tolerant to large quantities of alcohol. By the time a second quadruple Bombay Sapphire has disappeared, his sexual threat has long since waned. Oswald, the conversational terrier, is giving him a thorough going-over, to the amusement of Astrid.

But George is back with some more bad news:

"I AM DEEPLY SORRY EVERYBODY. FRANK FROM THE VILLAGE HAS GOT HIMSELF WEDGED." With British restraint, all refrain from groaning at his Lordship's announcement but the misery is clear—no more food for bloody ages. More wine is circulated and the babble reaches a higher pitch.

Kamran shuffles off in the direction of Polly the Welsh, and Marc eventually disappears (probably to have a lie down), leaving the floor pretty clear. Oswald entertains Barbarella and Astrid with a discussion on "the art of seduction," which reminds you of your grand plan—to win Charlotte's young heart and revive Barbie's old jealousy. And so, using Snuffy as a foil to your wit, you bedazzle Charlotte with the speed and dexterity of your mind. The conversation flits from colonial India (Snuffy, of course, was an army wife) to politics to High Renaissance art to . . . but

Charlotte is yawning as she tucks into some more wine. Time to be a little more direct.

But Oswald is confiding in Barbarella at the end of the table: "I'll demonstrate on Astrid when she comes back from the loo . . . the key is nostril flaring, next most important, pupil dilation. It's a Hindu trick of course, like everything worth trying. Knew what they were up to did the Indians, that's why there are so many of the blighters."

And to your chagrin you realize that Catherine is standing, and Charlotte is rising.

"Lord Ravenshaw has a rather lovely Henry Moore; Charlotte is going to show me . . ."

"We'll be five minutes tops," this last from Charlotte restores your confidence. And anyway Kamran has returned, fresh (no doubt) from failure.

"So the Welsh soil proved a bit stony for your plow?" Kamran smiles, never willing to admit defeat. "I'm a tad surprised. She looked desperate enough to pull Oswald earlier . . . You must be losing your touch."

You crook a thumb in the direction of Oswald only to notice him grunting lecherously at Astrid. His gnarled liver-spotted hand strokes her fleshy arm and you have to look away.

Kamran defends himself. "Actually we struck a deal. Coke for a blow job."

"Kamran Jazeer, famed lover of thousands, paying for sex . . ."

Kam smiles broadly. "Barnaby, you're so distasteful, always thinking of commerce. This is just a novel way to take drugs."

The light begins to dawn. "When you say some coke, how much do you mean?"

"Quite a lot actually, she may have got a better bargain than she realized . . . a foreskinful."

*

Scene 193

The switch to the present tense, the slightly ragged breathing . . . It doesn't take a genius to figure out what's going on. You turn away in horror at Kamran's smile. Oswald is leading Astrid away by the hand. God. Where's Barbarella when you need her?

Go to Scene 209

Scene 194

The garden, though demonstrating the same absurd formality as the house, possesses more charm. The hedges may be a little crisp and the patio terrace a little regimented, but with the addition of a hundred assorted guests the welcome has a warm inviting air. The addition of half a dozen champagne waiters adds to the welcoming ambience, and against a backdrop of humming idle chatter you instinctively home upon a cool, sparkling flute.

But you have little time to absorb the atmosphere. A moment's people-watching alerts you to the early arrival of Annabel. She screeches above the hubbub and greets you like the long-time friend she has never been. As she bounds across the croquet lawn you can't help feeling a pang as you remember how slim and tall she is. Facially she isn't stunning (despite the nose job she had when you were at school), but she is well presented and few men would be able to avert their eyes from her 42" legs for sufficiently long to notice that her eyes are a little close together, or her foundation a little thicker of late.

But no time to wallow in bitchiness; double kiss done, she is forcing you to conversation. "Barbie, darling, you look wonderful. Will tells me that you've been drinking since lunchtime. I expected you'd be flat on your back."

She opens with a direct attack, but Barnaby, bless him, is coming to your aid with his usual misplaced intentions. "You know Barbarella, got the liver of a whale."

Scene 194

Annabel smiles at his analogy and you realize, with sudden fatigue, that you don't have the heart for this fight just now.

"Annabel, darling, it's so good to see you. We're all so excited about the wedding." You don't pause but extract yourself with, "I can't wait to chat but I've *got* to go to the loo." And without hesitation you are gone, leaving Barnaby to his fate.

Go to Scene 210

Scene 195

"WHAT DO YOU MEAN, STUCK?"

The poor kitchen-hand fails to register a sound at your far end, but the gist is clear from Olympia's strident tones: "IT CAN'T BE STUCK. George, *do* something about it."

And George, Sixth Lord Ravenshaw, trots off obediently to sort out the domestic crisis. Olympia calms herself and addresses the hungry throng.

"My apologies everybody," she sighs theatrically, "half the main course appears to be stuck in the lift from the kitchen. They probably haven't been serviced since before the war."

This with a glower at her husband's empty seat. She effects a twittering gaggle of conversation from the ninety-odd guests, no less so than at your, far end.

"God, but I'm starving," booms Astrid.

And her social ineptitude manages to distract you from your own hunger. Oswald launches into an appropriate anecdote, relating the time he spent stuck in a lift with an African princess, and your *faux pas*, you hope, is all but forgotten.

Presently his Lordship returns and announces that the main course will be some while. A man called Frank is coming from the village with his tool kit, but tuck into the wine and try to drink through the hunger is the general advice.

And so you do. Lady Fotherington produces a bottle of Bombay Sapphire from her bag and orders up seven ice-filled glasses and a lime. "Bombay Sapphire is a wonderful appetite suppressant, but it must be drunk neat."

You doubt her wisdom but don't decline. Then, from across the table comes the bombshell that finally shatters your peace of mind.

"You have a Henry Moore in the *jardin*? But I must see it. Please to show me now."

And Marc jumps to his record-breaking webbed feet, virtually grabbing the delectable Charlotte in his haste. She won't last more than five minutes alone with that lecher in "*le jardin*." You could cry at the injustice of it all. Instead, you wring your hands as she is whisked away by the foreign devil. You imagine him resting a hand on her inner arm, lightly touching her bottom as she peers unknowingly at the statue (no doubt of a reclining female). You shudder at the thought of Charlotte shuddering beneath his touch. And damn his eyes and lungs—could you ever compete sexually with a man who needs only one breath to your seven? Can you cope with being second best?

"Astrid-I'd-forgotten-you're-a-huge-Henry-Moore-fan-you-must-go-with-them," you splurt out.

Astrid blinks at you.

Barbarella, your irrepressible ally, kicks her under the table and Astrid comes up trumps. "I would love to meet Henry Moore, yes."

And so you buy yourself time. Marc is suspiciously unfazed as he takes Astrid on his free arm and waltzes off to the garden. Good God, he can't be planning to tup them both?

"What a wanker." Barbarella fills the vacuum left in Marc-Pacaud's wake.

"Yes, he is somewhat . . . French. It seems such a shame, you and Charlotte were getting on so well. Still, faint heart never won fair lady." Lady Fotherington pats your hand in a grandmotherly way. "Waiter, more ice. No, not slush—proper ice. I don't want watery gin."

Sympathy from women has always brought on a black mood (well, ever since the day you lost your virginity) and the sympathy of an octogenarian dowager can only make things worse. Your tortured soul longs for release from the bonds of love. You hate her you love her you hate her . . . you want her . . . YOU MUST HAVE CHARLOTTE.

The whimper you produce doesn't go unnoticed.

"Barnie, pull yourself together." This from Barbarella who decides she's had enough of your lusting, and strolls off in search of fresh company. Kamran provides, if anything, even less solace, "plenty more fish, you've still got your health, etc.," and roams forth in the general direction of Polly the Welsh strumpet.

And so you are left alone with the two oldest people in the world. Whilst others walk the walk on the sexual tightrope, you talk the talk of defeat, battered on the rocks below. The dinner party seems to be breaking up from lack of food and alcoholic abstinence. All you can do is retreat to your glass of neat gin, and brood.

Snuffy senses your despair. "Barnaby, stop it at once. Self-pity is hideous in anybody, let alone a courting lover."

Oswald joins the Barnaby-baiting. "Yerrrs, come come young fella, just because you are not as deft in the game of love as you would like, no need to give up completely you know. There will be some four-eyed librarian out there who will waggle her pear at you."

You wail as you realize that these two have put you down as a love dunce. Too late you discover that lust has halved your IQ.

This is hopeless. Your plan to seduce Charlotte, and at the same time render Barbarella desperate with jealousy, has backfired totally. You've been caught between two stools, that much is clear. You just have to decide once and for all—Charlotte or

Scene 195

Barbarella. Nubile nineteen, or trusty twenty-seven? Girl, or woman?

Choose Barbarella, put aside childish things and try to win back your one true love. **Go to Scene 175**

Charlotte's no child; and maybe she's the one. If you don't fight for her now, you'll never know. **Go to Scene 257**

Or do you give up on females altogether? **Go to Scene 199**

Scene 196

"So what's this party, Catherine?"

"It's at Godfrey's fat-cat mansion. You know, *offshore* Godfrey, the guy who donated £2 million to the Labour Party before the last election and only pays nothing in income tax. Come on, it'll be hilarious."

You've made your mind up, Barbie, it's kill-or-cure time for Catherine. Edward Bunger, minister without morality, is just another desperate, middle-aged bastard who wants his bread buttered both ways. The fact that he's making Catherine suffer as a result doesn't seem to worry him. Well, it's time he did start worrying, and Barbie, you're just the girl to put the fear of God into him.

"Barnie, Will, shut up for a minute and listen. I think we should go to the party. We can go to the West India Club anytime; but tonight I think we should show Catherine a bit of solidarity." You squeeze Cat's hand and share a touching smile. Argument over.

Catherine finds Edward B., secures six invites to the party, and obtains the address with a vigor born of hope. By the time she returns, the boat party is really beginning to dissipate and you join the departing straggle of people up and onto the Embankment. Catherine is whisked away by Edward in his chauffeur-driven Daimler and she waves happily from the back seat. The rest of you wait for a black cab.

Go to Scene 78

Scene 197

The turquoise-brushed walls boom, and the limed-oak floor shrieks in contradiction. The churlishly overdecorated fireplace begs for mercy as it peers from beneath a primary school harvest festival display.

"Good God, it's like a *Changing Rooms* snuff movie."

Too late. You have splurted. With horror you observe her eager, expectant face turn to a frown.

Then, the beautiful, adorable, noble Charlotte shifts the frown with a becoming sigh and half smiles her inflated lips in invitation. "I *thought* Mummy was being a little overkind. Trouble is, I only seem to be good at one thing."

With the innocence of a middle-aged prostitute she unzips your fly and slips her cool slender fingers around your attentive manhood.

"I've never met anyone like you before." She pulls you tenderly over to the four-poster bed by your lead.

"You are so open. That French twat wouldn't know erotic if I sat on his face."

She giggles at her naughtiness, then strips you tenderly but expertly. The ease of your conquest slows your wits. Her eager beauty stuns you. She easily pushes you back onto the soft plump gingham duvet, kisses you tenderly with those lips, and gnaws at your flesh with long sharp canines.

The next events tumble before your sloth brain. She grips and claws at your wrists, bites at your chest and fixes you with vixen eyes. You are too lust-lorn to resist when she pushes your wrists above you . . . and attaches them to the bed with bespoke straps.

You wonder at her efficiency for microseconds before your legs are pulled roughly apart and strapped in the same manner. The sharp nail as it is drawn over your ribs and sternum makes you wince. And with practiced ease Charlotte plunges a gag into your open mouth.

Thirty seconds tops. From clothed to bound. She must practice on her teddy bear. But events are happening too quickly for your fuddled brain. The gag is a little spooky, but you can't say you weren't forewarned by the rumors. And now you can't say anything.

And then, somehow, it doesn't matter. For Charlotte, at last, is stripping.

She removes panties first, smothering your face with their odor. The dress floats off with a flicked wrist and she stands naked at the foot of the bed. You strain against your bonds to see the most glorious of all sights.

For there, before you, she stands, knees slightly bent, quivering, trying not to buckle. Her elfin face is drunk with lust and the speed of her crooked hand defies nature herself. Charlotte strums. Eventually she slows to a pause and, with panther intent, mounts the bed. Sitting above your gagged face, she continues, this time sparing a hand for you. The intoxicating smell lobotomizes your eager brain. Her hands never cease. Despite your utmost efforts you fail to disgorge the gag for a quick lick. And then it is too late. She plunges her ripe bottom on to your gesticulating face and you hear her through buttock earmuffs: "I couldn't believe how blatant you were at dinner. When I heard you talking about asphyxiation I could have . . ."

But as she rubs you with greater speed with one hand, the other switches to grab your nose.

Scene 197

No time for a breath, you fight against her weight for air. She pushes back down and you hear a groan. The more you buck the greater her cries. Then she bites your thigh and you feel sharp teeth almost penetrate skin. The cry in your throat is locked though, tight behind its gag. The hand moves ever faster and you can't help thinking of Marc and the dowager. You are going to come with a fearful fury, your eyes are aching, all you can sense is her hand, still rubbing, the stars come and then . . .

All fades.

The (Dead) End

How sordid. Play again, and try *to be more careful. At this rate Barnie will never get anywhere* near *the Perfect Ending.*

Scene 198

After a bare ten minutes you have everything to perfection. Oswald's surprisingly fertile mind adds ingenious nuances to Snuffy's daring plan. You contemplate what you have to do with some dread. It won't be easy, but Oswald and Snuffy have 170 years experience to fall back on, Kamran has always been a winner, and even Astrid's presence is somehow comforting. The others are coming back, sit up straight and prepare for war.

Oswald crosses the Rubicon before you have time to worry any more. "Ladies and gentlemen, if it is OK with you, Olympia, I suggest—as an additional distraction from our hunger—that we play a game. Ravenshaw House has a long tradition of 'sardines.'" The suggestion is greeted with a low murmur of tipsy approval. "Olympia, do you have a deck of cards? We need them to choose who hides."

Sure enough Olympia efficiently whistles up a pack of cards. And with great aplomb and no little dexterity Oswald holds court with witty banter as he strolls the length of the gallery, dealing out the deck.

"Lady Fotherington. Would you care to choose a card at random."

And so Snuffy, with a natural acting talent, plays her part in the plan. Seventy-three years after her own, fateful game of sardines in a Hampshire country house in 1929. "I choose . . . the queen of hearts."

Scene 198

With a hubbub of noise the ninety-odd guests look down at their cards. You don't bother of course, you casually look across at Will. He smiles and lethargically waves his card, the red queen, in the air. "I've got it, I've got it." He jumps to his feet, and with a last smile to the guests, calls out, "Give me fifty," and with one last handshake from Oswald, leaves the room.

Another trill of excitement ripples through the middle-aged diners as the chanting count begins. "ONE, TWO, THREE." You glance down the length of the table with a smile, most of these people probably haven't played a game of sardines since the sixties.

"SEVEN, EIGHT, NINE . . ." You glance across at Annabel. She is counting along with the rest, but at the same time she is staring at you, calculating. She knows you are up to something.

"TWENTY-THREE, TWENTY-FOUR . . ." You smile a winning primary school smile to deflect her penetrating glare, but it does no good. She sees all. She knows all.

"THIRTY-NINE, FORTY . . ." You move to the edge of your seat, kick off high heels and get ready for the race. Annabel sees you and discards her own footwear.

"FORTY-EIGHT, FORTY-NINE, FIFTY."

Go to Scene 20

Scene 199

Snuffy pours you another gin. Then another. The main course never seems to arrive, but you couldn't eat it anyway. The last you remember, before waking up by one of the tennis courts, is the bottom of an Armitage Shanks bowl . . .

The (Bottled) End

It can only get better than this, Reader. You're not a failure until you give up. Go back, try again, and get whatever you can.

Scene 200

A few more maladroit footsteps and you assume that you've arrived at the final destination. You are seated on a chair.

"Sww duu ei gaet a droenk?"

Um, try removing the helmet. You make moves to lift it off, but a hand is placed heavily, forcing it down. Barnaby speaks up.

"Baby, this is the Devil. Beside me is your Angel, but if you want to have fun with a stranger I suggest we keep your eyes covered. The rules dictate that I may speak, but the Angel may not. When we have finished with you, the Angel's identity will be revealed."

This all sounds rather sexy, but you can't answer back.

"I'm about to remove the helmet and bow-tie so that I can replace them with a proper blindfold. You've got to promise not to look. If you do, I'll get nasty."

The helmet is being removed. You're dying to open your eyes, to see where you are and to discover the identity of the Angel, but are equally determined not to ruin the fun. You keep your eyes cautiously closed, and a wicked smile resting on your lips. Think of the possibilities. It might be Barnie's work colleague, Ben, with the cute eyes, sensitive hands, and flamenco torso. Or maybe it's his old school mate, Harvey, with the big jaw and strange lolling tongue . . .

"Angel or Devil?"

"Um, either . . ."

Someone approaches (please be Ben), but you are not sure who. With weighty force you are pushed down onto something soft, like a mattress. You guess this means you get the Devil first. Piece of cake—you can handle the Essex boy.

"Come on then, tiger. Show me how bad the Devil can really be."

Nothing like a bit of cajoling to get this fantasy fired up. Oh, here goes. Say goodbye to your dress as it is literally torn over your head. Even though you know with whom you are contending, you now feel slightly defenseless—and a little nervous.

"Barnie, I mean Devil, you aren't going to hur—"

That sentence is stopped in its prime by something being placed in your mouth—oh God, it's a gag. This has never been part of your repertoire before. Ten out of ten for originality. Seconds ago you felt slightly vulnerable, now you feel entirely exposed. Someone is pinning down your arms. It must be the Angel, as the Devil seems to be wasting no time. He is forcing himself on you like a teenager, not waiting or even trying to satisfy anyone but himself. Pushing your legs upwards, he enters with a gasp (yours). You weren't quite ready for that.

Left to the indulgence of the Romford Devil you are unable to cry out, or even move.

"If you want a change, you only need ask for it." The gag is removed abruptly. You seize your chance.

"Angel."

The pace slows. The hands are removed from your arms and the Devil withdraws. You lie there expectantly, writhing playfully on the bed. Let's see what the Angel will do.

You feel a finger dragging itself up the length of your leg, ever so gradually. It leads up over your knee and between your thighs, then soothingly across your clitoris, pausing to stroke and burrow. Now this is more like it. It must be Ben. The finger then drags itself across toned midriff and towards your breasts; they're crying for attention.

The Angel repeats the finger trail with his tongue. You moan, eagerly intent on putting up a porn-star performance despite the lack of a camera (you hope). Your show is interrupted by a male voice, "Devil."

Hold on. The rules have changed. You weakly protest.

"No, look, I didn't ask for the Devil."

Your protestations are ineffectual as the Devil mounts you for a second time. This time you are turned on to all fours.

"Angel, Angel," you cry in desperation.

The Devil swears. Nice try, Barnaby.

The Angel returns for another round, this time using his hands to full effect. He is smearing something on to your skin. The nearest thing you can compare it to is a Dead Sea mud wrap (not for a second that you have cellulite). The substance is cold and pulls against the skin. The Angel slides it across your chest, kneading it rhythmically. On your bottom, you can feel another pair of helping hands as the Devil throws off his evil mantle to assist the Angel. Saint Peter would be so proud.

It's now two on one. You are literally being smothered with attention as more of the cool mud is smeared on to your skin. Efforts are being made to cover every part of your body, and the feeling of four hands running over your skin sends you into sensorial reveries.

Heaven and Hell work in harmony and you lap it up. Why haven't you played this game before? If you knew that Barnaby could bring you so much fulfillment, you might never have let him go. Who knows what really went wrong between you? But will he still consider you as girlfriend material after this rather sordid episode?

As you continue to moan and writhe with alarming professionalism, you fail to notice that the hands have stopped smearing. You also fail to hear a faint click as a door closes. Eventually, the suspicion valve is released and you sense that you might be alone.

"Barnie, are you there? Barnaby?"

Your immediate reaction is to remove the blindfold but your arms resist. Whatever has been smeared on your delicious body, has virtually set. With quite a struggle, you push off the blindfold by rubbing it against your right shoulder.

SHIT.

One quick glance reveals the identity of the hideaway *and* your Angel. You've been here before. Barbarella, you are currently aboard the *Anomie*—Kamran's little love boat on the river.

Don't strain yourself to move, it's futile. Barnaby and Kamran have smeared you in quick-dry plaster. How could they do this? As you kneel, motionless, encased in your cast, you fight the rising panic. The bastards will be sitting in their favorite greasy café two hundred yards away with a cup of caffeine and the Sunday papers. You could roll on to your back but you'd just lie there, with four limbs in the air, like a begging dog. How humiliating. Best stay as you are and try not to fall asleep.

Oh, Barbarella, when will you ever learn? God punishes the wicked by giving us what we wish for . . .

The (Uncomfortable) End

You can't leave Barbie like this, Reader. She is nubile, young, and just aching for fun. Have some sympathy and play again . .

Scene 201

Your stomach rumbles again. And a third time. Then, with bowel-clenching horror, you run to the bathroom and reach the loo with seconds to spare. A five-second, Jericho-trashing trumpet salute and it's all over.

"Barnaby, are you OK?"

Oh God, Catherine is knocking on the door.

"Yeah, sorry, I'm just feeling a bit sick. I ate a crab canapé earlier and it tasted a bit funny. I think I'll be OK in a—"

You don't finish, or rather, your crashing bowels decide to finish for you—with a thunderous symphony. How embarrassing.

"OK, as long as you're all right . . . I might just jump in a cab and go home, I'm pretty done in. Let's do the video another night."

Shangri La-de-da. Three flushes, and some heavy demarbling, later and you're still too nervous to leave the bathroom. You try texting Kamran, to find out what was in the smoothie, but the bastard doesn't answer . . .

How utterly humiliating. You could be here hours—plenty enough time to figure out what Kamran's secret ingredient is. Just think back . . . There was something vaguely familiar about that strange texture . . .

The (Messy) End

How can you leave Barnie like this, Reader? Quick, play again. And this time think twice about accepting anything *from Kamran.*

Scene 202

Quite right, you're obviously in touch with your feminine side. With that kind of thinking you can only be Barbarella . . .

Barnaby, your lost love, is like any other man. He's bound to be tempted by a skinny blonde with a cash flow crisis. But you can offer him so much more. You check your dress, smooth it down over a slightly menstrual tummy, and barge in.

You open the door . . . *and find your father lying naked on the bed*. He squints at you against the bright corridor light.

"Babs, what are you doing here? Tell Maruskha I'm ready when she is. And shut the door, would you. Thanks, my little pumpkin."

Your sleeping body judders a violent objection.

Reader, it's about to begin. Looks like you've chosen to be Barbarella. Don't worry, this Freudian nightmare won't last long. The day will come soon enough, so take a breath, count ten pelvic floor squeezes—and when you're ready **Go to Scene 2.**

Scene 203

And so, with your cunning scheme hanging above the poor snail-eater like a Damoclean sword, you three toast with the last of the Bombay Sapphire and await the return of Marc-Pacaud.

Barbie returns first, and you all brief her with gusto, ". . . just make sure that you stand up and leave the room as soon as I kick you under the table."

Then, finally, when you fear you can bear it no longer, Astrid, Marc, and a rosy-cheeked Charlotte emerge from the garden; smiling and flushed from the cooling night air. Before you can act, your attention is drawn to a scuffle of activity at the far end of the room.

"I AM DEEPLY SORRY, EVERYBODY—FRANK FROM THE VILLAGE HAS GOT HIMSELF WEDGED IN THE LIFT." With British restraint, all refrain from groaning at Lord George's announcement, but the misery is clear—no more food for bloody ages. More wine is circulated and the babble reaches a higher pitch.

Time for execution . . .

"Marc, tell me, in your own country you must be a major figure. I seem to remember that 'holding of the breath' is a big thing in France, up there with push-bike racing." You spill the opening gambit casually; Marc responds.

"Oh yes, it is somewhat embarrassing for my father to have a son who is a 'pinup.' But really the holding of the breath it is no great thing. Compared to say a *docteur* or . . . a *pompier*, how you zay . . . the fyer-man."

You sense your moment.

"Oh, Marc, you must be kidding us. Surely if you are the champion of all of France then you must have superman abilities. How long can you hold your breath for? Two minutes? Three?"

Barbarella shifts beside you, she suspects this could be entertaining.

"No, no. Three minutes is normal. Two minutes even an old man could do," this with a hand waved in the direction of Oswald. "I can hold my breath for five minutes twenty-seven seconds."

You work it out—one hour's cunnilingus on eleven breaths; Charlotte seems lost in thought.

"Over five minutes? . . . Astonishing. You can't be normal. I can barely credit it. You must show us . . ."

And so the challenge is laid down.

Go to Scene 231

Scene 204

Quite right, Reader. You're obviously in touch with your masculine side. With that kind of thinking you can only be Barnaby . . .

You're only human. And if your dearest Barbarella wants to get up to this sort of thing in your dreams then she has to expect an audience. There will be plenty of time to win her back when you wake up, and in the meantime you might pick up a few pointers. From the way Maruskha caresses the lid onto your cappuccino every morning she's bound to demonstrate some expertise.

You open the door . . . *only to find your mother lying naked on the bed*. She shades her eyes against the bright corridor light and eventually recognizes you.

"Oh it's you, Barnaby. Shut the door, there's a draft. If you see your father tell him Maruskha and I are waiting."

Your night erection stutters to flaccid.

Reader, it's about to begin. Looks like you've chosen to be Barnaby. Don't worry, this Freudian nightmare won't last long. The day will come soon enough, so take a breath, think about Britney touching her toes, and count to ten. When you're ready
Go to Scene 1

Scene 205

"Really? You'd let me redesign your flat?" She hesitates but maintains her grip on your arm. "But you haven't even seen anything I've done." She thinks . . . and excitedly drags you towards the house.

"Come and see my bedroom; I only finished it a few weeks ago," and she skips lithely away, dragging you all the while—back into the house via some unlocked French windows, along a small hallway, up some winding side stairs, and into the isolated tranquillity of her bedroom.

Go (quickly) to Scene 197

Scene 206

Are you mad?

Every child learns in the primary school playground that if you die in a dream then you die in real life.

OK, that may not be scientifically proven, but your thinking is unsuited to spending even so much as a day with Barnaby and Barbarella. Please, put the book down; if you still have the receipt then take it back to the shop—swap it for a romance novel or, better still, a comfortable John Grisham. Take your brain out put, the kettle on, and settle for a nice afternoon far from the ugliness of reality.

Reader, count your blessings, for this is . . .

The (Premature) End

Or you could take a deep breath, put your conscience to one side, and go back to the beginning . . .

Scene 207

Oh dear—you may have got your wires crossed.

"You're such a tosser, Barnie."

Kamran looks as though he could punch you; instead, he walks from the room, shaking his head.

Barbarella looks at you as though you've just mugged a granny. "I just don't believe anything you say any more."

She and Catherine leave in silence.

You find a decanter of scotch and fill a glass.

The (Lonesome) End

You should know better, Reader. Have a heart and play again . . .

Scene 208

Finbar, with a burst of energy, races around in circles and bit by bit draws you to the front of the house. Then he shoots forward and bounds to the bottom of the front steps. If the dog is right, Will must have circled the house before reentering the front door. You help the aging dog up the steep stairs and find yourself in the grand entrance hall. You can hear the sound of voices down the corridor and curse Finbar for his lack of speed. But the dog's nose draws you inexorably upwards and westwards, away from the voices. Then, along one particularly thin and distant corridor on the second floor, Finbar stops and howls at the low ceiling.

You look up, and there, barely visible, is the square outline of an attic hatch. It has a small brass handle, which you pull downwards to reveal an unfolding ladder. Finbar barks excitedly and with some hesitation you pick up your faithful friend and ascend into the gloom.

You poke a head up. Nothing.

But Fin is sniffing like an ItGirl in a loo. He's on to something—and so you clamber onto wooden boards, place Fin gently down, and desperately squint your eyes. A voice whispers breathlessly in your ear, "I knew you'd find me first." It is Will; he tries to pull you up.

"No, take the bloody dog first. He'll give the game away, sitting there." So you pass up the exhausted Finbar. Finally, Will grapples you up the ladder before closing the hatch.

"Will, we've got to talk," but he doesn't pay you any attention. He has been cooped up with a fistful of rodent musk for too long. "Barbarella, shush." He presses strong hands down your sides, you catch a whiff of a strange ambergrisian scent that pops blinding stars of light onto your frontal lobe. Your head feels numb but strangely alert, and like a blind man your other senses become sensitized to such an extent that you can hear Will's light breath in your ear, feel his trousers rubbing against the back of your knee, his fingertips on your throat, the dog tongue on your ankle.

You waste valuable seconds to gently kick the dog away, but it moves straight onto Will. With the enthusiasm of a Pfizer-assisted Californian pensioner, old Finbar has, in Will's leg, refound love.

"What the fu—" The dog barks with the rejection. Will almost falls over and your sensuously drowning head is dragged to the surface in a rushing torrent of noise, for the hatch is opening. Someone has heard you—and from the bright light below appears the reedy head of dear, darling Annabel.

She smiles up at you in victory. Will holds out a hand to help her up and soon the hatch is shut once more. In the darkness you sit in companionable silence, and wait to be found.

The (Threesome) End

Reader, you were almost there. The Perfect End was within your grasp and you blew it. Still, now that you know how Barbarella's mind works, you might have a better chance if you go back to the prologue and try out in the eager body of Barnaby . . .

Scene 209

Charlotte, your beloved . . . she has returned . . .

Even the sight of Snuffy gladdens. She looks a bit perturbed to see that Kamran has taken her seat, but he is beyond caring. He starts to make whimpering noises.

Lady Fotherington sits next to him and strikes up conversation. "So young man, where in India are you from?"

"Kashmnnnuur."

And Snuffy, oblivious to the odd pronunciation, takes up the conversational mantle as Kamran sits back, smiles warmly, and dozily listens. "Reginald was posted to Kashmir back in '34, just after Mahatma's little outing to . . ."

You doubt he can hear a thing. You return your attentions to the lovely Charlotte.

"Charlotte, where did you go for your year abroad?" You fill her glass and try not to feel pedophilic.

And so she talks, at first of Malawi, then her future. ("I've got a place at Exeter to study history of art, but I'm not sure. It all seems so self-indulgent. Mummy thinks I could be an interior designer.") And as she talks she drinks.

Frank from the village is eventually pulled from the lift, but the main course seems no nearer. Dessert makes an appearance after awhile, but by then most are too drunk to know what to do with it.

Charlotte continues to talk and drink; with eager senses you note a slight slurring to her speech. Kamran is arguing hammer and tongs with Lady Fotherington, and you're wondering absently about Polly when you notice a slight whimper from Charlotte mid-sentence. A certain raggedness of breath. She continues to talk but the words make little sense . . . and with a mounting horror (and erection) you realize that Polly is still at work.

This really is too much. You're beginning to feel like a eunuch at the Playboy Mansion. If Polly is as skilled as you fear, you might as well pack up and go home. Time to call a halt to Polly's warm-up routine, and bring on the main act.

Do you suggest some entertainment to relieve the boredom? Polly is Welsh, she could sing perhaps. **Go to Scene 227**

Or suggest Charlotte takes you to see the garden. **Go to Scene 211**

Scene 210

You duck into the house in search of some solitude and note with mixed feelings that the formal gallery has been chosen as the site of the evening's dining experience. It is less imposing, more windowed, and generally less miserable than the rest of the house, but you can't help remembering that the last time you were here, years ago, was the culmination of a happy night of drunken lovemaking with the now soon-to-be-married Will.

You approach the table with the usual mixture of nervous misgivings and aroused curiosity, and with relief you note that Barnaby will be sitting to your left, but to your right is the rather curious-sounding Lady Fotherington. Two girls together. Obviously the late arrival of Annabel has upset Olympia's seating plans and you smile with the dual thought that not only is Olympia less than Nigella-perfect, but that she will be cursing Annabel for her late acceptance.

An elderly female voice interrupts your thoughts. "Just put them down there, boy. No, not like that. Give them here. And get me a proper glass . . . no, not a pint glass, a tall glass, for gin. And ice."

She settles herself in that way peculiar to old people, and looks you up and down: "Well, well. Some young blood for a change. Pleased to meet you. Lady Fotherington, but call me Snuffy, everybody does." She sees confusion. "Snuffy . . . as in the movies." And with a glinting eye she proffers a firm hand.

You take to her immediately. A great beauty in her youth, "Snuffy" turns out to be a living history lesson. She can only vaguely remember the Great War but relates stories of the twenties that would have made Evelyn Waugh chew the rubber off the top of his pencil. The late thirties and forties were spent in "Injia" where she was on speaking terms with "Little Mahatma—such a happy little man." She talks for a while longer about her environmental work ("I shot a tiger back in '32 and feel the need to make up for it"), but with the unerring insensitivity of the old she spots your lack of wedding ring and brings the conversation to a more mundane level.

"So, I see that you're still 'fancy-free,' " she says, nodding down at your left hand. You nod feebly and await the inevitable chastisement, but instead Snuffy proves to be full of surprises: "Well done, there's nothing worse than seeing a girl tied down before she's ready. Of course, in my day if you were single at twenty-five you took up cross-stitch and retired to the country. Just promise me you won't settle down just because everyone else is. I often wish I'd never married Horace, God rest his soul."

With relief you take advantage of your new confidante. "Don't worry, I certainly won't get married for the sake of it. I'm stupidly fussy when it comes to men."

"Quite right, dear, I had twenty-three proposals before I consented to Horace. Of course, that was well above average." Snuffy glazes over at the memories of youth. You imagine her in the 1920s—impossibly glamorous, courted by the grandest men of her day . . . and then you spot her shaking hand as it curls, liver-spotted, around a gin glass. Your own mortality hits you like the surf on a windy Cornish beach. One day you won't be worrying about how bloated your stomach looks or whether you're getting cellulite, you'll be worrying whether you can walk up the stairs without help, or whether the rheumatoid arthritis in your hips means they need to be replaced. And as the cold wave of realization recedes, you are left sitting with a strange dawning thought. Maybe there's no such thing as Mr. Right, and maybe the list of Mr. Acceptables is shrinking with every marriage. You think about the four wedding invitations sitting at home and a cold glow of panic flushes your face. And with that particular resilience possessed only by the female of the species—you change your mind. Barnaby is a lost cause, and after him Will is the closest thing to love you have ever known.

And the idiot has just got engaged.

Time to make a life-changing decision, Barbie. He may be second best, work shy, and have the emotional depth of Keanu Reeves . . . but you can change him, or maybe you could learn to be less demanding. And, without prompting, an image of Will pops into your head. He's wearing his frayed M&S shortie-briefs and matching Marks socks. You can tell a lot about a man by his underwear. A conflicting image of Barnaby floats into view, but you can't quite remember what pants he used to wear. Are you sane? Picking a husband by the label in their underwear.

Get on with it, Barbie. No time like the present.

Be steadfast and true. Leave Will to the dogs and hunt down Barnaby. Tell Barnie that you want to have his babies. **Go to Scene 212**

Oh, fickle girl. Give up on Barnaby, Will is your true love now. **Go to Scene 90**

Scene 211

Charlotte doesn't hesitate at your suggestion and soon you find yourself in the garden. It's even more lovely empty of people. Not a chirrup of gossip breaks through the calm as you meander into its darkest recesses. Tall, clinically topiaried hedges now conceal you from the house, and as you follow Charlotte further, she continues to drink and talk incessantly.

"These are my favorite." She points to some nondescript flowers. "In August the butterflies get drunk on the nectar and lie on this path. When I was young I used to sit here with them and balance them in my hair."

You love her. You imagine her dancing gleefully, a woodland nymph, naked and strong, leaping from rock to rock, beloved of all the woodland creatures; she springs into a sunny glade beckoning you to touch her forbidden fruit, to slide a hand over a shoulder, to feel her shudder as it mounts her perfect breast, then hear her inhale as you slide down further, over the flat bronzed tummy, her mound . . . but she is still talking.

"There is something so romantic about midsummer's night, don't you think?" Good God. Virtually an embossed invite.

"The thought of you kicking off your heels and flitting through this garden like a woodland sprite, you mean," you suggest eagerly. "I would chase you, yet, you would forever remain out of my lusting reach." The time is right, you grab a tit.

Go to Scene 260

Scene 212

Very interesting decision.

"Sorry, Snuffy, I need to see someone. I've left it too long already."

Snuffy pats your hand. "It's a boy, isn't it? I can see it in your face." She smiles. "Go on then, you stupid girl, don't waste time talking to me."

You sprint to the garden. The guests are starting to move into the house and you have to fight against the crowd. Eventually you spot Barnaby, where you left him, chatting awkwardly to Annabel. You don't hesitate. "Annabel, just bugger off, would you? I need to talk to Barnaby and you're boring him shitless." You feel a whole lot better for that—should have done it years ago. Released love has liberated you. For once Annabel doesn't have a cutting retort and you drag Barnaby to one side.

"Sorry, Barnie, shouldn't have left you . . . but I had to do some thinking."

He doesn't speak, but smiles expectantly.

"Barnie, I want to get back together. I want the whole world to know that I love you . . . Barnie, will you marry me?"

You don't go down on one knee, but from the expression of horror on Barnaby's face, you might as well have done. He takes a step back, shaking his head. You don't wait for an answer.

Tears flowing, you run to your room and there wail into a

pillow, shedding tears for the mutilation of your love life and reputation.

You poor fool, Barbarella. You've well and truly blown it. Do you not know anything about the opposite sex? There's a reason why the 29th February comes only once in every four years. Pope Gregory XIII was a man.

The (Humiliating) End

Oh Reader, felled at the last hurdle. The Perfect Ending is out there, but you went about it the wrong way. You've obviously got talent, so play again, and don't try to run before you can walk.

Scene 213

You take the door on the left. It creaks as it opens but, alas, not nearly loud enough to distract the occupants. The sight within etches in your memory before you have time to scream in horror. The reedy, naked body of an octogenarian, chasing your rotund, Belgian friend round the room with a Pfizer-fueled pointer.

You grab Astrid by the naked arm as she races by (her dress is up round her waist) and slam the door on the skin-covered skeleton. By the time you run down the steps and into Will's Land Rover, all but one breast is covered.

Go to Scene 217

Scene 214

You take a sip of your drink while eyeing up the room, but before you can spot anything promising, a black-tied gentleman blocks your view.

"Hello, Barbarella. I must say, Catherine's description didn't do you justice."

Oh, Christ. It's Edward, Catherine's betrayer.

You can't think of an interesting response, and, being female, decide not to make one. Taking your arm, the minister steers you away to the nearest porthole.

Go to Scene 76

Scene 215

You decide ridicule is the best way forward.

"Tell me, Marc, I read once of a diver who could communicate with ze dolphins" (you can't help imitating his dodgy French accent). "Can you talk to zese creatures?"

"The dolphins are like brothers to me. They are my family. I have talked with them for as long as I can remember."

"Oh, how interesting. What do you talk about?" Astrid joins the conversation. You couldn't have put it better yourself.

"We talk of ze joy of swimming free in ze blue, of the sorrow of losing a brother to ze tuna nets, we talk of many things."

"Tell me, do dolphins bore easily?" This from Oswald, joining the fray.

Marc turns to face Oswald head on, the young stag ready to take on the elder. "I onlee wish you could see for yourself, the dignity and intelligence of zese creatures, their capacity for compassion, for onderstandeeng."

He smiles a thin-lipped smile of compassion. "I would offer for to have you join me, but the physical exertion for one so agèd . . ."

Fish-boy leaves it there, the insult hanging. Oswald can't help a harrumph escaping from the back of his throat. Marc turns once more to Charlotte. "But you, Charlotte, you are young."

Barbarella lets out a squawk at being overlooked.

"You would be able to take the incredible pressures, the heady rush from flying through water on the back of a dolphin. You see, in the deep, every touch, every sensation is magnified a hundredfold."

Charlotte blushes delightfully under his heavy-lidded gaze. Something has to be done.

"It all sounds rather erotic to me." You decide to flush the Eurobounder into the open. "Are you sure this sort of auto-asphyxiation is completely healthy; after all, look what it did to Michael Hutchence and Paula Yates. He died and she was pretty shriveled by the end."

Brilliant, Barnie, at once showing Marc-Pacaud to be a prurient licentious pervert and finding time to have a dig at Paula Yates.

But you should have trod more lightly. Marc is not so easily put back in his box.

"Barnaby, I do not understand what you mean by this 'ortoasfixeeayshun.' It is a perverted bad thing? *C'est dégoûtant, non?* I do not think we should talk of such things in mixed company. I apologize, your ladyship, Barbarella . . . Charlotte."

There is silence, punctuated only by sniffing from Mr. and Mrs. City Banker, a slight, embarrassed cough from the Lady Fotherington, and glinting daggers of light from Marc's impeccable smile. He has turned you. More so than if you had stood on your chair and shouted, "I am a pervert," he has made you look a fool. You can't even bear to see Charlotte's reaction.

Before you can rally, Olympia stills all with a shrilling wail.

Go to Scene 195

Scene 216

Go for the one who looks as though he's having the most fun—the next man to laugh gets you. There, that's him, catalogue good looks, talking to the sports minister. Make sure your drink is near replacing, think goddess, and go forth.

Go to Scene 150

Scene 217

"Quickly, you idiots," Will shouts rather unnecessarily, and you slam the car door shut. You do a quick head count and realize that everyone has made it; the six are reunited and ready to flee the wrath of Olympia. Will steps down forcibly on the accelerator, and, with wheels spinning in the gravel, you make a hasty departure for London.

The journey back to town is of little note. For some reason Barbie is so annoyed that she spends most of it in stony silence. You suppress the disturbing memories of copulating couples and vow to return for the lovely Charlotte (and your bike).

But before long, you are flying towards Hammersmith; it's time to look to the future. Will, chastened by an evening talking to aging relatives, is eager for action. Astrid and Kamran are well primed. Will suggests a casino.

"Unlucky in love and all that. It'd be such a waste to call it a night now."

Three of you agree with enthusiasm. Catherine, thoughtfully subdued, smiles meekly and concedes to the majority, but Barbie, still annoyed, puts a dampener on proceedings.

"You guys go where you want, just drop me off first. I'm knackered."

Suddenly your energy levels plummet and two thoughts fill your mind.

You and Barbarella are over. After all the arguments, all the years and months of dancing round each other, the teasing and taunting, it's over. No more bonus shags, no more sleepless nights, no more delicious text messages. Over.

And it doesn't matter. You have—at last—moved on. Charlotte will now fill your waking thoughts; *she* will provide thought for the sleepless nights, *her* mobile will beep in response to your lurid messages.

"Actually, drop me off as well. I need to get up early to go and pick up my bike."

Well. After all those silly games, it looks like you've gone and blown it with Barbarella for good. And what's worse, you now seem to be in love with a spoilt, nineteen-year-old brat. Best get some sleep; you've got a busy day tomorrow.

The End (of an Era)

Looks like you just don't understand women, Reader. Why don't you get into Barbarella's mind and body for a while? Go back to the prologue and play again—you might learn something . . .

Scene 218

Without another word to Astrid, you storm out of the toilets. There they all are, near the exit—Kamran talking to Barnaby (no doubt spreading more lies), Will arguing with Annabel. Catherine looking awkward.

Time for a big, fat scene.

"Kamran, have you got a canoe in your pocket or are you just pleased to see Barnaby?" Pause. "Don't you think you should tell Barnie the truth, Kam?"

Everyone hears it. Kamran and Barnaby turn in shock. Only Will makes a sound, a kind of strangulated nervous laugh. Barnaby responds first. "Barbie, what are you on about?" He turns to Kamran—but the Asian can't look him in the eye—and suddenly you know for sure that it's all true. For cringingly long moments nothing happens. Then, words failing, Kamran turns, and runs off the boat.

Barnaby looks at you in disbelief. You barely comprehend his contorted voice. "You complete bitch, what the fuck was that all about?" and Barnaby is gone, chasing onto the Embankment in search of Kamran. You're left with a puzzled Will, a smiling Annabel, and Catherine, staring at the floor. Will breaks the silence.

"Well, I think that went well," he jokes in his usual embarrassed way. But the cackle of laughter from Annabel is too much to bear. Catherine takes your hand, says goodnight for both of you, and leads you away and in search of a cab.

The rest is a blur. After a silent taxi journey you traipse into your flat. In the house the tears flow. Catherine is sensible enough to sneak off to bed and you are left alone with your reflection in the bathroom mirror. It tells a sorry tale.

Barbarella, what a mess. Looks like you've blown two friendships and any chance of getting back with Barnaby. Maybe you should think about laying off the coke for a while. Perhaps a couple of weeks at a nice clinic in the country. There's that great place in Cumbria where your mother's friend went to get off booze. All the best people go there.

The (Fucked Up) End

That was pretty dim. With thinking that simple you might be better off playing Barnaby . . .

Scene 219

Back in the bedroom you start your routine.

"My God. I'll be fired . . . I'm meeting my boss in ten minutes."

Step one: Rush round the room, dragging on a suit, uncufflinked shirt flapping. The sleeping contentment leaves her face and you can't help feeling a pang of guilt as she sits up, concerned.

Step two: Pause, smile your practiced Rob Lowe smile, and visibly relax. Half an octave lower and through tenderly smiling lips you murmur, "You were amazing last night," and force your eyes to smile. You uncontrollably drop onto the bed and kiss her lips, only to withdraw with a nervous, lips together, smile.

"Stay and sleep, you look tired." Touch the side of her face with light fingertips. "I've *got* to go." You turn to leave.

"Can I call you?" you ask with an expertly tentative quaver. "Will you leave your number?"

"That would be great."

Step three: You exit, but with rehearsed timing turn and race back to the bed. "You're fantastic," you growl breathlessly and, as if under the control of some atavistic urge, push her lips apart with your tongue.

Disengage, lusty look, grab at right breast, one more kiss. "God, I'm going to be *so* late." You smile as if you couldn't care less. Rush to the door, last look back. She really is hideous. Gleeful, boyish smile. Exit.

All under five minutes.

She'll love you at least until Tuesday. Then it will turn to hate via regret. But until Tuesday you will be loved, and to be loved is to be a god. You'll be immortal all day Monday.

You start your Ducatti with a flick and it growls into life with all the braggadocio of a high performance, twin-cylinder, 750cc, 0 to 60 in 3.2 seconds (and a top speed of 182 mph) Italian sex prop. It's red, vibrates a lot, and scares the hell out of anything sitting on it, including you.

Your mother's right, it's a death trap, but you can't give it up—the bike is embedded in your mating routine. Too many have fallen for its purring power, and besides, the day you bought it ended a twelve-week dry spell. You've faced reality and the bitter truth is that you are twenty-nine, starting to sag, and need every pulling aid you can find. With that thought, you hit the revs tentatively and speed out of Clapham and towards the river.

Within fifteen minutes, you are safely in Chelsea, sitting aboard the *Anomie*, the houseboat Kamran sometimes calls home. He calls it "the Love Boat" to his male friends, but to impressionable females, smitten by his Bohemian chic, he calls it home. He neglects to tell them most nights he stays in your spare room—instead, he talks of the hypnotic ebb of the tides, of feeling close to nature, and the inspiration he can find in water . . .

"My work is becoming stilted. I had thought to give up art for good. But when I look at you I begin to work the clay in my mind. If I could capture your face, your body . . ." is Kam's favorite line. You can't quite believe it works, but Kamran does have the advantage of heavy lashed, brooding eyes set in an angular, handsome face. With the reek of the Thames, the jumble of artistic paraphernalia, the rock of the boat, and plenty of alcohol, you can imagine most women would buy it. Some might even believe it.

Scene 219

Kamran is too good a friend to begrudge you a shower and some of his clothes, even while he is entertaining. The girl emerging from the shower is one of his regular guests, and with little fuss, she is dressed and gone. You envy Kamran his luck.

When you both first met at university, Kam was a borderline nerd. But with graduation came his father's life-changing announcement that Kamran was believed ready for marriage; five years of sexual feeding-frenzy later and the hunt for a suitable "arrangement" is all but over. In a few months' time, Kamran either marries a bent-toothed monster or kills his elderly father with sorrow (or at the very least causes a seizure in his check-signing hand).

So time is of the essence; no sooner have you filled in last night's blanks (she is called Agatha or Agnes or Angus) than the weekend must roll its next saga. A pub in Chelsea beckons; Barbarella, an ex-paramour, awaits you at the Admiral Bodering-ton. Fortified with coffee and toast, the two of you venture forth like knights of old, sunlight glittering from your black armor (back-of-a-lorry Cutler and Gross wraparounds, £110), ready to do battle. Stout-hearted young Barnaby, the weekend is still young and the wheel of love is ready to spin . . .

Go to Scene 169

Scene 220

You're able to maintain some dignity and gradually ease yourself closer to upright. Intent on asserting authority, you address the minister by his Christian name.

"Edward, is there something in particular you wish to ask me?"

Edward smiles condescendingly. "Tell me first what you do for a living."

You object to putting off the inevitable—small talk is boring—but you decide to humor him with an answer.

Do you tell the truth? **Go to Scene 132**

Do you lie? **Go to Scene 136**

Scene 221

But a Julie Andrews ending should always be a happy ending—and this will be no exception. Wait patiently, silent as a Von Trapp Family Singer hiding from evil Rolf, and let Mary Poppins work her Disney magic . . .

Catherine nudges you awake. "Barnie . . . wake up . . . bed."

The final word breaks you into consciousness and you blink your eyes. The film is still rolling on the TV screen—Julie is romping around in curtains—but you realize with relief that Catherine is ready for sleep. Yawning, you apologize.

"Sorry, I must have fallen asleep."

Catherine smiles. She talks, but with a strangely muted voice—for some reason you can barely hear her. You take hold of her hand. Then you realize, possibly from lying with your head pressed hard against the sofa, you can hardly hear anything out of your right ear—it's ringing with tinnitus. You waggle a finger in it furiously, but to no avail. Maybe it was a natural defense against Julie's singing. Either way, Catherine is still talking. You'd better pay attention, lean closer with your good ear and try not to ball things up. Just think Mother Superior compassion, and listen.

"I've . . . . idiot, ... amazing man, ... but . . . . just . . . . . . sleaze . . . . feel . . . . . . themselves . . . . . . time? . . . keep shagging . . . . show . . . . Why?"

She goes on and on. With your ringing ear you can barely hear one word in four. You twist the good ear forward ostentatiously, desperate to figure out what the hell she is talking about. In the pit of your stomach a rising panic spurts acid—what if you never get rid of the ringing? What if Barnaby the wit, Barnaby the great conversationalist and all-round center of attention goes deaf? You'll never pull again. Mind you, Catherine doesn't seem to be running out of steam, and as you strain to figure her words, she continues to prattle.

For a near-eternity she goes on, but you know enough to nod and murmur periodically. Eventually the tears flow and clutching her to your chest you squeeze in such tight embrace that, with a pop, the blockage in your right ear is freed. Like a miracle, the ringing stops, and the first thing you hear is Edelweiss, and Catherine sobbing.

"Barnie, you've been amazing." Lifting her tear-streaked chin, she plants a firm kiss on your lips. "You're not like other men. Barbarella doesn't know when she's hit the jackpot."

She cuddles closer, pressing her slender frame hard against you—and with mounting arousal you stare blankly at the TV. Catherine grips as though her life depended on your emotional sustenance, and seeing her squirm in your white cotton T-shirt and stripy blue boxer shorts you can't help but pulse an erection in a single beat. She clings, tight as a baby orangutan, your eyes lose focus, and everything blurs . . .

. . . Christopher Plummer—Captain Von Trapp—Whistle-blowing Naval Legend—Firm Hand—the Baroness—the Garden—Late at Night—Catherine, stripped, sixteen going on seventeen. The remote control lands with a thud, and with the ease of the Nazi occupation of Austria, you thrust down into her.

Catherine sucks and nibbles at your lips, breathing like a sprinter. You grab the curve of her skinny hip, feeling for soft flesh through the cotton boxers. She wriggles at your touch and eases onto your lap. You slip a hand under the T-shirt, feeling liquid-soft breast. More than a handful, but let's face it, you've always been greedy. Doe a deer. It goose-bumps into hardness. The hills are alive. She gropes madly at your shirt, desperate for bare flesh, ripping buttons with her small fists. You are Rodgers, she is Hammerstein. She thrusts and slides her groin on your thigh. Ave fucking Maria.

The (Proper) Julie Andrews End

Good skills, Reader. Barnaby was lucky to have you. Maybe you should try playing as Barbarella. Now that you've perfected the Catherine-seduction who knows where you could end up? It's worth a try . . .

Scene 222

You are loath to provide Kamran with what he would call "wanking material." And, cursing your schizophrenic prudishness, you gaze longingly through the bars at Jay.

"Look, Kam, I don't think this is such a good idea. Why don't you climb over here and I'll walk round until we find somewhere easier to get in."

Kamran doesn't look as upset as you'd expect. With monkey agility he pulls himself up and over. He points to your left.

"Go round that way and we'll meet by the front."

Kam and Jay disappear into the darkness—and then there is one. A chill breeze rustles leaves and brings goose bumps. Suddenly this doesn't seem like such a good idea. You trip hurriedly round to the front of the zoo, but even though you run, it seems to take an age. By the time you arrive there's no one to be seen.

"*JAY . . . KAMRAN* . . . Are you there?" You try to shout and whisper at the same time but there's no response.

"JAY . . . KAMRAN . . ."

Half an hour later, you give up. They've either been eaten or are playing boy-jokes and, frankly, you're not in the mood for either. Fortunately your flat isn't too far to walk, even in heels. The only satisfaction you have is knowing that Jay must be even more miserable than you to have missed out.

*

Scene 222

Where the hell could they have got to? There's no understanding it. You dread to think how bored Jay and Kamran must be, stuck in the zoo together . . .

Oh well, home alone, Barbarella.

The (Disappointing) End

Poor Barbie. You just don't seem to be up to the job, Reader. Maybe you're more in touch with your masculine side. You could go back to the prologue and show Barnie a good time . . .

Scene 223

The smoothie slips down in one. The subtle egg undertones blend with an unfamiliar, bitter taste, but the rough texture is actually quite nice—like the bits in Tropicana orange juice, only smaller. You suspiciously eye a broadly smiling Kamran.

"What's it supposed to do?"

"What doesn't it do? With that inside you this is going to be a serious night to remember—we're talking unique boom-boom, my friend. Know what I mean?" Kamran smiles lecherously, just in case you don't. "And best of all, I've found a secret ingredient to guarantee you won't get a hangover. It's—"

But Will is fretfully urging you into action and there's no time for further explanation. He jostles you both down the stairs.

O foolhardy one—you drank Kamran's devil-brew. Whatever the effect (and it may take hours before you realize the full potency of this stuff), jacta alea esto, *let the die be cast—here and now. Whatever the Fates have now woven into your silken thread, for good or ill, you'll just have to lump it . . .*

But for now, **go to Scene 99**

Scene 224

With the grace of a pregnant ballerina, you are hoisted over the fence. Unfortunately one of the spikes tears your Stella McCartney on the back seam. Rather than be sad, you decide to capitalize on it—any excuse to be an exhibitionist.

And so you stroll. It's for nights like this that you adore London. Admittedly it's not the warmest, driest, or easiest place to live. But when you have a New York model on your arm, the moon is shining, and you've just brought down the current government, you can't help but love it, even if Kamran is trailing along. Talking of which, time to lose the gooseberry.

"What was that noise?" Like a prewar heroine you cling desperately to Jay's arm and hiss a whisper, "Kamran, there's a noise—coming from over there," and point vaguely ahead.

Kamran, eager with machismo, doesn't hesitate and neither do you. Covering Jay's mouth you manhandle him into some nearby shrubbery.

You lie there, together, panting.

"Barbie . . . Jay . . . Where the fuck are you?"

Kamran isn't persistent in his search. Maybe he's spooked, or maybe he just realizes when three's a crowd. Either way, Kamran soon vanishes and you are left in the strong arms of Mr. Perfect.

Why is it that you always meet the perfect man at the last minute? Something clicks as you exchange stories. Within half an hour, you've got a pretty good picture of this man, and you like every bit of it. Feeling lighthearted, your conversation really loosens up. All inhibitions were lost somewhere in the bushes, so Jay's suggestion isn't totally unexpected: "Do ya fancy a rush, Barbarella? Why don't we 'do it' in the reptile house?"

You can't help but smile. "Let me think about it?"

Jay grins patiently, waiting as you eye him up and down, biting a lip with obvious deliberation.

Eventually he can't wait any longer. "How you doin'?"

You laugh, recognizing the Joey-line from *Friends*, only to realize Jay meant it in earnest. True, there are certain similarities . . . you love Joey. And now you love Jay.

Do you proceed to the reptile house? **Go to Scene 118**

Do you take a reality check and take Jay back to St. John's Wood? **Go to Scene 50**

Scene 225

You feel nothing, that is, until Charlotte's hands press on your torso and her lips pucker a kiss on your battered face. Her warm fingertips run across your eyes and down to your lips with celerity, teasingly probing and reaching for your tongue. You daren't move, lest you distract her. Her breasts rise and fall with breathless haste and as you look helplessly up into her young, flawless face—and see her lust scrawled across it—your heart palpitates with exhilaration.

Your head is full of fluffy evanescent clouds. Don't even try to think, no girl has ever made you feel this way before; it must really be some form of Midsummer Magic. Robin Goodfellow has been with you tonight, and placed love-dust in the eyes of the divine Charlotte.

And she truly is making you feel godly. Your body floats independently of your head, the wandering cupidity of her hands continuing to stroke your fervid brow. She places her arm under your neck, pulling you towards her breasts, ready to mount. You moan.

Again Charlotte pushes your chest. You take it as your cue to start thrusting. Grabbing her neck, you pull her down and onto you. Again you feel her lips against yours.

It's too much for both of you. Charlotte can no longer control herself: "Oh God, Barnie, oh God!" You thrust faster and again she cries, "Barnie! Talk to me, Barnie!"

Whatever You Want

She wants you to talk dirty; you rack your mind for selective filth—anything to prolong this exquisite performance.

"Charlotte, sit on my face."

"Thank God! Can you hear me, Barnie, please, Barnie open your eyes!"

But you can't, you don't want it to stop. That is, until you realize it never even started.

"Barnie, thank God you've come round. I thought you'd had some kind of fit! You were writhing like a madman. I was terrified. I tried everything, even the kiss of life. But don't worry, stay here and I'll get a doctor. Just stay calm . . . Just stay calm."

Perhaps from the disappointment, for a second time, all fades.

The (Stunned) End

You've not made the best choices for our hero, Reader. Please, give him another chance by playing again.

Scene 226

Well done, Barbarella, Annabel is a tricky customer, best play your cards close to your chest. If Kamran is a traitor to your love then forewarned is forearmed, if not (and true, the whole thing smells a bit fishy), then least said soonest mended.

That's all good advice, just keep your eyes peeled and your ears open. Nothing is more valuable than information, when the time comes be ready . . .

But for now, Mata Hari, slide back into the thick of it, and keep a watching brief.

Go to Scene 24

Scene 227

You reluctantly leave Charlotte to her fun and draw Kamran to one side. You whisper your dastardly plan into his eager ear.

Kamran does the rest. After pulling the two girls apart and ascertaining that Polly can indeed sing, he removes Polly from the gallery. You follow. In the quiet of a large library the two of you brief Polly.

"You're a rugby lass, what rousing songs do you know that'll liven people up a bit?"

Polly seems to know what she's doing, so you leave her to take care of any final touches and resume your places at the table.

The diners are well beyond decorum by now. Olympia has disappeared, no doubt to batter "Frank from the village" for his ineptitude, and you note with satisfaction that Polly in her bra and knickers should be a huge hit. The odd few dullards still appear sober, despite the lack of food, but even sober, the sight of 34 Fs should win them over.

And just when you begin to worry that Polly is chickening out, she appears clad in a gentleman's coat and matching top hat.

She steps on a chair, totters on four-inch stilettos, and onto the table . . .

I saw the light on the night that I passed by her window
I saw the flickering shadows of love on her blind
Sheeeeee was my woman.
As she deceived me I watched and went out of my mind

Scene 227

The hat spins off, the coat falls. Polly . . . in all her underwired beauty.

My, my, my, Delilahhhhhhh

Then the moment the front row has been aching for—the bra pings off with a quick snap of fingers and the momentous force of gravity.

Why, why, why, Delilah

But before Kamran has time to cry, "Show us your panty beard," and before the burgeoning Polly can finish a trumpet solo, Olympia returns. She cuffs the grinning Lord George with a look.

"WHAT IN GOD'S NAME ARE YOU DOING? GET DOWN FROM THERE, YOU HARLOT."

Polly's finale is, if anything, even more dramatic than her entrance.

Forgive me, Delilah, I just couldn't take any more

She slips becomingly and lands in the lap of a weasel City banker, before finally slumping to the floor in a drugged faint.

And before you can muse on the size of Kamran's foreskin, Will is rushing the length of the table to the rescue.

"Did you guys have something to do with this?"

You both nod, grinning like morons.

"Shit, if Olympia finds out she'll rip out my spleen. Get the others and meet me out front. I'll have the engine running."

Kamran, with the instincts of a serial adulterer, is out like a shot. You follow.

You've no idea where to look for Barbarella, but a quick sortie to the upper floor identifies a muffled groan. You follow tentatively and finally locate the source in a distant corridor in the east wing. You steel yourself to enter, when a higher-pitched squeal erupts from the door behind you. This corridor is witnessing some serious action.

Kamran takes charge. "One each, Barnie. Do you want the left or the right?"

Your call.

Do you take the left door? **Go to Scene 213**

Do you take the right door? **Go to Scene 191**

Scene 228

Restraint.

A somewhat unexpected appearance in our story (at least in this form). Nonetheless, you must be commended for showing such good sense. Catherine will be all the better for a good eight hours.

"Maybe you're right, Cat, give it up. Let's get out of this bloody awful party."

You don't even bother to tell the others that you're leaving. Instead the three of you skip away without a goodbye, grab a curb-crawling minicab and are back to St. John's Wood inside twenty-five minutes.

Time for some Häagen-Dazs with Baileys and *When Harry Met Sally* on DVD . . .

"You know about a man like you know about a good melon."

Jolly good advice.

The (Sensible) End

Sensible shoes, Reader. You might as well go back and live with your parents. Take a break, think it over, and if you want Barbie to have a little fun—play again.

Scene 229

"Oh dear. What a pity. He was doing so well." Oswald makes his apologies. "Sorry, everybody, seems young Marc is a bit out of condition. He'll be back for the Olympics, no doubt."

Barbarella never even made it to the door. Oswald turns to her and says, "Someone needs to take Marc upstairs and give him a once-over." She consents eagerly, and you note with soaring pleasure that Charlotte puts up little resistance.

And so, on Hermes' sandals you fly casually to the other side of the table, pausing only to collect some wisdom from dear Uncle Oswald: "Flare your nostrils and dilate your pupils—never fails."

You offer Charlotte the last of your gin, and idly maneuver her into your web ("So, what did you do on your year abroad?").

The party is really beginning to break up. Kamran has disappeared, you presume with Polly; Will is still trapped by an aging aunt, and you can't help but notice that Uncle Oswald is bedazzling Astrid.

But concentrate on the job in hand, Barnaby, your love is before you, she has finished your gin and is talking about her teaching job in Malawi. You move her back on to red wine and into the garden. There, all the better to see her taut figure in the shimmer of the full moon.

The garden is even lovelier empty of people. Not a chirrup of gossip breaks through the calm as you meander into its darkest recesses. High, clinically topiaried hedges now conceal you from the house, and as you follow Charlotte, she continues to drink and talk incessantly: "These are my favorite." She points to some nondescript purple flowers. "In August the butterflies get drunk on the nectar and lie on this path. When I was young I used to sit here with them and balance them in my hair."

You love her. You imagine her dancing gleefully as a woodland nymph, naked and strong, leaping from rock to rock, beloved of all the woodland creatures. She leaps into a sunny glade beckoning you to touch her forbidden fruit, to slide a hand over a shoulder, to feel her shudder as it mounts her perfect breast, then hear her inhale as you slide down further, over the bronze flat tummy, her mound . . . but she is still talking: "I don't think I'll go to university. I've got a place at Exeter to study history of art, but that all seems so pointless, so self-indulgent."

"There's nothing wrong with self-indulgence." You try to maneuver her on to your favorite subject, but to no avail:

"But I can't see myself giving up London life. Mummy thinks I could become an interior designer . . ."

Of course there are only two answers to that:

"My place needs a bit of an overhaul. I'd love it if you could help me out." **Go to Scene 205**

Or do you just grab at a tit? **Go to Scene 260**

Scene 230

Oh dear.

Your inelegance is sometimes astounding. Intent on reasserting authority, you address him by his Christian name.

"Edward, is there something in particular you wish to ask me?"

"Indeed, there is." He puts out a hand and you take it instinctively. Surprisingly strong, he pulls you towards him. "Tell me, where do you buy that marvelously transparent underwear?"

There's no real answer to that, and while you're trying to think of a pithy response Edward slides his hand up over your hips, intent on verifying his first glimpse. You close your eyes, still trying to conjure a riposte, but enjoying the sensation as it sets your thighs tingling. He pulls you down on to his lap and teasingly kisses you—judging if his gamble has paid off.

And you don't give him any reason to believe it hasn't. Older men are supposed to make better lovers, but you don't want to risk full nudity, not with the lights on, and so you start to unzip his fly. But Edward has other ideas, he firmly guides your hand away and into his jacket pocket. Together you pull out a rather large cigar tube.

"Barbie, can I tempt you?" he asks.

Of course, you're always open to temptation. The speeches will shield any noise you may wish to make.

*

Scene 230

Barbie, what are you doing? Not a Bill C.? How are you going to explain this to Catherine? Well, at least keep the noise down and hurry up about it. And for God's sake keep your eyes shut, haven't you noticed he's ginger? When you're quite finished everyone will be waiting back at the party . . .

Go to Scene 140

Scene 231

Marc takes up the gauntlet, little knowing what danger he faces.

"Hnnph, I will show to you now if you wish."

And so saying he removes his jacket to display a *Men's Health* physique. It shouts, "Fifty Ways to Make Your Lover Crumble"; it cries out, "An Inch on Your Biceps in a Weekend"; it taunts, "Eat Chips and Lose Weight." It does nothing to deter Oswald. He can smell blood.

"Bravo, sir, a spot of entertainment is just what we need to ignore the hunger pangs. Have you got a watch? I'll time." And with expertise to shame a Parisian pickpocket, Marc is relieved of his Patek Philippe—and with it, his last chance of survival.

By now, Oswald is in complete control. He bangs the table with an empty gin tumbler, and commands a hush over the gathering.

"Ladies and gentlemen, for your entertainment and distraction Mr. Marc Pacman from France, a world-famous exponent of breath-holding, is to honor us with an exhibition of his talents. Olympia, my dearest, I propose this could kill some time between courses?"

For once Olympia is glad of some assistance and urges Oswald to continue.

"Please remain seated, but please accord some silence for the young Frenchman. Ladies and gentlemen, I give you Marc."

True to form Marc stands and accepts the attention. You note with ill-concealed concern that Charlotte looks up in teenage rapture as Marc loosens his bow-tie, yet leaves it trailing about his unbuttoned collar. (OK, we've all done it.)

She lets free a silent gasp from still pink cheeks. You give way to a fresh surge of jealousy. But Oswald is at hand; you have nothing to fear.

"When you are ready, young man."

And as Marc gives over to a bout of hyperventilating, Oswald signals "*Commence!*" in a bad French accent.

And there, before you all, this wonder of nature gasps a final breath—and smiles at the lovely Charlotte.

Before you can think "die bastard," Oswald continues with his work.

"Marc has the supernatural ability, he tells us, to hold his breath for an astonishing five minutes thirty seconds."

The diners murmur in astonishment and approval. Oswald continues to warm to his theme. "Ordinary mortals such as an old man like myself could probably manage a bare three."

And so Oswald talks distractingly with some ease. Barbarella meanwhile, in glorious splendor, and well briefed by the mastermind dowager, is at work, pouting, smiling, and oozing across the table. Beneath the tablecloth, though, a more serious game is afoot . . . a stockinged foot in fact. Marc is stuck in a trap, and the sinuous foot is to deal the death blow. It coils up the inside of Marc's leg, turns at the knee junction and drives on into a happy groin. There, with skill known only to a few, the supple toes drum the beat of desire.

Above, Barbarella continues to smile. And to those who fail to detect her subtle lip licking nothing appears untoward. Certainly Charlotte, you notice with mixed emotion, fails to understand her inability to maintain Marc's attention.

Marc smiles gently back at Barbarella—and holds his breath.

With ninety seconds gone, Oswald instills a sense of drama. "An entire minute everybody, an entire minute."

A gentle ripple of polite applause erupts from the British reserve. Few notice Oswald's inaccurate timekeeping. And so the minutes pass. Charlotte's with increasing confusion, Marc's with increasing pleasure, yours with increasing spite, and Oswald's with increasing timekeeping confusion.

"Two minutes," he cries with false astonishment after three minutes forty has elapsed. "Pretty soon an old smoker like myself would be dead . . . for our friend Marc . . . he is at only the beginning."

More foot artistry below the table and the blood is draining from Marc's other vital organs. He stops smiling and starts to concentrate. If only he can get to four minutes he can blame the Concorde flight for lack of condition and save face. Must concentrate . . . a little longer . . .

With gibbon dexterity the foot unzips the fly, finds little resistance from tight, thonged briefs and . . . enters the forbidden domain. Marc lets out a whimper of precious air.

The Patek Philippe registers five minutes.

"Three minutes, ladies and gentlemen, even a young man such as young Barnaby here would begin feeling the effects of oxygen starvation now." Oswald lays it on. "Swimming vision, aching behind the eyes, and yet this athlete, he feels no such thing. He is barely halfway."

Marc's erection is sucking away his life. The foot kneads, it strokes, and it is everywhere—and, teasingly, nowhere. Barbarella sits and gnaws at her lip like a she-panther in heat. The vision of Barbarella's beauty swims in front of aching eyes . . .

You kick her gently and she stands.

Barbarella stands.

And yet she kneads.

And she excuses herself and leaves to powder.

Scene 231

And yet the foot still burrows.

And yet . . . yet . . . there is the dowager. She is smiling, and biting her lip . . .

Marc-Pacaud slumps across the table.

Go to Scene 229

Scene 232

You couldn't agree more. After seven years working in London you have more debt and less to show for it than ever. Tonight could be payout time. Joining Will on the Embankment, you find him negotiating with a cabbie. Six into five doesn't go.

"Come on, it's only just off Edgware. We'll make it worth your while." The driver looks dubious, but as you arrive Will turns to you and smiles. "And *she* only weighs six stone."

You beam radiantly at the lie, and the intensity of your delight almost wins over the cabbie—but not quite.

"Look . . . I could lose my licen . . ." He trails off at the sight of Astrid approaching with Barnaby.

"Five will be fine," you concede with good grace. Turning to Barnaby, "You're still OK to ride your bike, aren't you, Barnie?"

He's a man, of course he is, and soon the five of you are whisked away, leaving Barnaby searching for his bike keys. Through the back end of Victoria, up and off the Edgware Road the cab drops you in a somberly gentrified street.

The door before you looks typical of a thousand residences in this part of London, but Will knocks a dah-dit-dit-dit-dah and it opens to reveal a six five, muscle-clad doorman. He stands, enormously silhouetted against the glitz and lights of the interior, and nods an acknowledgment to Will. "Good evening, Mr. Burton. Come in, sir."

Go to Scene 36

Scene 233

Lose. Lose. Lose. It's becoming insane. Finally, long after your pile of cash has shrunk back to below its meager starting level, you get a decent hand. The chandelier lurches another spin to the left—go for it big time. Banking everything on three knaves, you push your modest-sized pile forward; much depleted certainly, but still enough to win everything back—and more.

"I call you, Nigel."

Astrid gulps down her drink and gawps at the fat nemesis, her face a fretful shade of purple. How will her father take it when she moves back to Belgium with a 20,000 euro credit-card bill.

"Are you sure, Barbarella—don't you want to save a few dollars back just in case?"

"Shut up, Astrid. I know what I'm doing."

Jenner smiles at both of you, and tosses five upturned cards on to the table.

"Three queens," he looks you in the eye, "and some dross."

Bugger.

You look imploringly at Astrid. You need the sort of distraction that only an behemoth Belgian can provide. Whether she understands your plea, or whether something snaps in her narcotic-riddled mind you can't guess: "No No No No," she wails and flings herself onto the table, desperately clutching at the piled cash. Jenner responds first, wrestling with her like a boar in a pit.

"You stupid cow, get off the table before you break it."

But the strain on her dress is too much. One by one, threads of Lycra groan, then snap. Astrid's chest crashes out, and catches Jenner on the side of his head. Will runs around to help Astrid back into her dress, but is tripped by Newt who thinks he's trying to steal the cash. The oil baron strides forward instead, but a chair is pushed into his groin by the Arab team. Bodi and Wasim dash like Tintin and Haddock at the cry of the Castafiore.

The tragedy of the situation is that Astrid remains stupidly unaware, screaming above the commotion: "THERE'S ONLY TWO QUEENS AND A KING. LOOK, YOU HAVE MADE A MISTAKE. LOOK, BARBIE, IT'S A MISTAKE."

But you can't answer. You can only feebly motion at her and squeeze out a sympathetic smile. And as the croupier runs to get a floor manager and Kamran holds on for dear life, the chandelier screeches a chilling warning. Strain, creak, strain, creak—the sound of a light shaft slowly disengaging from a two-hundred-year-old set of bolts. A chandelier can only go so far . . .

Go to Scene 70

Scene 234

Jumping up, you present yourself formally, as if crashing your bike were an everyday occurrence.

"Barnaby, friend of Will's, pleased to meet you." You offer a hand. "Sorry about the flowers, I keep doing that, I'm afraid . . . Every time I see someone remotely good-looking, my throttle wrist tenses and I drive into a wall, or flowerbed, or . . . whatever."

You trail off lamely, look slightly embarrassed, and pull a flower stalk out of your collar. You present her with the crumpled flower.

When it comes to this sort of love game, Barnaby, you're Tropicana in a fridge-full of Sunny Delight. You are, simply, the best. It took you two seconds to fall in love, another four to realize that you'd made a monumental cock-up by driving into a border of chrysanthemums, but only three to figure that even a nineteen-year-old would have some maternal instinct for a bruised-but-smiling, self-deprecating, but essentially all-right-looking, good-humored ass.

The psychology is clear. Be the kind, loving father she has never really known and allow her to mother you as she has never really been mothered, and then make love vigorously while she's too busy smiling to contradict you.

"I've only had it a week and I've already crashed four times," you lie as you shake her hand, and then stagger towards your still-running bastard of a bike—spurning her assistance.

"I haven't hit quite that many revs before, though," you joke pathetically, maintaining eye contact to make the point.

"Barnaby," you hear her voice for the first time, "are you sure you're all right?" She tries to look sincere, but can't help breaking out into a gummy thirteen-year-old laugh.

Stage One: your heart breaks anew and you stagger, this time genuinely (if only from lust) towards her.

"I'd better take you inside and clean you up a bit." She leads you with motherly tenderness and you lean on her with the desire of a thousand stoats.

Stage Two: having asserted your twin paternal roles the next step is to convince her of your intelligence, easy humor, and general desirability.

Stages Three and Four will leave her in little doubt as to your more specific abilities, but that will probably have to wait. It's all a little rushed perhaps, but when the cry of Priapus breaks upon a calm summer evening, you must answer his call like a hound to the horn.

With a frown she looks you up and down to determine your physical state. "There's a spare room in the west wing; it's far, I'm afraid. Are you sure you can make it?"

With a bare nod and smile you proceed, insisting on carrying your small rucksack despite a steadfast wince. And so you creak up a flight of stairs and over to the west wing. She bounces by your side and you titillate her with easy wit. Eventually, you arrive in a poky guest room reserved for unfavored relatives. Tiny windows render it murky even on this balmy evening, and the gloom of the décor contrasts strikingly with the easy but brilliant beauty of your new object of desire.

She energetically shows you the *en suite*, urges you to "join everybody in the garden as soon as you're ready" and with slightly nervous and unseemly haste, makes to leave. Every fiber in your being screams, "*Stay.*"

Don't you think you're racing ahead of yourself? You've only just met the girl. And all morning you were busy mooning over your unrequited love for Barbarella. No wonder you never get anywhere if you're this inconstant. Oh well, that's a twenties male for you.

It's probably asking too much of you to reject your lustful feelings for Charlotte altogether—you are only a man—but you could probably hold back for half an hour until Barbarella arrives. Charlotte will do wonders for Barbarella's jealousy levels, and, let's be honest, it's usually the best way to win someone back.

It's up to you. You can let your hormones run away with you (she is nineteen after all) or you could try a cold shower—and save it all for when Barbie arrives.

Are you a ravening beast? Put in some groundwork with Charlotte early—maneuver her on to the bed and attempt a brief finger buffet. **Go to Scene 93**

Or can you tame the base hunger? Stay steadfast and true to Barbarella (at least for half an hour) and let the temptress leave untasted. **Go to Scene 173**

Scene 235

"Read these lips, I've got a massive headache and I need a cab."

You push his snuffling face from between your legs. A blond fringe flops down over Dave's frown.

"But, Barbie . . ."

"Dave, last night was fun, but it shouldn't have happened. We work together."

Dave doesn't bother to respond. He dives back under the duvet and continues his burrowing.

"Dave, enough . . . Dave . . ."

You did your best. But there are some things a girl just can't control (resist). Oh well, it might help clear Barbie's pounding head. **Go to Scene 114**

Scene 236

A quick cab back to Clapham to retrieve your dinner jacket. A sobering shower and a pint of orange juice is all you need to revive. Then, a cab back to the pub, jump on your waiting bike, and you're soon heading along the M4. You forsake leathers in favor of arriving *à la* Bond. Besides, you haven't had your dinner jacket cleaned since the IT Recruitment Awards Dinner and it sorely needs an airing.

The others have opted for Will's Land Rover, and although you envy them their relaxed carriage, you are determined to arrive with at least a thirty-minute head start on Kamran and Will (she is only his "stepniece," remember—Will's sister is the new arrival in the family, and the Burtons have a history of "confused" lineage). If Charlotte's reputation is anything to go by, you will have bagged the beauty before Barbarella has finished applying her Clinique miracle mask.

And so you arrive.

The winding drive takes you past a line of cypresses, and the fit-inducing strobe of the still warm sun as it flickers through the passing trees inexplicably reminds you of your youth. And so you speed onwards and catch a first sight of the house.

The formal front lawn ends at imposingly colonnaded steps. And there, in the jaws of the nineteenth-century gothic foible of a house, as if about to be eaten by its hideous gargoyle frontage, stands a peering beauty.

She's wearing a floating, pale-blue, summer dress—and it's just asking for a summer breeze to lift it above her narrow waist, flat stomach, and boulder-like breasts, to reveal a tanned-all-over G-stringed figurine clutching at the sky after her fast-disappearing gossamer-light dress . . . Too late you register the sliding back wheel, the crunch of dissipating gravel, the whirl of sky and the smell of earth and crushed chrysanthemums.

The dark summer sky fills your visor and your limbs are frozen in the terror of anticipation as you gently test each for damage. But before you have time to give a self-pitying groan, Charlotte's lilting laugh rouses you from the shock. And with the anger of hurt pride, you thrust your helmet off so quickly your ears ring and you can't hear her first words.

You don't need to—all you need is to see the lips she uses to form them. Soft, naturally pink, unnaturally plump, with the top one pushed up and flat as if by an invisible phallus. She can't stop smiling, and as she bends down to restrain you from moving . . . you fall in love (lust).

Go to Scene 234

Scene 237

Time to end the dream.

"That's it. I quit. It's been an absolute pleasure playing with you misfits, but I think I need to socialize with some people more my own age." You stand and look knowingly at Barnaby. "Barnie, I want to go."

"But . . ."

Jenner doesn't let him finish. With spitting excitement, he says, "Barbarella, don't be such a sourpuss. Tell you what, why don't we play one last hand? I'll give you a chance to win everything." He looks down at his vast pile. "I reckon there must be over a hundred and fifty thousand here. One hand, Barbarella. My hundred and fifty, against your remaining pocket change . . . and half an hour of fun upstairs."

He smiles and your stomach churns.

"What happens upstairs?" Astrid asks Jenner, but he just stares, daring you. Barnaby laughs, Will frowns, and the chandelier rattles gentle encouragement. You hesitate, computing the odds.

Catherine rounds the table to grab your hand. "No, Barbie, this is ridiculous. It's disgusting. Come on, let's go."

Jenner gloats. "What's to decide, Barbarella? Don't tell me you've lost your nerve? One hundred and fifty thousand for half an hour, that's indecent . . . You're probably not worth that in Turkish liras."

One hundred and fifty thousand pounds (tax-free). That could buy a place in the country (OK, in Wales); or you could get out of the rat race completely, settle down with Barnaby in Devon, buy a dog, grow organic vegetables, and start a family . . . You look at Barnaby—he's nodding.

Barbie, get real. This is ridiculous. It's not as if you need the money. If you don't get fired, you'll be able to pay off your credit cards by the time you're thirty-five—easy. Turn your back on Nigel J. Imagine if you lose—those wet lips spitting with enthusiasm, the white, distended body jumping aboard . . . How could you look Barnaby in the eye after that?

The lady's not for whoring. Take Barnaby by the hand and leave this sordid mess far behind. Remain a talented amateur, Barbarella. **Go to Scene 247**

But what if you won? One hundred and fifty thousand pounds! Go on (with) the game, Barbarella. It's only prostitution if you lose. **Go to Scene 138**

Scene 238

In the minutes it takes to drag Kamran, Astrid, and Catherine from the dance floor, your mind has raced through a hundred plans. Kamran sees that rescuing Will could prove to be a dress rehearsal for his own marital salvation and is filled with enthusiasm. While he encourages Catherine and Astrid, your mind tarries on a play by Shakespeare. Midsummer has always made you think of the Bard, ever since you were forced to copy out an entire play during a week of detention one long sunny June.

Now, Willy Shakespeare, he knew a thing or two about the human condition. If a crappy plot has worked for four hundred years then there's no reason it shouldn't work tonight. If only you could remember how the play ended. You explain to the gang in a quiet corner, but Kamran misses the point: "No that wasn't *Twelfth Night*, it was *Much Ado* . . ."

You interrupt before he can demonstrate the benefit of a purchased education. "Yeah, whatever, Kam. The point is, can you get hold of Will's mobile without him noticing?"

"I can." Catherine steps forward. Pretty chin is thrust upwards and you remember how much Will still dotes on her. You look around at the smiling drunken faces; Astrid—keen to feel part of the gang; Cat—eager for rebound love; and Kamran—finding hope for his own redemption. But bugger, Will has spotted your skulking huddle and has come to join you.

"Guys, this party is tragic. And have you seen? Annabel has

turned up. Looks like my last cannon salute to liberty will have to be a bit feeble."

Catherine jumps in. "Not necessarily." She grabs Wills by the arm and whisks him up on to the deck and away. You pause to a count of three before continuing with the instructions. "Astrid, can you grab a man, any man, but preferably someone older than your father? When we give you the signal, arrange to meet him in the far-left cabin."

This is almost too easy. Kamran, fully briefed, sneaks after Will and Cat, while Astrid enthusiastically hunts down a victim. But you also have a role in this Shakespearian tragicomedy. You, Barnaby, must lock antlers with your foe, upset her enough, so that when the chance comes she'll be desperate to leave the party . . . and fall into your trap. Like a cheetah, you must force your victim away from the safety of the herd, and so you rejoin Annabel, and a rather strained Barbarella, by the bar.

"Where have you been?"

"You know, just a bit of wheeling and a-dealing, plotting and a-scheming . . ." Annabel assumes that you're sufficiently vulgar to have been drumming up recruitment business, but Barbarella knows you better. She smiles and grabs hold of your hand in a possessive, forgiving gesture. The conversation obviously hasn't developed far beyond the earlier points scoring.

"Annabel is so excited about the wedding she hasn't stopped talking about it."

"Oh God, how thoughtless of me. Barbie, you must find talking about weddings painful," Annabel feigns. "Your time will come, I'm sure it will."

This could go on all night. Barnie, it's up to you to overcome the stalemate. You need to find a weakness, something to probe at. It needn't be large; Annabel is too strong an opponent to have any gaping flaws. No, all you need is a small chink, an emotional paper cut to sting with your citric tongue. What do you know about Annabel? She has a flat chest—not great, but a start. Oh yeah, her parents offered her a nose job as a fourteenth birthday present. Rumor has it that she picked out Daryl Hannah for the surgeon to copy. The other rumor has it that she has fought with bulimia ever since . . . but that's unsubstantiated, and even you wouldn't use that.

"I wouldn't worry about it, Barbarella. Personally, I think we're all too young to be settling down. In fact the only reason I can see for getting married these days is to find someone to pay for cosmetic surgery," just enough pause for even the dim-witted to register, "and you two are hardly old enough to be racking up huge bills."

Barbarella understands your line and laughs naturally. Annabel goes on the offensive. "Barnaby, you are so sweetly naïve. It probably doesn't matter to your family," this time *she* pauses for emphasis, "but with mine there are traditions and bloodlines to keep up. I'm an only child and my father would be devastated if he thought there would be no grandchild to inherit the estate. I mean, Barnie, to some people an estate means two hundred acres in Wiltshire, but to others it means a Ford Mondeo."

She snorts at her own joke and you redden as you think of your dad driving about in his G-reg Vauxhall Astra Estate. But you don't have time to dwell on the insult; Annabel is flowing. "Barbarella's mother must feel the same. You can't be too careful, you know. In maternal terms thirty is *old* . . . especially after years of contraceptive hormones."

She finishes with a cold stiletto blade to the heart. "I read the other day that if you take the morning-after pill it can halve your chances of having a baby. Imagine what would happen if you'd taken two . . ."

She laughs again, this time looking at Barbie. Barbarella, rather famously, had to take two morning-after pills one heady lower-sixth summer term. She manages a smile, but it's rather thin.

Come on, Barnie, you can do better than this. Cut Medusa's head off with your scything wit. Just try not to look her in the eye . . .

"So you're going to have children straight away? Christ, Will must have had a bang to the head."

Annabel flinches a little as she realizes that she may have overstepped the mark in her eagerness to insult.

"Your children will be gorgeous though," you flatter, but with a bitter aftertaste, "as long as they get your nose and not William's great hooter."

You laugh pleasantly and she plays along with a smile of her own, but you see the famous "Darryl" twitch with the attention.

Time to put this to bed. "I can't believe Will didn't tell us that you are planning on having babies straight away."

Barbie adds, "We're not talking shotguns, are we?" and you all laugh with mixed degrees of enjoyment. You make sure the pressure doesn't let up.

"No, seriously, when did you two decide you wanted to have a family?"

This last is too direct to avoid, and Annabel is forced painfully to come clean. "Well, we haven't actually made any decisions yet, I was just talking long-term plans. I'm sure we'll wait for quite a while before doing the baby thing."

"Thank God, that really would have made me feel old."

Then the finish.

"And I can't believe Will would be happy sharing a house with a spoiled brat who does nothing but vomit all the time."

There, you said it. You didn't mean to, but she wanted to play rough. Barbie, taken by a fit of the giggles, laughs uncontrollably behind her hand.

Then, right on cue, Annabel's mobile bleeps with a text message. Relieved, she delves into her bag, and like a battered boxer retreats to read the small screen. You watch carefully, urging her to believe . . .

Then, with enormous relief, you hear her say the magic words. "Sorry, I'm demanded elsewhere. It was great meeting up with you guys. No doubt I'll see you both later."

And like a bad memory, or smell, she fades away. Barbarella looks at you and tries to guess at the origin of your rather curious smirk. You decide to let her in on the rest of the plan.

Go to Scene 81

Scene 239

Tails, you lost . . . and yet you won.

Well, if it's tails then Barnaby gets his wish first, and to be honest you're dying to know what he wrote. With a sudden rush of nerves you fumble with the scrap of paper, decipher Barnaby's untidy scrawl, and read out loud.

"I want you to seduce a girl, bind and blindfold her . . . then let me join in." How bloody typical. "Barnaby. You're so predictable."

You laugh at Barnie's boyish enthusiasm, but bitterly. So much for wanting you back. You offer to do anything for him and all he can think to ask is for you to find somebody else. Bastard. You can take the boy out of the gutter, but you can't take the gutter out of the boy.

And then an idea hits you. Astrid.

You grab the mobile from the bottom of your bag and speed-dial Catherine. Taking care not to be overheard you check out what's up. "Cat, it's me. Where are you?"

"Barbie, what the fuck happened to you? You just ran off and left us all."

"Cat, leave it, I'll explain later. Look, where are you?"

"I'm at home, I'm trying to get Astrid down to her room. She's passed out on your bed. She's totally out of it."

This is too good to be true.

"Cat, leave her. Don't worry about me, I can always sleep downstairs in her bed."

Scene 239

"You sure? We might be able to move her together. I'm just worried she's going to be sick."

"Cat, I'm positive. Look, leave a bucket next to the bed and go to sleep. I'll see you in the morning."

"OK, I'll see you tomorrow."

"Night night."

Catherine clicks off, but your mind is positively humming with activity. Thinking ahead you dial again, this time you call Snappy's Tomato Pizza: "Hi, could I order a Four Seasons Pizza for one please and a large rocket salad . . . thirty minutes? That'll be fine."

Oh, Barbarella, this is positively Dangerous Liaisons. *Mind you, it serves Barnaby right for being so boorish. If you can pull this one off we'll be impressed.*

Go to Scene 245

Scene 240

You pull the slip of paper from your trouser pocket. Barbarella grins. "Barnaby, why didn't you say? Your own little request is giving me nipple rub."

She pulls the thin piece of paper from the top of her dress and holds it up to the moonlight, as though second-guessing your fantasy through the paper.

"Heads or tails," Barbie grins at you, "it's the only way to be fair. Guess right and you go first. Guess wrong and *I* have some fun."

You dazedly contemplate her sexual imagination. Wow, this is something unique—a genuine no-lose situation. Even if you guess wrong, you're set for a road trip along Barbarella's deepest, darkest desires. She toys with a small coin, and your emotions . . .

Pick up a coin. Yes, a real coin, this is a genuine no-lose situation, remember. There's no point in cheating. Call heads or tails (out loud, you're not to be trusted) and toss the coin high—let Fortuna decide:

Get it right? **Go to Scene 63**

Get it wrong? **Go to Scene 107**

Did you drop it? **Go to Scene 254**

Scene 241

The London streets rush by in a blur and slowly your mind begins to focus. Barbarella, you still have one choice to make. You should, by now, be aware of why you and Barnaby are alone. It was meant to be, the evening has run its inevitable course. After a few minutes thought, you tap Barnaby on the shoulder; time to stop. He duly pulls over, halfway across Chelsea Bridge, and lets you dismount. You reach into the top of your dress—a folded piece of paper nestles there securely. You pull it out, but don't open it.

"Barnaby, the mere thought of your fantasy is giving me nipple rub."

Barnaby pulls your piece of paper from his trouser pocket.

"And yours is giving me an erection. So who goes first?"

"There's only one way to do this fairly. We'll toss for it."

Time for heads or tails. What do you mean you don't carry change? Ask Barnaby, he must have a coin. OK, think carefully. The last choice of the evening. Bring it all to a close.

You naturally go for heads, say it as calmly as you can, and spin a coin high into the air. You miss the catch and it clatters and rolls into the road. You both run after it . . .

So toss a coin, but don't cheat. The Fatae, Moerae—the Fates—whatever you want to call them, Clotho, Atropos, and Lachesis, have woven your destiny into a length of yarn. Toss the coin to read their will.

Heads, you win. **Go to Scene 38**

Tails . . . you win. **Go to Scene 239**

Scene 242

The hardest part about making money out of the West India is getting in. Tonight, Will has left your name with the doorman, and you have no trouble. You fly through open doors and are whisked courteously to the inner sanctum.

The club itself is stunningly fitted in deep oaks and mahoganies. The austerity of the wood is calmed with silk Persian rugs and *chaises longues* draped in rich fabrics and rich women. Your favorite part has always been the superbly stocked bar, including its choice in barmaids. All are bright students desperate to pay off loans, and willing to flirt outrageously with the clientele. You spot a new little brunette, on tiptoes, reaching for a bottle. Perfect for making Barbie jealous. You decide to introduce yourself.

But before you get anywhere, Barbarella is presenting a trayful of brandy glasses and Will is lighting you a cigar.

"Bit of an odd crowd in tonight—no Americans. We'll have to sharpen up to stand any chance of minting it. Now, I've been thinking about how we can make a killing and . . ."

You feign interest in Will's rant, but are really more interested in Barbarella. The day's events are obviously taking their toll because she's staring into space, daydreaming. Kamran is equally uninterested, hawking at the rich elderly and poor young, caught between two desires. *And then you catch him.*

Blatantly he clocks Barbarella up and down, ogling every

detail, every curve of flesh and dip of bone, sucking up the mental image. And all with a passion so powerfully etched on his face . . . that he almost looks angry.

Kamran is in love with Barbarella. Of course he is—any man with a pulse would be—and Kam most certainly has a pulse (he's on the Victoria's Secret mailing list, for heaven's sake). That explains why he's always getting in between you and Barbie. But before you can dwell on your discovery, Will's drawl ignites a flicker of interest: "Ra Ra, Ra Ra Ra cheat; Ra Ra Ra, made an absolutely stonking fortune, Ra Ra, Ha Ha Ha."

Desperately your brain and ears focus. Thoughts of Barbie and Kamran can wait. This is about money, and for once Will has something important to say.

"The old bloke was a total cheat, he introduced the 'cubby.' Fantastic fun. Giles and I used to hide in there and watch them play in the stud . . ."

"Hold on." Will's diatribe is meaningless code, but if you can translate into English, the potential of the cubby seems interesting. "Start at the beginning. Who is Giles and what is the 'cubby'?"

And so Will takes a deep breath and, patronizingly at first, but then with youthful enthusiasm, he takes you through his childhood tale.

Go to Scene 161

Scene 243

OK, you've had numerous, highly similar bets in the past (usually for less than a tenner), but this time you're most certainly innocent. For some reason, bitch-Catherine has taken it upon herself to split you and Barbarella up—before you've even got back together. She's obviously so bloody bitter about her own failed love life that she can't stand the thought of Barbie having a boyfriend. Either that or . . . no, surely not . . . surely she doesn't want you for herself? With that small encouraging thought, you stomp angrily back into the house.

Back in the dining room, the diners are well beyond decorum, but you don't give them a second glance. Barbarella has rejoined Catherine and you storm up to both of them.

"Barbie, we've got to sort this out, whatever you've heard is total lies. I'm going to the library and I'll wait there five minutes. If you don't come, I'm out of here."

Barbarella stares at you petulantly.

"Five minutes, Barbie, and then I'm out of here."

And so you exit for the library, grabbing Kamran—your witness for the defense—as you go.

Once in the library, you don't have to wait long; Barbie and Catherine are hot on your heels. You decide to take the initiative.

"Catherine, I have never made a bet about getting Barbie into bed—and you know it."

Catherine flushes. "Barnie, I just told Barbie what I heard. If you don't believe me then ask your sidekick. He was the one going on about it."

All eyes turn on Kamran, sitting in a red leather reading chair, nursing a glass of brandy.

"I have *no* idea what you're talking about."

All eyes turn back to Catherine.

"He's a fucking liar. I heard him telling Snuffy."

You look at Kamran, grasping for a clue. He smiles, but not with his usual composure. An imposing grandfather clock ticks on to the hour; eleven resonant dongs echo round the solemn library. The silence hangs. Kamran, Catherine, and Barbarella look at you expectantly.

Ask not for whom the bell tolls, this is crunch time. For ages now, you've had the feeling that someone's trying to stop you getting back together with Barbarella. You were worried it was Will at first, but not now. Catherine is the one spreading poison. But is she the criminal mastermind? Or just a pawn in another's game? Exercise the little gray cells, and look at the evidence.

Sitting among the ashes of another burnt-out relationship, does she want you for herself? Or is it that she can't bear her best friend to be happy?

Or does Kamran want Barbie for himself? Could there be some other reason for stitching you up?

This is a big one, you only get one crack at this, cast your mind back, look at all the evidence and, remember, Miss Marple could solve this in a nanosecond.

"Catherine, just because you can't hold down a relationship doesn't mean you should try to split me and Barbie up. We belong together." (Sincere frown to Barbie.) **Go to Scene 258**

*

Scene 243

"Catherine, I think I understand why you said it—and I'm really flattered. But I'm in love with Barbie." (Endearing smile to Barbie.) **Go to Scene 181**

"Kam, mate, I completely understand why you did it. I'd probably do the same thing. But Barbie wants me, not you." (Knowing smile to Barbie.) **Go to Scene 207**

"Kam, what's going on here, mate? Why did you do it? Is there something you need to tell me?" (Perplexed frown to Barbie.) **Go to Scene 249**

Scene 244

Quite right. Fools rush in. Barnaby is more of a "softly softly" kind of a guy. You've laid some solid foundations and now is the time to build. From now on, concentrate everything on Barbarella. Woo her, confuse her, do anything to win her and by the end of the evening you'll have her eating out of your hand.

Even sticking strictly to second gear, you make short shrift of the journey. You don't quite manage to catch up with the others, but have no problem finding the rather grand Georgian house that is home to the West India.

The West India Club is one of Will's favorite haunts—full of poor sophisticates and rich trash, each symbiotically feeding off the other. Will adores the place because he can strut his pedigree and supplement his income at the same time (there's only so much money an alcoholic can make from selling wine). Barbarella is pretty indifferent—the place is packed with filthy rich males, but most will be fat, ugly, or just generally filthy. You despise it on principle, but at the same time can never quite resist.

Take a breather. In the game of love, you've been a poor loser all evening, but luck must change. Courage! And shuffle the cards. If you don't turn up the queen of hearts, you might deal yourself a running flush and walk away with lots of lovely cash instead. So steel your frayed nerves, for gambling is not for the weak, and this club is swilling with cash. It's not often you get an invite, so nose to the trough, and scoff your fill . . .

With a sudden panic you realize that Will may be using his newfound freedom to leech onto Barbarella. You run up the austere stone steps and to the front door.

Go to Scene 242

Scene 245

You're back home in fifteen minutes. Entering first, you check that Catherine has gone to bed. Thankfully she has. This will be much easier without her awkward questions.

You mix some drinks, add a double measure of vodka to Barnie's, in order to dull his wits further, and then wait. Barnaby is obviously excited; he can barely string a sentence together. The realization, that Barnaby is more thrilled about sleeping with a random stranger than he has ever been about sleeping with you, sends a sharp stab of further annoyance. You look at him, drumming fingers on the armrest of an armchair, and such an overwhelming feeling of hatred overcomes you that you're forced to leave the room.

"I might have a quick shower. If the doorbell rings then for God's sake leave it and go into the kitchen so she doesn't see you."

A shower does little to cool your burning sense of vengeance. If anything, by the time you return, you are more adamant than ever. Barnaby will learn a lesson he'll never forget. If he thinks he can walk all over your feelings, treat you like some slut, and then two-time you to your face, then he's got another think coming.

The doorbell interrupts your stream of mental bile. Shit, it'll wake Catherine, you hadn't thought of that.

"For Christ sake, Barnie, get out of sight. Hide in the kitchen and don't stick your nose out until I come and get you."

Scene 245

Shutting the kitchen door, sure enough, you turn to find Catherine squinting at you. She's wearing her flannelette pajamas.

"Cat, sorry, it's just the pizza guy." You look embarrassed. "I got the munchies."

Cat sighs, turns, and goes back to bed. So far so good, the pizza delivery guy is given a hefty tip and, with a small pizza box under one arm and a plastic tub of salad in the other, you enter your bedroom for the first time. With some trepidation you creep in, dreading to think what state Astrid is in.

And there she lies, sprawled like a road-kill, on top of the duvet. Either Cat helped her undress or she managed herself because she's naked. You look away, in the interest of appetite, and settle down on the floor to eat some pizza. The thought of Barnaby working himself up into a frenzy persuades you to take your time. The pizza is delicious (revenge, it seems, is a dish best served hot with olives, capers, and a cheese topping), but the salad has to wait—you don't have a fork and it doesn't come with dressing. And so you make yourself comfortable, gently serenaded by Astrid's heavy breathing and the occasional snore.

Pizza eaten, you decide to go and check on Barnaby in the kitchen. He's got the itch, that much is obvious, but you fend him off with some brilliant acting.

"I am a goddess . . . almost home and dry, just don't forget, you owe me big time. The cow has flown south, I repeat, the red cow has flown south, all systems go, all systems go."

You start up the empty microwave for a five-minute spin and with the flushed cheeks of victory, whisper loudly in his ear.

"The object is now bound to my four-poster with stockings—and has an old sarong tied round her head. Give me five minutes to warm her up," a quick pointed look at the microwave timer, "and the little tigress is all yours."

You leave, clutching a bottle of extra virgin and a fork.

The salad is rapidly crunched through. You have ample time to float a sarong over Astrid's head and tip some olive oil on her abundant thigh. The microwave must have dinged because the bedroom door is creaking open. Barnaby is entering. You grab him, "She's all yours, *chiquito*. Don't let me down—I've got a reputation to consider," and make a hurried exit.

Within seconds you are out into the hallway with a key to Astrid's basement flat. It's a pity you couldn't hang around, the look of horror on Barnaby's face would have been priceless. Down in Astrid's one-room flat you get yourself a glass of water and wonder how long it will take Barnaby to figure out what he's landed. You listen, and with some satisfaction realize that in the dark he must still be totally unawares. Stupid dick, serves him right. He'll be absolutely mortified when he finds out. And he won't be so quick to take you for granted in the future. With that comforting thought, you plump Astrid's thin pillow, and settle down to sleep.

The (Bitter) End

You've helped Barbie prove her point, Reader. But what about giving her something to smile about? Start again, and this time choose carefully. The Perfect Ending is out there.

Scene 246

You've never seen Will look as vulnerable as he does now. "Barn, my Coutts card . . . it bounced. I'm broke."

He doesn't need to add anything, but the grip of confession has him. "Yaboowine.net went into receivership on Wednesday. That's why I agreed to marry Annabel."

You try to offer a solution. "What about Ronnie B.?"

Will smiles gravely at your old joke, but if anything the thought of his father sinks him deeper into despair. "Dad sent some money over, but it's barely touched the overdraft. I daren't tell him how much I owe . . . It would kill him. Coutts have repossessed my cards."

He burbles on incoherently, but you barely listen. Will, with tears in his eyes, has, for the first time in your friendship, asked *you* for help. Don't let him down, Barnie.

"It's all right, mate. We'll win back your freedom with a couple of good hands." You put a brotherly arm around him and head off to the gaming tables.

And so you spend the next half-hour, on Will's instruction, playing the *vingt et un* tables. You lose $80, but pick up some mental speed and also the nubile Daisy, a brunette in a cream, tan-accentuating dress. She promises more from behind than she can deliver face-on, but you don't mind. She has a raucous laugh, a gym-worked body, and you sense that she'll bring good luck.

But the clock strikes two and you must away to the stud. Will gives your shoulder a silent squeeze and you move away from the comfort of Daisy's small talk.

"Just thought I'd better mention it," Will whispers, "I put your MBNA card down for double contribution. It seemed to go through OK."

Go to Scene 35

Scene 247

"Your offer is very tempting, Nigel. But I don't think there are enough narcotics in London to persuade me to go anywhere near your repellent body, let alone your head."

"OK, Barbie, everyone has a price. Two-fifty."

It's your turn to smile. "'Nigel, my desperate little friend, do yourself a favor—spend it on liposuction."

You don't even need to ask Barnaby, he follows you from the room like a well-trained Labrador. The club is still full, but you barely notice; within seconds you're in the street and on Barnie's bike. Barnaby turns. "We're broke—you do know that, don't you?" He pauses and, with false melodrama, adds, "Ah well, who needs money when we've got each other?" You squeeze Barnaby's comfortable midriff and rest your head on his back. "Where do you want to go then?"

"Just take me for a spin, my lover. I need some fresh air."

Barnie ignites the engine and the bike begins its embracing throb. The gearbox clunks and you surge forward.

Go to Scene 241

Scene 248

Quite right. Never look a gift horse in the mouth, even when she does actually look like a horse. You regulate your breathing, compose your face in the mirror, and try to think lustful thoughts.

But it's no good. A sudden flashback overwhelms you—a massive, dimpled, cottage-cheese bottom, you wobbling it with glee. Your stomach lurches and a cold sweat creeps through your skin.

It's no good. You did your best, but there are some things a guy just can't control (stomach). Oh well, there's always Plan B.

Go to Scene 219

Scene 249

Oh dear—you may have just blown it.

"Barnie, you're so bloody clueless. Do you need me to spell it out?"

Kamran looks as though you've punched him; he walks from the room with lowered head. You could swear that you see a tear flick on to his cheek.

"What was that all about?" you ask Barbarella, but she just looks at Catherine.

"Oh dear. We'd better see if he's OK."

They both leave in silence. You find a decanter of scotch and fill a glass. Best drink through the confusion. It'll all be all right in the morning.

Looks like you guessed right, but fat lot of good it's done Barnaby. He's just too male and too dim to see the truth . . . Oh well, he'll drink himself fit to puke and everything will be forgotten by the morning.

The (Blind Drunk) End

Reader, best steer clear of all this confusion. This is simple—Barbie's hot and Barnie's raring—so do the right thing: play again, and do whatever it takes . . .

Scene 250

Back at the party, you catch your breath, grab a glass of wine, and take some time to survey the state of play. The crowds are already starting to thin now that the speeches are over, and after the evening's early disasters, you don't have the stomach for more action—at least not just yet. Instead, you morosely find a seat by an empty table and contemplate life. The evening has taken its toll and, standing alone with your unhealthy thoughts of life-failure, you feel the gnawing self-doubt rise like bile.

Barbie's made it clear. Whatever there was between you is over, and your ego, never particularly robust, has all the flabby despair of a month-old party balloon. There's no avoiding the stark truth, Barnaby. You're in love with Barbarella.

And the stupid bitch couldn't care less.

That's been the trouble for the last two years. You love her insecurities, fears, and failings. The way she refuses to ever acknowledge that she cared about you; the way she sometimes cried after making love. She needs you, and together, you were invincible. It's not about settling down, but teaming up. You could take on the world with Barbie by your side.

But what's this? You must have been lost in self-reflection for longer than you realized. Barbarella is bearing down upon you, helloing and smiling.

"Barnie, what have you been up to? Terrible, isn't it? We should have gone to Will's party."

Scene 250

You barely get a chance to interject, but it doesn't matter. As Barbarella talks, you just sit, gazing into her sparkling blue eyes and watching her collagen-rich lips pout as they form words.

"Oh my *God*!"

The blasphemy breaks your thought; Barbarella is staring over your shoulder in horrified disbelief.

Go to Scene 133

Scene 251

Kamran nabs you by the punch bowl.

"Barn, we've got to get out of here. Carol keeps touching my chest."

But before you can discuss, the very woman herself is before you. "Oh, Kammy, you must introduce me to your lovely friend."

And so you're introduced to Carol. She turns out to be a middle-aged horror story.

"I've been trying to persuade your sculptor friend to come upstairs and see my Egon Schiele sketches. Maybe we should all go up together."

Oh God, this woman has clearly forgotten how old she is. You look to Kamran for some escape plan, but instead all he can offer is, "Yeah, OK."

Carol grips you both by the hand and leads you out of the hall and upstairs. You're helpless, a rabbit caught in the glare of a juggernaut's headlights. Your mind is jabbering with mortified embarrassment and you desperately try to get Kamran's attention, but he's being drawn forward like a Stepford Wife. Carol leads you both along the upper hall, and to the far end of the house.

No one will hear you scream.

The ridiculous thought pops into your head and forces a laugh. With yards to spare, it lifts your mental paralysis.

"Ooh, the loo, you guys go on, I'll join you in a sec."

Scene 251

Without waiting for a reply, you duck back and into the bathroom, firmly lock the door and prepare for a long wait.

Probably two hours to be completely safe. Carol should have passed out by then. You'll have plenty of time to consider the speed of God's retribution on your selfish soul.

The (Evil Sinner) End

It's in poor taste, Reader, to leave our hero high and dry. Play again and show him the brighter side of life (and your thinking) . . .

Scene 252

You look imploringly at Barbarella, but before she has time to react, Kamran opens his big gob. Before you can fill it with a fist, he says, "Don't worry. I'll go with you," and joins you on the pavement. Barbarella and the others wave through the rear window as the cab pulls away. "So where are you parked, Barn?"

The gods thought otherwise, Barnie. Seems to be the story of your life; struggling to get it together with Barbie, only to be thwarted at every turn. Well, you've learned a valuable lesson—there's no point trying to wrest sweetmeats from the clutches of Providence until she's ready. There's nothing for it but to get on your bike.

You've ridden with Kam a thousand times. With little fuss, you both mount the Ducatti and leisurely pick your way east and north to the Bayswater Road. You don't need Kamran's directions, but go through the pretense as he guides you on through Leinster Square, and finally to a halt outside a grand Georgian house, home to the West India.

A sudden panic grips as you realize that Will may be using his newfound freedom to leech onto Barbarella. You run up the austere granite steps and to the front door.

Go to Scene 242

Scene 253

Desperate stuff. Still, she might think it's romantic.

Neither of you can stop smiling as she tucks the note into the front of her dress.

Go to Scene 67

Scene 254

Well, don't just sit there. No one else is going to pick it up. Get on all fours and check to see if you called correctly. Risk carpet burns, humiliation, your back and knees, risk everything to spin the roulette wheel of love.

For today and today alone—in the Gaming Den of Life—everyone's a winner (baby).

Get it right? Lucky devil. **Go to Scene 63**

Get it wrong? Lucky bugger. **Go to Scene 107**

Scene 255

"Are you all right?"

You rub your stomach and smile. "Yeah, fine, must be mixing too many drinks. Come on, better get out of here before Barbarella catches us."

The trip back to your place in Clapham seems to take an age. In the back of the cab Catherine rests her head on your chest and by the time you arrive you are both almost asleep.

Better put some coffee on, and put something lively in the video player, Barnaby. You're virtually home and dry so don't seize up now. Get the up-lighting just right, pour two generous nightcaps, and persuade Catherine that she'd be more comfortable wearing some of your boxers and a T-shirt. Just make sure you get the right film. No, not a porno, but something with a strong love interest, and a hearty sex scene not too far in . . .

You decide to raid Kamran's secret video stash. He sleeps in your spare room whenever he's sick of the houseboat (i.e., most of the winter) and keeps a lot of stuff there. His videos are hidden in a wicker basket at the end of the bed. Most of them will be horrifically unsuitable, but there must be some mainstream stuff in there as well. So you leave Catherine curled up on the sofa and go sneak a look.

Scene 255

The top layer of videos is pretty much as you'd expect—Debbie *et al.*, doing this and that—but as you rummage deeper . . .

"Oh my God." It's Catherine's voice and she's looking over your shoulder. "Is that *Thoroughly Modern Millie*?"

There's no denying it. Closeted away at the bottom of Kam's blue movie collection is a selection of classics: Julie Andrews, Cary Grant, Audrey Hepburn, they're all there. There's even a copy of *The Sound of Music*. "Fantastic, that's my favorite film of all time. Can we watch it? . . . Oh go on, Barnie—you'll love it."

Oh raspberries, you don't really have much choice, do you? Within five minutes, the video is whirring and your chances of competing with Julie Andrews for Cat's affections are just about nil. What is Kamran doing with all this rubbish? They must be an ex-girlfriend's or something. Ah well, if you're lucky you might be able to fall asleep before Catherine starts singing along.

The (Julie Andrews) End

Go to Scene 221

Scene 256

You open your good eye, expecting to see the voluptuous Polly full of trembling contrition, or better still, the terrified, dewy-eyed vision of your loved one, Charlotte. Instead, the eager look of ex-ambassador Oswald Dryton-Gore fixes itself like a limpet. The stab of pain, as his eager fingers probe your eyelids apart, makes you cry out. The cry brings Charlotte to your side.

"Barnaby, you poor thing, twice in one day." She tends and clutches your damaged head to her bosom.

"Maybe third time lucky," you mutter under your breath, wincing at the pain.

But Oswald is the wit of the hour; even as Charlotte clutches you and calls for a bag of ice, she laughs to hear him witter about the dangers of public life. And then, before you know it, Barbarella has arrived and Kamran and Will and the others. Barbie insists on looking after you and Charlotte is gone.

Go to Scene 187

Scene 257

Deep breath, Barnie, clear your head of the inexorably perfect Marc-Pacaud. Instead, think of Agincourt, Crécy, Waterloo.

With a clear eye, you look Snuffy in the eye and declare, "Charlotte will be mine. Oh yes, she will be mine."

"Barnaby, that Frenchman is what we used to call a 'lounge lizard.' Have another snifter." She loads up your glass.

"You can't let him waltz away with the cherry," she waves a hand in the direction of Charlotte's empty chair. "To be honest, if it were me, sixty years ago, I like to think I would have seen through such a greased ego . . . but then I didn't really know what oral sex was until my second marriage."

Oswald adds his two-penn'th. "Humiliation, you need to dish a good dose of humiliation."

"Decimate his self-esteem forever and ever," you finish his sentence and surprise yourself with the depth of feeling.

"Quite. The basic rules of humiliation are pretty straightforward. One: spot your victim's vanities. Two: flatter them to absurdity. Three: laugh smugly while he makes a complete tit of himself."

Your mind starts working, and so does your cohort's. It doesn't take the three of you long to plot the decimation of Marc-Pacaud's self-esteem . . . forever.

Go to Scene 203

Scene 258

Oh dear.

"You're such a wanker, Barnie."

Catherine's punch takes you totally by surprise. The small clenched fist smacks you on the side of your nose and the shock of it causes your legs to crumple. You collapse to the ground and she runs from the room in tears. Barbarella looks at you as though you've just had a bowel movement, and follows her friend.

Kamran crouches over you, in obvious concern as you sit up unsteadily.

"Oh shit, I think she's broken it."

With a tissue over your bleeding nose and head tilted back you and Kam go to find a doctor.

The (Bloody) End

What a mess. Reader, you really should start again and watch your step. Barnie needs you. Carpe diem . . . thrills and spills await.

Scene 259

You attempt a smile, and then, like a Hollywood hero, you go to your fate with raised chin and steady stare.

"Do I get a pop at Polly afterwards," you quip, but through the wadded tobacco it emerges as a mumble, lost beneath the hubbub of anticipation.

Oswald, very obviously a showman of some skill, hushes the gathering throng with some well-chosen words.

"The Cuban missile crisis. The world on the brink of disaster. We could have witnessed Armageddon . . . if it were not for this novel idea of diplomacy. You see, no one could ever hit a cigar from that distance with a champagne cork."

He pauses to breathe.

"So you see the bet was all but won. The Ruskies would withdraw, Kennedy would be a hero, and the world would be safe again. Khrushchev knew he would have to withdraw eventually of course; this little ruse allowed him to do so with good grace and gave him the outside chance of hurting Gregson—whom he detested. That was the brilliance of my plan . . . Nikki and Gregson absolutely hated each other. Gregson was man enough to face the brunt of Communist Russia on the chin. Actually, he still has a scar." Then a last word to you: "Stop mumbling, man, and think of the free world."

Go to Scene 183

Scene 260

You lunge; she gasps . . . and giggles, running deeper into the garden.

Like the nymph of your dreams she flits between trees, kicking off her heels. She skips on snow-white toes over the soft lawn and warm path. Finally you corner her in a yew-circled alcove.

She laughs, panting against a large mounted sundial. You turn her, and she arches in appreciation as you kiss the nape of her neck.

With deliberately slow hands you lift her dress to reveal edible buttocks. The G-string resists for five seconds before she is bent over the sundial, bottom bare and glinting soft in the moonlight.

On tippy-toes you raise your height to the required level, unzip your pant-free penis . . . and feel your foot slide on something squishy. A frog or salamander, it matters little. Your foot slides.

You lose balance, grasping at her shining buttocks—they are too firm, too smooth, too curved. Your hand slips off them like a baby-oiled blonde off the bonnet of a Ferrari, your head crashes against the hard stone of the sundial mounting. You hear the crack of bone on stone—and then, mercifully, nothing

Go to Scene 225

Scene 261

You leave Fin to his one-dog fox hunt and slide up some side stairs to the west-wing landing. Time for some serious thinking; you don't have time to go into every bedroom. Where would Will hide? Then you remember. That heady week you spent trying to christen every room, only one eluded you—the west-wing attic. You only found out that it existed on the last day and by then Will was spent.

With a pounding heart you race up steep steps to the second floor; athletic legs pumping, you sprint to the far corridor of the farthest wing. The last place anyone will look. With fizzing chest you pull at the bronze-handled hatch and a ladder pokes down out of the dark. It extends smoothly and with trepidation you ascend.

You clamber into the attic and squint desperately, trying to make out some shape in the gloom, but see nothing. Gentle hands cup your breasts, and a loud whisper laughs in your ear. "I was hoping it would be you."

You turn and place a full kiss on Will's smile. The odor of Indonesian rodent glands fills your nostrils. Blinding flashes wipe clean your frontal lobes and you find yourself sinking into the quicksands of passion, desperately clinging to Will for support.

"I love you," you manage croakily, and with immense willpower you draw yourself away, gather jumbled thoughts, and succinctly make your irrefutable argument: "Don't marry Annabel . . . she's a stupid cow." You trail off pathetically, "Marry me."

Will, far from rushing to embrace and swear undying love, bites his lip, pulls up the ladder, and shuts the hatch. He turns to you and, in the gloom, you make out a tense smile.

"Barbie, I love you too, but I can't marry you. I'm bankrupt." He coughs with emotion. "I'm a loser, Barbie, and you can do better than me. Marry Barnaby."

He's ranting now. You plant a kiss on his forehead and you hug each other tightly in the dark. After long minutes you make a decision. "Will, I'll sell my car. We'll sell everything. I don't care what we have to do, just don't marry that stupid, stupid bitch."

Finally you break down in tears and Will squeezes you with desperate love-filled arms. In the gentle darkness you whisper of love and think of the future: walking the dogs together on rainy afternoons, weekend parties with droning dragonflies, diving the Maldives in search of adventure.

You can hear Will smiling as he gently eases your zip.

Barbarella. No more pages to turn. This tale was a love story after all, it just has an unexpected leading man. But as you lie, remember, be very quiet—for our tale is due a happy consummation (and there's no lock on the hatch). Grasp young William to your bosom and hold him tight, for now he is thine, and you are his.

We will leave you thus, forever joined. 'Tis only left to observe, "In this world no life without love is worth, or may endure."

Truly This Is
The (Perfect) End

Scene 262

After all those months, mentally rehearsing this moment, the sudden relief of revealing your love is euphoric. And don't let any of the evening's events make you doubt it for a second. There'll always be pretty girls ready to tempt you, but unlike with Barbarella, the pleasure would be short-lived. This is what it's all about.

Barbie doesn't laugh—which is good—but she doesn't talk—which is bad. You smile at her, attempting an early Bruce Willis half-smile of self-deprecation. But the old trick doesn't want to come out of the box. Instead, you find yourself looking down at her with such a desperate breathless hope that all semblance of dignity is gone.

Too rash, too unadvised, too sudden. Your self-worth dangles by its ankles over the side of Waterloo Bridge. It looks down in horror at the whirling, sucking eddy of the Thames. You look Barbarella in her steel gray-blue eyes and pray . . .

And then she cries. With a half laugh at first and then with great sobbing stomach-blowing sobs, and you know as surely as Captain Corelli can play the mandolin that this is a love story. A harsh, modern tale of gratification, yes, but a love story nonetheless.

You put your arm around her quivering shoulders and squeeze tightly. She smiles up at you, with no embarrassment.

"I love you too," she states simply.

And suddenly dreams of a wisteria-covered house in Norfolk, a healthy few acres, and a cozy local pub don't seem quite so far away. And with foreknowledge of tables for two and companionable gardening and hiking holidays in Umbria, you mount your bike, and with love's light wings, go back to her place.

Barnaby. No more pages to turn. This tale was a love story after all. Perhaps not a wholesome, fattening, Sunday roast of a love story. No. A ready meal at best, but it meets the need.

Gather the rose of love while yet there's time, for the gods are capricious. One drunken slip of a motorbike wheel (and you are due it) and this comedy will turn to tragedy. But no . . . that would be treason to your love and we have not the stomach for it. Instead, our tale is due a happy end; let us see you slip into the night with hammering hearts and smiling eye. Play up, play up, and play on, for love is the greatest game of all.

Just remember, "In this world no life without love is worth, or may endure."

Truly This Is
The (Perfect) End